*To my dear husband **Rajiv**,*
*and to my daughters, **Karunya** and **Lavanya***
who always encouraged me to be authentic,
and follow my dream.

A ROSE from a dream

A NOVEL BY

Kanchana Krishnan Ayyar

Kanchi Books

http://www.kanchibooks.com

A Rose from a Dream

Written by
Kanchana Krishnan Ayyar
Copyright © 2017 Kanchana Krishnan Ayyar

Library of Congress Control Number: 2016918015
ISBN-13: 978-0-9838765-6-4
ISBN-10: 0-9838765-6-8
Edited by Jim Fairchild
Cover design by Feroza Unvala
Cover photograph by Karunya Krishnan
Format and Style by Sudipto Basu

Published by Kanchi Books

Kanchi
Books

http://www.kanchibooks.com

Contents

Section-II : 1946-1947

Section-III : 1947-1952

AUTHOR'S NOTE

Anyone who has read my first book, *When the Lotus Blooms*, can tell it contains a piece of my heart. Writing has become part of my life for the last decade. It rewards and nourishes in ways that cannot be fully explained by the spoken word. One rule I have set for myself is to be authentic no matter what I write. My writing comes in spurts and gets crystallized in moments of inspiration when stories are revealed to me in images so real, I actually visualize and explain what I see.

In writing *A Rose from a Dream*, my inspiration relied on a deep connection with my ancestors. There were periods where I saw nothing, and therefore wrote nothing. The anecdotes and stories in these novels are real life dramas that perhaps have occurred in each one of our lives at some point. I have drawn on the turbulent historical milieu of the 1940s, a period of significant turmoil worldwide. I particularly wanted to draw attention to the Bengal Famine in which over three million reportedly perished; an event which sadly skipped the attention of popular media in large measure.

In this book I have continued the path of a few characters from my previous book and left out others. There is no particular rationale for this. As I explained earlier, I write what I see.

I am extremely grateful to my peer editors, Pavithra Varadarajan and Karunya Krishnan, who read the raw manuscript and offered their invaluable advice prior to the formal edit. Thank you Jim, my editor, for having so much faith in my storytelling ability. Your editing has helped me become a more professional writer. My deepest gratitude to my husband Rajiv for the final edit, for knowing in many instances what I really wanted to say and rewriting it. A huge shout out to my dear friend Janevi for her help on the glossary. An effusive and warm hug to my soulmate and dear friend Feroza, who sees what I envision and creates the perfect book cover. Lastly, I am utterly grateful to my mother Kamakshi Ayyar: it is her stories that fire my imagination.

An Introduction

A Rose from a Dream completes Kanchana Krishnan's magnificent saga of two families who survive India's tumultuous political and social turmoil during the first half of the twentieth century. Based on Krishnan's own family chronicle, these two novels are a must-read for anyone interested in an authentic account of this period. The first novel, *When the Lotus Blooms*, deals with the last days of the British Raj and ends just before India's independence. Mahadevan Ayyar, an Oxford-educated administrator in the British system, and his wife Dharmu have discarded their Brahmin heritage for a life of relative wealth and comfort. On the other hand, Partha and his wife Rajam come from a traditional Brahmin family of declining fortunes. *A Rose from a Dream* continues the story begun in *When the Lotus Blooms*, covering India's struggle for Independence in the 1940s, as the British divide India into two savagely opposed cultures—India and Pakistan—and then abandon them to the bloody riots that leave both countries in a shambles. Like its predecessor, *Dream* follows a richly and compassionately imagined cast of diverse characters caught in a web of change. In the aftermath of these events, Kandu Ayyar and Kamu Parthasarathy come together just as a new India is bursting from its cocoon. The blending of this couple's modern and traditional backgrounds represent a positive vision of India's uncertain future.

Dr. James Fairchild
Associate Professor of Literature
Maharishi University of Management

CHARACTERS

KAMU'S FAMILY

Kamu: (Kamakshi) Main protagonist: Rajam and Partha's only child

Rajam: (Rajalakshmi) The main protagonist, Kamu's mother

Partha: (Parthasarathy) Rajam's devoted husband

Maithili: Rajam's second born who died in infancy

Nagamma: Partha's mother

Munuswamy Iyer: Partha's father

Siva: Partha's older brother

Sushila: Siva's wife

Thambu: Partha's younger brother

Vaalam: Thambu's wife

Kannan: Partha's youngest brother

Sachi: Kannan's wife

Pattu: Partha's sister, Nagamma's only daughter

Swami: (Swaminathan Iyer) Rajam's father (Inspector)

Mangalam: Rajam's mother

Kunju: Rajam's older sister

Venkat, Visu, Natarajan: Kunju's sons

Sundari, Lalitha, Jayam: Kunju's daughters

Mani: Rajam's younger brother

Parvathi: (Chithi) Rajam's maternal aunt–Mangalam's younger sister

Balu, Ramji: Sushila and Siva's sons

KANDU'S FAMILY

Kandu: Main protagonist (Mahadevan Nilakantan Ayyar)

Dharmu: (Dharmambal) Kandu's mother

Mahadevan: Kandu's father

Vani: Kandu's oldest sister

Ganesh: Vani's husband

Rukmini: (Rukku) Dharmu's younger daughter

Arun: (Arunachalam) Rukku's husband

Rao Bahadur M. Nilakantan Ayyar: Mahadevan's father

Sitalakshmi: Mahadevan's mother

Appanshayal: Mahadevan's grandfather

Shankar, Dandapani, Ganesh: Mahadevan's brothers

Kannan: Mahadevan's youngest brother

Laali: Kannan's wife

Shyamala: Rukku and Arun's daughter

Visvanathan Iyer: Dharmu's father

Gayatriammal: Dharmu's mother

Venkat: Dharmu's brother

Seetha: Venkat's wife

KOVILADI KAMALAMBA'S FAMILY

Koviladi Kamalamba: (Amma)The matriarch of a Devadasi (courtesan) household

Balamani: (Bala)A young dancer preparing for her Arangetram

Vyjayanthi: A courtesan

Vasanthasena: (Vasanti)A courtesan

Mohan: A young flautist

Muthu: (Karadi) the muscleman of the household, Kamalamba's cousin

Selvan: Muthu's father

Radhai: Mohan's father

Shanthimati Amma: Kamalamba's mother

Saroja: Bala's mother

Raja Varman: Saroja's husband, Kamalamba's former benefactor

OTHER CHARACTERS

Vaithee Chakrabarti: Revathi's uncle married to Meera

Meera: Dharmu's maid now married to Vaithee

Prashant and Pushkin: Vaithee's children

Nandu: Velandi's oldest son who becomes an assassin

Velandi: The cleaner, belonging to a caste of untouchables

Muhammad Salih: An old friend of Swaminathan from Vizhupuram

Biswa: A revolutionary

Rani Chatterjee: Dharmu's friend

Sudipto Chatterjee: Rani's husband

Deb Chatterjee: Rani and Sudipto's son

Vanchinathan Iyer: a famous revolutionary

Subramania Bharathi: A revered tamil poet and revolutionary

Tucky, Dilip, Mickey, Mani: Kandu's friends

Viju, Vatsu, Shathi, Pancham: Kamu's friends

Ramu: A priest, also Kamu's friend

Shaila: Vani's friend

Govindhan: Kandu's faithful servant

Advocate Panchu: Sushila's paramour

Sundar Sastrigal: Family priest

SECTION-I
1942-1945

CHAPTER ONE

RAJAM
MADRAS – APRIL 1942

THE KABULIWALLAH

Hearing a commotion outside, Rajam rushed out beyond their ground floor verandah into the common courtyard. There were at least fifty of her neighbors, all speaking simultaneously in one loud cacophony. Her brother-in-law Kannan was in front of the group carrying Kamu, who looked a little baffled. Rajam nervously wiped her wet hands, dampening her already moist maroon, cotton sari as the group congregated outside the netted balcony. Kannan placed Kamu gingerly on the ground, and the little girl quickly sidled towards Rajam, hiding in the folds of her sari. As she slipped one small, quivering hand into her mother's, she looked up at her with soulful eyes now widened in fear, dominating her petite seven-year-old face.

"*Yenna*? What happened? What did Kamu do now?" Rajam enquired.

"You need to watch your child more closely!" said one.

"You don't know how lucky you are," added another.

"The *devas* and angels are watching over you."

"The Kabuliwallah took her away. Thanks heavens Shekhar saw them."

"Isn't it enough losing one child that you are so careless with the other?"

Rajam winced at their comments. The wound was still fresh and it hurt to even think about her little Maithili. Moving her attention away from her recent loss, she tried to focus on what her neighbors were collectively attempting to articulate. Her head swiveled from side to side in an endeavor to get a handle on the situation. Between the comments of the neighbors and quizzing a reluctant Kamu in private, Rajam partially understood what occurred.

Kamu was miraculously rescued after being abducted by the Kabuliwallah. No one trusted these tall, strapping Pathans with flaming red hair, who roamed the streets of Madras, lending money to hapless, poor Brahmins who could not get cheap credit elsewhere. It was not uncommon to chance upon a thin Brahmin man two feet off the floor, held against the wall in the vice grip of the Kabuliwallah's large fists, as he threatened the poor man in broken Tamil, demanding his money back. Her husband, Partha, had learned the hard way when a loan of fifteen rupees became a hundred in a matter of months. No matter how difficult times were, Partha now steered clear of the Kabuliwallah.

Just half an hour ago, Rajam had been watching Kamu playing in the open courtyard with her cousins. She was the only girl in the group and refused to be left out. The boys were playing a game they called *Seven stones*, and reluctantly included her but, Kamu knew what to do. She waited till the ball rolled in her direction and then grasped it firmly in her strong palms, quickly placing it under her as she squatted on the muddy floor. The boys begged and cajoled her but she was steadfast. She knew the ball was safe under the folds of her *pāvādai*, and even though she was tiny, none of them would have the guts to pry it away, as that would mean lifting her skirts. Rajam smiled admiring her guile. Kamu knew how to go after what she wanted.

Rajam needed to prepare lunch and returned to the kitchen, knowing the boys would watch over Kamu. She had warned her overactive child often enough with dire consequences if she left the safety of the courtyard, but every now and again Kamu would scamper down the street to see her grandmother Nagamma Paati, who lived just two doors away. She was young and had no ideas of dangers lurking around the corner and no concept of anything *bad* happening to her. In many ways Kamu reminded Rajam of herself as a child. Rajam was a tomboy, fearless until a chance encounter with a fierce *sāmiyār* introduced the concept of panic and fear into her innocent life. A hard lesson with long-lasting impressions. She developed a lifelong phobia of these wandering, ash-smeared mendicants, one that stayed with her into adulthood.

Like her mother, Kamu was adventurous and bold. Adored by everyone around her, she added a sparkle to any conversation with her unique sense of humor and spontaneity. Kamu was also easily bored. After winning this battle of wits with her cousins, she played for a while and then got distracted by an ambling, colorful bullock cart passing by the gate. She wandered up to the entrance and peered out, looking at all the people walking up and down the street. Her uncle Kannan as usual balanced precariously on his ramshackle bicycle with his group of friends—*Mylapore rowdies* they called themselves. They were eyeing all the girls walking down the street, not sparing even the married ones. Their comments and raucous laughter wafted down the street, but Kamu could not make any sense of it and she turned her attention elsewhere.

Most of the women were either going or returning from the temple down the street. The hub of social were the temples, and all the women on *Mundakanni Amman Kovil Street* usually visited the Devi temple in the morning and the main

Shiva temple, *Kabāleeshwarar Kovil* in the evenings. Kamu hummed a tuneless song while playing with the gold chain around her neck, when someone stopped directly in front of her, blocking her vision. She had seen him walk the streets before in his loose, baggy pants under a shapeless, flowing shirt, both of which must have been white once upon a time. His long, flowing beard and hair were a strange orangish-red, and Kamu was intrigued rather than frightened by him. Amma called him the Kabuliwallah, and she was scared of him, but looking at the man smiling down at her, Kamu was not alarmed. Nothing worried her. She looked up at him boldly as he walked up to the gate and bent down to speak to her.

"Hello pretty girl," he said in broken Tamil.

"Hullo," she replied. "You look funny." The Kabuliwallah either didn't understand or just ignored the comment. He asked her if she wanted *rasagollas*. Kamu loved these delectable sweets. Amma's friend, Mrs. Chatterjee, the Bengali lady from Alwarpet, always sent some over when she made them. A delicacy from Bengal, they were not easily available in local stores, and Kamu wondered how the Kabuliwallah managed to chance on them. He said he knew a small shop near the temple which recently started selling these sweets. It was really close by and they could go there and be back before anyone missed them. For a moment, Kamu paused to think. Somewhere in the back of her mind she knew she wasn't supposed to walk off with strangers, but the temptation was too great. It was almost noon and she was hungry. She paused in a fleeting whiff of indecision. *Perhaps nothing would happen. Amma would probably never realize she had left.* The prospect of biting into juicy, soft, white rasagollas made her mouth water. Falling for the ruse, Kamu trotted behind the lanky Kabuliwallah and hopped onto his bike.

As they turned the corner, Shekhar, their neighbor, spotted them and yelled out. He knew Kamu was in the wrong place, and definitely with the wrong man, and was not about to let it pass. Shekhar shouted at the top of his voice running after the bike, "*Niruthu! kuzhandhaiye thookindu poraan, bloody rascal!*" urging people to stop the man abducting a child. As he shouted, more people joined in, surrounding the bike and bringing it to a grinding halt. Kannan was also part of the group that gleefully dragged the Kabuliwallah off his bike, beat and kicked him, revenge for all the times they had been at the receiving end of his pounding fists. Kamu watched bewildered. Once the police constable arrived, the crowd happily handed the scoundrel over to his custody and turned their attention to Kamu, whose lips by now had curled up in an angry pout.

She knew there would be no rasagollas today!

CHAPTER TWO

RAJAM
MADRAS – APRIL 1942

REMEMBERING MAITHILI

"Amma, don't hug me so tight," Kamu protested. But Rajam could not help herself. Kamu was such a precious gift. Her birth was a blessing from *Kamakshiamman*. For so many years after marriage, Rajam longed to have a child, but month after month her periods arrived like clockwork. She prayed to every God and Goddess, but it seemed the Divine was busy elsewhere. At the time, she was seventeen years old and had been married for five years. She should have given birth to at least a couple of children by then, and her inability to conceive was viewed with disdain by her mother-in-law Nagamma, and anxiously by her mother Mangalam. Nagamma never missed an opportunity to pass a contemptuous comment, and over time, Rajam's sensitivity to it transformed into an all-consuming phobia, an illogical fear of being forever barren. Moreover, she knew that women who didn't conceive had no place in society, and many men would take a second wife in order to have children. Rajam knew how much Partha loved her, but also acknowledged how much he respected his mother. Would her innuendoes be successful in poisoning Partha's mind and persuade him to abandon Rajam and take a second wife? No ... she could never allow that. She had to bear a child, and the Divine had to shine some light on her so far unfruitful destiny.

She was in the depths of depression and willing to do anything to have a baby. At around this time, her father arranged a special meeting with Shankaracharya, the spiritual head of the Shankara Madham of Kanchipuram, and when Rajam met him at the opening of a *Madham* (Center) in Chidambaram, he gave her some sacred *Meru*, fragrant sandalwood, which he blessed with special prayers. Then he told her she would have a child who should be named Kamakshi after the presiding Goddess of Kanchipuram. Yet, in spite of these divine blessings, her period arrived the following month. This threw her into a whirl of depression. She had been so sure she would be with child immediately; so getting her period questioned her faith in the Divine. Rajam was desperate, and when a dear friend presented her with a rare bloom called the Brahmakamalam, the lotus of Brahma, she watered it faithfully each day. Her friend said this was a magical bloom, and if she cared for the plant, it would answer her prayers. Rajam was ready to do anything to become pregnant even if it meant placing one's faith in the blooming of a lotus. Finally, whether it was the grace of the Guru, the magic of the Brahmakamalam, or her destiny, Rajam soon discovered she was pregnant. That year, there were two fateful bloomings of the lotus plant. She conceived Kamu on the night the Brahmakamalam first bloomed, a magical night that she and Partha shared under the moonlit, star-filled sky. She knew this baby would be a girl, whom she would name Kamakshi, and that is exactly what happened. The night the Brahmakamalam bloomed a second time, Rajam gave birth to a beautiful girl and Kamu became her precious gift to treasure.

Rajam never expected another child and felt surprised and grateful when she delivered another attractive girl, whom she named Maithili. Frail from birth, Maithili was exceptionally beautiful with curly locks and large expressive eyes and so, immediately became everyone's favorite. Rajam's eyes wandered to the pooja altar where Maithili's only photograph, taken right after her first birthday, stared down at her, now unfortunately adorned with a string of flowers, commemorating her passing on. Rajam walked over and wistfully stared at her child who had died not three months ago, never destined to live past childhood.

"Amma why did Maithili die? Rajam was jolted out of her reverie by Kamu's question. Rajam never brought the Brahmakamalam with her to Madras. Was that why Maithili died? Who knew? Searching for the right response to this very question that repeated over and over in her mind like a soundless mantra, she replied in a voice quivering with emotion. "God loved her too much and wanted her back."

"So then does God not love me? How come I am allowed to live?" Rajam had no answer. Who understood the mysterious ways of the Universe? Who knew what the future held in store? Why some were picked to live until they were ancient and others plucked from life even before they uttered their first word? It was all the play of Karma. Maithili lived for a short time on this earth, leaving behind a vacuum that perhaps would never be filled. How many nights Rajam had stayed up unable to sleep, overwhelmed with guilt. Perhaps she could have been more watchful, maybe they should have searched for an English doctor to find out what ailment beset the poor child. Ever since the baby turned one, her belly was distended and she could not digest milk. The *Vaidhyar* asked instead that she be fed with rice *Kanji*, the starchy mixture definitely easier for the child to digest. He said she had liver problems. Who knew that a short fall from the staircase would spell doom for this tiny unfortunate? When Rajam reached her side a minute later, it was already too late. Maithili had already breathed her last. It was unreal. One minute she had been playing on the stairs with Kamu and the next she had fallen down two steps. Two measly steps! No one knew if the fall killed her or whether she died prior to falling down the stairs. But it didn't really matter. Conjecture only gave the mind license to heap further guilt on her and she was exhausted by its burden. Maithili was gone and nothing would bring her back.

"You, my dear, are here to make me the happiest mother in the world." Rajam declared, wiping the tears from her eyes and hugging Kamu tight. "You were born to make everyone around you happy." Kamu basked in the warmth of her mother's embrace, a smile lighting up her face.

Rajam held her at arm's length. "Promise me right now that you will never leave the house with a stranger any more. Promise me!" Kamu pinched the skin on her throat and swore solemnly. She was a little scared, but only by the reaction of the neighbors. Thankfully she had no idea of the evils of the world; those were adult nightmares and she was not privy to them as yet.

So much had transpired since Partha moved to Madras. Partha's older brother Siva had arranged a job for him in the same Japanese company, Mitsui, and they moved here shortly after Kamu's birth. Initially, living by themselves felt strange, but the two rooms they rented were small yet adequate for the three of them. Inevitably one of Partha's brothers or some of their children slept over. Siva and his wife Sushila lived in the same compound, but their home was bigger, with a back courtyard and a small terrace. Siva had found work for their sister Pattu's husband, and Nagamma chose to live with her and her brood of four children. They lived a few houses down the street, and Kamu spent most of the day with her cousins. It was much more exciting with a lot more activity, and Rajam soon found she had a lot of time to spare. Partha's brother Thambu had recently married. He too had finally given up on his studies and as usual Siva had the onerous duty of finding him a clerical job in the same Japanese company. Of all the brothers, Thambu had grown up with very conservative ideas on religion and living. Rajam was religious herself, but she too, like the other family members, felt his religious observations sometimes bordered on pure superstition, filled with taboos and strong notions on right and wrong. The youngest, Kannan, was by far the handsomest of the four and knew it. Like his brothers, he too had little interest in studies and was happy to while away his time just hanging around with friends and whistling at girls. Though blustery and full of himself on the outside, he concealed a soft and gentle nature that surfaced spontaneously around people. He was always around to do Rajam's chores, hang pictures or repair pipes, that is, when he found some time spare from his jaunts with friends. He stopped his studies in spite of his brother's protests and found odd jobs here and there. Siva had secured Kannan an interview for a job as a peon in his company, but who knew if Kannan's interest would hold for long?

Rajam missed her father and her sister Kunju. Her mother Mangalam passed away a few years ago succumbing to a stroke. Now Kunju took care of her father, who had retired from the Police force a year ago. They had moved from their old home into the *agrahāram*, away from the center of the city. Rajam visited her father at least twice a year. Although she missed her mother terribly she knew her father's suffering was far greater. For the first few years his work had kept him busy and helped fill the vacuum. Now that he was officially retired, his entire focus centered on taking care of Kunju's six children.

A couple of years after her mother passed on, Rajam conceived again. She was elated at the unexpected good fortune. Partha and she shared a special loving relationship and now that he was earning well, life was very comfortable for them. Kamu was her constant source of joy, and she spent the whole day attending to the family. The new baby made the household complete. What a beautiful baby Maithili was, fair with soft, ivory skin and large soulful eyes that spoke to you in wordless legends. But now that short-lived saga was over. Maithili was gone and Rajam had to go on with Partha and Kamu.

"Rajam! Kamu! Where are you?" There was urgency in Partha's voice and Rajam hoped nothing untoward had occurred. It was just past noon, and Partha should still have been at work. Ever since the beginning of the month, the atmosphere in Madras had been tense. 1942 had been a year of upheaval. Although Rajam was not very concerned, she knew of a war raging in Europe. But recently, there had been air raids on the ports of Vishakhapatnam and Kakinada. Rumors were rife in the city that Madras harbor would be bombed again. Many elders recalled the horror of September 1914, when the S.M.S Emden, a German Ship, had bombed the Madras harbor, setting the Burmah Oil company tankers on fire, engulfing the city in black fumes. The memory for some was still fresh, and many people had already left the city. The Governor of Madras, Sir Arthur Hope, expected the worst, and there were rumors of a complete evacuation of the city. For the last couple of weeks, every citizen of Madras listened to the radio at every opportunity for updates. Britain and Japan were now locked in a struggle for Burma and that probably meant job loss for all three brothers. Siva, Partha and Thambu; all three worked for Mitsui and Company and knew it was just a matter of time before the British banned every Japanese Company based in India. Perhaps that's what happened. The axe had finally fallen. Maybe that's why Partha's voice held such an urgent tone.

Rajam felt a cold sensation of fear as doubts of an uncertain future crept into her mind. The last few years had been so comfortable, but she knew that everything could change dramatically. With all four brothers jobless what would they do? Where would they go? She would probably have to return to her father's home and add to his already overflowing burden. This was proving to be a year filled with disasters. War, the death of Maithili, and now God knows what. Attempting to control her trembling hands she grabbed Kamu and ran to the entrance, dreading Partha's announcement.

CHAPTER THREE

RAJAM
MADRAS – APRIL 1942

EVACUATION OF MADRAS

"*Yenna*, what happened, how come so early?" Rajam asked. "Come on, come on, we have to hurry. They are expecting the Japanese to bomb the harbor any day and we must pack and move."

"Move where?"

"We are all taking the train to Cuddalore. Jagadeesh Iyer, your Chithappa is expecting us."

"And the others?"

"Siva and Sushila are taking everyone else to her sister's place in Salem. Thambu, Kannan, and Balu will come with us."

A flurry of activity followed. Rajam was nonplussed. What should she take and what would she leave behind? What if looters came during their absence and took everything? But Partha was firm. No silver vessels. Only the jewelry and clothes. There was no time. The train departed at 5 o'clock and they would have to leave with just a couple of trunks. After lunch Rajam began sorting her clothes. She packed one trunk with clothes and jewelry and then ran out to check what the others were doing.

Sushila looked hot and bothered with a scowl on her face. "*Vaa* Rajam ... you heard the news. It's crazy. Not a single cart is available to take us. God alone knows what we are going to do. Everyone is panicking. Just look outside. You could never have witnessed so much activity in your life."

Rajam went to the terrace and surveyed the pandemonium on the street below. Everyone seemed to be rushing everywhere. There were cycles and bullock carts loaded with luggage, and it seemed as if the whole city was on the move. Even Kannan was navigating his bike skillfully between the rushing throngs of humanity instead of his usual purposeless meander. Rajam came down from the terrace and ran towards Pattu's home. Even before she entered, she could hear Nagamma's booming voice directing operations. Her husband Munuswamy was asleep on his easy chair through all the deafening commotion. As he aged, he slept longer hours, only surfacing to eat and bathe. He was old and quite frail and Rajam wondered how he would fare on this train ride to Salem.

"Come Rajam," Nagamma welcomed, glancing at her momentarily before barking further directions. "Take the rice cooker and don't forget to hide the silver."

"What silver?" Pattu enquired. "Nothing but this small silver container for *kumkumam* remains. Thieves will be sorely disappointed if they break into this home," she added wryly. Pattu had gone through some very hard times with her husband unable to find gainful employment. Each month she was forced to sell her silver vessels to put food on the table. That didn't stop her from producing a child each year and all of them were very demanding and needy. Poor Pattu, she never rested. Now with Nagamma there, the list of chores increased even more. The two of them constantly argued, yet one could sense they understood each other.

The house was a mess. They were not close to ready. All three steel trunks were lying open, half packed, with Pattu attempting to add things in between attending to her children's bathroom needs. It seemed as though the pandemonium from the streets had entered and completely taken over this household.

Between them there were seven trunks and over a dozen passengers. Even if they did manage to rent a bullock cart, it would serve no purpose. How were they going to find their way to the station? Rajam stayed for a while and helped a little but she needed to get home and finish her own packing. By the time she returned Siva had arrived. He waved to her and shouted out. "Rajam be ready to leave in two hours. Advocate Panchu is lending us his car. He has a big Dodge with ample luggage space. Even so, it will have to make two trips to the train station. We will leave first and then the car will return for Pattu and family."

Rajam was relieved. This was a godsend. Advocate Panchu was a family friend and a very senior judge in the High court. In spite of his appointment as judge, people still referred to him as Advocate, using his first job as a title. An hour later, Partha padlocked the front door and they were on their way to Egmore Station. Though the train station was barely a few kilometers away, the car made halting progress. It seemed as though the whole city were on the streets of Madras, but they reached with enough of time to spare. Their train departed at five, and Siva's left at seven. The men they carried all the trunks between them as there were no coolies to be found. Rajam and Sushila followed closely. The platform was teeming with hundreds of evacuees and the noise was phenomenal. Holding Kamu's hand in a vice grip, Rajam slowly made her way to the waiting train. It was a short train ride, and they would soon reach their destination. Rajam could not make sense of what was happening. Almost half an hour later they sat down in the compartment counting all their luggage: two steel trunks, two tiffin carriers, and six pieces of hand baggage including Rajam's pooja box. She never went anywhere without that. Kannan and Thambu had already made friends with some boys in the next compartment and had disappeared. Partha wiped his brow and sat down with a heaving sigh of relief. It had been a crazy, action-packed day. Getting tickets out of the city was a nightmare, and it was nothing short of a miracle that they were actually seated on an outbound train. The Ticket Collector was at the door checking everyone's tickets and refusing last minute passengers who begged to get on the train.

As the train chugged out of Madras, Rajam looked out at the dismal countryside wondering if she would ever return. Would Madras be bombed? Even if they did return, would Partha have a job? Everything in her life seemed to echo the quaking motion of the train. She could not find any rhythm either in her thoughts or emotions. Everything seemed chaotic and totally out of sync. Kamu, who had her face pressed against the dusty window, turned towards Rajam, her eyes twinkling in delight.

"What fun Amma!" she exclaimed. "I love trips. We are going to have so much fun!"

Rajam smiled. Oh to be a child again!

CHAPTER FOUR

KANDU
SHIMLA – APRIL 1942

THE SUMMER SOJOURN

Kandu had carefully cut a picture of Adolf Hitler to add to his collection of *Political Maniacs*. His chubby fingers interfered with his cutting skill especially when blunt scissors made a simple task daunting. He scoured and devoured the newspapers each day for stories about the War. For three years, war had been raging in Europe and now, it seemed as though it was truly becoming a global battle with England and Japan attacking one another, bringing the skirmishes onto the shores of the Indian subcontinent. Each day he made an entry in his diary of major events taking place in Europe, recording highlights in cryptic one-liners. His list seemed to indicate that Europe was united under twisted schizophrenics, and Kandu was glad he lived far away. Daddy only permitted him to cut pictures from newspapers that were at least a month old. He was done with the pile and could leave it along with the stack meant for the *kabādiwāllāh* who bought old newspapers and bottles each month from all the families on this street.

His pen ran out of ink and he arose from his seat by the bay window of their Shimla home and sauntered into Daddy's study but all he could find was a red pencil. It would have to do. He wanted to finish this entry before taking sugar cubes down to the stable for his favorite horse, Thunder.

No introduction needed for this bloke. He is Adolf who has bitten off more than he can chew. Kandu didn't know if that sounded right but it was already written and he couldn't erase a red pencil mark. *(Tell it to the schoolboys, population, and the marines).* That didn't sound right either. He wasn't quite sure if his twelve-year-old peers in school were even interested in Hitler and the war. It was not a very impressive caption but Kandu was not focused. They had moved to Shimla a week ago and the household had not really settled. They were in the midst of unpacking and there were boxes everywhere. The servants seemed overworked and it annoyed him when he couldn't find a fresh pair of underwear this morning.

Which reminded him, "Govindhan ..." he yelled for the servant. "Unpack *kiya*?"

"Govindhan ... *mera kapda*?"

Haa baba abhi karta hoon. Govindhan was very obliging. He was Kandu's constant companion and tried to get to everything, only he never really finished what he started and ended up being yelled at by someone in the household. He was the sweeper–cum–valet–cum–odds–and–ends person. Nothing really functioned in the Ayyar household without him. Govindhan ran to Kandu's room and meticulously refolded Kandu's clothes and stacked them in the large wooden cupboard. Kandu sneezed as the musty smell of the closet wafted past his nose. He had left the cupboard doors open but the effects of being closed for six months would take its own time to wear off. Govindhan had finished with only half the clothes when he heard Dharmu yelling for him from the store room. *Ayaa memsahib,* he yelled back and scampered off. There he goes, mused Kandu, *half-job Govindhan.* But his underwear was unpacked, and it felt good to wear a clean pair.

It was really disorienting for everyone in the household to spend half the year in Delhi and the summer in Shimla. By March, the mercury would begin rising on the dry, northern plains and the packing would commence. The entire British government shifted to the hills of Himachal and settled in the cooler hill station of Shimla for the duration of summer. Some took trains to Kalka and horse *tonga* the rest of the way and others rode in the plush comfort of cars. The luggage arrived later, carried manually uphill and delivered to the families by the local Kulu coolies. Mahadevan constantly complained about the expense involved in such a move, but he could scarcely register a formal complaint. This was the British Raj and they were the rulers of the land and could afford to live like kings. Their overwhelming concern about the weather and their comfort was paramount, even at the expense of the Indian Treasury.

Kandu loved the weather in Shimla, always cool and sunny. Even when the rain rolled in, the mist over the hilltops presented a mesmerizing sight. Kandu spent most of the day sitting by the large bay window which marked one end of the living room. The window extended all the way across the width of the hall and housed a beautiful seat with comfortable velvet cushions. This was Kandu's permanent haunt. It overlooked the street and Kandu spent many hours looking at passersby and admiring the verdant valley. He inevitably sat here after five in the evening to catch the first glimpse of Daddy slowly plodding uphill. Poor Daddy! He was too fat and the walk home from work was good exercise, which he may have even enjoyed if only he were twenty pounds lighter.

Kandu walked across to the window and glanced out. The hillside was dotted with homes, and to the east he could see the spire of Christ Church that marked one end of the Mall Road. For the first few years Kandu was not allowed to walk there as Mahadevan didn't have the requisite seniority to hobnob with the whites. But after Mahadevan was promoted to the rank of Secretary in '38, the family was permitted to use this fancy thoroughfare. Evening strolls on Mall Road became part of the family's routine which Kandu loved, especially when they stopped by the candy store.

He glanced at his watch. It was 5:15. Daddy was late. Figuring he could spend some time with the horse, he ran into the pantry and stole a few sugar cubes. Then down two flights of stairs and into the stables at the rear of the house. Kandu breathed in deeply. He loved the smell of horses, and the hay, and even the horse dung had its own special odor. From childhood he had associated people and things with fragrances, and Shimla was intrinsically connected to horse smells. The groom had just finished brushing Thunder down and greeted Kandu as did the large grey mare with a gentle *hrrumph*.

"Hello Thunder," Kandu whispered rubbing his velvety neck. "Did you miss me?" Smelling the sugar, Thunder pushed his nose towards Kandu's pant pockets. Kandu pulled out the sugar cubes and watched the horse pick it off his palm. He always wondered what would happen if Thunder used his teeth. He had such large teeth but always puckered his lips and gently lifted the cubes off Kandu's hand. It was a nuzzly, ticklish sensation that Kandu absolutely loved.

Kandu heard Mahadevan's cough even though he was way downhill. The cold Delhi weather, combined with the smoke from *chulas*, the stoves locals used to heat coal and keep warm, made Delhi winter smog unhealthy, and not one winter passed without Mahadevan coming down with a hacking cough. Ever since his London days, he had a weakness in the chest, and the slightest cold brought on the wheezing and inevitably lapsed into bronchitis, leaving him coughing for months. The climb uphill was especially strenuous, making him breathe deeply and inducing a deep, chesty cough. Kandu turned and ran down the hill to greet his father.

"Hello Daddy!" he said cheerily. "Shall I hold your briefcase? Did you bring the newspaper?"

Stopping momentarily to catch his breath Mahadevan hugged his son and handed his brown leather attaché case to him. Kandu flipped open the flap and began scanning the headlines even while walking.

"Don't walk and read, it's bad for your eyes. You can look at it at home." But Kandu didn't hear him.

"Ready for school?" Mahadevan continued. Catching the last word, Kandu looked up. "I can't wait for school; it's so boring at home. Do you think Tucky and Deb would have arrived by now? I'm dying to meet them again." Kandu, being the youngest, had fended for himself ever since they moved from Rangpur, as his sisters were promptly enrolled in a boarding school in Kurseong nestled in the hills near Darjeeling. His oldest sister Vani got married the previous year, and Rukku now studied in Tara Hall, a boarding school for girls in Shimla. She had exams this week and was expected home soon, and Kandu anxiously awaited her return. He had plenty of friends but only a few had arrived in Shimla, and this meant utter tedium for Kandu. Finally, they reached the gates flanked by two stone pillars which held the words *Hari Niwas:* abode of Krishna. Kandu cheerfully bounded up the stairs to his quiet corner at the bay window, ready to discover what Hitler had done today.

CHAPTER FIVE

DHARMU
SHIMLA – APRIL 1942

SETTLING IN

D harmu could not contain her excitement today. They were invited to the grand Viceregal Hall, as Viceroy Linlithgow and Lady Doreen had extended an invitation to them for the very first Ball of the season. It was scheduled two Saturdays from today, yet Dharmu was already planning for the event. Mahadevan never had the seniority to deserve such an invitation for many years but his recent promotion had changed so many things. The balls and garden parties at the Viceregal residence were the high point in the social lives of the local gentry and Dharmu recalled the very first time she received an invitation card a year ago. She was so gratified and proud, she kept it in her purse and showed it to everyone she met.

Dharmu held her diamond necklace and ruby choker against her skin and admired the jewelry in the mirror, unable to decide between the two. Everyone would be in their hand-picked gowns and saris sporting their finest jewelry and she needed to look her best. Since it was the very first Ball of the season, impressions were everything. Yet she wanted to make the right impression and not appear gaudy or overdressed. Mahadevan had gifted a new diamond necklace for her that almost reached her waist and she had not worn it yet. Perhaps she would use this event as an opportunity to show it off. Everyone was sure to notice it sparkling under the brilliant chandeliers that lit up the Grand Ballroom.

Dharmu carefully put the jewelry back into the steel safe and turned her attention to her saris. She was never very adventurous with her clothing and remained conservative, knowing that saris were just more respectable and natural to her. She never thought of wearing dresses like many of the Calcutta ladies. She couldn't conceive of removing her *pottu*, a sign of marriage, and realized she would look ludicrous in a dress and a huge pottu on her forehead. On her last trip to the south, she had picked up over a dozen saris and now needed to decide what best complemented her diamonds. She wished the girls were here.

Their comments were much more constructive. Vani had a good eye for color and would have made this decision in minutes. After vacillating some more, she finally she picked a rose pink sari with a bottle green border that had little gold paisleys embroidered all over. It was grand enough, yet the color was subtle, and the diamonds would set off the deep green border.

She had come a long way from the gauche, hesitant girl in Rangpur. She now spoke English perfectly and had learned to play croquet, tennis, and bridge. Living in Nadia and Calcutta was a learning experience, especially after she met Rani Chatterjee. Rani had been a godsend; she had taught Dharmu all the requisite niceties to function in European society. Rani was bold and very westernized and wore dresses and sleeveless shirts and crops, but then had the figure to match it. She was so gorgeous, with her tawny complexion and smoky eyes. She looked like a model at parties in western clothes with a Campari in one hand and a cigarette perched on the edge of a silver holder, dangling in the other. Dharmu felt like a villager next to her and didn't bargain on Rani actually being a nice person. She was so accustomed to the anglicized Bengali ladies taking every opportunity to make her feel like the country bumpkin, that she expected no less from Rani. It was a pleasant surprise when they hit it off, and over the next few years Rani became her mentor and best friend. Rani taught her how to play bridge and even found a tennis instructor who instructed some of the officers' wives a few days a week. Calcutta social life revolved around the Gymkhana Club, where the ladies played bridge and tennis during the day and men met for cocktails and poker in the evenings. It was the hub of all activity and slowly Dharmu found herself quite at ease with the wives of senior officers as well as the English ladies. Dharmu discovered a natural ability to hit the ball, and even though she wore a sari to play, she managed to be at the top of her tennis league.

Tennis and Bridge brought her into the circuit of coffee mornings and tea parties, and she became an integral part of the social circle of young officer's wives. With constant contact in such circles, her self-esteem increased monumentally. Even though she had gained some weight, it did not deter her. She was always impeccably dressed and hosted some of the best garden parties on the lawns of their Tughlak Road home in Delhi.

Yes, she certainly had come a long way.

She heard Mahadevan's classic cough, and after quickly checking that all her clothes were neatly arranged, she made her way to the living room.

The Shimla home was much smaller than her house on Tughlak road, but it was enough for the three of them. Thankfully there were four bedrooms, but the hall and dining rooms were small. The weather in Shimla was so perfect that most often they took their meals outside on the patio, overlooking a terrace garden. There were large French doors that opened up from the dining room onto the patio and Dharmu still had the set of wicker furniture she used in Rangpur, renewed with a fresh coat of white paint. The air in Shimla was dry and crisp. Spring was in the air and the weather was picture perfect. It was still light, and they still had time to enjoy the outdoors before being forced to retire indoors by mosquitoes and bugs that appeared in droves after dusk.

Mahadevan was already seated outside when Dharmu walked in.

"How was your day?" she enquired.

"It was quiet. Many people haven't moved as yet and the office feels as though we are on vacation."

"Has the Viceroy arrived?"

"Oh yes. They moved in last week, but he is on leave, so everyone is using this week to take a break from work. We even had our lunch served on the lawns. It was delightful. I have some letters. I think Vani has written to you."

Dharmu opened the letter in dread. Vani had been married for almost a year, and they hadn't seen her since. When the alliance for her marriage was brought to them, she was not happy. Her husband Ganesh was a doctor who had studied medicine in Europe. He was dapper and very westernized and had a reputable job as the private physician for the Maharaja of Mysore. All that sounded very exciting, but Vani was terribly disappointed when she saw his photograph. He was dark with a small face and a hooked nose and was unbelievably thin. Vani had grown up into a beautiful young woman and felt she deserved better. Both Mahadevan and Dharmu believed that marrying a doctor who held such a prestigious position should not be turned down for something as unimportant and transient as outward appearance. They may not be able to promise her a better match. He was well dressed, educated and well-spoken and, besides, Vani wasn't getting any younger. After months of tears and persuasion, Vani relented and the marriage had taken place the previous year. After that, Vani's letters home were somber and dry. She was filled with resentment and never forgave her parents for marrying her off to someone she didn't love. With a deep sigh Dharmu opened her letter.

Dear Amma and Appa,

By the time you receive this letter you would be settled in Shimla. Mysore is getting hotter by the minute and with no ventilation in these two rooms the heat is becoming unbearable.

I can't believe you didn't see what a mistake you were making when you married me off like this. You cannot understand how hard it is to wake up and see Ganesh's face each morning. I know you said love would come but I have no idea when and how. He is a nice and kind man but so is every Tom, Dick and Harry on the streets but that doesn't mean one has to marry them. I hate Mysore, I hate the people, Kannada is a crude sounding language and I wish I could wring my mother-in-law's neck. She has the most annoying voice and her demands are ceaseless. It's not fair that you didn't have to live with in-laws and I do. Please, please let me come home for the summer. I need a break to be able to breathe.

I am done with my ranting and raving. What's the point? It's not as if I can change anything. I just have to accept my destiny. Unfortunately, you sent us to convent schools and we learned to think, which I now believe was a miserable idea. If you planned to marry us off in this manner to the first person who walked in the door, why the hell did you educate us?

Well, like I said earlier, I am done with ranting and raving. Now for the good news or however you want to take it. I have missed my periods and I believe I am pregnant. I am thoroughly miserable as the bathroom is all the way at the end of the garden and I need to pee ever so often. In this day and age who builds the bathroom as an outhouse? I truly live in a village with villagers. I bought a chamber pot and use it at night. By morning the room smells disgusting and I have to empty it myself as the old crony (my mother-in-law) won't allow parayans to enter the rooms. I have half a mind to ask her to empty it but of course I can't.

So my dear Mummy and Daddy, I hope you are satisfied to hear I am thoroughly miserable and you realize you played with my life and deliberately thrust me into this life of drudgery. Please don't do the same with Rukku. Of course dear Kandu will marry a princess and live like a King. Of that I have no doubt.

I am sorry to write all this but sometimes I feel as if my head will burst with all the suffering I have to endure. I do hope Daddy can send a ticket for me to come to Shimla. I really could do with the break.

And once again I'm sorry
P.S. I hope you are too. And I still love you.
Your loving daughter,
Vani

Dharmu slapped the letter down on the table, angry with Vani for blaming them for her misery. Every girl had to marry. Some people had poor health, others nasty in-laws and still others wayward husbands. Everyone had their own destiny, so how was she to blame for everything?

Mahadevan sipped his tea and looked at Dharmu knowing instinctively that here was another tirade from Vani. It had been this way ever since she married.

"So she still hasn't settled down then."

"No. As usual she hates her life, her marriage and I think she hates us all."

"No, don't think that way. She is going through a period of adjustment. Who else can she blame? After all we pushed her into this marriage."

"That may be, but how were we to know where the bathroom in their house was? In any case she doesn't have to live there forever. Things will change, and in the meantime like all other women all over the world, she needs to adjust."

There was a pause and Mahadevan sat silent. Had he made a mistake? Would she do anything drastic if she was too unhappy? This was not good, and he feared for her mental and physical safety.

"How is her health?" he enquired.

"She's pregnant," Dharmu replied, as if merely stating a matter of fact.

"Oh dear, that is great! Why didn't you say that in the first place? This is fantastic! We are going to be grandparents." Mahadevan's face broke into a wide grin. He was truly happy to hear this piece of good news. "I'm sure this will make things appear different. A child will give her something to care for. She is just spoiled with too much luxury and cannot put up with any hardship. I'll send her a ticket to visit us," he added with his customary uncanny ability to know what people around him wanted or needed.

"Let the first trimester pass, then she can come. Rukku will also be here and they can talk to each other. Otherwise she'll eat my head. I tell you, thank goodness for Kandu. He is such low maintenance. He never bothers me."

"Don't say that, Dharmu; they are still our daughters. If you have children, you have to deal with problems."

"Not anymore ... she is married. She needs to deal with her own problems. Who helped me out? My mother never knew what I went through. Each person is in charge of their own life," Dharmu added with an angry scowl.

"That may have been true in your generation, but as a mother you need to be sympathetic."

"She gets my back up with all this blame."

"Come on now, forget about it. We can think of Vani when she writes next."

As Mahadevan picked up a magazine to browse, Dharmu did the same and all thoughts of Vani were conveniently shelved for the time being.

A strong breeze blew by the patio and Vani's letter which so far had sat on the breakfast table lifted in the breeze, soared into the skies over the garden and into the valley beyond.

CHAPTER SIX

MAHADEVAN
SHIMLA – APRIL 1942

THE RIDE BY THE MAIDĀN

"**D**addy I'm bored. Can we go for a horseback ride? There is still light and we can come back in an hour, in time for dinner." Kandu had been idling all day trying to find ways to fill his time, but Dharmu and all the servants were occupied unpacking and organizing the house, which left no time for him.

Reluctantly, Mahadevan lifted himself out of the comfort of the wicker chair and yelled at Govindhan to bring his riding gear. By the time they reached the stables, Charanjit, the groom, had two horses saddled and was ready to accompany them. They trotted slowly downhill with Charanjit jogging along. Kandu felt mighty proud, dreaming he was a Raja riding for *shikār*, the royal hunt. They would not be able to ride at full gallop until they reached the *maidān* which was the only expanse of flat land in Shimla. It wasn't as large as the Annandale Maidān, but would have to suffice today. It was late and sunset was less than an hour away. Besides, Mahadevan was tired and only agreed to accompany Kandu under duress. Riding had never been his favorite pastime, and he only rode because horses had easier access in Shimla's smaller pathways. He had a hard time mounting the horse, particularly now with his added weight, and the trotting jostled his innards, a very uncomfortable feeling. As they moved away from the largely residential areas and into the British Cantonment with all the office buildings, the horses shifted into a brisk trot. Mahadevan never really developed any rhythm while riding, and Kandu needed to control himself from laughing out loud. Daddy looked truly unhappy with his belly jiggling like jelly, and Kandu realized he only rode to humor him.

When they reached the maidān, they were surprised to see it crowded with people. From their white cotton apparel Mahadevan recognized that this was a meeting of the INC (Indian National Congress). Obviously, with the government moving to Shimla, the Congress had shifted their agitations here, to bring government attention to the growing demand from Indians for full freedom. Gandhiji was gearing up for a major call of *Quit India*, and peaceful demonstrations like this were mushrooming in every corner of the country. Mahadevan turned to Kandu, who looked worried.

"I had no idea that the Congress was organizing a rally. Maybe we should ride somewhere else. I don't want to get caught in an angry mob." Almost as if they had heard him, a group of boisterous young men suddenly surrounded them.

"Oy brown *sahib*, all dressed in British clothes," jeered one, as he held onto Mahadevan's horse, much to Charanjit's chagrin. Red in the face, he asked the boys to move on and not cause trouble. He told them that sahib was an officer and that they shouldn't mess with him, this leading to more comments and agitation among them.

"Our own people are traitors, sold to the British."

"Not traitors yaar, slaves," added another angrily.

"Not slaves, arse-lickers. Oy brown sahib, are you an arse-licker?" This led to a titter of laughter. Mahadevan knew that responding would further agitate them. It needed little to convert a peaceful group into an angry mob, and he didn't want Kandu to be harmed in any way.

Mahadevan was flustered. They had touched on a raw nerve. He had always been at crossroads about his allegiance to the British. Now that the Independence movement was gaining momentum, it led to an upsurge of even more feelings of guilt and betrayal. His best defense had been to ignore it. Over the years he never acknowledged these negative thoughts, as they prevented him from functioning with integrity at work. He could never do full justice to his job if he lived with animosity. So he learned to divorce his emotional allegiance to his motherland from his work ethic. Immersing himself completely in the British way of life made him forget his deep-seated regret of career choice. It was too late for change. He knew he did not have the courage or strength of conviction to resign from office and join the movement like Nehru or other freedom fighters. Recognizing his lack of courage, he accepted that the path of revolution was not for him. Yet he never openly spoke about it and never passed judgment in front of others, as that would bring to the forefront an open acknowledgement of moral cowardice and it served no purpose other than to demean his self-respect and confidence, both of which were sorely needed for any Indian that worked as an underling in British service. His thoughts were interrupted by angry questions by the mob.

"Why do you wear those *Angrezi* clothes. Use *Khadi* like us."

"You should be ashamed of yourself. Don't you have any self-respect?" "If I were you I would rather commit suicide than sell my soul to the foreigners."

"*Arre,* don't waste your breath on these brown sahibs. They will enjoy with the British while we die for the country and once we have freedom they will enjoy that too."

Mahadevan now was truly uncomfortable. He had never really talked about the freedom movement with Kandu and knew these comments would definitely impact the young boy. Unfortunately, everything they said was credible, and Mahadevan knew he would have a hard time defending his position to Kandu. Hopefully he wouldn't need to if Kandu didn't bring it up. He turned to glance at his son's face and, on detecting a look of fear in Kandu's eyes, recognized that he needed to get away from here as fast as possible. He spurred his horse into a trot, forcing the group to part, and Kandu followed him quickly with Charanjit fending off the invasive arms of the young men who attempted to touch the boy and frighten him. For a while they didn't speak. They cantered down the road away from the township and stopped their horses under a copse of trees. Mahadevan dismounted and sat on the stone wall facing the darkening valley below. Kandu joined him and remained silent, knowing that his father was upset. Finally, he broke the deafening silence.

"Daddy, why do you let those boys upset you. They are just ruffians and you shouldn't mind what they say. You say that to me when I get into a fight in school after someone calls me darkie, and now you are not following your own advice."

Mahadevan turned to his son, knowing he was right. Kandu was sometimes wise beyond his years. But he deserved an explanation. "It's not easy Kandu, especially since Gandhiji will soon announce the Quit India movement. They will ask for the British to leave Indian soil permanently, and that might affect my job.

"Is that a good thing? How will we run this country? Don't we need the British to keep things in order?" Kandu was echoing common British sentiment. He read newspapers voraciously, but his information was from the British dailies. Mahadevan did not subscribe to the local vernacular newspapers as its editorials only led to more mental turmoil. On occasion, whenever there was a national incident, he picked one up to learn more about the local sentiment.

"If the British do quit India, and they will, the new Government may decide to make changes that could involve retiring current civil servants. I don't think they can run the country without us, but one never knows." He felt the anxiety associated with uncertainty of the times and realized Kandu was too young to have apprehension about the future, but the damaging words had left his mouth, echoing his own fears.

"Daddy this worries me. Without the British, it's going to be very different. They bring so much order into everything. They have laws and rules."

"Aha!" exclaimed Mahadevan. "They like us to believe they maintain order, but the reality is that they create chaos in the first place.

"Divide and rule. I know about that. I have read about that strategy in Macaulay's essays. They use it to cause rifts between us, between the rich and poor, Muslim and Hindu." Kandu paused to reflect. He never really thought of independence from the British and that too from the perspective of a native. He didn't feel like a native. He felt British but knew that to them he was just another darkie. How many times had he got into scuffles in school when he reacted violently to his white school mates disdainfully dismissing him as one! It made no real sense to work for the British, and this thought really confused him.

"So then, Daddy, why do you work for them? You are so clever—you could be a great lawyer or even run your own business. Why choose to work for people who deliberately make us feel small?"

"What else can I do, Kandu? What will happen to all of you if I give up my job and go to jail? You are all used to this good life—the house, cars, servants, horses, parties, great schools. How can I take that away from you?"

Kandu saw the point. After all, a man had a duty in life to take care of his family, and Daddy was only doing his job. Then he recalled the comments by the ruffians.

"Are you an arse-licker?" he asked his father.

Mahadevan threw his head back and burst into laughter. "I don't know that I am. I just do my job. Remember the letter I showed you that Abraham Lincoln wrote to his son in which he said to sell your skills to the highest bidder?"

"… but never sell your soul." Kandu completed.

"These men are all unemployed youth. They want someone to blame. But I cannot take responsibility for two hundred years of British rule just because I work for the ICS. Besides, our work is so fundamental. It is the bureaucracy that actually runs this country, and this will become crucial when we get independence. The new government will have the machinery to run itself. I just hope the new leaders realize that."

"Do you ever feel guilty about working for the British?"

"Sure I do. I wish things were different. But I made a choice long ago and I really can't do much to change it, so there's no point feeling guilty. In our hearts we know we want independence. In our souls we long to be free. We will support the movement though we cannot shout it out from rooftops and there's no shame in that."

"You know what Daddy; I think it's enough of British rule. I'm sick of the British. I'm tired of fighting with British kids who hate my skin color. I wish they would leave and the class be filled with our own people. At least then we would all be equal."

"Even then you will find something to squabble about. Never forget they call you names because it makes them feel superior by putting you down. You are no darkie, you are a Brahmin, an Aryan, you are light-skinned compared to other Indians. Don't focus so much on color and race. Instead you have to develop lofty ideals beyond race and color."

"I know. Look at what Hitler is doing in Germany? Millions are dying there because of their race. Its despicable that one group of people think they are better than the others and then they try to decimate them. But I really think there are Hitlers all over the world, in India, in America, all over!"

"What do you mean?" queried Mahadevan unable to figure out his son's train of thought.

"The white men who kept blacks as slaves and tortured them for two hundred years? That was not one Hitler, that was a whole society of Hitlers who believed Negroes were animals and whipped and tortured and lynched them for years. Do you know some 50 or 60,000 people died in their Civil war, all to abolish slavery?"

"Are you sure of the numbers? Oh dear! So much blood had to spill to clear the debt of evil. Everyone pays for their wicked deeds in the end. The South did, the Germans also will," pondered Mahadevan.

"And the British? Here too, so many people are dying from hunger. You know that."

Mahadevan knew only too well. He was well aware of the British maneuvering prices for rice and wheat beyond the reach of the public. Widespread poverty and hunger were now commonplace. They would do anything to divert people's attention from the Independence movement, and he feared a disaster much bigger than the impending genocide in Europe. But he couldn't talk about that to Kandu.

Mahadevan stood up. They had been so involved in their discussion that they missed the sunset. "Come on, Kandu enough of this heavy talk. Everyone gets what they deserve, and you, my dear boy, deserve a hot bath followed by a hot meal."

The two mounted the horses again and made their way home feeling thoroughly exhausted, but Kandu was pretty sure this wasn't physical exhaustion. It was much more the burden of having the misfortune of misplaced allegiance, the liability of being British trapped in an Indian body.

CHAPTER SEVEN

SWAMINATHAN
THANJAVUR – AUGUST 1942

TIME MOVES ON

S waminathan put down the historic copy of *Swadeshimitran* and stared into the distance. Today, August 8th, would be remembered with reverence by every Indian citizen forever. Finally, the Congress Party had mustered up enough courage to launch and pass a resolution asking the British to Quit-India in a peaceful withdrawal. Gandhi and other important leaders along with sixty thousand additional INC supporters had been arrested. Swaminathan had been closely following the movements in the country and around the world. He had much less information about the latest trends in the nationalist movement now after his retirement from the police force. Earlier, as long as he was working, he met people constantly and there was always some lively deliberation over any incident taking place in the country. Life had changed with retirement and he did not meet his old friends ever since they moved out of the official accommodation to a smaller home in the suburbs. Things were quieter here and, although he had some acquaintances, they were not close enough to sit and debate politics. So, instead, he relied on the infrequent dropping-in of old friends, or on his weekly visits to the marketplace, where he could join a group of people deep in discussion. These events were sporadic and unsatisfying, and he filled the vacuum of intelligent dialogue by voraciously reading every newspaper editorial, and if that didn't suffice, there were always memories.

Three full years had whizzed by since Mangalam's demise. Rajam and Kamu were visiting, having arrived here after the Madras evacuation. They had spent a month in Cuddalore with his brother's family but on their return to Madras just as everyone feared, all three brothers lost their jobs. Swaminathan always worried about Partha working for a Japanese firm and knew in his heart as soon as the British announced India's active participation in the war that this proclamation would spell doom for every Japanese company. It took about three months for Partha to finally find a job in an ammunitions factory in Poona, and he left Madras immediately. Rajam and Kamu came to Thanjavur as Mangalam's death anniversary was coming up and Rajam wanted to spend some time with her father before her move to Poona. Once Partha found decent accommodation, he would call for them to join him.

Swaminathan sank back into the comfort of the easy chair and extended his swollen feet, resting them on a small foot stool. The last few years seemed to have flown by almost in a blur. For the first few years after his daughter Kunju was widowed and had moved into their Chidambaram home, his wife Mangalam took care of their needs for the most part. He was due to retire, but with eight mouths to feed, he knew he could not afford to until his son, Mani, also found work. Mani dropped out of school and found odd jobs here and there. He could never hold onto a job for any length of time, and Swaminathan had given up on the idea that his son would care for him in his old age. Mani would always be a wastrel with no ambition or motivation. It was disappointing, but Swaminathan had no choice other than to request his boss for an extension. His application was accepted, but his next posting was as Inspector of Thanjavur District. So once again they packed and moved further south to the city of Thanjavur.

Mangalam's health continued to deteriorate, and the move to a new house proved to be too strenuous for her. She now exhibited all the symptoms of hypertension, and the headaches and swollen feet kept her in bed recuperating most of the time. Kunju had completely taken over the running of the household with Chithi's help. Thank heavens for Parvathi Chithi, who still functioned at her peak with mechanical efficiency, churning out simple yet nourishing meals for the whole family. She ran the kitchen on a shoestring budget, and no one seemed to notice the watered down *sāmbār* and *thayirshādham* or the diluted coffee. Even if they did, no one complained. There was so much love in the household with compassionate and caring elders that the children flowered and added to the joy in the household. The additional burden of caring for Kunju and his grandchildren was sometimes overwhelming for Swaminathan, who should have retired by now, enjoying his pension in relative comfort. But he carried this obligation with his unchanging stoic attitude brought on by years of discipline working in the police force. He had no choice but to shoulder his responsibility with grace, because to question his situation could only bring on additional mental dilemmas which served no earthly purpose.

Mangalam had resigned herself to a quiet life, not walking around much, yet participating in every decision affecting the household from her command center in her bedroom. She hated eating salt-free food, but the English doctor was adamant. He told Swaminathan in no uncertain terms about the dangers of her consuming high levels of salt. For a while Parvathi kept some food apart especially for her, but over time, as her health improved, Mangalam would revert to eating what was cooked for the rest of the family. The stroke that eventually took her life came suddenly. Her movement and speech were severely affected. Swaminathan sent an urgent telegram asking Rajam to come back as soon as possible, but even before she got on the train, Mangalam had breathed her last. The Almighty was kind and took her away less than a week after the stroke. In many ways Swaminathan was grateful she was not confined to her bed for a long time in a coma. She had been so active all her life, Swaminathan could not bear to look at her in such a terrible state. He felt helpless and, although it twisted his heart to watch her suffer, he could not leave her side. Taking her to a hospital was not an option, and with no preventive medication, her end came quickly.

Swaminathan wiped the tears rolling down his cheeks. When he married, he assumed Mangalam being several years younger would outlive him, but she was blessed to die a *sumangali* and had probably won a hallowed spot in heaven; that's what the elders believed was the good fortune of a married woman whose death preceded her husband's. The reality for him was solitude with no one to share his thoughts and suffering. While he battled loneliness, he could never really ever be alone, not with a household filled with growing children.

Swaminathan stretched his aching legs and stared into the distance. The *thinnai* was his chosen place to repose no matter where he lived. He loved the outdoors, and sitting on the open verandah in front of the home allowed him to observe the comings and goings on the busy street. Besides, the light was perfect here and he could read his newspapers in peace. He picked up the newspaper once again to read the editorial on the Quit-India resolution.

"What an exciting day!" he exclaimed. Here I am lamenting Mangalam's loss, and the country is poised for actual freedom from the foreigners. Perhaps I might just live to see the Tricolor flag fly in freedom. *Vande Mātaram!* he bellowed in joyful abandon.

CHAPTER EIGHT

SWAMINATHAN AND RAJAM
THANJAVUR 1942

THE LEGEND OF VANCHI IYER

Rajam was startled by her father suddenly bursting into the national freedom cry. The coffee she was carrying spilt on her fingers scalding them, and she almost dropped the hot *davara* and tumbler.

"Gosh Appa, you scared me. What's got into you?"

Swaminathan burst into laughter. "Freedom fever my child. It's what the nation celebrates right now. *Vidudalai!*" He felt foolish being caught in a private moment. He was sure the ladies were otherwise occupied in the kitchen and only shouted thinking he was alone.

"Have you not read the papers? Quit India … *Bharat chodo*. Finally, Gandhi had the courage to ask for full freedom. It is a historic day for India, and the newspapers are full of stories." Swaminathan handed an English newspaper to Rajam.

"Where have I had the time between the kitchen and the kids?" replied Rajam, picking up the Tamil daily instead. English was not her forte. She could read English perfectly well but did not really enjoy herself as she struggled to decipher the meanings of words. Tamil was much more comfortable, and the editorials way more colorful.

"Thatha…." screamed Kamu running outside to gleefully sit on her grandpa's lap. She rubbed the back of her hand over the soft wrinkles cascading under his chin, something she did unconsciously every time she was near him. Soon Kunju, Chithi and the children joined them, and a lively discussion on politics ensued as each one tried to get heard above the loud laughs and yells of the younger kids who were playing. Swaminathan basked in the comfort of family, beaming from ear to ear. This was his topic and he was the authority here. The conversation moved from national politics to the local movement. Swaminathan had plenty of dealings with revolutionaries and had the unfortunate experience of being on the wrong side of the law. Venkat, Kunju's oldest son, wanted to join the INC, which thirstily enrolled fiery young men. Swaminathan had told him that he would have to wait until he was eighteen, and that day was not far away. "Thatha, you should introduce me to your friends Velu and Pandyan. I really think I'm old enough to join the INC."

"Venkat, you need to think more of your studies and wait a while before you become a revolutionary."

"But if I wait, the freedom struggle will be over and I would have missed all the fun," Venkat protested.

"At your age, you can be very emotional and move away from Gandhi's non-violent path. I have seen so many people die for no reason—all because of their zeal and misplaced heroism," Swaminathan stated wistfully.

"Did you know any famous ones?" asked Venkat, always excited by his grandfather's interesting anecdotes. Swaminathan was a natural story teller and loved an audience. After retirement all he had was memories, and so far the children were interested, but he knew it was a matter of time before they thought of his stories as an old man's ramblings. He decided a long time ago never to open up on anything unless specifically requested. He kept his stories for himself, for his private ruminations, something he had a lot of time for these days.

"The only one I remember is Vanchinathan, and that was back in 1911. I was there when he died." Swaminathan said softly, as he recalled with clarity that fateful night when the revolutionary Vanchi Iyer shot Collector Ashe.

"What?" exclaimed Venkat, who had been to Maniyachi station and heard about the assassination of the Collector whom they called Ashe Durai. "I didn't know this. You have to tell us this story."

"Your Thatha has seen many things. Everything is locked in his head, and if you don't ask he will not tell you. Come on tell us about Vanchinathan," urged Chithi.

"Don't remind me. I have too many regrets about that day. Unfortunately, I arrived too late at Maniyachi station and I could not help him."

"My goodness Thatha, you are full of surprises. Come on tell us what really happened," pleaded Rajam wanting to hear more.

"It's a long story." Swaminathan said, his mind shifting back in time.

"Never mind, we have all the time if you have the inclination. Vanchi is such a famous man, I can't believe you were involved," said Venkat, his voice betraying his excitement.

With a pretense of great reluctance, Swami began his story.

"Back then I had a temporary posting in Thirunelveli. King George V was to celebrate his coronation, and there was a terrible reaction to this all over India.

Thirunelveli, as you know, has always been a hotbed of underground activity. To add to that, Gandhi had little influence over the revolutionaries of the south. They wanted more action. They were not ready to wait for freedom. Most of them had been followers of Bipin Chandra Pal, who as you know took a more proactive approach, to put it mildly. He was one of the first freedom fighters from the north to come to the south and talk to the people. All the meetings were held in secret, and they were very volatile, spirited and inspiring. As a result, the youth got galvanized into action and began boycotts, morchas, and all kinds of other anti-government actions. Some of these had violent outcomes, but you know all that.

Ashe was the Collector of Thirunelveli, and he suppressed the revolts with brutal ferocity. He was a terrible man. For us Indians, it was very painful to *lāthi-charge* our fellow Tamilians. But since I was a police officer, duty came first. But Ashe didn't stop there. He unleashed a reign of terror on the citizens of Thirunelveli, entering homes, making random arrests, and people were horrified. There was a shoot-on-sight curfew, and people could not move around freely. Everyone was viewed with suspicion, and neighbors were ratting on neighbors. The community was very unhappy, justifiably so, and they hated Ashe. Every day there would be news of another person taken in for police questioning, and I cannot even begin to tell you about the plight of those who were taken into police custody. Ashe himself interrogated the prisoners, as he knew we were not as heavy-handed with them as he was. What I witnessed in that town, and what I was forced to inflict on my fellow citizens, defies reason and comprehension. There were many times when I was on the verge of quitting my job and joining the revolutionaries, but I had my family to think of, and I thought to myself that I would use my position as a police officer to help and save my brethren. Those bitter memories have often tortured me, and I am sure it will take me several lifetimes to recover. But enough about me, let me get back to the story.

As always, oppression led to more violence. The people of Thirunelveli wanted revenge, and the plotting began for the assassination of Ashe. I recall that our police barracks were attacked with kerosene bombs. Many officers were hurt, but I was one of the lucky ones. They even attempted to torch the Collector's house.

In the midst of all this, was Vanchinathan Iyer. I had seen him several times. Thirunelveli is a small town, and it was my job to keep track of known revolutionaries. He used to work as a clerk in the Forest department of Travancore. If only he had stuck to that, things might have turned out differently for him. I had heard through informants that he'd been to Madras and was seen in the company of V.V.S. Iyer, a well-known revolutionary. It was from him that Vanchinathan learned to shoot a gun. After returning to Thirunelveli, he began stalking Ashe, following his movements closely. There were many occasions when I saw him around town and could easily have approached him, and perhaps dissuaded him from carrying out his plot. I had no fondness for Ashe, but by killing him, Vanchi was guaranteed a quick walk to the gallows, and I hated to see such a tragic end to such a bright man. I have never stopped regretting I never took advantage of the many opportunities to deter Vanchi Iyer. But in retrospect, my advice may not have meant much to a fanatic, who was hell-bent on getting rid of Ashe.

There were rumors that some high ranking official would be targeted on June 11th, coinciding with the Coronation of King George, and on that day, Ashe, wisely stayed home. However, a week later, thinking things had quieted down, he planned an official trip with his wife to the hill station of Kodai Kanal. They were to leave from Thirunelveli, but enroute, had to change trains at Maniyachi station, and that is where Vanchi planned to shoot him. Early morning, my informant stormed into the station telling me that Vanchi had left the previous day, and was waiting for Ashe at Maniyachi. I took a group of constables, and we rushed out to intercept Vanchi and perhaps save the day. But time was against us, and by the time we reached Maniyachi by road, the dirty deed or the heroic one, depending on your perspective, had already taken place.

Vanchi and his brother-in-law, Shankar, had been waiting for the train to pull into the station. The Collector and his wife got down from the train and started walking across the platform to board the next train. His *sepoys* were still inside the train bringing out the luggage. Vanchi could not believe his luck. Taking advantage of the situation, he came up to Ashe and shot him three times at point blank range. As the wounded Collector clutched his bleeding chest, Vanchi ran to the end of the station to make his escape. The station was so crowded that no one knew who had shot him. There was so much confusion and screaming, the sepoys protecting the Collector could not see exactly who had done the deed. But Vanchi made the fateful mistake of returning to check if in fact the Collector was dead and saw him lying in the arms of his wife. Satisfied, he turned and for a second time tried to get away, but someone in the crowd screamed out calling him the assassin, and the sepoys began the chase. At the far end of the station, Vanchi turned like a stag at bay. He watched the soldiers approaching, followed by a huge crowd. He realized that there was no escaping, so he did the only other thing he was trained to do in such a situation. He reached for his revolver and shouting out the freedom cry, "Vande Mātaram," shot himself through the throat. I learned all this from spectators.

When we reached the station, I ran to the platform and saw the huge crowd at one end of the station. I knew right away that I had arrived too late. As I ran towards the crowd, I passed the Collector's wife, sobbing helplessly, holding the bleeding corpse that had once been her husband. I did not stop, but ordered two of my constables to help her, and continued running, pushing my way through the crowds. I was right. I had arrived too late. Vanchi's body had fallen over the edge of the platform, and his blood was soaking the earth around him. His body was contorted, but there was a smile on his face. As he left his body, he had done so knowing his mission was accomplished. Another martyr for the cause of India's freedom.

And there you have it, the legend of Vanchinathan Iyer."

For a while, nobody spoke. The group was still lost in the gripping drama of the story. Why did he die? Did he die in vain? Would people remember his brave act? Was violence the answer? Their minds were lost in a whirlwind of unanswered questions.

Then Venkat broke the silence, voicing what was in all their minds.

"Thatha, do you think India will ever be free?"

Swami did not reply. He did not need to. They knew the answer to that rhetorical question. It was just matter of time.

CHAPTER NINE

KOVILADI KAMALAMBA
THANJAVUR – OCTOBER 1942

THE DEVADASI HOME

Dhalaanku thakadhiku thaka thandinginathom. Kamalamba's voice rang out, marking the beginning of a particularly difficult dance pattern that her niece Balamani was having trouble with.

"Come on," she urged. "Sit down even more. The beat is *chathushram*, four beats, and you are still doing *thisrai* from the previous *jathi*. Are you stupid?" The frustration was apparent in her voice which was reaching a scary crescendo. Kamalamba was in the process of teaching Balamani a *varnam*, which would be the highlight of her performance. A difficult piece, the varnam was dedicated to Lord Shiva, which was interspersed with complicated *jathis*, rhythmic dance patterns that demonstrated the dancer's expertise. Bala had started her dance lessons almost as soon as she could walk and had been preparing for her debut performance for the last year. She was exhausted. Practice began at four in the morning and it was now close to noon. Other than a few sips of water, she had eaten nothing, as the dancing was so rigorous it made her sick to ingest anything. Her thighs were quivering in *aramandi,* the half seated posture used for traditional Bharata Natyam dance, which brought her down to virtually half her height. It required strength and endurance and her quads were still under-developed and reacting to overuse. Bala had been preparing for her *pottukattu* ceremony at the Thanjavur Periya Kovil (Brihadeesvara Shiva Temple). She would be performing her debut dance repertoire, her *arangetram,* in front of over of two hundred invited patrons. This was going to be a very important day for her, as a marriage ceremony to Lord Shiva would be performed by the high priest at the temple, after which she would become a *nithya sumangali.* She would be considered married for eternity, as the Lord in the temple was eternal, and she would forever be his *dāsi,* his slave.

Bala didn't know who fathered her but felt he must have belonged to a high caste, as her skin was fair and her features indicative of being high-born. Her mother died at childbirth and Kamalamba became her foster mother. On her birth the celebrations continued for a week, as Devadasis mourn the birth of a son and celebrate the birth of a daughter. When a daughter is sold to a patron, this holds promise of fortune and wealth for the entire clan. The girls were raised to be courtesans and temple dancers, learning dance and music, and were even instructed in the erotic secrets of the Kama sutra, as their life would be dedicated to serve their client and keep him happy.

They lived in a palatial house gifted to Kamalamba by a long-gone patron—an extended family of fifteen men and women. Bala didn't really know how she was related to the other women in the household. She called them all *Akka*, the respectful term for elder sisters—and everyone referred to Kamalamba as *Amma*. Other than the seven women, there were men who were the *Nattuvanārs*, official musicians who accompanied all the dance performances. The most powerful was Muthu, and Bala was terrified of him. He took care of the finances, arranged the dance recitals, pottukattu ceremonies and arangetrams, taking time to travel to nearby farms to connect with local *Jameendārs* and *Mirāzdārs*, inviting these rich landowners to events, and collecting food and gifts from them on behalf of the ladies whom they supported. He arranged the weekly soirées and ensured the Mirāzdārs' entry and exit was conducted with as much secrecy as possible. Muthu was not very tall but exceptionally imposing with his shiny black skin, red eyes, oiled black curly hair and a large handlebar moustache, which he twirled at sporadic intervals, to signal to everyone around his importance in the household. Kamalamba needed him to do her dirty work to keep the money flowing in from their patrons and ensure the girls were well taken care of.

Bala glanced at Muthu nervously and shivered when she saw him glowering at her. His large arms were plastered against his barrel shaped chest. One podgy hand adorned with several gold rings left its immense resting place to reach for the twisted moustache, and Bala fearfully sank down a few aching inches into her aramandi, but her legs were tremulous and she slipped down to the floor. Looking at everyone's shocked faces, she knew she was in trouble and burst into tears.

Mohan, a young flutist, part of the orchestra, felt her angst. He had a soft spot in his heart for her but knew he needed to mask his feelings, as she could never be his. Not in this lifetime. She was a Devadasi, born to offer herself to the highest bidder. He knew her first patron would probably be an ugly, overweight, middle aged debauch, and it hurt even to think about it. She was only twelve years old and would have to wait for her menstrual period to arrive before she submitted to that unfortunate destiny.

"Amma, let her rest now. We are also tired. Maybe we can begin again later," he ventured, hoping Kamalamba would relent.

Kamalamba looked at Muthu, whose hand had now descended from the moustache, signaling it was alright to stop. She touched the chime cymbals to her eyes, indicating that Bala could now end her lesson.

Bala's eyes closed in gratitude, and she energetically finished her closing obeisance. She nodded to Mohan acknowledging his timely assistance and ran into her room. Bala shared a room with two of her older sisters, Vasanthasena and Vyjayanthi, both of whom had recently secured new patrons. Vasanti as she was referred to, was adorning her hair after a luxurious oil bath, and the room smelt of *sāmbrāni*, the incense she had recently used to dry it. Bala ran to her bed and began crying afresh. She was overwhelmed with all the preparation. Her body was not used to so much dance and her muscles protested. The pain in her thighs was so intense that she could scarcely think straight.

"What happened? Too much dance? Did the Karadi not let you rest?" Vasanti asked, referring to their secret nickname for Muthu. He looked like a large, black bear, and the name they chose for him was apt.

"Every time I looked at him hoping to get a break, he twirled his silly moustache, which meant I couldn't stop. What do they think I am? Some bullock that can be made to work nonstop? I'm sure that even bullocks get more rest. I can't do this Vasanti. My whole body hurts." Bala buried her head in the soft pillow drenching it with her tears.

Vasanti recalled the time she was training for her pottukattu not so long ago and shuddered, grateful it was all over. The training had to be rigorous and the dance steps in perfect rhythm to the *nattuvāngam* and *mridangam*. Kamalamba was well-known for her dance prowess and her reputation was at stake. She knew the girls were young, but the ceremony had to be conducted pre-puberty, so she needed to be a hard task master.

"Don't worry. Once you know the varnam, the other pieces will be easy. The pure dance items are always the hardest. You have to know the piece well enough to perform it in your sleep. Only then will your performance be flawless."

"I'm so tired of all this. I don't want to do the pottukattu and I don't want to have a patron." Bala ranted, raising her voice in sheer frustration.

"Shh…." said Vasanti quickly closing the door. "Someone will hear you."

"Why can't I be like other girls and have a normal life? Meena next door goes to school. I want to do that too; I want to learn."

"Shh," Vasanti said, cradling Bala's head in her lap and wiping the sweat off her neck and face with a soft towel.

"You and I, we can't do anything to change our destiny. We are born Devadasis and we will die like that. Everyone around knows which caste we belong to. Even if we try to run away, they will not let us live normal lives. Amma has so many friends in the police who will find us no matter where we run. You know how Muthu beat Vyjayanthi when she ran away last year? You remember that don't you?"

How could Bala forget? It was she that was assigned to wiping the blood off the floor after Muthu was done with teaching Vyjayanthi a lesson. It took more than six months for her wounds to heal before she looked normal. Even before Vyjayanthi's psychological lesions healed, Amma had found a rich Mirāzdār from Salem to visit her. The three girls slept together and were unfailingly woken up by Vyjayanthi's nightmares and sobbing. No. There was no escape.

"Don't even think of running away. It's just not worth it. Just accept your destiny and maybe one day you will have your own home and be an Amma like Kamalamba Amma."

"I would never do that. I would rather die than make small girls dance and entertain fat, old men. I want to marry and have a family. Why can't I marry like other ordinary girls?"

"You will. And what better husband than the Lord himself?"

"But he isn't real and he can't love me and hold me or even talk to me. I don't see the point in that."

"Don't aspire for love from a man, foolish child. That is not for Devadasis. We love each other and that's all that matters. The most dangerous situation for us is to fall in love with our patrons. They are all married men and would never consider leaving their wives for us. Don't even entertain that thought. You know what happened with your own mother, don't you?"

Bala stared up at her with a blank expression and Vasanti knew she had made a mistake. Amma never liked to talk about it, but the gossip grapevine held no secrets. Obviously no one had said anything to Bala, and she was not about to be the first. If Amma wished, she would reveal the story.

"What happened to my mother? Tell me." Bala pleaded.

"Nothing. I meant to Kamalamba Amma, not your mother. You know about her first patron don't you?"

"Why can't you tell me? I know you are hiding something. I want to know her story." Bala pouted angrily, annoyed at being treated like a child and kept in the dark.

"I can't tell you. Muthu would kill me. Just know that she was fortunate to be loved by a real man and she tasted paradise on earth. Now come on, take a quick bath and I'll rub some coconut oil with camphor on your legs. It will ease the pain."

Bala sat up and stared vacantly across the room. She sat down in front of the large wooden carved mirror and looked at herself. A few stray locks had escaped from the tight bun and framed her heart shaped face. She leaned forward and admired her grey, doe shaped eyes with naturally curled lashes. Then she ran her fingers along her long arched eyebrows and down her pert and slightly hooked nose until they outlined her full lips and pointed chin. In the glow from the candles, her skin shone like polished ivory. She was beautiful. She turned around and looked at Vasanti.

"What do you do at night with the patrons? Do you dance for them?" she asked innocently.

Vasanti dropped her shaking head into the palms of her hands. No one had told this poor child what her destiny was. In what words could she explain to a twelve-year-old what her main occupation would be for the rest of her youth?

CHAPTER TEN

DHARMU
SHIMLA – JULY 1942

THE VICEREGAL BALL

D harmu pulled the cashmere stole tightly around her shoulders, realizing quickly this was feeble protection against the cool Shimla night air. She turned to wave to Kandu, who as usual had his nose plastered against the bay window. She hated leaving him and going out in the evenings, but today she was not worried. Rani's son Deb and Kandu's best friend Tucky were to spend the night with him, and he was quite happy to see off his parents. Kandu was used to their hectic social life. Once the girls had left, it became lonely for him in the evenings and initially, he hated that they left him to the mercy of servants several times a week. Over time, he got used to being by himself, depending on the battalion of servants to keep himself entertained.

Dharmu looked resplendent in her pink and green Kānjeevaram silk sari. It was definitely a good choice. Her diamond earrings, large as English pennies, glimmered even in the waning sunlight. She had used her best diamond nose rings, and the necklace spoke for itself. Her wrists sported two dozen brilliant glass bangles matching her sari that she had picked up in the busy streets of the Chandni Chowk Bazaar in Delhi; colorful green, gold, and white stone bangles that clinked daintily each time she moved. She looked down at her fingers and admired the half dozen diamond rings adorning them. She definitely looked like a Queen. Beside her, Mahadevan was seated in full Government regalia. He had shaved and bathed, and the smell of English cologne overpowered her own perfume. They had hired a carriage for the evening as had most other invitees. Although they had a Dodge sedan, it merely dropped them off at the Kalka station because these large cars had difficulty navigating the hilly terrain. As long as they were in Shimla, they preferred walking or renting a horse buggy. The journey to the Viceregal Lodge was not long, but the road was steep and the ride wobbly. Today everything looked festive. Bright oil torches lit the way for almost half a mile, and at the end of the road Dharmu could see the lights from the mansion shining brightly, partially illuminating the darkening sky.

They had to wait behind a long line of carriages and cars before they could alight at the magnificent entrance. There were carriages everywhere, some ordinary ones like theirs, but others were fancy with flags and emblems, gold and silver paint, and Dharmu knew many local Rajas and their glamorous queens were in attendance. She gleaned this from the number of Rolls Royces and other fancy cars parked in the distance. She was really excited. Perhaps she would meet the Raja of Jammu and Kashmir or maybe the svelte Maharaja of Patiala. Mahadevan mentioned a long list of invitees, but the names of the Rajas were too long, too complicated and too similar sounding. She had a hard time remembering north Indian names and invariably used the wrong one. Turbaned doormen in impeccable uniforms opened the carriage doors and helped them descend from the coach, and then with her heart pattering, she held onto Mahadevan's arm and entered the brilliantly lit Grand Ballroom.

Strains of a Viennese waltz performed by a live orchestra greeted them, and they paused for a moment, taking in the brilliance of the panorama in front of them. The vibrant and diverse colors and clothes dazzling under the electric lights and chandeliers made Dharmu's head swim momentarily. There were handsome European couples dancing at one end while groups of fascinatingly dressed men and women huddled around. Uniformed waiters carried drinks and cocktail snacks, and at the far end under the Grand staircase, she could spot the Viceroy and his elegant wife. The Viceroy was resplendent in his white uniform with shiny brass buttons and stripes, and next to him Lady Doreen looked rather plain in a long, flowing, purple dress with a fashioned rose holding one strap of her gown and leaving her neck and other shoulder bare. She had sparkly earrings, but other than that she had no jewelry on. Really! European women had no dress sense. They always dressed so simply. At best they wore a string of pearls or a decorative brooch. This was in direct contrast to all the Indian ladies in brightly colored silk saris shimmering with sequins and gold and silver embroidery. Some of the royalty had necklaces that cascaded from the throat to their waist. Today everyone was dressed in their finest with their best saris and gowns complemented by their choicest jewelry.

Dharmu waited nervously in line to greet the Viceroy. She had practiced her curtsy several times today, making sure she managed to complete it without the end of her sari falling off her shoulder. She had fastened it with a brooch just in case it slipped. Today had to be perfect. She was taking no chances. *How do you do Lady Doreen or was it Doris? Oh dear!* "Yenna what's her name, Doris or Doreen?" she whispered to her husband.

Mahadevan frowned at her. "How many times do I have to tell you? Don't you make a mistake! Just say *how do you do*, forget about her name. I don't want you to make a fool of yourself." Dharmu's palms were moist in anticipation until finally, it was their turn.

"Ah Ayyar ... Nice to see you. All settled in?" the Viceroy enquired.

"Yes sir. Thank you for asking. May I present my wife Dharmambal, whom I believe you have met?" That was Dharmu's cue to drop into a curtsy. Thankfully the routine was completed quickly without a hitch and then Dharmu could actually enjoy the event and meet some people. She grabbed a martini from a passing waiter and downed it in one gulp. All this waiting had parched her throat. And with all that tension between Doreen and Doris, she really needed that drink.

She could spot the Maharaja of Patiala, tall and elegant in a white embroidered *shervani* suit with a pink turban dripping with strings of pearls and centered with a large emerald. That turban itself must be worth a lakh of rupees and the necklace in uncut emeralds and diamonds was priceless. It was probably one of the many pieces of famous jewelry the family possessed. After all, the last rightful owner of the famous Koh-I-Noor diamond was his ancestor Maharaja Ranjith Singh of Lahore. In 1859 when the British raised their flag over the city of Lahore, the Sikh kingdom became part of the British Empire. One of the clauses in the treaty involved the transfer of ownership of the diamond. The crown prince sailed to London accompanied by a British surgeon who was knighted for his efforts in convincing the prince to personally present the priceless diamond to the Crown. On reaching London, the young prince presented it in a grand ceremony as a gift to Queen Victoria along with the almost equally priceless Timur ruby. What a gift! —And the prince supposedly feigned delight while offering it to the Monarch— gratitude to the usurpers of his land and treasury!

During a visit to England a few years previously, Dharmu had experienced a deep sense of emptiness on seeing the Koh-I-Noor diamond in the Tower of London adorning the Queens's crown and scepter. The British had wasted no time in breaking down the priceless gem to embellish their symbols of power. She knew that systematically the English were looting everything from jewels and money to self-esteem and their way of life. The glory and wealth that belonged to India was fast becoming a faded memory. And here she was joining in the revelry, grateful to be on the invitee list of a British viceroy. Dharmu shook herself out of her thoughts. She was not about to ponder such dark and demeaning matters. Not today. Today she was going to enjoy herself. In any case serious issues such as these only flitted momentarily through her consciousness. She was here and determined to eat and drink and make merry.

Dharmu looked around for familiar faces, but it was not until a whole hour passed that she spotted Rani, elegant as usual in a purple *Banārsi* sari and her signature sleeveless blouse. She had her hair puffed up in a bouffant with two kiss-curls framing her face. As usual, she was surrounded by a dozen men, and from the sparkle in her eyes and the raucous laughter around her, it was clear who was the belle of the ball. Next to her, Sudipto was in a dark, three-piece suit. Like most Indian couples, in Dharmu's opinion, Sudipto and Rani were ill matched. Sudipto was short and fair with a Hitler moustache and thick, black glasses. His slim build and pallid personality was further dwarfed by his scintillating wife. It was Rani that got him the attention he needed to climb the social ladder, and he used her social skills to make up for his deficiencies on that front. Left to himself, he would probably have chosen to become a scholar, given his intellectual leanings. He was reticent and spoke with a pronounced Bengali accent, but his hard work and razor sharp mind quickly brought a series of promotions. He was the Under-Secretary in the Home Department, an envied and sought-after position in Government. Socially inept, he left this arena to his vivacious and beautiful wife who could melt a stone with her charms.

Rani waved to Dharmu, asking her to join the group. Already on her third martini, Dharmu was grateful when dinner was announced. A huge *shamiana* was set up outside with flaming torches illuminating the culinary spread. Every type of meat and vegetable had found its way onto the buffet, making it hard to imagine the country was on the brink of the worst famine in history. Dharmu and Rani filled their plates and sat down with the other ICS wives. Rani was not terribly popular in this group, as rumor had it that Rani's charms were being used in inappropriate ways to help Sudipto. Rani didn't have the time or intent to dispute their claims and, instead, had a grand time fanning the flames and referring to the British officers in endearing terms.

"Ooh! Look at Bob with that cute moustache," she remarked loudly, and a dozen eyebrows went up. "See the guy he is talking to? He is the Rajah of Chail. We have an invite next weekend for a croquet game following the cricket match at the Annandale grounds. I am so excited because Bob will be there too. Unfortunately, Sudipto will not be coming, he has some official business," she lamented a little too loudly and the dozen eyebrows now merged with hairlines. Robert Wilson was rumored to be her current paramour, and she was enjoying the ladies' discomfort. *Poor souls with colorless lives and drab appearances. At least this would give them something to talk about.* As they walked away from the table, they could see heads coming together, and Rani laughed scornfully and she sashayed across the lawn swaying her hips seductively.

"You shouldn't do this, Rani," Dharmu scolded, knowing that by association these women shunned her too. "You know the rumors are not true. Why do you encourage the talk?"

"It's exciting. I love to rile up the old ladies. It adds sparkle to their boring day."

"All I can say is that it will come back to bite you."

"Oh stop, Dharmu, with your goodie-two-shoes routine. It's fun to be naughty. I love the thrill it gives me."

After her third post-dinner sherry, it was time to go home. Dharmu felt unsteady as she climbed into the carriage, but she was happy and singing away. Every couple of minutes Mahadevan, who had also put away quite a few, kept telling her to be quiet but she wasn't bothered. Once at home, navigating the stairs to their bedroom proved to be quite a challenge for the couple, and Govindhan had to support them.

The singing disturbed Kandu's sleep. He opened his room door a crack and watched Govindhan half carry, half drag his drunken mother to her room. A tear from each eye and trickled down his plump cheeks. He was not sad, just angry and disappointed. He wiped them with the back of his hand and stumbled back to bed.

CHAPTER ELEVEN

KANDU AND TUCKY
SHIMLA 1942

BOYS WILL BE BOYS

Deb and Tucky had arrived half an hour ago, and Kandu couldn't wait for his parents to leave. He was annoyed having to babysit Deb, but Rani Aunty thought it would be nice for young Deb to have company as they had just moved into the house next door and Deb was a little disoriented. Deb was only eight years old but very circumspect and mature for his age. He took after his father, small framed and highly intelligent. An unruly mop of hair sat awkwardly on his head looking down on a small, inscrutable face. Three quarters of his face was hidden by the round, horn-rimmed glasses Deb wore. He loved being around Kandu and really didn't need much attention. He was happy to read or play cards and never fussed about anything. It was hard to imagine he was Rani Aunty's son.

Just thinking about Rani Aunty made Kandu weak in the knees. She was like a movie star. She had short bobbed hair and wore red lipstick like Marlene Dietrich. Well, it looked black on the screen, but Kandu could swear all movie stars wore red lipstick. She had the most perfect figure and Kandu couldn't help thinking she was God's gift to mankind. Tucky definitely had a crush on her, and Kandu wasn't quite sure how he felt. When she visited, he always hung around. Rani Aunty's conversation was so exciting. She had this high pitched sweet, "tinkling bells" kind of voice and her laugh just warmed his soul. She showed her sparkly teeth and threw her head back, laughing almost from her gut. Most often Kandu was so focused on her appearance, he missed the conversation. He laughed when she did, although he had no idea what was so funny. He often dreamed of how nice it would be if he were older and she were his girlfriend. Maybe he did have a crush on her. Well … maybe a small one. She was his mother's friend and it wasn't right to admire older women. Unfortunately, all twelve-year-old boys did dream of older women because twelve-year-old girls didn't conjure dreams. The ones he knew were nondescript, thin, bespectacled, or plain stupid.

Kandu turned around after seeing his parents ride away. Tucky had been yelling for him every few seconds, but Kandu had to wait until he was sure they were alone. Tucky beckoned to him to come up the stairs to the terrace. Kandu turned to look at Deb. He was seated upright in the chair, his nose buried in a book. His shorts came halfway down his knobby knees and his feet were moving like windshield wipers. There was some connection between his feet and mind, and the more he was engrossed, the faster the wipers moved. He had crinkled up his small nose, and Kandu wondered how it took the weight of those round, horn-rimmed spectacles.

"Deb, will you be okay? I am going to the bathroom. I'll be back shortly." Deb stared up vacantly from his book and nodded nonchalantly, following which Kandu bolted past his room into the landing which led up to the roof. Tucky was at the top of the stairs. It was dusk and in the dimming light Kandu could only discern him outlined against the open door. "Will the shrimp be okay? I hope he doesn't come up here."

"Yes, don't worry" Kandu replied. "His feet are going at 60 kms. per hour. What did you want? What nefarious activity have you planned today?"

"Fool, Kandu, hurry up. You're going to miss the action. She came out of the bathroom in her towel a minute ago and if we wait, the whole show will be over."

"Are you mad? Deb is downstairs and we are ogling *his* Mom. What if she looks up? Bugger, if she catches us I'm dead. She's my Mom's friend and I'm watching her unclothed."

"She won't see us. I have these binoculars I borrowed from my Dad. Come on. You can see the freckles on her nose."

Kandu was not sure if this was the right thing to do. He had been up to the terrace the other day. It was his other special haunt and he loved to just sit here and admire the view. This is where Mummy kept her prize rose bushes, which was her latest fascination. Their elevated home looked down on the Chatterjee bungalow. From the eastern corner just over the tree line he could see the windows of the master bedroom. The bathroom had shuttered windows, but adjoining the bathroom was what appeared to be a dressing room with open windows, and Kandu who was seated on the parapet, nearly fell over the side when he saw Rani Aunty seated on a stool in front of her dressing table with just a towel wrapped around her. He knew he should look away, but his eyes seemed to have a mind of their own and would not tear away. He just sat and stared at her bare shoulders hoping she wouldn't take off the towel. Ever since he mentioned it to Tucky, his friend couldn't stop thinking about it either. He had been making all kinds of voyeuristic plans all week and today he had arrived with grim determination and immediately made a bee-line for the terrace. Kandu had no idea he had a pair of binoculars but by the look on Tucky's face it seemed worth the effort.

They ran to the corner and could see the light on in the dressing room but she had disappeared.

"Shit … she's gone. How much I was yelling? You should have come earlier *sala!*" Tucky swore in sheer frustration.

"I couldn't. My parents were leaving and Deb had just arrived." Tucky had half his body over the edge of the parapet, his prominent chin now set at an impossible angle.

"Okay here she is," he whispered, his voice crackling in anticipation.

"No wait … Hell, I can see her pointy boobs in a white bra. Oh shit, shit, shit."

Kandu tried once again to pry the binoculars from Tucky but he would not let go.

"Oh man! She is a bombshell! What a waste of sweet meat. That Sudipto is one lucky man to bang such a fabulous lady." This conjured up weird images in Kandu's mind of Sudipto intellectually making love to Rani Aunty, and he urgently pushed it out of his head. Tucky, who was obsessed with sexual fantasies forced Kandu to think of things that made him feel terribly guilty. It was wrong to look at half naked women, especially when they were double your age and one of your mother's best friends. Besides, Kandu was terrified of getting caught. "This is bad, Tucky, we shouldn't even be here. What if Deb sees us?" But Tucky was too absorbed and could not tear himself away. "Two more minutes," he begged. Kandu grabbed the binoculars, but by now she had donned her blouse.

Dekha? Tucky asked. "Mount Kilimanjaro … I love you!" he crooned. Tucky was crazy. Rani had a good bust line, but Mt. Kilimanjaro?

"Gone," Kandu replied dejectedly. "Blouse and now sari is on."

"Shit, this is better than watching a movie. You lucky bugger. I think I am coming here every week."

Kandu handed the binoculars to Tucky but as he was turning to leave, his shirt got caught on a thorn in the rose plant. Kandu reached down to disentangle his shirt when he saw the red rose. It was in full bloom and looked as if it had been fashioned in velvet. Three big dewdrops sat suspended on its inner petals making it appear even more inviolable. Something stirred within him and he felt unsettled. *The rose … What was it reminiscent of? A dream … a girl?* He knew that the image of a red rose was important but could not make the connection. Pulling his shirt free, Kandu ran down the stairs into the living room.

The windshield wipers were going at full steam. Deb was as engrossed in whatever he was reading as when Kandu had left him. Thank heaven.

Govindhan announced dinner: Fried fish and tartar sauce with boiled carrots and peas and lemon soufflé for dessert. Tucky kept prodding Kandu through the evening and annoying Deb with probing questions about Rani Aunty. He even asked the poor boy at one point how well he knew Mt. Kilimanjaro. After dinner they played games of chess and cards and around midnight they lay down to sleep. Tucky slipped into deep sleep almost immediately with a smile on his face. Kandu supposed that tonight his dreams would be sweet. As they were about to fall asleep Deb whispered to Kandu, "Kandu, does your mother love your father?"

Kandu looked at him in surprise wondering what was troubling Deb. "I suppose so. I haven't really thought much about that. Why do you ask?"

"Does your mom have a boyfriend?" Deb whispered rubbing the back of his hand against his leaking nose.

"No Deb, she would never have one, she is married." There was silence. After a few moments Kandu asked softly, "Why, Deb, what's the matter?"

"I think my mother has a boyfriend."

Kandu was stunned. He felt betrayed hearing this news, and he was not even related to Rani Aunty. He was just her loyal puppy dog. He could only imagine what young Deb was going through.

"You must be mistaken. It can't be. Rani Aunty would never betray Sudipto Uncle. Who is it? Tell me his name?" Deb was about to tell him but then thought the better of it and muttered, "I can't tell."

Kandu slammed back onto the pillow wondering how he would sleep after this piece of devastating news when he heard the door open and strains of some Tamil film song wafted up the stairs. His parents were home. He walked up to the door, and what he saw upset him as it usually did. He had witnessed this very scene so many times. Two fat tears rolled down his cheeks, but he couldn't tell if they made their appearance because of his disappointment with his drunken mother or Rani Aunty's betrayal. It didn't really matter. He turned and stumbled back to bed. In a few minutes he slept and as he slept he dreamed …

He saw her once again running down the hillside towards him, a red rose in her hands. She stopped a few feet away from him and smiled. "I'm here," she whispered, her voice soft and sweet. He stood firm, his brow furrowed as he looked at her questioningly, trying to figure out who she was. His short pudgy arms akimbo, he demanded to know her name.

"Your friend, didn't you know that already?" was her cheeky reply.

"My special friend?" asked Kandu, the words slipping out on their own volition. She smiled and said nothing, merely turned around, ready to return from where she had come.

"Wait," he called out, eager to stop her. "Come back. Don't go so fast. If you are my friend, then let's play."

She shook her head. "Not yet, it's not time yet."

"Then when? When will you come back?"

"Soon," she said, shrugging her tiny shoulders. "I'm still small, I'm not ready." Kandu didn't quite understand why she had to leave so soon, and if she had to go so fast, then why had she bothered to come? But he wanted a special friend very much. "Will you come back for sure?" he asked again, eager to meet her once more.

"You know I will," she said as she turned again to scamper off.

"But you will have grown; so how will I recognize you?"

She placed the red rose gingerly in his hands and then turned, swiftly making her way back towards the hillside, her dainty anklets jingling as she carefully stepped in between bunches of Brahmakamalams.

"A red rose. Will you have a red rose with you?" he yelled out, needing to know but she was out of earshot, so with determination he ran after her. She stopped and turned around smiling at him, her eyes dancing and sparkling with mischief. He ran as fast as his short legs would carry him, but he tripped on a fallen vine and fell heavily to the ground before he could reach her.

Kandu woke up with a start. That was it! *The red rose* he mumbled to himself and then snuggled down again, drifting into delicious slumber.

CHAPTER TWELVE

MAHADEVAN
SHIMLA 1942

AN UNEXPECTED LETTER

The first sip of clear, light, Darjeeling tea cleared his head almost immediately. He knew he'd had far too much to drink last night and should sleep it off, but force of habit awakened him at the crack of dawn. The household was quiet when he stepped onto the street and walked downhill, part of his daily constitutional. It was wonderful to catch the first breath of fresh air and the morning sights of Shimla awakening. A few neighbors were out walking their dogs and the die-hard exercisers were briskly walking up and down the winding roads that typified the Shimla terrain. He reached the bend in the road, and as he paused to admire the pink skyline, a deep sense of peace dawned within him. He inhaled the morning crisp air a bit too deeply, triggering a cough which cleared the phlegm in his chest even as it made the throb in his temple more pronounced.

The town seemed to rouse leisurely this Sunday morning. A few women with ruddy faces carried bags of vegetables on their backs as they made their way to the marketplace. Some coolies urged their unwilling mules uphill, their movements slow and halfhearted as they trudged along towards their destination. He could see the end of the Mall road, and it looked pretty deserted. The morning service at the church would not commence till ten o'clock when crowds of English men and women would converge here. Ironically, the sound of temple bells broke the silence, and he wondered where they came from. Sounds bounced off the hills making it almost impossible to sense their origin, but the resonance reminded him of his native place in Nagarcoil and almost automatically he began practicing *Nadi Shodhana*, alternate nostril breathing, which his grandfather Appanshayal had taught him. In through the left ... hold ... out through the right ... hold ... in through the right ... hold ... out through the left. Appanshayal had passed away three years ago and Nagarcoil would never be the same for Mahadevan. In many ways Appanshayal mirrored the noble values of fair play and justice that his grandfather Nilakantan symbolized. He didn't make it for the funeral, as his journey from Calcutta took three days, but was present for and reverently participated in the rituals which followed. Almost the entire village had attended the funeral rites. Appanshayal was well known and well liked by everyone, and his loss was sincerely felt by everybody in the village.

When Mahadevan returned home after his walk, everyone was still asleep, but Govindhan greeted him and a few minutes later brought out his tea and toast along with the mail and the morning paper. Mahadevan scanned the headlines, biting into the crisp toast slathered with butter and orange marmalade. He turned his attention to the mail. There were a few bills and a letter with several postmarks which appeared to have originated in Bengal. It was from Vaithee, who had worked for a short while as his assistant in Rangpur. After they left, Mahadevan had not heard from him and this was indeed a surprise.

Dear Sir,

You must be surprised to hear from me. It has been almost six years since you left Rangpur and many important events have taken place in my life. I joined the Anushilan group here shortly after the horrific execution of our beloved leader Surya Sen and have involved myself completely in the dream of a free Bharat.

Mahadevan knew this was not good news. The Anushilan group was a militant faction with Stalinist leanings that relied on subversive anti-government activities. They had been named in several terrorist acts all over the country, especially in Bengal, and were notoriously involved in setting off bombs all over the state and even assassinating British officials. Vaithee harbored a wild side, although no one could tell from his demeanor. Mahadevan always felt he had suffered deeply in life and had moved to Bengal to escape something. Why else would a Tamil-speaking south-Indian live in the Chittagong Hills? Mahadevan never asked him and Vaithee was so diligent in his work ethic that Mahadevan had no complaints. Besides, he had worked for him only for the last few months, and Mahadevan was at the time so tied up in wrapping up his own affairs that he didn't feel the urgency to probe into Vaithee's personal life. If Vaithee was part of this group, then undoubtedly he was involved in violent activities. Perhaps he should tear up this letter. As a Government servant, Mahadevan felt it would come to no good if he were found in possession of a letter from a member of an outlawed terrorist organization. Mahadevan sighed in discontent but continued reading. Honestly, some people were so misguided.

You will be happy to hear that I also got married and perhaps even more surprised to hear that my wife is none other than your previous maid

Meera. Shortly after you left, Meera came to the office. She was with child and wanted to contact you to see if she could move to Calcutta and work with you. Her family had rejected her, and the current Collector had no use for a woman so heavily pregnant, so he sacked her. She came to the office not having any place to have her baby. I took pity on her and allowed her to live in my quarters. After the birth of her son, she stayed with me for a while and cooked and cleaned for me and over time I decided to marry her. We are expecting another child soon.

Last year I resigned my post in the Government, as most of my comrades were boycotting everything British, and I got an office job with a local doctor. We continue to live in Rangpur, although my work with my group takes me to Calcutta and Dacca. The kind doctor is also part of the same group, and this works well for me as I know Meera is taken care of when I am away. She works as a cook in their home, and our child has the opportunity of going to school.

The situation in Rangpur is tense. The waterways are empty after the British destroyed all the boats. The Japanese are on the Burma border, and the authorities believe that by destroying boats they can slow down the enemy encroachment into the rest of the country. In the meantime, the local people are starving with no access to river fishing and, recently, even basic food like rice is in short supply. With no fish and little rice, you can imagine what the situation here forebodes. I don't know what the Angrezi are thinking, but starving the locals to death seems to be high on their agenda.

On a lighter note, you will also be happy to learn that I speak Bengali like a native. I have almost forgotten that my roots are in the south. I can never go back. My family would never accept Meera. We are rejected by society and fulfill that need in each other.

I hope your family is well. Please do visit us if you come to Rangpur and give my regards to your Mrs.

With fond regards

Vaithee Chakrabarti

P.S. I changed my last name

Mahadevan was quite stunned by all the news in the letter. Vaithee was a freedom fighter—a terrorist in the eyes of the British and he had married Meera! Dharmu loved Meera and had asked her to accompany them, but Meera at the time did not want to leave Rangpur. He had no idea she had been pregnant, but then he hardly had any contact with her. She was Dharmu's and the children's maid, and he scarcely noticed her even when she was around. Perhaps Dharmu knew about her pregnancy and didn't mention it. Anyway, it was a good thing Vaithee married her. She would have been rejected by her family for having a baby out of wedlock, and Vaithee was a loner too which made them ideally matched. Who knew what his story was? They were ideally suited to one another, and it pleased Mahadevan that they had found their peace together.

Mahadevan was troubled by the news about the waterways. He had heard about plans to destroy boats along the Ganges waterway, so even if the Japanese took Burma, they would find it extremely difficult to enter the plains. How foolish and misguided this was. The waterways were the main access for supplies into the Sunderbans. The locals depended on them for all their basic needs. The area was marshland, and the rains caused floods yearly, so naturally the roads were in shambles and not viable for major transport. There were rumors of food scarcity in Bengal, but as most of his friends worked for the Government, they were ensured adequate food rations. Unfortunately, drought and famine were the affliction of the poor; the rich could always afford to feed themselves. The Japanese had cut off all rice supplies from Burma, which constituted a substantial part of the total supply of rice, the staple Bengali diet. If the rice crop failed this year too, it would be catastrophic. Rumors of scarcity were rife, and people had started hoarding, causing an unnatural spike in the cost of rice. This promised to be a difficult year and Mahadevan was fearful. Sudipto would probably have a better idea of what was happening in Bengal, and Mahadevan made a mental note to speak to him about it the next time they met.

Mahadevan scanned the headlines: *Influx of refugees into Calcutta. Cripps mission a failure. Nehru accepts Parsi son-in-law despite prior objections.* This was interesting. The article had a photograph of Indira, Nehru's daughter sitting next to her husband Feroze in a ceremony that was officiated by someone who definitely looked like a Kashmiri Pundit. The article stated that, despite family opposition, the marriage between Indira Priyadarshini Nehru and Feroze Gandhi took place at Anand Bhavan on March 26th, 1942. Nehru was initially opposed to the union, as he believed that Feroze would be unable to maintain the high standard of living Indira was accustomed to, but when he realized how determined the young couple were, he gave his blessing. There was a quote from Mahatma Gandhi as well, blessing the couple and admiring Feroze's devotion and care for Nehru's wife Kamala, especially when she was unwell. Apparently, Gandhi was instrumental in persuading Nehru to gracefully accept his out-of-caste son-in-law. The article went on to discuss Feroze's relationship with Kamala Nehru and his tireless work for the INC.

Mahadevan put the paper down and smiled. Nehru was no Gandhi, who made his wife clean toilets to prove that such menial jobs were not solely the burden of untouchables. In spite of his strong nationalist fervor, when it came down to his daughter, Nehru must have wanted a good Kashmiri Pundit son-in-law. It was strange that despite all the education and exposure to western thought, the idea of caste was so ingrained in every Indian; the notion of marrying out of one's caste was unthinkable. Perhaps this is why, despite so much incursion and invasion, Indian society persisted and prevailed and would probably do so for thousands of years more. To most Indians, marrying within one's caste was just the right thing to do, and few people really wanted to change that. There was fear of excommunication, not only from parents but from one's extended family. Besides, it was just easier when you married someone who ate the same food, prayed to the same God and spoke the same language. When looking for a suitable boy for Vani, Mahadevan didn't dream of choosing a boy from a lower sub-caste. He had to be a Brahmin and an Iyer at that. That's how things worked and they had worked well for eons.

For years' parents simply chose your life partner, and even if you didn't like the person, you made the marriage work because marriage was not about love so much as it was a sacred commitment. You married to have a companion in your old age and children who would care for you. All this love business was for westerners who did not have happy marriages and divorced their husbands! What an alarming thought! That word alone was taboo. You married for life, good or bad. Indira was setting a dangerous precedent by marrying out of caste. But that was Nehru's problem. Vani had married an Iyer, and so would Rukku and Kandu. That was a certainty. No questions asked or entertained. Even if they fell in love, it would have to be with an Iyer; of that he would make sure. There were certain principles that defined a race, a group, and a family, and marrying within one's community was one of them.

He looked down at another photograph of Nehru looking all somber and couldn't help smiling. Poor Nehru!

CHAPTER THIRTEEN

RAJAM
THANJAVUR – JANUARY 1943

INSIDE RAJAM'S HEAD

Rajam lay on her side watching the room brighten as the moon inched its way into the square living room window and now surprisingly sat dead center, framed like a photograph in the middle of the window. She could hear Kunju's and Chithi's gentle snores and discern the rhythmic rise and fall of seven soft chests, all sound asleep. As usual, everyone had lined up in the hall—Kunju and Rajam at each end and Parvathi Chithi somewhere in the middle with the children on either side. Rajam sighed deeply and reverted her tired eyes back to the window, watching, mesmerized, until the moon partially disappeared from sight. She hadn't slept much after midnight. For some reason unknown to her, she was just anxious. There was really no cause to be worried. After all, Partha had found a job in the munitions factory at Kirkee, and it was just a matter of time before she joined him. Being home with her father and sister was like returning to a sanctuary. She felt so safe and so cared for. As long as her father was alive, there was no reason to be concerned. Yet the anxiety gnawed at her insides and she tossed and turned on the thin mattress. No matter how she slept, it was uncomfortable. The floor was increasingly hard, or was the mattress thinning? Either way, she could identify each bone in her body, and the pain in her pelvis was particularly sharp. This in spite of some fat added on these last few years—she considered herself somewhere between rotund and chubby, but certainly not fat.

The night was interminably long, the hours stretching ahead with nothing to do. What was worse, in the last couple of hours she had visited the toilet thrice, and that gave her even more anxiety. As she turned on the light, she noticed two cockroaches on the ceiling and had to finish her business really fast with her eyes peeled to the ceiling in case they decided to descend. Cockroaches were so ugly and so unnecessary and Rajam hated them. Why did God have to create a creature whose sole purpose was to terrorize all humans? Cockroaches served no earthly function and every year they seemed to be growing larger.

It was now past two o'clock. Only a couple of hours before her father awoke. She decided to chant some mantras hoping the monotony of chanting would lull her to sleep. She must have dozed for a while because when she opened her eyes there seemed to be more light in the room. How strange! Just a few hours ago all she could make out in the diffused night lighting were indiscernible shapes and now, with a little sunlight, objects in the room were suddenly appearing out of nowhere. It was almost as if God had just infused life into them. Pillars, plants, chairs and nightstands were all making their presence known one at a time.

Appa was already up. Somewhere in the distance she could hear Kunju and her father speaking in hushed tones so as not to awaken the rest of the household. Rajam's head was heavy, and as she ambled to the bathroom, she hoped the cockroaches had retired for the day.

Kunju handed her a steaming tumbler of hot filter coffee. "How did you sleep, Rajam? I thought I heard you go to the bathroom at night." No one went to the bathroom at night. The *Kollaipakkam* was at the back of the house and at night they avoided going if they could help it. The children were terrified of vermin and even more afraid of ghosts. Everyone made certain they had squeezed out every single drop from their bladders before turning in.

"Ugh! So many cockroaches. I wish we could do something about that. Appa why don't you find out if there is any English remedy we can use to kill cockroaches?"

"No remedy will work Rajam. Cockroaches have always been around and will be long after humans stop inhabiting this earth. It's impossible to eradicate them. The toilets are open, the drain and sewage outside is open, and naturally vermin find their way here. Be thankful it's only at night," replied Swami, pausing to stir the vegetables cooking in the pan ready to be added to the roasted *rava*. Obviously Kunju had decided to make *upma* for breakfast.

Feeling a lot better after the coffee, Rajam joined Kunju in the kitchen, cutting vegetables in preparation for lunch as Kunju attended to the simmering upma. It was nice that Kunju decided the menu for the day. Back in Madras, Rajam agonized each day over deciding what to make. Whenever she made a particularly delectable lunch, Kamu would come home from Nagamma's saying she had already eaten thayirshādam. Rajam would dejectedly put the food away for dinner but often, if Partha didn't join them at night, Rajam would be forced to throw the food out or give it to the parayan. Almost sensing her mother's absence, Kamu awoke, and soon Kunju's kids straggled in for their morning milk or coffee, first the girls and then the boys in various stages of undress.

Rajam knew there had to be some substance to her sense of foreboding. She felt uneasy but really could not find any reason for her discomfort. Everyone else seemed to be in good spirits that morning, and she had no wish to darken their mood by announcing she felt something was about to go wrong this day. Besides, she had felt this way so often in the past and, so far, nothing tragic had occurred. Perhaps it was just hormones.

The telegram arrived around noon. MUNUSWAMY PASSED AWAY. STOP. COME TO MADRAS. STOP. URGENT.

Munuswamy, Rajam's father-in-law, had finally passed on. His last few years had been spent on that easy chair. He slept almost through the day, and it must have taken a while for others to figure out he had died. He had lived a full life and played with his grandchildren, and really, his life should be celebrated, but Rajam felt duty bound to cry. She squeezed her eyes and tried to make the tears appear, but nothing was happening. Finally, only a memory of Nagamma's menacing glare brought the appropriate tears to her eyes.

Kamu would stay with Kunju while Swaminathan accompanied Rajam to Madras. Being a *sambandhi* (in-law) he needed to attend the funeral if he could and stay for at least 13 days after the passing. Rajam was happy he would be there with her. She hated death. It scared her even more than sāmiyārs did. Something dark and murky entered the home where a death occurred. Perhaps other ghosts and spirits came to visit. Who knew? The energy in the house was bad with no lamp being lit to dispel darkness and invite the divine into the home. This would only be permitted after the ceremony on the thirteenth day and, until then, the atmosphere was going to be dismal and scary. The thought of spending two weeks in mourning made Rajam even more fretful. Once again, she could sense her inability to remain still. Her fingers and toes twitched and flexed almost on their own. Now she was touching her nose, then scratching her head. Movement, movement all the time, propelled by the rush of thoughts invading her mind.

Kunju glanced up at her. Rajam was staring into the distance and moving and twitching non-stop. She had not seen these symptoms for the last week, although they were visible when Rajam first arrived. Kunju rose and hugged Rajam tight. Then she held her fingers firmly in her own, not allowing them to twitch. She had seen Rajam's transformation after marriage from a bold, fearless child into a fidgety and anxious woman. Just the thought of being around Nagamma triggered this response. Rajam lived so much more in her head than in this world. All her fears and anxieties were imagined. She had pantomimes going on in her head about what Nagamma would say and how she would respond. This meant she never really heard what anyone spoke to her, moved from one unfinished task to the next impossible one, and was always in a heightened state of stress. The tenor of her voice had changed and she seemed to border on shouting if anyone remotely challenged anything she said.

This had begun to irritate Partha. With so much change and upheaval in recent years, he had his own basket of problems. He had done his best to allay Rajam's unreal fears for the past fifteen years. He even made sure Nagamma didn't live with them. What more could he do? Rajam was always preoccupied and never remembered to do things in a timely fashion. What annoyed Partha more was her continual need to play the victim. It was almost as if she enjoyed being pitied and loved complaining. He had a short tempered boss, his work was hard enough, and he had no patience for Rajam's moaning at the end of the day. The evenings were full of squabbles in raised voices, ending with them sleeping with their backs to each other. Love had taken a back seat in their relationship. Thank heavens Kamu was young and almost permanently with her grandmother and cousins down the street. Hopefully moving to Poona would be good for all of them. Nagamma would not be around to interfere, and Rajam could perhaps relax and become the person she used to be.

Rajam and Kamu had already been here a month, and Partha had not sent any money yet. The milkman had not been paid for a month and the provision store for over six months. Kunju was concerned about her father, who carried this burden and shame of debt and the resultant stress. It would be good to get some money from Partha. Perhaps next month. It was pointless worrying. Something would work out. It always did.

"Rajam, go pack; your train leaves at lunchtime. Don't worry about Kamu. She will be fine with Chithi and myself."

"I know," murmured Rajam "Partha will be there. I hope he gets some good accommodation and we can move soon."

"I'm sure you will have some good news. When an old person passes in any family, it brings good luck to others. At least that's what they say."

Rajam turned to leave. As she passed by the door Kunju said, "Remind Partha to send some money. I mean … if he can … if he has some."

"I will. I know it's been difficult. Don't worry I won't have to stay too long."

"Do we ever worry about you staying here? You and Kamu hardly eat. It's the rest of us. God alone knows when Mani will start earning. He has gone to meet Appa's friend in Chidambaram. Hopefully this time he will keep the job. It's too much of a strain for Appa, managing everything. I have half a mind to ask Venkat to quit school and start working."

"No! Never do that. At least *he* must go to college. Never make him quit."

Rajam went to the steel trunk and pulled out a silver plate adding it to her clothes packed for Madras. If Partha gave her no money she knew what she had to do.

CHAPTER FOURTEEN

NAGAMMA
MADRAS – JANUARY 1943

THE BURDEN OF WIDOWHOOD

Nagamma sat in the corner of the room feeling a little dazed. People were coming in and leaving and she really couldn't register who they were and didn't even care. Her husband Munuswamy had passed away that afternoon. The events of the day kept replaying in her head and she couldn't stop her mind from going back to it time and again. Every time she revisited the event, it wrenched at her heart and she felt a pang of sheer guilt, or was it terror? She had served him lunch a little after noon, following which he sank down further into the easy chair ready for his nap. At three o'clock she brought his coffee and left it by the table. "*Yenna* don't keep sleeping. Get up and drink your coffee when it's hot. I'm not about to reheat it, so move!" she ordered. Then, murmuring under her breath about his laziness and his obesity, she returned to the kitchen. While rinsing out the coffee tumblers, she realized she hadn't picked up Munuswamy's and so returned to the living room incensed to find him still sleeping, now with his mouth wide open. She hated when he did that. Who slept for so long? All day and all night. She couldn't help but burst out. "You are nothing but a wastrel. Sleep, sleep, sleep, that's all you do. You can't even shift your elephant like bulk to drink your own coffee. What do think, I'm going to pour it down your gullet? *Pha! Porum!* I'm tired of you. God knows when I'll get freedom from the likes of you." But Munuswamy would not stir. Normally he would have opened his eyes and silently downed the coffee in one gulp, cold or hot, and his refusal to move made Nagamma extremely irate. She pounced on him "*Ketela?* Are you deaf now? Why do you not answer?" Again Munuswamy did not respond. Nagamma felt a light twinge of fear, but she was not about to pay any attention to that. How dare Munuswamy blatantly ignore her? She bent down and prodded his swollen belly, which shook like jelly, but still Munuswamy was silent. "*Yenna* answer me … wake up … Pattu! Come here … see why he is not waking up. *Yenna*, wake up!" Nagamma shook him like a leaf in a storm, her booming voice now weakening to a false treble as she began panicking, suspecting the worst. Pattu rushed in, shocked to see Nagamma screaming and shaking her father. She knew instantly on looking at his placid face that he had passed. "Amma stop!" she yelled, trying to pry away her mother's hands, but Nagamma would not let go. She continued begging her husband to move and open his eyes, shaking him and slapping his face. It took all of five people to drag a sobbing Nagamma away from her dead husband.

It had never crossed her mind that he would dare die and leave her, without checking first if it was okay with her. Munuswamy had made his final decision, perhaps for the first time, on his own. Her bitter, acidic words kept echoing in her brain. How could she have been so cruel even at the time of his death? She couldn't stop shaking her head from side to side like a mad woman and beating her chest till it hurt to breathe. This was unforgiveable, and she could not come to terms with it. Pattu and the children were surprised to see their mother's reaction to her husband passing. In all their life they had never seen her display anything close to sadness, and it was beyond shocking seeing her break down like this.

It took Nagamma a while to calm down. Many things needed to be done and Pattu rushed to call for help. The sons had to be called to be present for the last rites, and neighbors rushed in eager to help. In an hour Siva arrived, followed by Kannan, who wept copious tears on his mother's shoulder. Partha and Thambu were both in Poona and would arrive only the following day. The body needed to be preserved on ice, so that all four sons could attend the funeral and pay their last respects, and arrangements were made for that.

Nagamma sank down into the corner staring at his swollen body, now covered with a white sheet. He looked so calm, almost as if he were sleeping in that easy chair of his. For the last two years his knees had been hurting and it was difficult for him to get up after a meal. He had given up work years ago and had retired to his easy chair, his throne, placed strategically by the front door so he could watch the world go by on the busy Mylapore street. From this vantage point by the door, he could also survey the activity of the household, and watch and even enjoy the skirmishes between mother and daughter. Yet he never cared to participate. He had become the lonely bystander, happy to observe silently the happenings of his world. As his physical activity slowed down, the weight gain commenced. It was almost a vicious cycle. He was so fat he couldn't walk, and his inactivity made him even more bloated and swollen. Nagamma waited on him, helping him use the toilet and even assisted with his bathing. She brought him food and coffee whenever he asked for it. But her *seva* was always accompanied by some barb or bitter comment. She wanted her service to be recognized and appreciated verbally and couldn't get over the resentment of being his nursemaid.

In her mind he was a useless, good-for-nothing, and it was just a waste of her time waiting on him. Yet she insisted on attending to Munuswamy herself and would not allow the children to help.

She never thought she would mourn his death. They were never particularly close and hardly exchanged more than a few words with each other every day. Perhaps there had been a phase when there was a lot of warmth in their relationship, but Nagamma could scarcely recall that time. Life had just whizzed by without a moment for tenderness or even kindness. In life she didn't value him at all. Then why were tears rolling down her cheeks? Why did she feel so stranded and even scared? Fear was not an emotion that Nagamma recognized. She feared nothing and no one. Boldness and fortitude were hallmarks of her character. So then, why the tears? Perhaps it was widowhood that scared her.

Munuswamy had been her husband for as long as she could remember. Was it sixty or perhaps seventy years? She had lost count. He had always been around. She looked at the empty easy chair and tears welled up in her eyes. The emptiness was like a vacuum closing in on her, and she couldn't believe she would never see him again. She didn't think she ever loved him. He was just her husband. Her love was reserved for the children and grandchildren. All her life she viewed him as a mere nuisance. The only useful thing Munuswamy ever did was provide her with children. While she believed this wholeheartedly, she knew it wasn't true. She never went ahead with any of her decisions without running it by him. He was not as vociferous as she, but in his quiet way he always managed to be heard. Just a few words of caution followed by silence would set her thinking. Nagamma would reverse course at times but always maintained it was her decision and Munuswamy had nothing to do with it. And he was fine with not getting credit for anything. He had given up trying to fight her long ago. By acknowledging her unequivocally as the leader, the boss lady, the victor, Munuswamy was spared hours of listening to her booming voice argue and shout him down, making him feel miserable and helpless. Instead, he just took a sort of voluntary retirement from the marriage and withdrew to his easy chair in the thinnai. That chair was his refuge, his best companion. It supported his burgeoning form without as much as a murmur or a creak. It never complained and never reproached him. The rattan on the back of the chair was now misshapen and there was a soft dent where he habitually rested his head.

All those years had passed and they had only exchanged snatches of conversation. They never discussed the future, the future of the children, politics or religion. Nothing. Never. Two large tears snuck out of Nagamma's eyes and rolled down her ample nose to join the tiny pool on the living room floor just past her feet. She was now filled with regret. Munuswamy had been faithfully by her side, and she hadn't recognized the great friendship that they could have cultivated. Why had it been so important to establish control and to prove to herself that she needed no man? Why was it so important to her to be in control of everything and everyone around her? Munuswamy had done nothing to challenge her, yet she took so much pleasure in keeping him down. She never missed an opportunity to say something caustic. It now made no sense.

Nagamma reached down and with the tears that had collected on the floor wrote the words, *Yennai Mannichudungo.* Please forgive me.

CHAPTER FIFTEEN

KUNJU AND KAMU
THANJAVUR – FEBRUARY 1943

A GODSEND

Rajam and Swami had been gone a week now. It was time to stock up on provisions and Kunju had no desire to make that trip to the store. The store owner, Perumal, had not been paid for three months, and she wasn't sure if he would give her the rice, sugar, and lentils she needed to feed the family.

It was almost mid-morning. The children were all in school, all but Kamu, who was bored out of her mind, especially as her mother wasn't around to bother her. The morning started on the usual busy note with everyone dressing and eating before school, but once they left, it became eerily quiet in the house. Kamu had wandered around every room, climbed up and down the thinnai several times, counted all the cracks on the floor and was now at a loss for what to do next. Parvathi Chithi noticed her wandering aimlessly around the house and called her to sit down to play *"Othaiya Retaiya"* (ones or twos) with shells, her swollen arthritic knees grateful for the respite from standing and walking. After a half hour, Kamu was ready for a change of activity, and Chithi sent her to help Kunju finish cooking before noon as it would become unbearable to enter the kitchen after that. February was not that hot, but the coal fire stove kept the room hot long after they stopped cooking. Besides, like most kitchens in the south, there was one small window near the ceiling for the smoke, and no other outlet. This really kept the heat trapped, leaving the room several degrees warmer than the rest of the house. It was good that the kitchen was at one end of the house, so it's heat did not spread to the rest of the house.

Kamu squatted near the door and with intense focus began shelling peas. She was too young to attempt chopping vegetables on the *aruvāmanai*, but Kunju had to keep her occupied. She began cross legged and then every time Kunju turned around, she found Kamu in another posture. Now squatting on her feet, then leaning forward or lying on her stomach. Kamu had converted this simple task into a game and she kept the basin of peas three feet away and was throwing them in. That got too easy, and now she was on her back throwing the peas over her head. There were peas all over the floor and Kunju could not allow that. They did not have the luxury of wasting a single pea.

"That's enough Kamu, I've been watching you. Stop throwing the peas on the floor."

"No Periamma, I'm just playing with them," Kamu protested.

"No playing with food," Kunju insisted firmly. "We can't eat food that you step on, and there are peas everywhere. Chithi or myself are sure to slip and fall." Kamu giggled envisioning the sight. Chithi up in the air with her legs splayed in each direction and peas everywhere.

"You think that's funny? If anything happens to us, guess who will have to cook?"

Kamu tentatively pointed to herself, her eyes asking the question.

"Yes dearie, you! So pick up the peas and if you are bored, go read a book. We are almost done. I have to go shopping, so you can come too."

That clearly sounded like a better prospect than shelling peas. Kamu was exhausted from doing nothing. The walls of the house were closing in on her and she definitely could do with an outing. She diligently picked up all the strewn peas and put them into the basin. To be totally truthful, although the prospect was really funny, she didn't want either Periamma or Chithi to fall and break their head. That would be terrible!

Kunju picked up a notepad and a pencil to make a shopping list pausing to examine the array of semi-empty jars on the larder shelf. There really wasn't much to survey. Most jars were empty. They really needed everything. Over time, Kunju had created novel and different recipes to eliminate the use of the more expensive lentils which made the list more manageable and the price affordable. For the past year they cultivated a vegetable patch in the backyard and ate whatever was growing. *Podalangai* and peas or *vāzhaithandu* and *pooshinikai*. Their only luxury was the purchase of a sack of potatoes every three months. Potatoes didn't spoil and could be used to add consistency to her watery sāmbārs. Their typical meal was rice with a watery sāmbār, watered down thayirshādam with pickle. There was half a jar of rice and barely a cup of sugar left. Kunju's head drooped in disappointment. It was almost impossible to feed this entire household on such meager rations. She felt helpless and wished she could do something. But what? She couldn't get a job! She had only studied till sixth grade and had no other talents. Not that anyone was about to hire a woman for work. All she knew was the art of cooking.

Parvathi Chithi's warm hands on her shoulders brought her back to reality. "I know it's hard, but we have to try and make do with what we have. So what if we don't eat like royalty? At least we have a loving and caring family."

"I know. But love and care cannot satisfy the hunger in your stomach."

"What hunger? I don't know about you, but I have not starved once in this home. Every night I have slept with my belly full and so have the children. No one is complaining."

"That's because they don't know better. They don't recall the food we ate when Appa was in service and my mother was cooking. Every day a different *rasam*, different vegetables, even sweets. Life was so good. It's not fair that things have to be this hard for Appa towards the end of his life. I know he feels he's let us down." Chithi understood exactly how Kunju felt. To move down the socio-economic ladder was tough. To have lived well and have to let that go was perhaps the cruelest punishment. But what was the point in lamenting the past. The past was long gone and with it went the good times. This was their karmic down cycle, and hardship built endurance and character. It was only in tough times that people recalled the Divine. As long as things were good, God was there somewhere in the background, and no one ever thought about him with such urgency. Having lived so long, Chithi endured each day entrusting the Divine with her destiny. She depended on others to provide her food and shelter, and the Divine so far had never let her down. Things would look up. They had to. Life followed a rolling cycle. They had been down for so long that things were bound to get better. The trick was in thinking good thoughts, which was sometimes so difficult, especially when something as basic as providing daily meals became Herculean tasks. Yes, Chithi understood Kunju's angst completely. The poor child was born in a bad moon cycle, and life had cheated her of happiness. She had been widowed at the prime of her life and left with the burden of raising six children. Kunju's burden was now Swaminathan's and hers by default.

"Swami worries I know. But he's happy to care for you. Never once have I heard him complain. The children give him purpose in life. He shoulders his burden like a champion."

"I know. It should have been me taking care of him in this old age. Instead he is saddled with me and my brood."

"Don't say that. We are all in this together. God is watching over us. He will never let us down. He definitely has a plan."

"Well I hope he reveals this plan soon before we all starve to death."

"Shh ... don't ever say such things. The divine works in strange ways; he comes in front of you in different forms, when you least expect it. Don't worry, something will work out. You go to Perumal's and ask for just one month's credit, and say we will have something by next month." Kunju hugged Chithi, soaking in her positive energy and surprisingly, she felt better.

Kunju held Kamu's hand tight as they crossed the road into the main market square, dexterously avoiding bullock carts, cycles and ambling shoppers. Lost in the glitz of the bright shop windows, they tripped and bumped into everything. Kamu had asked to buy pencils, ink pens, peanuts, a straw doll, purple ribbons, a frock, a cow, horse, face powder, flowers, and dancing monkeys—almost everything available in the marketplace, and Kunju was tired of saying "no" every minute. Perumal's provision store was at the far end of the street. He seemed to have just opened, and luckily, it was not crowded.

Kunju went in and waited while he finished another customer's order. Perumal always sat at the front of the store, his podgy, hairy arms resting on the masala-speckled tabletop. Kunju wondered how he saw anything through his dirty, round spectacles. In stark contrast, his white shirt was brilliant and spotless and always freshly ironed. You could tell from the crisp fold marks on them. The lady read out her list: *Thovaram paruppu oru kilo, Paashi paruppu rendu kilo.* The list went on, and Perumal repeated each item writing it down meticulously, pausing to yell at each of his four assistants in turn to pack the provisions. "Eh Mali bring 4 kgs of coal. Lalu pack 2 kilos of paashi paruppu, Velu put it in the big basket…." Between them, they had a good system going. They never skipped a single item on the list and, even more surprisingly, the bill never ever had a single error, even if the list was two pages long.

Kamu kept pestering her. "Periamma *mithai,* Periamma *mithai,*" at regular intervals. If she continued long enough, Periamma was sure to relent. And she did. Happily sucking on a lollipop, she sank to her haunches watching the world go by on the busy street. Tired of sitting in the same position Kamu stood up and bent over and now admired the world upside down between her legs. It was really funny! The sky was completely flat, and people were actually walking on their heads. People's faces looked really comical upside down. How nice to live in a topsy-turvy world! She saw them walk in—an older lady and a young, beautiful girl in a peacock blue *pāvādai* with a deep maroon *dhāvani.* Kamu's topsy-turvy world was jolted when without warning this girl's face appeared six inches away from her own. "What are you doing upside down like that?" she asked, scaring Kamu out of her skin.

"Aaaaaaaah!" Kamu screamed. She straightened up and couldn't speak for a bit as the rush of blood to her head made the girl seem to swim in circles in front of her. "Oooh! That feels good. I was bored, so I thought I would look at the world upside down. I do that often you know? It's real fun. You should try it. Eyes on top of the head, the nose facing up, but it's the mouth that really looks sooo funny. By the way I'm Kamu, who are you?"

"My name is Bala," the beauty replied.

"You're so pretty," Kamu remarked, in open admiration.

"So are you," replied Bala pinching Kamu's cheeks. "Why aren't you in school?"

"Oh I'm here with my Thatha for only a few months. Then I'll go to Poona and go back to school. And why aren't you in school?" Kamu had touched a raw nerve, and Bala's lips twitched as she replied. "No school for me ... I'm a dancer."

"Really? I love dancing." So saying, she traipsed around the room singing *Thaaye Yasodha* ... using all the wrong lyrics, imitating someone she may have seen perform. Bala threw her head back and laughed, so thrilled to encounter such spontaneity, which only children were capable of.

Kunju's small box of provisions was ready.

"Your bill is 14 rupees," Perumal announced.

"Could you add that to our account? My father has gone for a bereavement, but he'll pay as soon as he comes."

"That's fine, but please pay something. Your account is now over hundred rupees. It's been six months since you paid me. I respect Inspector Saar, so I have been patient, but I have to feed my family too."

Kunju was shocked. How were they going to pay this bill? She looked at her purchases. Perhaps they could do with less rice and half the sugar. They didn't really need so much *ulunthu*. She proceeded to remove some unnecessary items. "How much is the rice?" she enquired.

"It's three rupees," Perumal replied.

"Okay take out half. We don't really need so much."

Watching this scene, Kamalamba felt sad. She could see by Kunju's appearance that she hailed from a good family. Perumal had referred to her father as Inspector. It was clear they had fallen on hard times. Removing all those items only reduced the bill by a few rupees. Kamalamba felt utterly grateful that she never had to worry about food. Her benefactors were all landowners, and abundant groceries arrived in overladen bullock carts from their farmlands. She only stopped by Perumal's to make special purchases. Not all Devadasis were blessed with good looks. Beauty meant rich patrons and the result was abundance in her household. It was sad to see this Brahmin lady struggling to make ends meet. Who knew her story? She looked so noble, and the child with her was so lovely. A rush of gratitude overwhelmed Kamalamba and she felt an urgent need to help out. But she had to do this without offending the lady. "Please don't take the rice out Perumal, or any of the other provisions. Please put it on my account. That is," she added, turning to Kunju, "if you don't mind me helping out."

Kunju looked at her, shocked. She was not accustomed to taking charity. What would Appa say? No! She couldn't accept it. That too from a stranger, and she told the lady so.

"We don't have to be strangers. My name is Kamalamba, and this is my daughter Balamani. See? Now we know each other and the rice is my gift to you. Surely you accept gifts?"

Kunju's eyes filled with tears. Such random kindness overwhelmed her. Chithi was right. God appears in different forms, and today, he came to her as Kamalamba.

CHAPTER SIXTEEN

VANI AND RUKKU
AKBAR ROAD, NEW DELHI – DECEMBER 1942

SISTER-SISTER

"**D**o you really have to wear a sari? I mean your husband isn't here and neither are your in-laws. There's no one here to tell you what to do. You can wear my slacks if you wish." But Vani didn't want to. It was mid-morning and the sun had lost its battle with the clouds, making the house damp and cold—uncomfortable for being up and about. Such weather called for snuggling under a *razai,* drinking hot *chai,* and nibbling on fried, onion *pakodas.* They were both in Rukku's room just lazing around. It was Sunday morning and Rukku was done with school for now. She would return to school in a month to take her Senior Cambridge exam, after which she was free to do whatever she pleased. Right now, with all the studying, the prospect of three months of leisure loomed like a hazy mirage in a hot desert, a comforting scenario compared to constantly burying her nose in some book.

Vani had arrived in Delhi a week ago. She had miscarried a few months before and had been too weak to travel. Her husband was a doctor, and had taken care of her adequately, yet Vani couldn't forgive her mother for not making the trip to be with her at the time. Shimla was far away from Mysore and travel during the monsoons was hard. Dharmu thought about it, but the journey was too daunting, and it would take a week to reach south India. It seemed at the time a better idea for Vani to join them a few months later in the comfort of their Delhi home. Vani's physical needs were taken care of, but the depression that followed almost swallowed her whole. She absolutely hated her life and felt abandoned by her parents, yet she'd been too weak even to write a letter. Since her arrival, for the past week, Dharmu and Vani were continually sparring and saying nasty things to one another and, frankly, Rukku was tired of it. Kandu had no patience for family drama and would make a hasty exit as soon as the conversation got tense, but Rukku couldn't do that. Every time she attempted to flee, either Vani or Mummy would stop and ask her for moral support to validate their actions and words. No matter what Rukku said and whom she sided with, it was always the wrong choice. At times her comments would backfire, causing them both to turn on her! Emotions were high, and everyone needed someone to blame. Since Daddy was at work and Kandu kept up his disappearing act, Rukku faced the brunt of the squabbling.

Today, Vani had said it all and lay depleted. She sat up in bed and pulled the razai a little closer around her, but nothing could warm her up in the cold December air. "Don't you think it just gets colder each year?"

Rukku burst out laughing. "No!" she snorted. "You've just gotten used to the warmth of the south. How long have you been married now?"

"Too long," Vani replied sullenly and Rukku knew she had put her foot in it. This was just the topic she wanted to avoid. Poor Vani, stuck in a loveless marriage. Rukku could tell she was unhappy, but it was no good fanning the fire. There was no point making her feel worse, especially since there was no instant remedy in sight. Vani was married and now, no matter how she felt, or what her husband was like, she had no choice but to remain there. Rukku knew how much she hated her life. Sometimes she wondered how Vani could bring herself to have sex with a man who was so unattractive to her. She could never do that. She had told herself a long time ago that if she married it would be for love. She would fight tooth and nail before being sold into a loveless marriage. "Why did you do it?" she asked Vani.

"Do what? Get married? I don't know. When they keep telling you it's your last chance, you somehow believe it. It wasn't as though I was going to be able to find my own man. How would I do that?"

"In college?" Rukku suggested indignantly.

"In a girl's college? No! I seriously doubt that I could have found anyone other than a menial jamadār there."

"Honestly I have never seen anyone so cynical about life. You have to figure out some way to stop being glum. Your mood is affecting everyone. No one wants to be around someone who constantly brings them down. Even Kandu has become clever about avoiding you."

"So what do you suggest I do? Take a lover?" Vani was indignant and her voice warbled with emotion.

Rukku blushed, startled by her impulsive response, but she was not to be outdone. "Well ... since you bring it up ... why not?"

Vani closed her eyes and for a moment imagined being held in the loving embrace of a handsome, virile man. One who understood her, who valued her hidden talents, one who had strong shoulders, a square jaw and a handlebar moustache. Her body reacted involuntarily, and she felt the heat rise in her loins and suffuse her face in a gentle blush. The idea made her feel complete, wanted and even loved.

"A lover," she purred inaudibly. *What an epiphany!*

CHAPTER SEVENTEEN

NANDU
ASSAM – DECEMBER 1942

THE ASSASSIN

He wasn't scared. He wasn't worried about the outcome. He felt calm. Calmer than he ever expected. He was dressed in a white dhoti and an open shirt and looked older than his years, but Nandu really had no idea how old he actually was. He could have been ten or fifteen years old, but the hardship he had endured in his short lifespan made him feel he had lived forever. This was his first real assignment and he wanted to ensure he made them proud. Nandu sat outside in the verandah waiting to be called in and had been there for the better part of an hour. He could hear the sound of tinkling silverware and porcelain. The sahib was eating a leisurely dinner, and it would be some time before he was invited in for the post-dinner entertainment.

He sauntered up to the fountain in the patio. The pool was placid with occasional ripples created when a wayward drop of water chose to escape its stony orifice. The eyes of the naked boy adorning the center of the fountain stared into the distance, his mouth slightly parted, allowing ample space for a water spout, his hands not caring to cover a naked torso barely concealed by encircling vines. Nandu stared up, taking in every inch of this sculpture of an Anglo-Saxon youth, his eyes as hard and cold as the marble fountain. He looked down into the water and saw the outline of his head. It was too dark for the moon to illuminate his slanted, icy eyes, small pug-like nose or his protruding lips, but the water clearly mirrored his ebony complexion.

After checking the *darwān* was not around, he sauntered to the edge of the balcony where Biswa waited for him hidden in the outlying foliage. Biswa had accompanied him to this remote location somewhere on a tea estate in Assam for this mission. He made sure Nandu bathed with soap and then dressed him in pure white clothes, a dhoti and kurta and lined his eyes with *kājal*. Then they prayed in front of Goddess Kali. Nandu didn't believe in Kali or any other Goddess, but he copied what Biswa did and even bent his head in feigned deference when

Biswa anointed his forehead with bright red vermillion, the color red signifying sacrifice to the Goddess for the sake of righteousness. The blood that would spill was no murder, it was justice for the multitude of girls and young boys this vile sahib had used and discarded.

Biswa went over the steps for the umpteenth time. Nandu knew exactly what he had to do and could perhaps now carry out this mission with his eyes closed. He had heard the same instructions so many times in the last two weeks. He didn't care what happened to him, and Biswa, recognizing this coldness of heart, instantly knew he was perfect for the job.

"He always sits on the edge of the bed. Then he will make you take off his pants and pleasure him with your mouth. Keep watching for him to close his eyes and slip the knife under the mattress. This will be your only chance to do this. Once your dhoti is off, you won't be able to and it must not be discovered. Don't be in a rush to finish early. Patience is the key. Wait until he finishes buggering you and is fast asleep. This is very important. Don't fail ... Kali is with you."

Nandu nodded and returned to his spot in the corner of the verandah. The darwān had not yet returned. He was probably asleep. Nothing really happened on the estates worth policing; the rape of girls and boys by an angrezi sahib was not worthy of any attention. This is why the locals appealed to Biswa to help them out. The sahib loved it here and had been living on the same estate for over a decade. His sexual appetite was notorious, and the countryside was overrun with his Anglo-Indian bastards. Girls and young men especially feared him and kept their eyes lowered when he passed by on his horse, in case they perked his interest. At first, when Biswa brought him the request, Vaithee was not about to pursue it. It was too bloody and would cause a lot of problems for his organization. His group was involved in assassination of important Government officials and, really, killing a one-time colonel in some remote tea estate did not suit their political agenda.

Vaithee was more involved in the planning and gathering of information and kept away from actual killing. That was relegated to another part of the group, where several young boys were trained for this very purpose. The young lads were perfect choices for assassinations. They were inconspicuous and could escape from the scene quickly, seamlessly blending in with crowds. They were all erstwhile thieves and pickpockets and came to the group with special talent. All that was needed was for these skills to be honed and polished. After much thought and a multitude of requests, he finally relented, thinking that there was no angrezi better than a dead angrezi. Nandu was picked because he was perfect for the job. His monitors said that he had a razor sharp brain, an attention to detail, but more importantly, he was devoid of emotion. He was of medium height with a slender build, which apparently was what the sahib liked. Besides, from what he had learned of the boy's past, this sexual act was nothing new for him.

No, Nandu didn't care that he was about to be buggered. So many had done it to him innumerable times that he finally stopped counting and could scarcely recall the faces of his ravishers. His anus was just another body part, as was his arm, and it was readily available as payment for food sometimes and a ride at other times. What did it matter? For a whole year Nandu travelled, sometimes stowing away on trains and at other times asking to be a cleaner on a truck. That year had transformed the innocent runaway child into a hardened, cynical man. So many times his tormentors had thrown the *rotis* onto the ground; some stomped on it and others peed on it. And Nandu would then pick it up, dust it off, and eat it. He was used to foraging from the garbage, and his survival instinct was strong. He had to eat, and he needed to keep moving. He had no idea what his final destination might be, but he knew he wanted to be as far away from home as possible. An eon ago he remembered crying into the dirt as he was being raped. His tears were a bodily reaction to pain, his salty tears drying instantly as they encountered the harsh, unyielding earth that offered little consolation. Soon the tears dried out and the pain receded. He was able to cut himself out of his body, and replace his feelings and emotions with stony indifference. He had to survive, and he did whatever it took. His body just was. He just was. Nothing really mattered.

His father Velandi would not be proud today. Thank heavens he died a while ago. Poverty had aged his father. He never really got over the death of his first wife Muniamma. He just wasted away, and mercifully exited his decaying body one day. The reek of his putrid flesh permeated everything in the house, and for weeks after he was gone the rancid stench remained. Sindhuriamma had been good to him for a while, but with no food in the house and Velandi raving like a lunatic, it was up to Nandu to scavenge the dustbins and bring home the rotting leftovers. For the first few years a few families hired him to clean their latrines, but he had never really apprenticed with his father and didn't exactly know how to do a good job. Besides he hated this repulsive trade. Nothing could cleanse the foul smell off his clothes, skin, and hair, and even though he grew accustomed to its special odor, he hated his life. Velandi had been supremely religious and had tried to impart these qualities in Nandu, but looking around him and seeing others live in comfort and wealth, Nandu couldn't come to terms with his father's punitive and unfair God. Two months after Velandi died, Nandu ran away.

Waiting to be summoned, Nandu had a rare recall of his painful childhood. He was sure no one had looked for him after he left. Sindhuriamma would have been glad to have one less mouth to feed. Now he was here—an assassin in the making. The door opened, and the bearer signaled for him to enter. Nandu took a deep breath and boldly walked into the large bungalow.

CHAPTER EIGHTEEN

RUKKU AND ARUN
AKBAR ROAD, NEW DELHI – DECEMBER 1942

THE HOLLYWOOD ROMANCE

K andu ran in all excited. "They're here, come on!" he yelled, before dashing off.

"Who?" snapped the girls in unison. They hadn't a clue about the happenings in the rest of the house. Here under the warm covers of the razai they had created their own isolated, perfectly comfortable world. Strangely, neither remembered their mother mention visitors. She must have forgotten. Usually she would have begun preparations a week before they had any visitors.

"Kannan Chithappa! He's here with his family." Kandu could barely conceal his excitement. He absolutely adored his dashing uncle but rarely got to meet him. Kannan had run away from the house and much against his father's wishes had joined the Royal Navy. That meant months away at sea, and somehow his leave never coincided with Kandu's annual visits to Nagarcoil. Kandu's childhood trips to Nagarcoil was filled with memories of Kannan's antics. Kannan was different from his brothers in that he was brave enough to stand up to his daunting father, Nilakantan. Of course, he always demonstrated the right amount of respect, but ultimately he did what his heart dictated. He was closer to Kandu in age—at least that's how Kandu felt back then, and always kept the family amused with his stories and antics. For years Kandu followed him like a doting puppy, hanging onto his every word and smiling and laughing at every joke. Now Kannan was married with two children, but his look of cheerful amusement as he walked in showed that marriage had not wiped the smile off his face.

Mahadevan was already outside welcoming his brother when Kandu noticed Kannan had not come alone. There were two carloads of people. Kannan's wife Laali and their young son were the first to get out of the car, but to his surprise, he noticed a baby in Laali's arms. No one had mentioned a new baby, not that Kandu even heard or took note of family gossip. Well … hopefully she was well behaved; he hated the sound of babies crying.

Kannan hugged him and was beaming from ear to ear by the time Dharmu and the girls arrived. The family reunion was raucous, everyone meeting and greeting, laughing and speaking. Dharmu took the baby from Laali. "Precious. She looks just like you. How old now?" she enquired.

"Three months and thankfully she still sleeps all the time."

Two orderlies brought in the suitcases, and Dharmu was busy barking instructions to the servants to prepare the rooms. The house was very large with six bedrooms, so housing them didn't pose a problem. The rooms needing dusting and new sheets, but with eight servants in the house, it would all be ready way before lunch.

Just then, a young man walked in carrying two bags of fruit, which he gave to the girls, Vani and Rukku. He must have been in his late teens and was dark complexioned like Laali. The girls accepted the gift with question marks in their eyes. They had no idea who he was. He certainly wasn't dressed like an orderly. Seeing their confusion, Laali burst out laughing. "This is my brother Arun, short for Arunachalam." Arun did a half shuffle and gestured something between a salute and namaste. At first glance, he appeared shy and well mannered.

Rukku couldn't stop staring. It was good no one was watching her. The attention at the moment was all on Arun, the newcomer in the family. He had perfect features, big eyes over a straight short nose and a small yet soft mouth. He was of medium height, and his shirt and pants enhanced his slim, athletic build. He seemed to bring with him the bright, warm sunshine. Rukku could hear her heart thumping loudly in her chest as if it wanted to exit her body. Everything she had read about in romance books, and then thought about and dreamed of, seemed to be happening to her. Her mind was confused, and she couldn't make sense of her thoughts entering and leaving. Her heart a flutter of excitement, her face hot and bright pink. All this in a matter of moments. Then, the entire room began to swim and she felt her knees tremble. The next thing she remembered was waking up on the sofa. A myriad of worried faces peered down at her, and someone had just rudely splashed cold water on her face. She sat up awkwardly. "Wh … what happened?"

"That's what I'd like to ask you," replied Dharmu. "Have you eaten since you woke up? It must be the empty stomach. You fainted face forward."

Mahadevan ran his hand across her forehead to check if she had a fever and added, "Thank God Arun was standing close; otherwise we would be dealing with a broken nose."

Oh Lord! What had she done? This was really awkward! She had to faint and that too into this strange boy's arms? How was she going to live this down? Oh

Lord, this was so embarrassing!

Vani handed her a glass of water and Rukku gulped it down. She glanced up at the amused expression on her sister's face. "What?" She asked.

"Someone's in love ... and just fell into her beau's arms," Vani whispered.

"Shut up. Don't begin all that nonsense. Anyway, he's too dark, and besides he is related to us, so Daddy and Mummy would throw a fit." Rukku was visibly nonplussed, and the words were streaming out in a ramble.

"What? Are you already considering marrying him? Aren't you a bit too young? I would definitely suggest waiting a bit," she chuckled. This was getting better and better and Vani had lots of fuel for future ribbing.

"Noooo...." Rukku whined, annoyed with herself for being infuriated with the incident. Vani was going to tease her, and if Kandu got wind of it, her life would become a living hell. She was surprised at her reaction on seeing the young man. This could well be a page from a *Women's World* romance book. Rukku was usually very composed. In the family she was the peacekeeper, the rational, sensible one. This was completely out of character. Perhaps it *was* the empty stomach. It had better be. She got up and ran to her room happy to hide in the safe refuge of the razai. Somewhere in the background she could hear voices, but she faded them out and hoped and prayed they had faded her out. A few minutes later there was a knock on the door. "Come in," she yelled, thinking it was Vani checking on her but no, oh no, *it was Arun!!!*

"Can I come in? How do you feel?" he enquired politely and then added as an afterthought, "After laying in my arms?"

Rukku was enraged. "I'm fine and you don't need to feel like a hero. You can certainly wipe that smirk off your face." This was no quiet, well behaved boy, and he had no business coming into her room. The guts of the boy daring to come *into* her bedroom and tease *her*! This was outrageous and she told him so! "How can you just come into my room like that?"

"I asked permission and you gave it," he remarked, his smirk now a hearty laugh.

This was true. But in her defense she thought it was Vani.

"It's not every day I get to save a damsel in distress." Now he was really teasing her and it made Rukku mad.

"You're no knight in shining armor. You are lucky you happened to be there. So don't go giving yourself unnecessary laurels." Rukku's beautiful face was now squished into a scowl.

"It's a shame you can't remember how it felt to be in my arms," he continued unabashed. Rukku was now on the point of tears. He was getting too bold and no one had ever spoken to Rukku like that, so she was at a loss for words. Rage was bubbling within her like lava and she burst out, "Leave ... leave now! Are you mocking me?"

"It's all a matter of perspective," he replied glibly, casually lounging against the door. "But I don't want you to faint again or else I might need to get under the covers to save you," he replied with a smirk on his face. Infuriated by his remarks, Rukku threw a book at him and he caught it deftly. This was getting more and more like a scene from a Hollywood movie, and the already weak and embarrassed Rukku just didn't know how to react. Her mind was thinking *I hate him* but her rebellious body longed for him to remain. Conflicting emotions battled within her, and all she could hear was a high pitched screaming in her ears. "I hate you ... get out!" she yelled. To which he smoothly replied, "No you don't ... but I'm off anyway. Don't miss me too much."

For a few minutes after he left, Rukku couldn't breathe. How dare he come in to her room and flirt with her. Didn't he know he was out of bounds? She was way younger than him and for god's sake, they were related. It was totally unacceptable. Rukku turned face down and pummeled the pillow, *I hate you, I hate you, I hate you!*

But deep down she knew she didn't. She knew he was going to be around a lot in her life. Something told her this was no chance meeting. All her life she swore to herself that she would only marry for love, and now the Universe, the divine, had manifested the very person she'd always longed for. In spite of her inexperience and immaturity, she knew he was the one she would marry.

CHAPTER NINETEEN

BALA AND KAMU
THANJAVUR – FEBRUARY 1943

THE TEMPLE OF PILLARS

Kamu sat up against the stone pillar at the temple poring over her slate, where she wrote beautifully formed words in Tamil. Her chalky hands had left stray telltale marks all over her face, but she was unmindful of that and focused on her lettering. When she moved to Poona, she would learn English at her new school. Appa said it was a convent, and the nuns insisted the children learn only in English. Unsure how long they would remain in Thanjavur, Rajam decided not to enroll her in school. Kunju Periamma reminded her of this all the time, and Rajam spent a couple of hours each day teaching Kamu to inscribe the complicated Tamil script. Kamu loved the sound of chalk on a slate and spent most of her free time sounding out and writing new and more involved words. It was hard because most often the required letter wasn't always the right one, as Tamil was not a phonetic language, but Kamu sounded her letters out anyway. She was so engrossed with writing and erasing that a whole hour slipped by very easily. Time meant nothing when you were seven years old, until you were bored; then it hung around endlessly.

Kunju loved coming to the temple, as this was her chance to meet her neighbors. They were here at least two or three times a week in spite of not living close to the Periya Kovil. Of course, on the other days Kunju went to the local Ganesh temple, but Kamu didn't always accompany her as it wasn't half as interesting. The temple complex was huge and the most interesting part were the pillars in the corridors around it. Kamu would snake her way in between and around the pillars, niftily clasping the jutting sculptures when she had to navigate the outer edge, and if Kunju found enough friends to chat with, Kamu would get time to count each and every pillar. It was strange that the numbers never remained constant. One time it was 350 another time 395. Today she had counted 397 pillars. More every time. This was certainly a mysterious temple of continually increasing pillars. She was getting better at it though, and could move pretty quickly.

They had already done the *poojai* and *pradakshanam* in the inner sanctum, and once Kunju started chatting with her friends, Kamu made a hasty exit. She quickly completed her serpentine pillar walk and picked the perfect column to sit against. It hurt her back a little to sit down against the ornately carved pillars, but she didn't mind it today as she was hunched over her slate. A favorite pastime with Kamu was deciphering the intricate sculptures and imitating dance poses. Each pillar was carved with a cluster of different statues and depicted scenes from Hindu epics. But what fascinated her more were the sculptures of dancers in complicated and graceful postures. She longed to learn to dance, but Amma had not put her in a class. Dancing was reserved for Devadasis, and only recently people from the upper castes were beginning to allow their daughters to learn the art form. Here in Thanjavur, there were many more opportunities to learn as, traditionally, a thousand years ago, the temple had boasted of more than four hundred royal courtesans. Their families continued to live here, and there were still many homes where the ancient culture thrived; homes like that of Koviladi Kamalamba.

Kamu knew she would remain in Thanjavur only for a short time, so there was no point in enrolling, but nothing stopped her from imitating the postures. She looked up and spied a beautiful frieze of a woman admiring herself in the mirror except that her body was twisted backwards. Kamu spread her feet wide attempting to copy the statue. Then she twirled her upper body away but quickly realized that with her face turned away, she couldn't see the sculpture, so then she turned around, wondering how to proceed. She figured it was better to start with her back to the statue, so when she twisted her body, she could see the figurine. She placed one hand in front as if holding a mirror and with the other, applied an imaginary *pottu* in the center of her forehead but was unstable and couldn't hold the pose; she could feel herself teetering on the edge of the platform.

Lucky that Bala happened to be walking by and caught her, breaking almost certainly, a very painful fall. "Saved you Kamu kutti. What in heaven were you trying?"

"Oh Bala Akka?" said Kamu breathing rapidly, excited to see her again. "I was imitating the poses in the temple. I always do that. If I do different ones each day, one day I can dance just like you," she said, a smile lighting up her face.

"You like to dance?"

"I really want to learn, but no one is there to teach me."

"Which statue were you copying?" she asked, placing her back on the ledge. Kamu pointed to it and once again awkwardly attempted the pose. Bala laughed and effortlessly sat low in aramandi and twisted her body fluidly so she virtually looked like a dancer in stone.

"Wow! You do this so easily." Kamu's expressive eyes widened in admiration.

"I should. I have been dancing as long as I can remember. In a few months I will have my Arangetram in this very temple." The very thought knotted her stomach and made her think of the hours of practice in store for her when she returned home.

"You are so lucky. I wish I could be you," remarked Kamu wistfully.

"No, don't ever wish that. Amma says you have to have done something very special in all your previous births to be born a Brahmin, so why would you ever want to be a Devadasi?"

"So I can dance. Easy," said Kamu bouncing up and down.

"Your face looks very colorful. Have you been playing with chalk?"

"Yes, I'm practicing my letters." She lifted up her slate high where the word "ettram" was scrawled in beautiful letters.

"What does it say?"

"Easy, "ettram." Can't you read it? You're bigger than me." Kamu was astonished. In her world everyone went to school.

Bala shook her head sadly. "No we learn to dance, but we are not allowed to go to school, so I can't learn to read and write."

Kamu took a flying leap off the ledge and gleefully wrapped her legs around Bala, who was a little taken aback by this sudden exhibition of exuberance. She whirled her around and then sat on the ledge with Kamu gleefully ensconced in her lap. Across the courtyard walking towards them they spied Kunju Periamma deep in conversation with Bala's Kamalamba Amma.

"So? What are you girls chatting about?" Kamalamba asked.

"Bala Akka showed me how well she dances," piped up Kamu immediately.

"And Kamu showed me how beautifully she writes." added Bala, a hopeful twinge in her voice.

"Good!" remarked Kamalamba. "Maybe you can teach one another your skills."

"Really?" said Kamu in disbelief, her eyes sparkling wildly. "Can I learn to dance? And could we teach Bala Akka to write?" Bala couldn't believe where this conversation was heading, all in the right direction. It was wise to stay silent and hope for the best.

"I don't see why not," piped in Kunju. "Bala, you don't go to school?"

"No Kunju," said Kamalamba, speaking on Bala's behalf. "Our kind are never accepted in schools; you should know that. And at home no one except Muthu knows how to read and write. He takes care of all our needs—accounts and letters—so we have nothing to do with all this literary stuff."

"Then maybe you should join the class too, Kamalamba. Kamu will be here for another couple of months and is quite bored during the day when my children are in school. Maybe she can come and learn a few dance exercises from you and then I can teach Bala and perhaps you how to write and read. How about numbers? Can you do maths? It's very important to know how to write and to count. How would you know what is written in letters to you and what about checking accounts?"

"I can't write numbers, but I do it in my head."

"Well that's not good enough. Let me teach your girls. It would be my way of paying you back."

Bala couldn't believe what she was hearing. She was going to learn how to read and write. How exciting! Already, she had delved into a world of dreams and seen herself sitting at a desk in a school. It was only when she looked around and saw her classmates were six year olds that she was rudely awakened. She would never be able to attend school. They did not allow people from lower castes to come there. No one from Kamalamba's family had ever attended school, and she mustn't dream, but on the brighter side, at the very least, she would learn to read and write and that was a beginning. Beaming from ear to ear, she left with Kamalamba to meet the priest. They were here to make arrangements for her upcoming pottukattu ceremony which would be conducted in a few months, and the date and timing needed to be fixed so they could plan the event properly. In a few months she would be married, except her husband was a stone lingam. The good thing is, she never would face widowhood. She would die a *"nithya sumangali,"* permanently married to the Lord.

She looked around at all the families in the temple in envy, young women with real flesh and blood husbands and children. And her eyes brimmed with tears. She didn't want any of this. She wanted to go to school and learn and read and go to the cinema. She wanted to marry a handsome young man and cook and clean for him. She wanted children to sing lullabies to and to hold and cherish. But she knew these were useless thoughts. All that was destined for her was a stone lingam.

CHAPTER TWENTY

RAJAM AND PARTHA
MADRAS – JANUARY 1943

DEALING WITH DEATH

Ten gloomy and difficult days had gone by. Death always affected Rajam, and the memory of her inert father-in-law made the nights unbearable. She kept reaching out to Partha at night for solace, but instead of responding, he would turn the other way and inch away from her. Rajam couldn't keep her eyes open because she saw dangers lurking everywhere. The street lights entered the room at a strange angle, creating ghostly shadows and swaying shapes. Closing her eyes was even worse because then her imagination ran riot, making Munuswamy appear floating into the room smiling at her ghoulishly. She hated death and all its connotation: cremation grounds, *Kabāligas* (Shiva worshippers) ghosts, ghouls and dreadfully vivid images that shook her innards until it became impossible to think straight.

The tenth day ceremony was tomorrow, and Siva and Partha had made all the arrangements. There had been a heated discussion whether to call the *ambattan* and shave Nagamma's head in a special ceremony which was customary in very conservative families. In spite of Thambu's insistence that Nagamma needed to follow tradition, both the older brothers held their ground. Partha in part had been greatly influenced by his father-in-law Swaminathan, who had always vehemently voiced his opinion against such barbaric customs. Yet, in spite of his pleas in his own home, Nagalakshmi Chithi always shaved her head and never wore a blouse. She had dressed like this for years now. Swaminathan had tried in vain to convince her otherwise, but she came from the old school that believed a widow had no place in society and needed to dress according to tradition, else ill fortune would beset the family—and no amount of arguments would persuade her otherwise. However, Kunju always wore colored saris and even a small black pottu at her father's insistence. He did not get his way with his sister-in-law, but with his daughter he had much more influence. Besides, Kunju's education and familiarity with western ideas made it easy for Swaminathan to influence her.

Partha was having a hard time with Thambu. He could not understand how Thambu preferred to see his mother in colorless saris when all her life Nagamma always wore beautifully colored, nine-yard madisars with a large kumkumam pottu adorning her forehead. She was never without adornment—a nose ring and big diamond earrings for the longest time. Then difficult times made her switch to sizeable pearl earrings, but her thick gold *thali*, a symbol of her married status, always adorned her neck. Partha was alright with her downgrading her jewelry, but he did not wish to see her in those ugly, coarse, mud colored saris that widows were forced to wear. Thambu had for some strange, unfathomable reason become almost fanatical in his religious beliefs. He prayed for three hours a day, went to the temple daily, but more incomprehensible was his finicky, dogmatic attitude to ritual. He wanted every single rite to be performed, and Lord knows no one in the family could afford to pay the priest for these long and arduous rituals. But now he was literally "standing on one foot" (A tamil saying), insisting they include the ceremony and bring in the ambattan for the ritual shaving of the widow. This in spite of pleas from everyone else that this was a cruel observance that had no place in their lives anymore. The air was fraught with tension. The long and bitter arguments thankfully took place in Siva's home and so far had not fallen on Nagamma's ears. She was in a very tender and vulnerable place and did not need to hear such cruel words. Hopefully, tomorrow Thambu would control himself and let this one go, but knowing him, he was sure to make a scene.

Rajam reached out to Partha, and this time he brushed her arm off and moved even further away. What was wrong? Ever since he came, he had been acting strangely, not looking her in the eye and avoiding every chance to be with her alone. It was almost as if he were deliberately avoiding her. Had he found another woman? Not being able to speak to him in private, Rajam was unable to ask him, but it bothered her. After all, they had been apart for four months now and the old Partha would have contrived an intimate moment somehow in the midst of all the gloom. Was he turned off her or had she put on too much weight? Rajam was really troubled. She had not yet raised the question of money and hoped he had some to give her. It would not be much, as he had only been working for three months now and the brothers were sharing all the funeral expenses. She would probably have to sell the silver plate to pay Kunju something. What a life! Fear of ghosts, a nonresponsive husband, and no money! Sometime in the early hours of the morning in sheer fatigue, Rajam dropped off to sleep.

But not for long. At the crack of dawn, the household was up and running, gearing up for the tenth day *kriya*[1]. The retinue of priests arrived and preparations began. Thambu stood in one corner, a scowl marring his face. He was still angry because the ambattan was not to be called. The other brothers ignored him, and Siva was performing the ceremony with due solemnity. The sound of mantras filled the air, but the vibrations they emitted were not good. Rajam could still feel the uneasiness that had plagued her from the moment she entered the home. The *pindam*[2], the fire and smoke, everything reeked of death and doom. The ladies had prepared the meal in advance. Normal food was never cooked in the house but instead, brought in from the neighbor's home as the fire in the kitchen could not be stoked until the ceremony *shubha sweekāram* on the thirteenth day was complete. They ate *vazhakāi* (raw banana) curry every day and Rajam was sick of it.

Finally, the priests left, satisfied with the generous *dakshina*. The money for the dakshina was mainly paid by Siva, Partha, and Thambu as Kannan was still not working.

As soon as the priests left the house, Thambu burst out. All his pent up anger came out in one long monologue. "There will be more death and devastation in this family. What kind of Brahmins are you that you cannot follow the most important customs in our tradition? One thing ... one thing I insisted on and you refused to comply. I tell you as long as Amma dresses like a sumangali nothing good will happen. What does she need to wear jewelry and fancy saris for now? She is a *mundam*—an *amangali* and seeing her with long hair and colored saris makes my blood boil...."

Suddenly there was a hushed silence in the room. There, framed in the doorway was Nagamma. She looked at Thambu with such venom in her eyes, he shriveled up and started dithering like the fool he was. He never meant to hurt his mother, just establish some say in the family and have his voice heard. Nagamma's chest was heaving with passion. She said nothing, but two large tears escaped her eyes and ran down her ample nose. She didn't bother to wipe them away. They were tears of rage. Partha and Siva made excuses for Thambu but she heard not a word. She turned and walked out of the house. After she left, the brothers turned on Thambu who by now was weeping like a child.

"I hope you're satisfied," Siva said coldly. "This is what you wanted isn't it? All her life she has lived to support us and make us comfortable. She was always such

---

1 *Kri* means task and *Kriya* means 'completed task'. These tasks are performed by the son on the death of his father.

2 Rice balls offered to pitṛs (ancestors) after death as part of *kriya*. The spirit of ancestors accepts this offering in the form of *pindam* which are then released into water together with the satiated spirit.

a proud woman, we wanted to spare her this agony. But you ... you stupid idiot you just wanted to bring her to her knees, you heartless ingrate. And now look at what you have done Thambu. You have no heart ... no heart at all." Thambu was so overwhelmed he couldn't speak.

"Go and get her!" Rajam yelled. "She is overwrought, and God knows what she will do." Partha ran out looking for his mother, but she was nowhere to be seen. Siva and Sushila went to their home hoping she was there, but it was locked and she wasn't sitting outside. She wouldn't have gone to the temple. She had *theetu* for a whole year, which meant she couldn't enter a temple, so it was no point looking there. They entered every home on Mundakanni Amman Kovil Street, but no one had seen her. Finally, they came home to regroup and decide what to do next. They had to find her.

It was close to lunchtime when they heard the gate open. Nagamma entered the room and in stunned silence the family simply stared at her. Her head was bald and covered with sandal paste. She wore a coarse, mud colored madisar and the blouse was gone. Deliberately she stood in front of Thambu, unscrewed her diamond nose ring and her pearl earrings and threw them at him. She stared down at him disdainfully and hissed, "Is this what you wanted? Do I look like a mundam now? Well ... I hope you are happy...."

Then, not pausing for a response she proudly walked right out of the room leaving its occupants bewildered and dumbstruck. Even in the ugliest moments, even when she was at a disadvantage, even when every attempt was made to bring her to her knees, Nagamma had the courage that warriors coveted. Her towering strength and inner pride engulfed any shred of weakness brought on by grief. No one, nothing could ever diminish the powerful inner strength that she embodied. Even widowhood, she would wear like a soldier's armor of steel. She was Nagamma!

CHAPTER TWENTY ONE

SWAMINATHAN
THANJAVUR – FEBRUARY 1943

A LONELY, OLD MAN

"Rajam ... Rajam ... Kunju ... what? Is everyone deaf today? My throat is so dry and there is no one to get water for this old man."

"Thatha you called?" Kamu came running.

"Kamu kutti, bring me some water. You'll get a thousand blessings from an old man." Kamu pranced in sideways and returned with water, and Swaminathan poured it down his parched throat making sure his lips didn't touch the tumbler. The sun was low on the horizon, and the streets were busy with people rushing back from work or going to the temple. Rushing, rushing, rushing. And all Swaminathan could do was sit and watch them. He had nowhere to go and really nothing to do. With his mind so inactive, he felt the aging process take a toll on his body. It seemed in recent years that it took him forever to get anything done. Even the simple process of sitting down in his easy chair and getting up made every bone in his body ache. He always prided himself on being independent, but now he needed help even for a glass of water. There was a time he could walk across the house in seconds and help himself to anything. As a policeman, he had chased a thousand criminals, but today even a simple *Surya Namaskaram* was too difficult to complete.

Old age is inevitable. No matter how hard you exercise and how well you eat, time eats away at your body; wrinkles appear out of nowhere, skin sags and muscles get weak. The only thing that Swami had was his mind, which somehow had remained alert and sharp. But he missed the conversations and really missed being useful. It seemed from morning to night he ambled around in the house and no sparkling conversation came up worth discussing. Sometimes, only sometimes, the grandkids would ask him to tell them a story from the past but they were less interested and more preoccupied with each passing day. Only Kamu's scintillating presence kept him alive. But she was going to move soon. He wished his old friends would drop by but they had grown old too and, like him, remained in their respective easy chairs on their thinnais. Swaminathan looked wistfully down the street; his eyes crinkled as he strained to recognize some familiar face. Kamu had drawn chalk lines on the floor and was playing hopscotch while singing all the time. Music and dance came naturally to her, and Swaminathan smiled at the innocence of childhood. The realities of the world had not hit Kamu yet, and she was happy for no particular reason. She took pleasure in any activity and never tired of searching for things to do. If she wasn't playing then she wrote on her slate or practiced *thaiya thai*, her dance exercises, in front of the mirror. She continually asked everyone if she was in aramandi or *kaal mandi*. Her thigh muscles were still weak and she could not comfortably sink low enough in aramandi, the classic and basic pose in Bharata Natyam. But that didn't deter her. She danced and practiced as if she were about to do an Arangetram next week. Swami was so busy watching her expressions he never realized someone stood at the gate until Kamu squealed, "Bala Akka how nice."

Right behind her followed Kamalamba who greeted Swaminathan; "*Namaskaram*, Mama, *sowkyama?* I came to ask you for some advice and also thought I would see Kunju."

"*Vaa vaa* ... Welcome ... sit down." Swami was beaming when he turned to Kamu, "Go call your Periamma. Tell her Kamalamba Amma is here and ask her to make some coffee as well."

Kunju came out immediately, and they sat in the thinnai talking like old times. Swami was really happy. This is how he liked things. People dropping in, chitchatting; this was what he longed for.

"Mama, you know I am so happy. I learned how to read numbers; Kunju has been a godsend. Our way of life is no secret to you, and you know my girls have many benefactors. Well, one of them came and asked if the 50 rupees he sent was enough. When I checked the accounts Muthu had entered only 25 rupees. Now when I asked Muthu, he was certain the Mirāzdār was mistaken. It was his manager who gave the money, so Muthu felt he must have skimmed the money off the top before handing the balance over. Now I am in a situation and don't know whom to believe." Kamalamba trusted Muthu with everything. She had never bothered to check what came and what left the house. The store room was always brimming with provisions and money never a concern. It completely unsettled her when she realized that she may have been cheated for a long time. In a way she was a little scared of Muthu. Technically she remained the matriarch, but the real muscle in the household was Muthu, and he had built himself quite a reputation and was considered irreplaceable. She relied on him a bit too much and just realized that things had slipped out of her control.

"Well, well … this is a difficult situation and you have to go with your gut. Once you involve the police it might turn ugly. What I suggest is that you insist on a written note from whoever gives you cash. That way you know what to expect."

"It isn't just cash. Last month in the store room we had plenty of provisions: bags of wheat, rice, pulses … and today when I checked, at least four or five bags are missing."

"And Muthu has the keys to the storehouse?" asked Swami, controlling this like a classic police investigation.

"Yes, he always has taken care of these things. He is my Periamma's son, and I have trusted him all these years to run the household. The grains and vegetables mostly come from the farms, and as I am busy with the girls and their dance classes, he does the inventory. Until today, I have never questioned his loyalty."

"Don't be too trusting." Swami paused to think, feeling suddenly important as he metaphorically donned his police inspector's hat. "Is there anyone else you trust who can keep an eye? Maybe he has started gambling or has plans to leave you."

Kamalamba thought about her household. All the musicians were related to her; among them Radhai was especially trustworthy. Radhai was Bala's *Mama*, her mother's own brother, and he had remained with the household. Then, when Kamalamba's mother passed and she took over the household, he was quietly at her side. "Yes yes … there's Radhai, whom I trust with my life. He's Bala's Mama and he is quiet but fiercely loyal." Kamalamba felt a sense of unease thinking about Bala's mother and all the past drama involving her and hoped her expression didn't betray her thoughts. Many times she was tempted to share her secret with Bala, but was scared of losing her. Bala was beautiful and would be her meal ticket for the next few years. She had threatened Radhai with terrible consequences, and so far he had kept the secret and she was going to keep it this way.

"Well," said Swami thoughtfully rubbing chin, "you will have to change the way your household works. Give the store room keys to Radhai and tell Muthu you need to see a paper signed by the Mirāzdār. That's the best you can do for now," Swami concluded as he looked at Rajam, who had brought coffee for the visitors. Kamu ran up to her and sat on her lap rubbing the back of her hand on her mother's soft cheeks.

Bala looked at them, her eyes misting up. What a perfect portrait they painted, mother and daughter. If only she could have had such a wonderful experience with her mother. No one ever talked about her. Amma said she died at childbirth leaving the baby in her care and, so far, she had believed it. Vyjayanthi and the other girls seemed to know more about her but just would never reveal anything.

It was all so mysterious, and she wished she could find out more. Amma was kind, but she never cuddled or caressed. She believed in tough love, while Bala longed to be held and touched the way Rajam was with Kamu. Kamu was really very lucky indeed. Her thoughts were rudely interrupted with a car stopping in front of the gate.

An older man slowly got down from the passenger seat. His clothes revealed he was Muslim and Swami took a few moments to realize who this was. His dearest friend from his Vizhupuram days, Muhammad Salih. Swami bounced out of his easy chair a lot faster than his usual crank up and rushed to the gate to embrace his friend. The two hugged and rocked and kissed one another on the cheeks repeatedly.

Just a few moments ago Swami was lamenting his loneliness, and as if the divine heard him, he had a flood of visitors. First his advice was sought by Kamalamba, and now almost like a miracle, Salih appeared from nowhere. When it rained, it poured.

CHAPTER TWENTY TWO

MAHADEVAN
CALCUTTA – FEBRUARY 1943

HOBNOBBING AT THE CLUB

A t lunchtime, the Calcutta Club was very busy. The bearers in their starchy, white uniforms complete with gloves and turbans, looked visibly harassed. They had their assigned tables, knew the taste of regulars; Johnny *Saab(Sahib)* liked a gin and tonic, Sudipto Saab a cold beer, Rahul Saab a stirred martini—and never once dared make a mistake. Every table was full and the double doors to the bar and kitchen swung incessantly. It was February, and the rose garden was in full bloom with flowers in all colors and shapes. Beside the rose garden, beds of dahlias, chrysanthemums, snapdragons, and dianthus swayed in riotous colors as the soft afternoon breeze blew through them. Calcutta Club was at its social best, and Mahadevan surveyed the scene before heading to a table with two empty chairs. He recognized a few of the British occupants but didn't really know them well. Mahadevan had been away from the Calcutta office for several years now, and there must have been several waves of transfers. ICS officers were moved every few years in case they got too comfortable. Mahadevan was currently working in Delhi but needed to return to Calcutta every few months for meetings.

Sudipto signaled to the bearer for his usual lager and, delighted to recognize a familiar face, sat down in the empty chair with Mahadevan and his cronies. "Good afternoon and how are we today?" he enquired as he lit his pipe and received a variety of polite responses.

"Mahadevan, I didn't realize you were in Calcutta. Are you staying at the Grand?"

"I just arrived this morning and I have a series of meetings after lunch. But I have family here and prefer to stay with them."

"Have you looked around? How was your ride from Howrah station?" Sudipto asked, one eyebrow raised in expectation of a bleak response.

"It's getting pretty grim, isn't it? Refugees are flooding the city. I had a hard time making it through the platform with all those supine, beaten away bodies. Most of them looked half dead. It was really depressing."

"It's so bad we can hardly walk on the Strand or around the Victoria Memorial without these emaciated fellows coming up and begging," remarked one of the cronies and Sudipto raised his eyebrows again, wondering if white folk were genetically insensitive.

Another occupant, whom Mahadevan knew vaguely as an arrogant SOB added, "It's preferable when it's fellows, but I simply cannot bear to look at the women with their children straddled on their waist. Honestly, their eyes have no expression, and they look as if they just walked out of their grave." There was a teeter of laughter followed by an awkward pause.

Mahadevan and Sudipto were certainly not amused. Throngs of refugees were ensconced at Howrah station hoping to receive a few paisas from weary, beaten travelers, and their plight was deplorable. Children starved to the bone, looking like walking skeletons. Famine had hit Bengal hard. The winter crop had completely failed, and there was no food to be found anywhere for the poor. No supplies were being brought into Calcutta, and as a result, large groups of malnourished, desperate folk had found their way into the streets. The Government policy of price control had seriously failed. With prices unregulated and supplies unavailable in the famine stricken state, the condition of the people defied description. People were dying in the country, and now as they thronged to the city, the death toll in the city was rising each day. Lord Linlithgow had toured the province and instated a Food committee, but its primary Food member Mr. N.R. Sarkar had just stepped down, fed up with the inefficient food policies. Unable to ameliorate the pain of his home state and his people, he had resigned office in protest. Sudipto had been called in for an emergency meeting to discuss a contingency plan and possible replacements.

"It's no laughing matter. This will probably be the worst famine in our entire history," he remarked dismally. Only Mahadevan paid attention to his comment. The others were laughing and joking flippantly, sharing a private moment.

"So what is Linlithgow doing about it?"

"We are talking. It seems that there is plenty of rice but merchants are hoarding to sell for profit. This is serious because we don't have the manpower to investigate."

"Finding these damn merchants can't be that hard."

"We have already opened a dozen granaries, but with the influx of thousands each day it's just not enough. It will only become worse." Sudipto shook his head feeling the sense of impending doom. "It's the countryside that is going to be the bigger problem. Who is going to visit each village and hound the merchants?

It's an impossible situation, and if something isn't done soon people will die in droves," he prophesized. "Already the morgues are overflowing. As time passes, we may not have facilities necessary to remove the dead from the streets."

Both Mahadevan and Sudipto were lost in thought and sipped their drinks silently. England was fully engaged in the war in Europe. So far they had heard about atrocities in concentration camps in Germany and Poland but chose to ignore it. So why would Churchill even bother about natives dying in a far off land?

"And England really doesn't care. Churchill is morally responsible for this mess," Mahadevan voiced his thoughts, in response to which Sudipto guffawed. "Are you crazy? He's a racist pig who called Gandhi a half-naked fakir. Besides, it's because of the War policy that waterways have been shut down and the supply chain broken. Damn right he's morally responsible. I can name a hundred other things he is responsible for, but the important thing is that we are in the grip of a drought and no one in bloody England gives a damn."

Sudipto was caught in the turmoil of his own thoughts when he thought of an amusing anecdote that was going around in ICS circles. "Did you hear this one? Krishna Menon was in a meeting with Churchill asking for full independence and in the midst of a heated debate apparently Churchill, with his jowls quivering in emotion, yelled passionately, *the sun will never set on the British Empire*. To which Krishna Menon coolly replied, *that's because even God doesn't trust an Englishman in the dark*."

Mahadevan and Sudipto laughed raucously and abruptly stopped when they noticed the others weren't smiling. The conversation was getting a bit heavy and unpleasant for them who didn't care to be bothered by the plight of the masses and certainly, they weren't going to be party to a conversation demeaning Churchill, that too by darkies. So they coldly excused themselves making their point clearly, leaving both Sudipto and Mahadevan thoroughly amused and secretly thrilled.

Sudipto gave their departing behinds a withering look and opened the newspaper. The front page was of course reserved for the war in Europe but on the second page, there were mentions of the mass exodus into Calcutta. And then an obituary on the last page for Colonel Ashton. Somewhere on the seventh or eighth page was a short article which astounded Sudipto. "Oh my gosh, Mahadevan, you have to read this? You were in Assam for a bit, did you know a fellow named Colonel Ashton?"

"I didn't really meet him, but I recall we had a complaint about him. Apparently he got some English girl pregnant and then refused to make an honest woman out of her. Why, what happened?"

"He was brutally murdered. It says here the body was discovered the next morning by the servants. He was covered in blood with his penis sticking out of his mouth."

"Ouch! That kind of triggers something. I think someone mentioned he had a penchant for local tea. Local girls, you know what I mean?"

"The walls were smeared with his blood saying *Jai Kali*. It must have been a crime of passion."

"Do they know who did this?"

"No, it says here that the investigation has reached a dead end. No one knows anything."

"Or they know and won't say anything."

Mahadevan looked down at his watch. "Time to head back. Can I give you a ride?"

"No, I have my own vehicle. By the way, Mahadevan, there are rumors that Linlithgow might go and we may have a new Viceroy."

"Any idea who?"

"No, not yet. Someone said Lord Wavell is a likely candidate. So be ready for some changes. Don't get too comfortable in Delhi."

As Mahadevan drove out onto the street, the car could barely move. About twenty people were banging on the windows asking for money. Men, women with children, scarcely dressed and bone thin. Mahadevan covered his eyes, unable to bear looking at their pitiful plight. He reached into his pocket and threw a handful of loose change into the street. As he turned around, he watched the rabble scrambling for the coins like mad dogs after meat.

CHAPTER TWENTY THREE

MEERA AND VAITHEE
RANGPUR – MARCH 1943

THE HUNGRY CHILD

"**M**eera! Meera! Where are you?" Vaithee had searched both rooms and the courtyard but he couldn't find her. The house was dark and the children stirred hearing him call out, but Meera didn't seem to be in the vicinity of the room.

"Wait here," he instructed Nandu, who was here in Rangpur for his next assignment. Vaithee cautiously proceeded towards the kitchen in the main house. Meera worked as a maid for Dr. Datta, and they lived in the servant's quarters. She mainly cooked for them and ran errands, and that left her enough time to care for her own children. Her son was almost eight years old and attended the free municipal school. Meera took him there in the morning, and in the afternoon Vaithee picked him up, leaving Meera free to work in the kitchen. Her daughter was just six months old, and the Dattas were kind enough to let her stay in the kitchen while Meera worked. They made a swing out of an old sari, which Vaithee suspended in the doorway, and all day long little Pushkin swung back and forth, crying only when she was hungry.

Meera's fortunes had certainly turned when she met Vaithee. He allowed her to escape from her prisonlike existence, a scary, dark place where she was pregnant with no one to help and nothing to eat. Early on in her pregnancy, she tried killing herself, but the Gods had not been ready to receive her yet. After her failed suicide attempt, she was stuck in her murky life with no option other than to surrender to God's will. After Kandu Baba's family left, she tried to get a job with the new Collector, but as soon as he learned she was pregnant, he showed her the door. For a month she wandered around aimlessly, scavenging from garbage heaps and then quite by luck, ran into Vaithee near his office. She recognized him instantly, as he regularly visited the house with papers for the Collector Babu to sign and was very surprised when he knew who she was. He saw her condition and gave her refuge in his quarters. She cooked for him and ate well after a long time and soon the baby in her belly grew strong and big. Their companionship turned to something more, and when Vaithee suggested they marry and give the unborn child a name, Meera's life transformed overnight. Her son Prashant was born a month later, and life was really wonderful. Heaven knows how they made the marriage work with Vaithee speaking only a few words in Bengali. Possibly their body chemistry made up for lack of conversation. Then one day, Vaithee came home and said they were vacating the Government quarters. He had quit his job and was going to become a freedom fighter. None of this made any sense to Meera, who didn't quite understand what all this talk of freedom even meant. Her entire world consisted of three people and her small room. Vaithee said he had met a Doctor Babu, and they were going to move to his house in the city.

All that happened a while ago. Doctor Babu was a secret revolutionary, which is how their paths crossed. Vaithee met the good doctor regularly, as he was also part of the Anushilan group although Doctor Babu was much higher up in the hierarchy, deciding policy and not overtly involving himself in the day to day workings. At night Meera went in to serve dinner and clean up and normally she was done by 8 p.m. They were extremely lucky to have the doctor as their benefactor as, with the drought in full swing, rice was almost nowhere to be found. Sometimes, news would come of one sack being sold in the black market, and then a mob would descend on the seller with a cupful going for the ridiculous price of ten rupees. The rich had their sources and managed to get provisions, even fresh vegetables, but meals were becoming more and more meager. Vaithee worried about the children and considered moving to Calcutta for a while just to ride out the famine, but he had a couple of loose ends to tie up, which is what he was doing tonight with Nandu.

Meera was sitting on the floor of the dark kitchen, her head in her hands. Vaithee approached treading softly. "Meera, *ki holo*? What happened? Why are you sitting here in the dark? Why aren't you in bed?"

Meera looked up at him, wretchedness written all over her face as she reached out her arms to him, sobbing helplessly. The two stood in a close embrace and Vaithee rubbed the back of head, trying to calm her down. "What happened … tell me what happened … *Thik aashe … ami ekhane asi … matha thanda rakho aar bolo ki hoise.* Come on now, calm down and tell me what it is. How can I help you if you don't speak?"

Meera composed herself finally and drank a sip of water. It took a while before she could speak, all the while, staring vacantly into the darkness.

"This evening I had finished cooking. *Memsaab* was ready, but Saab had not yet come out of his study. She filled his plate with rice, fish curry and vegetables and they began eating. The door was open and suddenly a young girl wearing only breeches rushed in through the open door and picked up the plate and ran out. I tell you, *ogo*, she had no flesh on her frame, *ebong tar mukher chamra tar harer saathey chipkiye silo*—even the skin on her face was clinging to the bones. She looked like a walking skeleton. I ran behind her to stop her but she had already reached the street and ten or twelve people appeared from nowhere and tried to pry the plate out of her tiny hands. Eventually the plate flew into the air and the food went flying everywhere and landed in the dirt. Then, like animals, all of them were on the floor licking the dirt for a morsel of rice. I was so stunned I couldn't move. *Por aro kharap hoite silo,* much worse. The young girl found a tiny piece of fish but two dogs started tearing at her. She popped the fish in her mouth and headed for the canal. I can still remember the expression on her face as she chewed the food. She mustn't have eaten in days and the food wasn't sitting well in her stomach because she turned to one side and retched. And then once she did this, she attempted to drink the water that had her vomit. I tell you, Boythee, it was horrible ... horrible! *Tomai kohi Boythee khoob kharap silo ... khoob kharap."* Meera was crying again uncontrollably. "Is this going to happen to us? Tell me ... is this the plight that awaits us? Will our children also starve to death? *Tumi amadergo basao, basao,* save us please...."

Meera was inconsolable. Vaithee held her and became even more resolute to finish his mission successfully. The drought and its frenzied effect were converting men into monsters. There were rumors that British officers were paying merchants to hoard grain and were profiting from sales. For several weeks he had been shadowing a merchant and finally after three weeks he followed him to the *godown,* which for sure housed grain, probably rice and wheat. The only problem lay in the three men guarding it day and night. Besides, the huge padlock and chain could never be broken. He would need to wait until the merchant unlocked the godown before putting his plan into action. He knew the man visited the godown for a weekly check every Monday night after everyone was asleep, so tonight was the night.

Vaithee and his compatriots had meticulously planned the attack all week and were now ready for action. He had left the rest of his team at the merchant's house and planned to go with Nandu directly to the godown where he would meet with Biswa and his team. He only returned home for a quick dinner, but after hearing this story, was in no mood for food, but Nandu would be hungry. "Meera, I'm going to take care of things and bring some food perhaps. Is there any food for Nandu?" Meera filled a plate with rice, dal, and fish. She was about to fill another for Vaithee but he stopped her, "*Naa ami khaiche esho tumi khao aar tarpor ghoomao.* Don't wait up for me." Nandu wolfed the food down in seconds and the two left for the godown.

The godown was in the outskirts of the city, and Vaithee took his bike. If you didn't know what to look for you would never notice the building hidden in the dense foliage. A perfect camouflage. Once they reached the edge of the forest, Vaithee hid his bike and the two walked into the jungle, worried that the sound of feet against crackling leaves would alert the guards. When they reached the godown, Biswa was waiting with two other boys.

"Any sign of him?" Vaithee asked, sitting down on his haunches.

"No, he hasn't arrived yet. There are two men in the front and one behind. I'll wait with these two. Maybe Nandu and you can take care of the one at the back." Biswa was the expert, and Vaithee would follow his lead.

"*Thik aache*, I'll wait for your signal. Remember, no movement until the door is unlocked and one guard has entered the building." Biswa nodded as Vaithee and Nandu got up and slowly made their way around the building.

The sound of the crickets was loud, but the mosquitoes were not having any luck with their weathered skin. Vaithee looked at Nandu. It was such a coincidence that Nandu was Tamil. Vaithee had not spoken his native tongue for years now. He felt good hearing the words effortlessly roll off his tongue and enjoyed the opportunity to speak to Nandu in Tamil. Vaithee had not met Nandu after his mission in Assam but Biswa had given him the details. Such a young boy and able to kill with no emotion. Killing took a toll on your psyche, and Vaithee still shivered thinking of the time he had killed Revathi's husband. He was young and in love with her, and besides, Raman had battered Revathi to death and gone scot free. Vaithee reassured himself, saying he merely provided justice but, still, killing was killing. It did not come naturally to him, and he felt pangs of remorse for years, especially when he remembered severing Raman's genitals and stuffing it in his mouth. Strangely, Nandu had done the same with Ashton.

"How did the mission in Assam go?" Vaithee whispered.

"It went as planned," replied Nandu nonchalantly.

"No one heard you?" Nandu shook his head "But they did see you and can identify you."

"That they can, but they won't. Everyone hated him."

"You were only supposed to slit his throat. Why did you slice off his penis and put it in his mouth?"

Nandu was silent for a while thinking about his response. "Retribution I suppose, for all the men who have buggered me in the past and, besides, I remembered."

"What did you remember?"

"That night in Vizhupuram in the mango grove … you thought you were alone … but I was there. *Naan ellaam paathen,* I saw everything."

Vaithee felt a cold fear grip his stomach. He had checked and was quite certain he had been alone, but even more baffling was Nandu revealing he was from Vizhupuram.

"You are from my hometown? And you saw what I did?"

"Yes. I also took the *aruvaal,* the knife you stuck in the tree and threw it into the river."

A low whistle interrupted their conversation, the signal from Biswa that someone was approaching. They heard low voices and waited silently for the signal to attack. Then, as the merchant spoke with the guard, they heard the sound of steel and of the chain slipping to the ground; both noises deafening in the jungle's silence. The godown was unlocked.

In a few seconds, the sound of the whistle came again. Nandu moved to the left as Vaithee slunk up from the right. Like panthers, they moved silently on the guard, Vaithee holding his hand over his mouth as Nandu slit his throat. They ran up front stepping over the second guard lying on the floor, his eyes opened wide in horror, the blood from his slit throat wetting the forest floor. The two boys were in the process of killing the third guard while the merchant screamed in terror. All around them were bags and bags of grain and vermin! More rats than he had seen in his entire life. Vaithee felt sick to his stomach. First, the sight of all this blood and now thousands of rats. Half the grain must have been eaten by these bloody rats while people starved to death. Vaithee held a knife to the merchant's throat, only permitting Nandu to slit it after the virtually incoherent man revealed the name of the British soldier behind this.

The next morning, villagers descended on the godown, cleaning it up like Amazon piranhas. Those that arrived late ate the rats.

CHAPTER TWENTY FOUR

KANDU AND TUCKY
DELHI – APRIL 1943

GROWN-UP STUFF

"Tucky no ... Stop! I'm not doing this." Kandu ran after Tucky through the house, out the back door and towards the garden.

"*Arre* Kandu, stop being a baby. You raise objections to anything I suggest. Have you any idea what planning it took to steal this from my Dad?"

"You're crazy! He's going to find out. You're really pushing your luck Tucky."

"No he won't. He hasn't so far. Come on, stop being dramatic. My Dad's a busy man, he is not going to count how many are in each tin."

"Each tin? How many does he have?"

"Two in the house and one in the car that I know of."

"Then what planning are you talking about? If he has tins all over the place, it should have been pretty easy to filch a few."

"Easy my ass! My house is crawling with servants who wouldn't think twice about ratting me out to curry favor with Dad."

"That's because you're so rude to them and kick them and stuff." Tucky stopped in his tracks and turned to face Kandu. "Man, if a servant deserves a kick then a kick is what he gets. Stop preaching."

Tucky found his way into a safe spot at the far end of the garden. He slumped under the tree gazing around to ensure they were out of plain sight. The garden was thick enough to prevent anyone peering through the windows from catching a glimpse of what they were up to. His jutting chin was set doggedly. He was determined to go through with it whether Kandu liked it or not. Kandu stood towering above him, hoping his power stance would give him some advantage. Tucky was a strange guy. They had so much in common and never short of things to talk about, however, Tucky had a wild streak which could not be reined in. He liked testing the limits and got a high from not getting caught. But Kandu usually didn't have the same luck. If he did something wrong, he always got caught red-handed. Tucky squinted up at him through his odd, oversized sun goggles, probably also filched from his Dad. "So are you in or not?"

"Do I have to decide right now? Can I think about it?"

"What think? Is this an office? Do I have to send a memo for your approval weeks in advance so you can consider in measured arguments and then veto my decision. *Arre* Kandu, what's to think?" He snapped his fingers repeatedly. "These pleasures are best enjoyed spontaneously. Listen to me, this is S-N-A-Z-Z-Y," he said spelling out the word for effect. "Everyone does it."

"Not thirteen year olds, adults do. This is for grownups," he argued, squatting down next to Tucky.

"Hey, man, we are in our teens, almost grown up. Look at you, big, strapping hulk, you are almost what … 5.8'? You look adult enough. Okay, so I'm a little behind, but really, I feel old enough. Have one … who is going to find out?"

Tucky could be extremely persuasive when he wanted. He should become a lawyer with his penchant for underhand stuff. But Kandu was still worried about getting caught. "What about the smell?" he asked.

Tucky reached into his pocket and took out a bottle of Cologne and some mints. "My dear friend, never enter the battlefield unarmed. I have everything we need," he said, displaying his arsenal.

But Kandu wasn't convinced. He was frightened of his father finding out. Besides, Vani was at home too and didn't stay in the room all the time. What if she decided to take a stroll in the garden? With his luck, that would probably happen. This was hard. A part of him wanted to try it, but another part was asking him to use his head. It felt there were two people in his head—God and the devil. I suppose it wouldn't hurt to try just one, but on the other hand, what if he liked it and it became a habit? But on the other hand (although he didn't have a third hand) he had no way of buying any. But then he could always send Govindhan to do his dirty work, but what if Govindhan told Daddy. I guess he could always bribe Govindhan. This was getting progressively worse, perhaps the most difficult situation he ever had to deal with.

"Tucky, this is only going to lead to trouble. I'm not a great liar, and I've thought about it real hard. I'll have to lie, bribe, hide, and lie some more and I think it's a bad idea."

"Okay," Tucky capitulated. "Suit yourself. But don't eat your heart when you see how snazzy I look."

"What's with this word snazzy?" Kandu asked, a trifle irritated.

"It's *the* word Kandu. Are you deaf? All the kids use it. Snazzy, killer-diller, etc.,etc.,etc."

Okay, so Kandu was going to be the simpleton, but with Tucky, he was always one. He just couldn't match Tucky's cunning and his penchant for outlandish things. Tucky was an only child, and his parents left him to his own devices a lot of the time. Only, Tucky used this time for devious things. He had always been like this, thinking up some prank or another. Kandu was naughty as a child. He still remembered how he scared people with cockroaches and spiders, but as he grew, his energy channeled into reading and writing, playing table tennis and billiards, and somehow, wicked ideas didn't germinate in his head. But he always had Tucky for useless suggestions. Like the time he wanted to put liquid paraffin in the *dal* right before dinner was served or when he hid all the light bulbs in the house. When the family returned from the Club at night, the house was in pitch darkness. Of course Tucky had left by then and Kandu hadn't a clue where he had stashed the light bulbs. Kandu of course was blamed, and when he tried to tell them it was Tucky, no one believed him—a guest would not have the gall to do something so dastardly. Kandu could probably write a book on Tucky's endless misadventures.

Tucky lit his cigarette and drew a deep breath. Then very deliberately he blew smoke rings like a Hollywood star. Kandu stared mesmerized. Tucky smiled triumphantly, his lower jaw jutting out even more prominently. It was a matter of time before Kandu capitulated.

"Tucky!" exclaimed Kandu. "You rascal, you have bloody done this before, haven't you?"

"Aha! Columbus discovered America! I suppose you recognize the expertise, don't you? Of course I've done it, old chap. Many times. At night when they sleep or are out at parties."

"When did you start?" Kandu thought he was Tucky's closest confidant and was miffed that he hadn't shared this part of his life.

"Around three months ago?"

"And when were you going to tell me?"

"I wasn't sure you would approve. Anyway, that's history. I'm here now, aren't I? Come on try it. It's so...."

"Snazzy," said Kandu gloomily.

Cigarette smoke smelled a lot different from the cigars Daddy smoked. That smoke was earthier, this smelled strange like ... how the house smelled after Rani Aunty left. "The smell reminds me of Rani Aunty, she always smokes," Kandu remarked.

"Aha! Rani with the famous Kilimanjaro peaks. How is she anyway?"

"She must be fine. I haven't seen her in a while. I think she meets Mum when I'm at school. They play tennis together."

"And what about little windshield wipers," he enquired, referring to Deb.

"No idea. Haven't seen him in a while either. He's stopped moving his feet like that. Now he twirls his hair. His head is full of bunches of knots. Looks weird."

"He's a weird one," agreed Tucky handing the cigarette to Kandu again. "Come on Kandu try it," he said, tempting him one last time.

After a brief moment of indecision, Kandu took the cigarette from him. He put it to his lips and inhaled deeply. Almost immediately he began coughing.

"That's okay, the cough disappears after some practice. Take another drag," he urged.

Kandu smoked the rest of the cigarette and then stubbed it out with some deliberation, a stupid smile adorning his face. The nicotine was making him feel light headed and woozy but he wasn't about to admit it.

"You did it, man," said Tucky slapping him on the back. "How do you feel?"

"Snazzy!" admitted Kandu, still feeling lightheaded and woozy. Perhaps that's what it meant when they said snazzy. Wow! This was an unfamiliar yet pleasant feeling. He tried standing up, but his legs felt a little wobbly, and he collapsed on the floor again, this time giggling foolishly.

Okay, time for camouflage," instructed Tucky. "Pop a mint and splash the cologne."

"You know it's strange to admit, but I actually like the taste in my mouth. This was fun. Now we just have to figure out how to get back into the house without anyone smelling us."

"Your family members smell you regularly?" questioned Tucky, and the two guffawed.

Fifteen minutes later, and a lot steadier, Kandu and Tucky walked back in, feeling pretty good. Vani and Rukku were in the living room but they didn't even glance up as the duo walked past them and into Kandu's room.

Tucky threw himself onto the bed, and Kandu glanced at himself in front of the mirror. He picked up his hat and placed it on his head at a rakish angle. Then he dangled a pencil in the corner of his mouth in place of a cigarette and pointed an imaginary gun at himself in the mirror. He looked good. Then he pirouetted around striking some more dashing poses, admiring the handsome picture he cut.

"Snazzy," he whispered, "real snazzy!"

CHAPTER TWENTY FIVE

SWAMINATHAN
THANJAVUR – FEBRUARY 1943

A CHANCE MEETING

S wami couldn't believe his dear friend Muhammad Salih was actually here after so many years. They shared countless memories from their younger days in Vizhupuram. At the time, Swami walked the fine line between helping his friends who were revolutionaries and staying true to his job as a public servant serving the British. Now he was retired and could freely proclaim his thirst for Independence. He sat back in his easy chair, a beatific smile spread across his face. "So Salih, tell me what is happening in your life?"

"Nothing much these days. I have nine grandchildren who keep me alert and happy."

"Yes, that is what helps us grow old gracefully. Rajam, bring some coffee and snacks for our guest." When Rajam returned with the coffee, all of Kunju's children came with her to greet their grandfather's old friend. Swami turned to his comrade, eager to talk about his favorite topic. "So Salih, what do you think? Will the British leave?"

"They have to, Swami; it's just a matter of time." He turned to the children, "Did you know your grandfather was a secret revolutionary? He has helped many freedom fighters escape imprisonment."

"Come on, Salih, you exaggerate," murmured Swami, a trifle embarrassed.

"No, really, ask him about Bharathiyar?"

"Who, Subramania Bharathi? Did you know him?" exclaimed Kamalamba, visibly impressed, as Bharatiyar's poetry was famous in Tamil Nadu, and many of his songs set to dance. In fact, she had been choreographing for one of his famous *Kannamma* songs that she was planning as part of the repertoire for Bala's Arangetram. What a coincidence!

"Well not exactly, but I did help him out one time." Swami's mind drifted off into the past as he thought of the great revolutionary who spent his entire life dreaming about freedom. "He died too early, and just as he was doing such great work," Swami said wistfully.

"And in such a terrible way. What are the chances of being trampled to death by an elephant? That too, a temple elephant. Something must have happened to scare the creature; they are normally so docile," Salih lamented.

"Well it's a good thing he did not die in a prison in British custody, if that's any consolation," was Swami's wry response. "Bharathiyar was such a gentle man, such a champion of non-violence; he did not deserve such a violent end." Swami was utterly grateful for that one unforgettable encounter with him.

"Story time!" yelled Venkat, knowing his grandfather was itching to share.

As usual, with sufficient reluctance Swami began, "Let me not bore you with my stories. I remember him well and it's wonderful to have fond memories of such a great man." Swami turned quiet, lost in thought as the many chance meetings with the great scholar flashed vividly across his mind. He had seen Bharathiyar several times as a youth when he was posted in Thirunelveli, especially at rallies, when the great poet addressed the audience with his flamboyant rhetoric, but his most memorable meeting took place on a train from Madras to Pondicherry.

"No no, please, I would love to hear it," pleaded Kamalamba.

Needing no more encouragement Swami began, "I was very young at the time. I remember being called in as part of the additional reinforcements needed during a controversial trial in Madras. The British were trying to build a case against an eminent lawyer named Pillai, an activist against the treachery of British Imperialism, especially amongst the workers of Coral Textile Mills in Thirunelveli district. Charges of sedition were brought against him, and in this famous trial, Bharathiyar was called in to give evidence. Pillai was found guilty, naturally, and charged with two life terms with hard labor. Orders were issued for the arrest of Subramania Bharathi on charges of abetting the crime, and it was believed he was in the process of fleeing British territory in an attempt to avoid arrest.

The police were informed he was aboard a train to Pondicherry, a town south of Madras in French territory. I was on the train along with a group of ten constables headed to Pondicherry with orders to apprehend Bharathiyar before the train exited British territory. After going through the front of the train, two constables and I entered the third class compartment. I was very tense, feeling uneasy about arresting someone as famous and well respected as Bharathiyar. In my career I had to do many things against my will and better judgment, which included arresting several freedom fighters on charges of treason against the British crown, but somehow this case felt different. I knew if I tried to help the fugitive escape, then I would be charge-sheeted, face dishonorable discharge from police duty, and lose all my pension and savings. But at the same time my heart was not in the mission. I felt so strongly about Bharathiyar's innocence that I couldn't help cursing myself for being on the wrong side of the fence. It was a terrible situation."

"Damned if you did and damned if you didn't," said Salih cynically.

"Exactly! I walked through the first compartment scanning everyone's faces, hoping against hope that I would not have to be the arresting officer. As I entered the second compartment, I noticed a man sitting in one corner, hunched over, his face peeping over his knees, with the end of his turban covering the lower half of his face. He was playing cards with the man sitting next to him. For a brief moment our eyes locked and there was the spark of instant recognition in both our eyes, before Bharathiyar lowered his, nonchalantly continuing his card game.

One look at his aristocratic face told me immediately who this was. His deliberately darkened skin, his soiled clothes, his dull turban, all part of his disguise, didn't fool me. There was no mistaking his small straight nose, luminous eyes, and high forehead. This man was definitely Bharathiyar. I felt a moment of rising panic. My mind started racing, thinking of what to do next. Should I apprehend him or take a risk and allow him to escape? I glanced at my constables. Had they noticed him?

Then I made a swift and risky decision. I told the constables that I would take care of this compartment, and they should move onto the next one, which was the last to be searched. The train would reach Pondicherry in half an hour. If I kept the constables occupied, then maybe, just maybe, I could help one fugitive escape and make my contribution by omission to the freedom cause. I walked to the end of the compartment and conferred with my constables, ordering them to report their findings to the other team. As soon as they left, I sat down on the narrow seat opposite Bharathiyar.

"Can I join in?" I requested, referring to the card game. He nodded and indicated I should sit down. After the round was over they dealt me a hand, and for a while no one spoke.

"In ten minutes the train will cross into French territory. Some people get off the train as it slows down, just before reaching the train station," I suggested and he understood my meaning but just continued playing.

A short while later Bharathiyar collected his belonging and stood up.

"Why?" he asked me.

"Why am I letting you go?" I countered.

"Yes. You could have arrested me a long time ago."

"I know. I really don't know why, other than this felt like the right thing to do," I said.

"I will always remember this," he replied as he headed for the exit.

"Likewise," I responded and watched Bharathiyar deftly jump off the train minutes before it reached the station.

"You are so lucky to have met him. What a great man, great poet," Salih remarked, breaking the silence.

"Actually Bala will be dancing to one of his songs. *Chinnan chiru kiliye*," Kamalamba added.

Bala's heart sank. One more dance? At least it wouldn't be as hard as the pure dance items. Padams were always easier because it was more acting than dance, and she preferred the dramatic Natya aspect to pure dance or Nritta.

Kunju starting singing *Chinnan chiru kiliye kannama* ... and Rajam joined in and so did Kamalamba. The children watched, amused, as they went from verse to verse, each one filling in as the other forgot the lyrics.

After the applause at the end, Kamalamba laughed, and exclaimed, "Wait till you see her dance. I hope you will be coming for her Arangetram?"

"Of course," said Swami. "Let us know."

Kamalamba and Bala left their house and headed home.

"Isn't it exciting, the things Swami Mama has seen!" Kamalamba agreed, but her mind was planning ahead. "Tomorrow I'll begin the new Padam. So many things to teach you, so many stories to share with you."

"About my mother?" Bala queried tentatively, knowing she was treading treacherous ground and the conversation could turn either way.

Kamalamba looked at her strangely but didn't respond.

"Will you tell me her story?" Bala pursued, a little bolder now.

"Perhaps ... one day ... when the time is right."

Bala was pleased. She would patiently wait for that elusive *"One day."*

CHAPTER TWENTY SIX

BALAMANI
THANJAVUR – MARCH 1943

MOHAN'S SECRET

Bala basked in the sun drying her long hair. She had danced for almost four hours and was thoroughly exhausted. She sat under the shade of a large *peepul* tree, cross legged on the parapet, practicing her writing on the dirt below. The soft March breeze was blowing through her hair and the sun every now and again peeped through the leaves and danced tantalizing shadows on her face. Mohan could not stop looking at her. She was just so beautiful. Mohan had loved her from the time he could remember. From her childhood he had protected her against all kinds of dangers, like the time she reached to pick flowers and didn't notice the garden snake in the bushes, or when he hid the broken pot in the garbage and wiped up the spilt butter milk so she wouldn't be blamed for it. As a child she was plump and fair but her eyes … oh her eyes had oceans hidden in their depths, as if they held some deep and dark secret. He longed to look into them and uncover the mystery but he never once willfully raised his eyes in her presence lest he offended her.

She was just the most accomplished dancer he had ever seen; her form and energy were extraordinary and her *abhinaya* unlike any other dancer he had seen before. Kamalamba Amma only had to describe the emotion one time and throes of passion would stream from her face. She used every part of her face to reveal the feeling—her eyebrows, her exquisite mouth, and her large eyes, of course, needed little urging to dance or cry. She even moved her nostrils and quivered her lips when she demonstrated a woman in emotional torment, causing his heart to swell and bringing tears to his eyes. But she could never know his real feelings towards her. As her cousin, he really should be feeling only brotherly love for her. But he could not control the emotions that rose within him every time he set eyes on her. Bala was Kamalamba Amma's greatest asset, and in two months would be sold to the highest bidder. Heaven knows which fat, old geezer would pay top rupee for her. The very thought made Mohan shudder. He couldn't bear to think of her in the arms of another even though he didn't feel worthy of her. There was no point building castles in the air; she would not be his, but he could at least admire her from afar.

Bala felt as though she were being watched and she looked in his direction startling him out of his trance. "Mohan? Why are you standing there behind the pillar? Come here and sit under the tree. It's so beautiful."

No, you are beautiful, he thought to himself as he made his way tentatively towards her.

"*Yenna?* Why do you stare at me? Do I have something in my hair? My teeth?"

Mohan lowered his eyes, ashamed at being caught staring. "No, I was just looking, I'm sorry," mortified at being caught in the act.

"You danced very well today. I think your Arangetram is going to be the talk of the town." All the time he shifted from one foot to the other, his toes playing with the dirt, keeping his eyes fixed on the floor.

"I guess," she said, looking down, her shoulders slumped, revealing her dejection.

"Why are you sad? You will be the center of attention. The whole town will be there to admire you. You should be elated."

"I don't know. Many things … I'm worried about who will be my benefactor. The girls say all kinds of things. I wish my mother was alive."

"How would that make any difference?"

"A mother would understand her child. I don't like this life. I don't want to be a dancer and be married to Shiva. I want to marry a real man like other girls and have children," she blurted out, revealing her inner most thoughts to another, perhaps for the first time.

And I want to be that man, Mohan thought and swallowed those words quickly.

"I want to study and become a teacher," she declared.

"Talk softly Bala, someone might hear you. Seriously, just don't say or do anything stupid. It's useless to dream. I dream too, but it's no point. You can't escape your life. Not as long as Karadi is here. Amma is kind to you, but if you raise any dust, she can become a monster, a *Bhadrakaali,* so don't ignite her wrath. I hope you don't say these things to the other girls. They would not hesitate to betray you to score points with Amma. That's how Karadi and Amma keep their control in this house. They pit one against the other. You have to give up these useless dreams. They won't help you at all," Mohan advised, making the longest speech to her in his life.

"And how do I know you won't betray me?"

"I would never. Not in a million years. I too want to study. In the big cities people are becoming doctors and engineers and I would love to do that. I play the flute because that's what my father wants. He was a flautist, so I am. I like it well enough but I too long to run away from this."

"So then let's run away," declared Bala, a sparkle in her eyes.

"Run away and go where? Are you crazy? We have no money and no place to go to. It would take Karadi all of five minutes to track us down, and he would probably break my fingers, so I can never play again, and believe me when I say he would beat you too. He's done it before. Don't think that because you're so pretty they would spare you. They will hit you in such a way that you don't spoil your face or legs. Trust me, I have seen his handiwork; even my father is terrified of him. No, no … we can never think of running away. It would only cause pain."

Bala looked down sadly and continued to write the word *kanavu* repeatedly. Dreams were all she could hope for. And she created all kinds of beautiful scenes in her head, of her living in a big city, riding in a car, but her most precious dream was meeting her mother. Mohan was right. It didn't help to dream of escaping. And meeting her mother … in all probability she was dead. "Did you ever meet my mother?" she asked Mohan, hoping for some tidbit of information.

"I vaguely recall her face, but I remember waking up one morning and she was gone. I also recollect asking where she was, but no one would say anything at the time and I never really asked again. I was too young then."

"Radhai Mama probably knows. Do you think he would tell you if you asked him?"

"No," he replied instantly. "He would never tell me something if Amma forbade it."

"Ask him, you never know," said Bala, hoping to make Mohan an ally to help her reveal the mystery.

"Bala, forget all of this and just focus on your dance." Bala just stuck out her tongue at him. Vasanti was crossing the yard to join them and seeing this, Mohan made a quick exit.

"What? Are you just relaxing?" asked Vasanti, sitting down next to Bala. "What was Mohan saying to you?"

"Nothing much. He said I dance well."

"He's moony over you," she remarked, tapping Bala on the head.

"What do you mean moony?"

"Haven't you noticed how he always stares at you?"

"No, never. He looks sometimes, but everyone looks," she countered.

"He is in love with you, I can tell by the gloss in his eyes," declared Vasanti.

"What gloss?" said Bala, thoroughly confused.

"Bala, you are too young, so naive, you have a lot of growing up to do. And in the next few months a lot is going to change in your life."

"I know, and I'm not sure I'm ready for it. Will I have to meet my benefactor immediately after the Arangetram?"

"That really depends. You haven't got your period yet, but some Mirāzdārs have fantasies of sleeping with virgins and may pay extra for you to bed them immediately," Vasanti replied.

There were three rooms in the back of the house that were used by benefactors. When they came, the girls were sent into the back. Bala never went there, but she had seen the rooms, the beds all decorated with velvet with soft cushions. It was supposed to look all fancy, but she didn't like the garish colors. She asked Vasanti tentatively, "Will I have to use the room at the back?" When Vasanti nodded yes, she asked, "And what will I have to do?"

Vasanti shifted uncomfortably. "That is not my job to tell you, Amma will explain everything when the time is right."

Right, Bala thought … One day … everything will be revealed one day! As Vasanti stood up to leave, she looked up and shot one last question. "Do you love your benefactor?"

"Never make that mistake. Bedding your benefactor is just a task that needs to be done. In any case, most of them are dark, ugly and fat, and it's impossible to fall in love with them. Reserve your love for your land of dreams," she said, a parting remark that made Bala's heart sink.

Within five minutes, two different opinions. Mohan had just told her to forget her dreams and Vasanti now said her happiness lay only in her world of dreams. Bala didn't know what she had to look forward to. Nothing was in her reach. No one told her anything. Why was she killing herself practicing dance if all that lay ahead was a fat, ugly man whom she wasn't supposed to love? Nothing made sense. One day … she thought, one day I will find out where my destiny lies. One day, the elusive one day … but she knew in her heart that it was nearer than others would have her believe.

CHAPTER TWENTY SEVEN

PARTHA
POONA – MARCH 1943

GUILT, GUILT, GUILT

Partha waited apprehensively at the railway station. He should have been excited. After all, Kamu and Rajam were going to join him to live in Poona after almost six months of living apart. He was eager to meet Kamu again; she must have grown, and he looked forward to listening to her nonstop chatter. But Rajam, he dreaded meeting. He felt worse about this because Rajam was faultless, yet he needed to stay away from her for two more weeks. How was he going to manage to keep her at arm's length when they lived alone in the house and shared the same room? Perhaps he could persuade Kamu to sleep in between them for a while. That was a good plan, and his nervousness lifted a little.

He looked at his watch. The train was delayed by half an hour. Maybe he should buy himself a cola. The platform was crowded, and he risked losing his seat if he went to the newspaper stand. Forget it. The cola could wait.

Sitting idly, he couldn't escape thoughts about his recent past. The more he resisted them, the more they persisted. His mind had an agenda of its own, and it seemed topmost on it, was to harass him. He was such an idiot with no self-control! He swore to himself he would never touch another drop of alcohol ever. If he just hadn't imbibed so much that night, he may have had some direction over the evening's nefarious proceedings. Just thinking about it made him cringe.

After many months of searching, Partha had landed a wonderful job at the Munitions Factory in Poona, thanks to a referral from Thambu, who had been working there for a while. The previous week, Thambu had received a better offer from Bombay at the Mazagaon Docks and had left their small quarters, allowing Partha to call for his family. He sent a telegram to Rajam asking for her and Kamu to join him after a month. Rajam had been asking to move to Poona for months now. She was tired of being in Thanjavur and worried about Kamu's schooling. Ideally, he would have preferred to postpone their arrival by longer if not for Sister Rebello, the headmistress at Kamu's new school, who had scheduled an interview in a month's time.

Partha wondered if Rajam got a sense he was pushing her away in Madras when his father died. He could always give an excuse, saying he was grief-stricken, the house was full of people, but knowing Rajam, she must have perceived his anxiety. She always found out everything, such a *Nosey Parker*. How was he going to hide it from her? She was sure to needle it out of him.

Partha thought back on the events of that day not two months ago. He had just been promoted at work and some of his friends were going to Bombay for a bachelors' weekend. When they used that word he should have known what they were planning. But, fool that he was, he went with them anyway. The last few months had been so stress filled, he felt it would be nice to get away and let off some steam, so he decided to join them. The evening began harmlessly, checking into the hotel. The sign outside was lopsided with a few letters missing and read K IS NA LOD E. That should have told him what to expect. It appeared a little sleazy but had three clean beds. They took a bus into the center of town to admire the "Queen's Necklace" on Marine Drive. They had recently installed new lights, and at night the sea-facing promenade sparkled like a diamond necklace; hence the name. Finally, they had lunch at an Irani restaurant called Naaz. After the second beer, Partha found himself merrily biting into a piece of chicken. When he realized what he had just eaten, he was appalled, but not shocked enough to stop eating. It actually tasted great, dripping with spices and curry.

They dozed at a bus stand on Marine Drive until the afternoon sun lost its intense glare and then made their way to see the Gateway of India, a magnificent stone edifice built to welcome Britain's King George V and Queen Mary to India for their state visit in 1911. One of them had a camera, and they took typical tourist photographs with the Gateway as a backdrop. They gaped at the magnificent Taj Mahal hotel, built by the Tatas to rival the city's grand Watson Hotel in the Esplanade, which was reserved for "whites only."

"Now this is where we should have checked in," Partha remarked.

"In your dreams. The daily rent will be a year's salary," one of his companions remarked dryly.

"Are we allowed to go in?" Partha queried.

"Are you in the mood to be insulted?" retorted his companion. Finally, they decided their safest bet was to take pictures in front. They certainly didn't wish to be stopped by the burly, turbaned gatekeepers. The afternoon was harmless enough with them just horsing around, cracking bawdy jokes and just having fun.

The problem started in the evening, when they entered the bar on Hornby Road. Partha never did well with alcohol, and the beer from the afternoon was still playing tricks with his brain, but he didn't want to appear backward, so he took one drink. It would have been perfect if he had just stopped with that but he was easily persuaded and pretty soon, he had downed six or seven. After the fifth he just stopped counting. He had a faint recollection of eating, drinking and talking and then heaven knows how they found their way to Grant Road's red light area. Partha sat outside a dingy room with his friends lolling around awaiting their turn with the woman inside.

Then it was Partha's turn. He recalled protesting but was pushed in and found himself in a dark room which stank of urine and semen. Supine on the bed was an Anglo-Indian girl, or so he thought, because she was fairer than the average Indian. She was smoking a cigarette and slapped the bed next to her indicating he should sit down. The sheets were crumpled and soiled too. The very sight made him want to turn around, but he didn't want his friends to think he was a sissy, so he sat on the edge of the bed barely allowing his behind to make contact with the surface.

"Come on," she said, "let's get it over with," as she lay back against the pillows with her feet spread-eagled.

Partha was nonplussed, not knowing what to do next.

"What are you waiting for? I haven't got all day. My time is money. *Patloon utaaro*. Take your pants off," she urged crudely. Partha hurriedly let his pants and underwear fall to the floor and climbed on top of her. Entering her, almost immediately he felt the grimy moistness of her vagina, but he pushed a couple of times and in two minutes was done. There was no place to wash up so he wiped himself thoroughly with a handkerchief.

The next morning as they returned by train to Poona, his hammering head registered the enormity of his misdeed and the fear of disease crept into his mind like a tiny virus. On his way back from work he bought a bottle of Dettol and immersed his penis in water with half the antiseptic poured in. The burning absolutely killed him, and he hoped all the germs had been burned off. But a week later the symptoms began. The British doctor in the army cantonment told him he had contracted syphilis. A new drug was available imported from the UK, but was very expensive. Partha didn't care. He was willing to spend all his salary if it saved him from the shame that lurked in his uncertain future. In the two weeks the doctor took to procure the drug, the disease had taken a strong footing in his body. What began as a small sore at the tip of his penis now converted to rash on the lower half of his body. As soon as he started taking the miracle drug, the symptoms began abating. Still, he needed to continue taking the pills even after his rash had cleared.

He had learned a very hard lesson. Luckily the doctor was resourceful enough to get this medicine, as it had only recently been introduced in the UK market. The divine had been very kind to him. He took his last dose today, but the doctor's checkup was next week. What a mess! And for one night, not even that, a few moments with a filthy woman. It just wasn't worth it. Partha's mental symptoms far outweighed his physical ones. He hated himself for complicating an otherwise simple life. He shuddered at the fear of possibly contaminating Rajam. Now she would arrive any minute, and he hoped his face didn't betray his frail emotional state.

At long last, he watched the train chug deliberately and loudly into the station. His moment of confrontation was here. Partha took a deep breath and stood up.

From now on he was going to remain sober, that much he knew. And he would never do anything he needed to hide from Rajam. That would keep him on the straight and narrow. A lot more composed after his "*Bhishman*"[3] celibacy vows, he walked towards the second class compartment of the arriving train.

---

3 Bhishma is the patriarch in the great Indian epic Mahabharata. Young Devavratha's father wishes to marry Sathyavati but her father wants assurance that his grandchildren will ascend the Kuru throne. So Devavratha takes a vow of celibacy (Brahmacharya) and is hailed as Bhishma.

CHAPTER TWENTY EIGHT

KANDU
SHIMLA – JUNE 1943

THE BETRAYAL

Deb and Kandu were lounging around in his room in the Chatterjee home, reading comic books. Kandu, although older, enjoyed being with Deb, as there was no pressure to talk. Most often they read comic books or played cards while listening to the radio. Sometimes the reception in Shimla was not good, and they ended up turning the radio off after listening to fifteen minutes of static. Deb was highly intelligent and from time to time made profound pronouncements which amused Kandu. Today's was "Hitler just destroyed the theory that vegetarians don't have the propensity to kill." How Deb discovered that detail was beyond Kandu. For the last three years Kandu had read each and every printed article about the war, but young Deb could probably write a thesis to corroborate his claim. Not that Hitler being vegetarian had any bearing on the day's proceedings.

Deb's grandparents were visiting, and Kandu realized how all grandparents are alike regardless of background. Grandmas soft and nurturing like his Sita Paati and Grandpas stern disciplinarians, like his Nilu Thatha. It was early evening and Kandu lethargically raised himself from the bed, preparing to return home. He stopped in his tracks when he heard loud, angry noises from downstairs. Deb simultaneously stopped twirling his locks and reading and opened his eyes wide, as he strained to hear what was being said, but since neither he nor Kandu could hear clearly they both ran to the top of the stairs and sat down, watching through the railings the drama unfold in the living room. Both Sudipto and his father were yelling at Rani in Bengali, "*Ki ashpardha* ... How dare you, sleazy whore?"

"Have you no shame? *Kono lojja nei? Tennis khelbi?* Want to play?" so saying, the old man threw a tennis ball in her direction, then picked it up and threw it at her again, this time harder, making her squeal and rub her belly.

They could hear Rani protesting, "*Na, na, amake chhere dao* ... leave me alone ... I'm sorry ... I made a mistake ... *Ami bhool korechi* ... Please forgive me." She was on the floor in the middle of the carpet, her hair tousled, sobbing heartrendingly, but the two men's demeanor failed to soften. This was followed by a cacophony with all three talking together trying to get heard. In the middle, Deb's grandmother walked in on them from the kitchen, looking visibly shaken. She picked up the tennis ball and looked admonishingly at her husband, the scene shocking her out of her customary reticence and making her actually speak to her husband. *"Ki korchho? Ki kore tumi oke marchho? Tao ekta tennis ball diye?* Stop it I say! Surely playing tennis is no crime for a woman. *Thamo! Chherre dao oke."*

Then his Grandpa retorted in his booming voice, *"Tennis khelche?* Yes, she was definitely playing tennis, but with the tennis instructor's balls? You stupid woman, Sudipto and I caught her at the train station running away with the tennis teacher! Happy? Your accomplished daughter-in-law has one more accomplishment: Cuckolding! *Shara poribarer badnam korchhe meita.* She is a shame to the family. So just shut your mouth and sit quietly," he screamed, shoving her back onto the sofa and turning his attention to the wretched heap at his feet.

Again there were more abuses. Kandu was thoroughly familiar with them as profanity is the first thing you pick up in a new language. "Whore! Slut! *Nichu jater beshya! Amar iccha korche tomake Benaras pathiye diyi.* Yes, let us just send her off to Benares. You have brought a bad name for the whole family." And then suddenly the old man slapped her hard across the face. Deb screamed and ran downstairs and Kandu frightened out of his wits ran down the stairs, bolted out the front door and made his way home. "Mummmmmyyyy ... Daddyyy ... are you there?" he yelled as he made his way upstairs.

"Coming," answered Dharmu, recognizing panic in his voice. "Your Dad is changing."

"Mummy, they are beating Rani Aunty up. Something is happening. You have to help her."

"What? Oh lord I hope she didn't do something stupid?" But Dharmu knew she must have.

Rani and Dharmu were very close. She knew Rani and Sudipto had a strained relationship. Rani was a natural flirt, and people in Shimla paired her with all kinds of Englishmen; the two would joke about it and feed the local gossip. But last summer, Dharmu suspected she was having an affair with the tennis coach. Rani was always playing tennis and continually missed her bridge mornings and Mahjong, and when they played tennis together, it didn't seem as if her game were improving. Many times when Dharmu sat at the Bay window, she saw the coach leave the house, looking furtively left and right and over his shoulder as if he were avoiding someone. Rani brushed it off each time, saying he was stringing a racket, or she had to write a letter of recommendation. She gave some excuse and then skillfully steered the conversation away. Dharmu would have dismissed the idea as being part of her fertile imagination if the young man hadn't turned up in Delhi as well. During their tennis classes, Dharmu noticed the looks and lingering touches between them and she still attributed it to Rani's enticing nature. It wasn't until she unexpectedly landed up in Rani's house and saw him exit the bedroom that her suspicions were confirmed. Rani was caught, almost in the act, and had to acknowledge it.

Rani declared her love for Tapan and swore she was not ashamed. For the first time in her life she felt appreciated. Sudipto was always so cold with her, and no matter how hard she had tried she could never get close to him. He never treated her like a woman. She was merely his trophy wife to help him get promotions. The afternoon progressed from lunch to tea with Rani releasing years of accumulated stress. She had been hiding and sneaking for so long, it felt good to confess. She felt the relationship developing into something deeper, and she wanted to be with him permanently.

Dharmu knew these types. They were like parasites feeding on rich women, going from one to the next. Poor Rani, blinded by love, couldn't see it. The sex must have been exciting. After all, Tapan was young and muscular and extremely good looking. Keep a rag next to an open fire and it's bound to smolder, and that's what happened with Rani. She was bored and lonely, primed for an affair.

Rani had nothing to do all day with Sudipto keeping long hours at work and Deb away at school. One day last summer Tapan dropped in, and when he touched her, she felt her whole body tingle, just like in the movies. Naturally she responded and then sleeping together seemed the most natural culmination. She felt no guilt then, only the thrill of a clandestine secret, but soon enough, the fear of being caught burned like a fire within her. Over the last two months she had lost a lot of weight and looked wan and preoccupied. She knew Sudipto was a proud man, and if he even suspected she was playing around, there would be hell to pay. But Rani was growing weary of this subterfuge, and last week she confessed to Dharmu that she planned to run away with Tapan. She was tired of all the lies and hiding and sneaking around. It was time to make a clean break.

Dharmu was appalled. This was the stupidest thing she had heard in years. Who gave up the life of marriage to a successful Secretary to British Government for a life of poverty with a tennis instructor? Dharmu told her not to be dim-witted. She had a good life and, besides, if she left, Sudipto would never allow her to see Deb again and that would kill the boy. He was so attached to his mother, he wouldn't last a day without her. Dharmu tried every angle and pleaded with her to break it off. It just wouldn't work. Tapan had no job other than tennis, and Rani had never worked a day in her life. What would they live on? Pretty soon sex wouldn't satisfy the hunger in their bellies, and Rani was quite used to the good things in life. What would she do then? If Tapan didn't think twice about sleeping with her, what if he tired of her and wanted another woman? A leopard never changed its spots. She warned her of all the dire calamities that would befall the family, and finally Rani agreed not to act on her whim. Dharmu thought that was the end of it, but obviously Rani had taken the plunge. She had to go and help her. "Mahadevan!" she yelled, galvanizing into action. Oblivious that she had on different slippers on each foot, she ran down the stairs, yelling over her shoulder. "I'm going. Get your father quickly and join me. You need to take care of Deb. He mustn't witness all these horrible things. It will leave a terrible scar."

The three rushed in to witness a traumatic scene. All these years they had met over elegant banquets and sipped their cocktails while making polite conversation, and now they feared that Sudipto might tell them to stay out of his personal affairs. Who could blame him, really? Sudipto was extremely conscious of status and Rani had been caught doing the unforgivable, which could seriously harm his career.

As they entered, they found Sudipto attempting to hit Rani with his belt, with Deb hanging in the air holding his arm back. In the meantime, Sudipto's father was feebly attempting to kick her supine form. He couldn't do it forcefully, not with his wife holding his leg with all her strength, and then suddenly he lost balance and fell down. Kandu felt like laughing. It was so comical. But he took a moment to control himself. This was serious stuff and he needed to take Deb out of here.

Deb screamed ceaselessly, "*Naa Baaaba koro naa.* Don't strike my mother."

"Stop it Sudipto!" Mahadevan yelled, yanking the belt out of his hand. "Have you lost your senses? How dare you raise your hand on Rani and that too with a belt? She's not your slave, she's your wife. Stop it I say."

Sudipto stopped in his tracks a trifle discomfited; he hated to be caught at such a distressing moment and certainly didn't want anyone, not even Mahadevan, to witness any weakness. "Mahadevan you'd best be on your way. This is my personal problem and I won't tolerate any interference," was his response in his clipped, British accent.

But Mahadevan was not intimidated, even though Sudipto was his superior. "Well I'm sorry, but part of being your friend includes my involvement, so if you have any objection, send it to me in a memo tomorrow morning. Right now, you need to behave in a civilized manner. She's your wife of more than ten years. Show her some decency."

"Wife? She's no wife. Fucking whore!" And his face screwed up as he tried to hit her again, but Dharmu had shielded Rani's body with her own. Kandu dragged Deb out of the melee and ran up the stairs with him, but Deb insisted on sitting on the stairs. He had been crying so hard his spectacles were completely clouded. Kandu cleaned them with his handkerchief and put his arm around his shoulders protectively.

"Why does she want to run away? Why would she leave me? Doesn't she love me?" he whispered, his voice pathetically weak.

Kandu had no words. "It's going to be fine. She's back and now she will remain with you. Of course she loves you. You won't understand grown up stuff. It's too complicated."

"I told you she didn't love my father. I saw them many times. My mom and that damn tennis fellow. I caught them kissing so many times. Everyone thinks I'm a fool, but I see things and I feel bad. Just because I don't talk they think I won't notice what's happening."

"So then why didn't you confront her?"

"I tried a couple of times but she told me she was sharing a secret with him. Big secret! You don't tell secrets mouth to mouth," he sobbed.

Kandu was shattered. He had idolized Rani for so long and now she had proved to be just another promiscuous woman. He didn't believe he could never again trust a woman completely. If Rani Aunty could do this, then any woman could. When the time came, he would watch over his wife very closely.

Everything calmed down in the Chatterjee household. Rani was in bed in the guest room sleeping with her mother-in-law. Sudipto sat quietly and sipped a stiff scotch. The events of the evening were too draining. Only time would heal all wounds, but eventually the pain would subside, leaving only traces of a bad dream.

Kandu returned home and went up to the balcony. It was dark and all was quiet.

Women! He thought as he inhaled deeply on a cigarette. They were so untrustworthy. Thank heavens he didn't like girls. When he married, eventually, he would keep his wife happy. He would make sure she was of strong moral character. And he wouldn't allow *pātu vādiyārs*, tennis coaches or English professors, within a ten-foot distance of her. "I wonder who I'll marry?" he blurted out inhaling deeply on his cigarette.

He moved to the corner from where he could see Rani Aunty's window, but all the lights were off. He tried to get past the rose bushes, but accidently pressed his forefinger on a thorn. A droplet of blood oozed out. He sucked on his finger and looked down at the rose bush. Only one small bud was blossoming. *A red rose* he pondered, *why does it intrigue me so?*

CHAPTER TWENTY NINE

RUKKU
SHIMLA – JUNE 1943

LOVE UNFOLDS

Rukku spotted the mailman at the end of the street and ran down two steps at a time. She had to catch him before he delivered the letters to the house. She couldn't help feeling it was so much easier in school. She never had to worry that someone might catch her. Letters addressed to her were just delivered without question, but here, at home, there were too many people. She had not told a soul that she and Arun had been corresponding regularly for the last six months. When she received the first few letters, they were still in Delhi, but the Ayah was her buddy, and Rukku convinced her to secretly deliver the letters to her. Ayah didn't join them here in Shimla so Govindhan picked up the mail and gave it directly to Kandu, who was home from school. Her only option was to catch the postman before he delivered the mail to their home.

Namaste Singhji, she said greeting him politely. *Mere liye kuch?*

Namaste bitiya, he replied, knowing very well what she was looking for as he went through the mail. *Yeh leejiye Rukminiji, aapki chitthi.*

Rukku grabbed it from him and her heart skipped a beat as she recognized the writing. She tucked it into her blouse and ran back. Then, safely ensconced in her bedroom, she began reading.

Dear Queenie, (His name for her)

Each day feels like a year without seeing you. I wish you would send me another photograph of yourself. This one is a little worn out from over handling, if you know what I mean. I can't wait for us to be married. Tell me you will. You have graduated from school, so it should not be a problem. I hope your stern father approves of me as a son-in-law. Of course I don't have his fancy qualifications, but I am completing my graduation in two years and should be able to get a job and support you. College is really boring when all I want is to hold you in my arms.

Will you be coming to Nagarcoil this year? I could find a way to be there. Perhaps I could persuade Laali to visit around the same time. Let me know of your plans. It will be much easier to pazhagufy, know each other intimately. The gardens in Nagarcoil have many hiding places.

Has your father decided where you will go to college? I hope it's here in Madras, although there isn't much chance I know, but I can still hope.

Nothing more will fit in this stupid inland letter, so unfortunately my love, I have to sign off. I live and breathe for you.

Yours and yours only

Arun (King)

Rukku put down the letter to glance at his photograph and she hugged herself tight. It was such a crazy feeling to be in love. Everything seemed brighter and more beautiful. She couldn't wait to broach the subject with Daddy. Perhaps she would wait a while. With all the drama at Rani's home, everyone was a little upset. No, definitely now was not a good time; it was prudent to wait. After all, Arun hadn't finished college and wasn't ready to support her. She had just completed her Junior Cambridge exams and did want at the very least to complete her Senior Cambridge before she married. Besides, her love life was confined to letter writing. She wanted to meet Arun at least once before she committed completely. But she was in love. She wanted to scream out from rooftops and proclaim her love for him but for now, she just curled up into a ball on her bed, plastering kisses on her pillow.

"Dharmu? Where are you?" She stirred hearing Daddy's voice. That was strange! Daddy home? It was barely lunchtime. His voice sounded agitated and urgent. She carefully hid her letter along with the others, wrapped up in a large handkerchief buried under her underwear.

"Hi Daddy? Home early?" she said, upbeat and happy to see him.

"Yes Rukku," he gasped, collapsing onto the sofa. "I have news for you. Call your brother and mother." Kandu as usual was on the terrace and Dharmu in the kitchen. Once they straggled in Mahadevan began. "It's here," he said, furiously waving a letter. "Transfer orders! I go to Calcutta as Secretary of Civil supplies." Each one of them had different reactions to the news and for a while no one spoke. Kandu was the least affected. It hardly made much of a difference to him where he stayed. As long as Mummy and Daddy were there, the house they lived in was home. Delhi, Calcutta, and Shimla were all just places and he did fine anywhere. Dharmu felt exhausted, thinking of the work it involved closing house and moving. She had done this so many times. Deciding what to keep and what to send was a mental exercise she loathed. But on the other hand, she loved the Calcutta social life. "When do we leave?" she asked, the exhaustion already audible in her voice.

"Immediately. I join next week and you can finish the packing here and in Delhi and then perhaps go and visit your parents in Dindigul and mine in Nagarcoil. The luggage will take at least a month to arrive. Calcutta is a mess, and I'll need some time to organize schooling for Kandu and college for Rukku."

Yippee! Thought Rukku. She would tell Arun to orchestrate a visit coinciding with hers, and finally they would get a chance to pazhagufy. Would they hug? Or kiss? She began visualizing their meeting; and she felt her whole body begin to heat up.

"Another move?" remarked Dharmu dourly. "Sudipto had warned you, but is this what you want?"

"Yes I knew it was imminent, but am I looking forward to it? Well, the situation in Calcutta is pretty tense, and I'm going to have my job cut out for me. Long hours, a new Viceroy—and this time I will report directly to him, what with the famine and all."

"And Sudipto and Rani? Will they be moving too?" Dharmu needed her friend, but right now Rani's need for her was greater, and she wanted to be around to help Rani through this difficult time.

"Yes, he leaves this week. The Calcutta posting is temporary because of the famine. He is not in the best frame of mind, but this is a really crucial job which won't leave him much time to think of domestic problems. I think Rani will be happier there with her family to support her. She won't be able to get back to her usual tricks."

Mahadevan sat on the porch with a glass of lemonade and went through the mail. There was a letter from Rangpur. He opened it and saw it was from Vaithee. What now?

Dear Mahadevan sir,

    Namaskarams from Rangpur.

    I hope you and your family are doing well. I addressed this letter to the Calcutta office and am praying this finds you. If you are reading this, you will know that the situation in Bengal has become intolerable. People are walking around the streets eating mud from the floor. Rivers are now so contaminated with rotting bodies as people do not have the means to cremate the dead. Rice is unavailable and even the river fish is making people sick. So far my family has been doing alright but the gentleman I live with who has been supporting us so far, is moving to Calcutta and as he plans to stay with relatives he cannot take us with him. I can somehow survive the famine, but I am humbly requesting that

you keep Meera and my two children as I worry about their survival.
Meera is a great cook and she can care for your family whom she knows
well. If we stay in Rangpur any longer, we would just be tempting fate
which may not be kind forever.

Please sir, do consider my humble prayer and with your kindness save
my family.

I hope to hear from you soon with good news.
I remain
Your humble servant
Vaithee Chakrabarti

Mahadevan put the letter down. Vaithee had chosen an opportune moment
to write. At least Dharmu was ensured one good servant to start things off. He
would write to Vaithee and tell him to make preparations to send his family to
Calcutta. Dharmu walked in just then holding her head in her hands. "I hate
moving, Mahadevan. Why do you do this to me?" she wailed.

"Come on Dharmu. All you need to do is pack two trunks of clothes you need
for a month. The movers will take care of the rest. By the way, I just received a
letter from Vaithee, you remember the clerk who worked for me in Rangpur? He
wants his wife Meera and her kids to come and live with us. I think that will be
fine; you will have your old maid again. The famine has hit Rangpur hard and
he wants to save his family."

Even this piece of news didn't make Dharmu smile. She didn't want to think
of famine. She had no concept of the depths of degradation the people of Bengal
had sunk to and frankly didn't care. Her worry was moving. "That's fine," she
said dismissing him.

"When do I have to start packing?"

"I have booked your rail tickets to Delhi for Friday. The movers will be here
Wednesday, and my secretary will take care of things and make sure it's all
coordinated."

Rukku sat in the corner of her room hurriedly writing to Arun. She was
happy, really happy. Her mind was already in Nagarcoil and she sang happily to
herself. Life was really exciting.

Kandu returned to the terrace where he smoked another cigarette, wistfully
staring at the Chatterjee Bungalow. He stubbed the cigarette out and threw it
over the side of the house. The rosebud had bloomed fully, and he plucked it
and placed it in his front pocket. The fragrance was overwhelming. Rani Aunty
had let him down but the rose was in full bloom, the fragrance reminding him
of cycles in life. Love blooms and fades like flowers. Calcutta would be exciting!

He was almost fourteen now. It was time to start thinking of girls and catch up on Tucky. *Forget Rani. Beautiful girls are awaiting your arrival, Kandu, so prepare yourself.*

For some reason Kandu felt compelled to save the rose. He placed it in a cup of water on his dresser, and when it started fading he pressed it within the folds of his diary with a comment reading, *Rose?*

CHAPTER THIRTY

MAHADEVAN
CALCUTTA – SEPTEMBER 1943

THE GRAND OAK CRUMBLES

Mahadevan went to his closet and pulled out the gold pocket watch his father had bought for him all those years ago when he was preparing to leave for the UK to sit for his ICS exams. His father Nilakantan had always been that Grand Oak tree under whose shade one felt safe. And now he was gone.

He had received the telegram late last night, and now at two in the morning he still couldn't sleep. Memories of his childhood kept tormenting him. It was so hard to come to terms with death. It was just so final. Even though he knew that one day his father would die, he was somehow completely unprepared for the rush of emotions. Anger that the gods had taken him away so early, regret that he hadn't gone home this summer to meet him one last time, fear that he would die too, and most of all guilt that perhaps he would not be able to perform his father's last funeral rites. All these mixed emotions were rising and falling within him. Normally he was a very composed person, this lack of control troubled him.

Ever since his move to Calcutta, life had been grim. The new Viceroy was a no-nonsense person and expected work to be done even before it was asked for. Long hours of work didn't irk Mahadevan so much. He was used to it and didn't mind doing what needed to be done. Perhaps the most difficult task was getting to the office. Bodies were strewn on the streets like garbage, and the city stank of death and doom. Some said the official count was a million, but in actuality close to three million had perished and more were dying each day. Yet, a steady stream of desperate refugees hoping for salvation continued to flood the city

Food supplies were slowly coming into the city, but most of it was purchased by the wealthy and the privileged, leaving the poor to face their grim fate. Food camps had been set up all over Calcutta, but the gruel they prepared in large vats hardly lasted an hour. It was a desperate situation, and the establishment was moving with less than sufficient interest and speed to avert the unfolding tragedy.

Kandu had started school and attended the prestigious St Xavier's Boys school, and Rukku was in Loreto Convent. They had settled into a routine as had Dharmu. Having Meera around had been a boon, although he was nervous about Vaithee visiting. He was too senior in the bureaucracy to be connected with any terrorist organization. He warned Vaithee of this and told him that Meera would be out on any hint of trouble. Vaithee had promised him that no one would hear of his comings and goings. He always used the back entrance and stayed in the quarters assigned to Meera.

Besides, right now alleviating the plight of famine victims had become Vaithee's top priority. Freedom struggles had taken a backseat. With no food in their bellies, no one had the stomach for patriotism. He had been successful in unlocking five more granaries in the Chittagong area and was amazed at the callousness of the local merchants at this time. The sight of skeletal bodies dotting the countryside would melt the hardest heart. If he could, Vaithee was ready to eliminate each one of them. Society was better off rid of such vermin. Nandu adored Vaithee and took every opportunity to be by his side. Vaithee had to merely mention something and Nandu would jump to action. He was like the God Nandu never knew, and he followed him like a faithful puppy doing his bidding without question.

Mahadevan sat outside in the verandah, his watch in his hand, remembering his father, and the tears would just not stop. He knew that going back to Nagarcoil might take three or four days of traveling, and he wondered if they would be able to wait for him for the funeral rites. As the eldest son he was expected to conduct the kriya on the death of his father and he hoped he would make it. He could not leave without permission. He needed to meet Lord Wavell and get an official release before he left. It was only four in the morning, and he had to somehow go through the next few grueling hours of uncertainty not knowing what the Great Lord would decide. Nothing happened in government offices until noon, and with some luck the Viceroy was in station and not back in the capital.

Kandu was inconsolable. He had just met with his grandfather over the summer and he seemed healthy enough then. Going back to Nagarcoil would never be the same again. Appanshayal was gone and now his beloved Thatha too. Life was just so unfair. Why did the people you love the most suddenly die? The fear of losing his parents gripped him, and he knew that one day he too would have to face that. He hoped it was a long way off and resolved to enjoy being with Daddy and Mummy as much as possible. It took him a while to fall asleep, yet he woke up at the crack of dawn. Daddy was still in his shorts and baniyan drinking tea and reading the morning news in the verandah of their Harrington House home.

"Dad, you're up? It's early. Will you be going to Nagarcoil today," Kandu asked, rubbing the sleep out of his eyes.

"I have to go into the office and get permission first," replied Mahadevan, putting down the newspaper.

"That's just a formality isn't it? I mean you have to go."

"Yes, but one that I need processed before making any plans to leave." For a while they sat staring into the distance. The sun had risen and the trees were changing color. Each one had his own stream of thoughts preoccupying him but their silence was bonded in grief. Both loved, feared, and respected Nilakanta Ayyar. He was a man of such sterling qualities, and Mahadevan respected his father so much that he attempted to embody all of his principles and values, and that's what centered him in an environment fraught with racial tension and other injustices.

"So what happens now?" asked Kandu breaking the deathly silence.

"Nothing. Life goes on. The grand Oak tree has fallen. And we must find shade under another."

"I'll really miss him. I don't ever want to go to Sita Gardens again," Kandu declared.

"Don't say that. What about Sita Paati? You have to go and visit your grandparents as long as they are alive. They live to be with grandchildren."

"What if you can't go for the cremation?" Kandu queried.

"I probably won't make it for the cremation. Even if I did leave today I would only reach in two days and they won't keep the body for that much time. Shankar will have to perform the rites. He lives right there."

"Will they hold it against you?"

"Knowing them, they might. But I know that my heart is there. The family will gossip, but that is something beyond my control." So saying, Mahadevan prepared to leave for the office.

Mahadevan never attended his father's funeral. His brothers held it against him for the rest of his life. Lord Wavell denied his permission for leave. *People are dying like flies on the streets of Calcutta, so what's one more death?* was his explanation.

SECTION-II
1946-1947

CHAPTER THIRTY ONE

BALA AND MOHAN
THANJAVUR – JUNE 1946

AND THEIR LOVE BLOSSOMS

Mohan held Bala tight in his arms, grateful for this brief moment of intimacy. No one could know about this, which is why they met at the far end of the back garden where the thick foliage hid them from plain view. Bala broke from the embrace to look up at him adoringly and whispered, "I still can't believe this. You love me in spite of everything."

"I have loved you from the time you were a tiny baby. How does growing up make a difference?" replied Mohan, gently cradling her face.

"I don't mean growing up. I mean … you know I'm no virgin … that I sleep with Mudaliar Saar," Bala lowered her eyes unable to meet his gaze. This fraction of her life was her shame, her miserable karma, and she could not speak of it with anyone, least of all Mohan.

Mohan closed his eyes tight, not wishing to be reminded of that which pained him the most. He was tormented by the Mirāzdār's monthly conjugal visits, and each time he heard Bala summoned on the Mirāzdār's arrival, he rushed to his room, threw himself onto the bed, and firmly clamped his palms over his ears. Yet the sound of her jingling anklets as she made her way into the back rooms resounded in his ears with thunderous resonance long after the clinking receded into the distance.

Bala's Arangetram took place three years ago. The temple was packed with people waiting to see her perform. An Arangetram from Kamalamba's home was always a prestigious affair as she herself was a renowned dancer. She had not hosted one for a while and the local population eagerly anticipated this next event. They admired young Balamani for her beauty and had gathered to enjoy an evening from one of the best. Bala's pottukattu ceremony was conducted in private, but Mohan heard of the many offers that came for her. Finally, after much bargaining, she was given to Ramanatha Mudaliar, one of the biggest landowners in the area. When Bala saw him for the first time, she started trembling and fainted. He was large—even larger than Karadi—and really overweight. They dragged her sobbing into the back rooms. It was a pitiful sight, one that remained imprinted in Mohan's memory. After the Mirāzdār left, Bala didn't eat for three days in protest. Mohan, naturally concerned, would periodically peep through the curtains in her room and each time saw her lying curled in a crumpled heap on her bed. Her pain affected him deeply, but much worse was his inability to ameliorate her suffering. Ultimately she had to accept the inevitable—she was a Devadasi, a prostitute, and this was her occupation. For over a year Bala's face remained tear-stained, her movements slothful and her complexion ashen. She barely acknowledged anyone and spoke only on occasion. She dreaded her benefactor's monthly visits and reluctantly made her way back, but over time, she got used to it. She had no option.

Those nights, Mohan cried himself to sleep. When he closed his eyes, images of Mudaliar's elephantine form squishing his Bala tormented him, yet his love for her grew. In spite of his overwhelming adoration for her, he managed to hide his feelings from her successfully for almost three years. But he couldn't hide it from his father Radhai, and especially not when he cried each time she slept with Mudaliar. His father was no fool. In the beginning, he ignored it, hoping Mohan would get over his infatuation but, when he saw this behavior persist, he knew he had to talk sense into his son.

One such night he came to Mohan and wiped his tears gently. "Foolish boy. Why do you waste your love on her? She is taken. She is tainted. I will find you a nice girl whom you can marry and live happily with. That will settle your wandering mind. It's immaterial what you desire, and if you want any peace of mind, get your attention away from Bala."

Mohan stared at his father in the darkness. He understood that his concern was genuine. After all, he was almost twenty and should have been married by now, but each time his father asked, Mohan would refuse. Now Radhai knew why.

"No Appa, I will never marry anyone if I can't marry Bala. I will wait forever." His tone was firm and his verdict final, that much his father sensed. Radhai shook his head in sadness. "Son, I have seen this play out so many times. Don't waste your love on one of ours. You are unnecessarily tormenting yourself. This will lead to no good. It can never happen ... you know that right?"

"Yes I do, but still, I can't control what I feel. I have loved her forever," he declared.

"This love is a bad thing. It causes rifts in families and especially in a Devadasi household it has no sanctuary. I have seen it play out badly all my life. *Karmam karmam,* first with my sister and now my son. What must I have done in my past life to witness this repeatedly and remain helpless."

Mohan sat bolt upright. He knew it. His father was very much involved in his aunt Saroja's disappearance. A hundred times Bala had pleaded with him to somehow get the real facts from his father, secure in the hope that her mother wasn't dead. This was his chance to find out more. "What happened with Saroja Athai? Tell me! You have to—for so many years I have been asking you and you always change the topic. I have to know." He shook his father, urging him to respond, but Radhai was unmoved. He would not speak.

"At least tell me if she is alive … please," he pleaded.

Radhai took a deep breath. He had held this secret for so long, it hurt to think about it. With a deep sigh he said at last, "She is alive, she is happy, but that's all I can tell you."

Mohan couldn't contain his excitement. *Saroja Athai alive! This was unbelievable!* He had to share this with Bala. Every time they spoke, she brought up the conversation of her mother. Every waking moment Bala thought about her mother and hoped by some miracle she was alive and would find a way to release her from this life of bondage. This hope enabled her to escape from her harsh reality. She had suffered so much for so long, stuck in a life she loathed, wondering who she was and who her father was, constantly seeking identity. This would definitely make her happy and provide some basis for optimism.

The following day he asked Bala to meet him at the far end of their garden, and when he told her what he knew, Bala spontaneously hugged him. That act was just too much for him to bear and he responded by smothering her with kisses, confessing his love for her. He had held back his river of emotions for so long, and now they flowed uncontained over the broken dam of propriety. Taken aback, Bala pushed him away, looking at him incredulously. *What Vasanti said was true then … Mohan loved her!* Too much was happening at the same time. She finally learned her mother *was* alive and now … Mohan was proclaiming his love for her. It was too much to digest.

Mohan was overcome with remorse and fell at her feet begging for forgiveness, but Bala was silent and trembling. She could not think straight. This new intimacy with him had caused disconcerting physical reactions within her for the first time, and she didn't understand what was happening. So she did what came naturally to her. She fled as fast as she could, leaving Mohan on the floor, confused and repentant. For a few weeks Mohan avoided her, and even if they met in the hallway, he kept his eyes peeled to the floor. Slowly, over the next few months she softened, and when she sought him out again, Mohan felt renewed energy coursing through his body changing his life forever. He knew he couldn't marry her but he had her love.

They met secretly near the temple, by the river or at the far end of the garden, but their intimacy never extended beyond a heartfelt embrace. Mohan would never demean her by demanding sex from her. Already, every shred of decency had been stripped from her, leaving her feeling used and spoiled. He adored her, worshipped her, and he would only bed her after they married in front of the fire. *Agni Sakshi*. Now as he held her, he imagined taking the *Sapthapadi,* sacred vows around the sacred fire with Bala in a red Kānjeevaram sari and him in a white, silk *veshti*—garlands of roses adorning their necks and *malli* and *kanakāmbaram,* bedecking her hair. He was so absorbed in his reverie that Karadi's voice stunned him and he turned incredulously with Bala still in his arms. He watched Karadi advance menacingly and couldn't believe they had been so careless to neglect hearing the sound of someone approaching. Karadi must have been watching and waiting to catch them red-handed. *Bloody rascal! Love pannariyaa? Kamannati ... pinniduven unnai,* he bellowed.

Bala and Mohan sprang apart, shocked that of all people, it was Karadi approaching. They knew it was over. This was the end. Before Mohan could protest, Karadi's fists had found his face and blood spattered all over his sky blue shirt. Karadi was hurling abuses, kicking and slapping him. Mohan tried to get up and say something in his defense and Bala was screaming *Dayavu seidhu niruthungo! Thappu pannitaen ... Mannichudungo.* For God's sake stop, I made a mistake, please forgive me.

But Karadi was unstoppable. This was what he excelled at, bringing miscreants to justice, and for the longest time he had waited for this opportune event, having suspected it for a while. It took barely a couple of minutes for him to haul Mohan, holding him by the scruff of his shirt, into the house before throwing him down at Kamalamba's feet.

Kamalamba tucked a freshly made *beeda* into the corner of her mouth and raised her head in alarm, one eyebrow cocked. "What happened ... what is this? Why are you beating him, *paavam,* he's such a harmless boy."

"Harmless?" Karadi roared. "I knew you should have kicked out Radhai and his son along with Saroja, but I was too young and my father didn't have the guts. They are all cut from the same fabric, born to disgrace this household. This harmless boy was in the garden embracing and kissing Bala. *Indha paavam love paneeturundhaan.* Karadi paused for effect waiting for his words to sink in. His resentment of Radhai was all consuming ever since he lost control of the storage room. It had cut off his access to extra cash. He knew he needed to bide his time and soon enough the right opportunity would surface. For a while now he had been watching them both, eager to get Radhai out of his way, and now his foolish, love-struck son had provided him with the perfect excuse.

Kamalamba's ears were ringing. Memories of a similar scene with Saroja sprang into her mind as though they took place just yesterday. Her wound had never healed and Bala was her revenge. Saroja had stolen the only man she ever loved and had a child by him. That was unforgiveable. Kamalamba had been for several years the most senior asset in the house. Her mother Shanthimati Amma ran things just like she was doing now. Kamalamba was young and beautiful and her dance prowess was legendary in these parts. She was overjoyed to get a benefactor who was from the Kerala Varman royal family, distantly related to the great artist Ravi Varman of Travancore. When she set eyes on him in his impeccable silk veshti with a rich, red shawl casually draped over one shoulder, she instantly fell in love with him. She didn't need to raise her eyes to admire the curly locks cascading to his shoulders in a glossy mane, or his royal, broad forehead and strikingly handsome face. His complexion was milk white, and as she gazed unabashedly at him sitting on the red velvet sofa, like a model in a Ravi Varma painting, she felt dizzy with love. Their coupling was magical and Kamalamba felt life had given her *sanjivani,* the secret nectar to immortality. She would be with him forever. It was rare fortune for a Devadasi to find love, and in her obsession with him she never noticed that he made no declaration of love for her, not even once. Quite by chance, he set eyes on Saroja, seated by the entrance applying *mardhani* to her feet. All Saroja needed to do was glance at him casually and their destinies became inextricably intertwined.

Saroja was the offspring of a *Chitpavan* Brahmin man, and received from his genes fair skin and the most incredible, alluring eyes. They were a deep, charcoal grey, with curly, long lashes, a feature she had passed on to Bala. She merely had to raise her eyes once and look into Raja Varma's for an instant for the fire to be kindled. However, Raja couldn't break his connection with Kamalamba as there would be extremely severe consequences. Karadi's father Selvan was a power house, an equally ferocious man when crossed, and Raja didn't want to get on his wrong side. For a rich man like Raja Varman, finding another love nest was not a problem. Kamalamba was suspicious when Raja kept asking questions about Saroja at every opportunity, and one day she saw Saroja leave the house by herself and followed her to the city. That was a huge mistake because, the memory of that day tormented her every day afterwards. The pain of seeing their passionate embrace tore her into pieces, and she flew into a jealous rage entering the house, breaking up their embrace and attacking Saroja, scratching her flawless face, hurling gutter abuses. She came home distraught and screaming incoherently, and like *Kaikeyi*[4] from the *Ramayana* created an ugly scene and demanded the family get rid of Saroja. She wanted Saroja dead.

The family congregated and attempted to find an amicable resolution to the problem at hand. This was a delicate matter that needed tactful handling. They couldn't afford to lose the patronage of the royal family, yet Kamalamba was her mother's pet, and needed to be comforted. Shanthimati couldn't bear seeing her beloved child in so much pain.

Radhai intervened on Saroja's behalf. He knew the situation was even more complicated. Saroja was pregnant with Raja's child and seeing Kamalamba ranting, he feared for Saroja's life. He racked his brain for a solution that would appease them all. He begged them to spare Saroja's life, imploring them to understand because she was five months pregnant. He begged for mercy, saying he would take care of her and when the baby was born and if it was a girl, she would belong to Kamalamba. Saroja would need to make this sacrifice in lieu of her life being spared and in return they needed to allow her to leave the house alive. Henceforth there would be no more contact with her; Raja Varman would take her to his home and set her up there and everyone would go about their lives.

Kamalamba wanted Saroja's blood and fought and screamed and ranted, but in the end, they all agreed to Radhai's terms. Shanthimati Amma insisted that Saroja stay in town until the child was born so they would not be cheated of their end of the deal. Saroja moved into Raja Varma's home, where Selvan guarded her night and day. He didn't trust anyone else. Radhai was allowed to visit her, but could only speak with her in Selvan's watchful presence.

With tears in her eyes, still weak from childbirth, Saroja kissed her lovely baby for the last time and, as promised, handed her over to Shanthimati. No one ever spoke of her or saw her again. Kamalamba was bitter and miserable for years. She wanted to wring Bala's throat, but the child simply adored her and followed her like a lamb. Gradually Kamalamba's heart melted, her resentment waned, and she realized that this child was blameless. She took Bala under her wing, loving her as if she were her own. It took a lot of effort on her part but she took solace that each time she looked at Bala or talked to her, she knew she had something Saroja would never have, and that somewhat ameliorated her wounded feelings. She had lost and won at the same time.

She would never ever let Bala go, as that would mean returning a trophy. She would rather kill her than return her to her mother. God knows where Saroja was

---

4   Kaikeyi saved her husband Dasaratha in war and he gave her two boons. Before Lord Rama's coronation, on advise of her maid Manthara, she demanded that her son Bharata be crowned King of Ayodhya, and Rama be banished from the kingdom.

or if she was even alive. She suspected that Radhai kept in touch, but he always swore his allegiance to Kamalamba and the household and assured her he had no idea of Saroja's whereabouts. Bala was hers now and forever, and now this pipsqueak of a boy was professing his love for her. How dare she blatantly carry on and that too with her own cousin, right under her nose! Kamalamba stood up and with every ounce of strength slapped Bala so hard she went reeling and would have fallen if Radhai hadn't caught her.

Radhai lay Bala down gingerly, watching her face puff up with the imprint of Kamalamba's fingers standing out angrily against her pale skin. He had warned Mohan that his love for Bala would only lead to pain and now here it was playing out. They would probably break his fingers so he could not play again. Kamalamba looked so angry he didn't know what she would order Muthu to do.

He held Kamalamba's feet and with utter humility pleaded on their behalf. "Kamalamba Amma, I have been faithful to you all these years. I have eaten your salt (*A Tamil saying*) and never once in all these years have I given you any reason to doubt me. I beg you, forgive them, they are young and foolish. I give you my personal guarantee that Mohan and Bala will never meet or talk or even look at one another. Please … please if you value even a scrap of my service to you, give them a chance."

Kamalamba spat red betel juice into her spittoon. She looked at him, one eyebrow raised, her face contorted in a nasty scorn. "Hmm," she murmured, pulling her legs away. "Get up … it doesn't feel right having you begging at my feet. One chance. One chance only. If I hear of Mohan coming even within six feet of Bala, my wrath will fall on you. I will have Muthu break every bone in his body and yours."

Radhai was shattered. He hoped Mohan had learned his lesson. Love made the young reckless. Somewhere in the recesses of his mind he knew he had to find a way to send Mohan away. There was a time bomb ticking with the two under the same roof, and he feared for his son's safety. He had saved Saroja and now he would save Mohan at all costs. He had a sinking feeling this wasn't going to be easy.

CHAPTER THIRTY TWO

RAJAM
MUMBAI – JUNE 1946

THE LETTER FROM HOME

Rajam lifted the tea off the stove when she heard the knock on the door. If it spilt over that would spell doom for the tiny stove, which in turn meant no food until she fixed it. The postman stuck his pen over his ear and peered at her over his eyeglasses. "Chitthi," he said dryly, handing over the letter to her, knowing she didn't understand much more Hindi than that. Rajam had joined Partha two years ago when he lost his job in Poona and had to move to Bombay in search of new employment. Thambu had gotten him a position at the Mazagaon Docks, and after a year of hard work, Partha was promoted to a slightly better paying job. Even so, because Bombay was a more expensive city than Poona, the money was insufficient for them to get their own separate accommodation, so they shared the room with Thambu. The two families took turns staying in Bombay. Rajam and Kamu stayed in Bombay for six months at a time, and when they left for Madras, Thambu's wife would join him. They lived in a *chawl* called Shanthinath Bhavan in King's Circle, Matunga, in one small room. The accommodation was barely sufficient for one family at a time, and though Rajam complained at times about the oppressive, cramped space, Kamu never protested. Rajam and Kamu shared the tiny cot placed on one side of the room, and the men took the floor. One end of the room housed a single kerosene stove, and Rajam hunched over this endlessly each day, cooking one dish at a time, the entire process painfully slow. It seemed she was cooking all day. Rajam was particularly uncomfortable with the bathroom, which was at the end of the corridor, common for all residents on the floor. Mornings were the worst, standing in line awaiting her turn. Pretty soon, Rajam learned to hold it all in till the office rush was over. The chawl was largely occupied by Gujarati families and the women from that community were especially clean. The bathrooms were surprisingly well maintained even though so many people used them each day.

She stepped outside onto the common balcony to get natural light to read her letter. The balconies ran all around the corridor allowing occupants to come outside and socialize. The community here was hard working and very welcoming. The women had even formed a ladies group and met monthly for a cooking demonstration or yoga class. Rajam was not very comfortable with Hindi but could understand more than she dared speak. Luckily, everything came to their doorstep: groceries, milk, vegetables, the morning paper, mail and sometimes even sari vendors would drop by. Rajam briefly glanced at the busy courtyard below. A bunch of boys were playing cricket in the narrow space, carefully avoiding lifting the ball high, so it was on and off drives only. Besides that, groups of women were bargaining with the vegetable vendor, carefully selecting their tomatoes and okra. Rajam would go down to get hers after reading Kunju's letter.

Kunju's letters were wonderful, full of news with lots of details. The best news today was that her brother Mani was to be married to ... *oh no ... Kunju's daughter!* Rajam put the letter down completely aghast. Of all the women in the world he had to pick his own niece. She was certain Appa must have given him quite a mouthful about that. Mani just couldn't get his act together. As a son, he turned out to be the biggest disappointment, not willing to study and not able to hold onto any job for more than a month. Shaking her disillusioned head, she continued reading.

Appa was terribly saddened when Mani sheepishly told him Jayam and he wished to be married. Right under our noses they had been romancing, and we were so caught up in our money issues, we never even realized what was happening. Appa slapped him on the head yelling, Mandu, madayaan, porki payyan, verai ponnu theda mudiyaliya? But as usual, Mani started crying and fell at his feet. Stupid fellow. Appa is too tired now to do much; he had no strength to hold out and finally agreed to the match. We have fixed the marriage for next month and are not really planning to call anyone, just the family and maybe Kamalamba and Bala. Please make sure you and Kamu arrive well in time to help me. Which brings me to the most difficult part of this letter. I know Partha just started working in this new company and I hope you will find it in your heart to help us out. We do need some money to conduct the wedding, at least to buy Mani a veshti and Jayam a sari and thali. I was hoping I could ask you to give five hundred rupees. Rajam's heart sank.

Lord, expenses again? How was Partha going to afford that? She would probably have to sell another piece of jewelry to get even half that money. Over the years she had sold most of her silver and a lot of her jewelry to make ends meet. *I suppose that's what dowries were for, to give a woman access to some extra cash,* she thought. Rajam had for the longest time held onto a beautiful gold and ruby *odiyānam,* her waist belt, a family heirloom which had been passed onto her from her grandmother's time and she intended to gift Kamu when the time came for her marriage. This was Kamu's only valuable piece of jewelry; everything else other than the chain and earrings she wore were long gone. Thank heavens Kamu was still young and they had time to prepare for her marriage. The good lord would provide them with some means to give her a decent dowry when it was time for Kamu to marry. I suppose the time had come to say goodbye to the odiyānam as well. That would fetch a lot of money and then Partha would only have to pay for their ticket home. Her jewelry and silver were in Thanjavur, which meant asking Kunju to open the locked trunk, take the odiyānam and get the best price for it.

Life was so hard, and Partha customarily flew into a rage every time Rajam brought up the topic of money. Last year he had to pay his share at his younger brother Kannan's wedding. As soon as Nagamma saw her youngest son was working, she quickly secured a match with Sushila's recommendation. They made a quick trip for the marriage to Sachi's village. The wedding was held in the agrahāram and attended by the entire village. Partha didn't enjoy himself too much, his mind was beset with financial worries. Their relationship had become fraught with tension. With little or no private space, it became impossible to discuss real issues, and conversations between them remained mundane. Rajam was concerned about Kamu's education. Right now she was enrolled in the sixth grade in SIES—the South Indian Education Society, but when she left for Thanjavur, school would get disrupted again. She wanted to discuss the option of them remaining in Thanjavur with her father or better still in Madras with Sushila so Kamu's education would not be disrupted. In the meantime, Partha could focus on his job and perhaps get a promotion and make enough money to get them their own place. Their marital life was non-existent. In Poona, Rajam sensed a certain indifference in Partha's attitude towards her and told him she was certain he had found someone else. He swore that wasn't the case and that it was the job that occupied him for long hours and left him stressed. He earned enough for them to eat well, but when the factory closed down, once again they had a crisis. Family was always there, a rooted support system and thankfully within a month, Thambu was able to find the job for Partha with Mazagaon Docks in Bombay. Rajam was lonely here. She missed her family and longed to go back south again.

She put the letter away and painstakingly cooked the evening meal. It was a blessing she didn't need to cook twice a day. She prepared an elaborate evening meal and packed the leftovers for the two men and Kamu for lunch.

"Mmm," said Kamu throwing her satchel on the floor, "mullangi sāmbār and vendekai curry. Can I eat now?"

Rajam prepared a plate for her and watched her eat huge mouthfuls, enjoying every bite. "Kamu," she spoke at last, adding a spoonful of yoghurt to the rice, "Mani Mama is to be married. We are going back. Can you believe this?"

"To Thanjavur?" gurgled Kamu, her mouth too full to speak clearly. Rajam nodded.

"And I can dance with Bala Akka?"

"You can dance all you want. I'm going to ask Appa if he wouldn't mind if we stayed there." Kamu ran out to wash her hands and then didn't return. She must have gone downstairs to play. Rajam lay down exhausted after a long session of cooking and cleaning. She closed her eyes and dreamed of being back home with her father and sister. Life was simple in Thanjavur, the meals meager yet filling. In the right company even watered down thayirshādam tasted like sweet *pāyasam.*

CHAPTER THIRTY THREE

RADHAI

2 WEEKS LATER

KRAUNCHA PAKSHIS: LOVE BIRDS

For the first time in Radhai's entire life the home that constituted his sanctuary felt alien to him. For as long as he could remember, he had been an integral part of this household serving Kamalamba's mother Shanthimati Amma. He maintained such a strong bond with the matriarch that even when his only sister was sent away, he felt compelled to stay and demonstrate his loyalty. When Kamalamba took over the household, he stood by her side offering advice and helping her whenever solicited. Reticence was his basic nature, and he was quite happy to just play the *thavil* and execute Kamalamba's bidding, speaking only when spoken to. But overnight, he had become a pariah in his own home. Kamalamba barely spoke to him, except to disdainfully spit out some instructions. Every time he turned around, one of Muthu's men seemed to be hanging around. Radhai got a distinct sense he was being watched. He knew Muthu resented him, but now he was quite certain he hated him. By taking over the stores, Radhai cut off Muthu's connection to the black market, and naturally Muthu couldn't forgive him for that. But Radhai didn't pay much attention to him. His conscience was clear. He only took on the task on Kamalamba's instructions and for the last few years, the store and accounts were in order. As he handed over the keys, the delight on Muthu's face was nauseating. Poor Kamalamba, she was siding with the devil, taking Radhai's honesty for granted and not realizing that Muthu would milk her dry. He belonged to the new generation that did not value traditional ideals of loyalty and respect. He was nothing more than a cold hearted *adiyaal*, good for beating people up and coercing them to do his bidding. Power was his morphine and he needed to get high on it each day.

He probably knew that the Devadasi's days were numbered. People were talking about a lady doctor in Madras who was forcefully trying to move a bill through parliament to outlaw the Devadasi system. The British for a while had regarded Devadasis as common prostitutes, *Nautch girls* they called them, and didn't understand the value of art, dance, and music that this community embodied. Devadasis didn't sell their bodies to random men. They were married to Shiva and had only one or perhaps two benefactors in their lifetime; only this bond could not be legalized by marriage. They were responsible for ensuring that ancient dance forms and music would continue to flourish. In the old days with the patronage of kings, their status was very high, especially if they were royal courtesans or *Rajadasis*. But with the advent of the British, royal kingdoms were disbanded and they were forced to take on patrons from lower castes to live and feed their families. For some years now Radhai had been advising Kamalamba to give up these old ways and, instead, establish a School of Dance.

Things were certainly changing, and people from other communities were now getting more interested in the arts. The household was filled with musicians and dancers, and had she started the school three or four years ago, she would have a new, reliable and legal source of income by now. He could sense the girls were tiring of this profession. They wanted to be educated and marry and felt Kamalamba was holding them back. Bala for certain hated being here and longed to escape. Once the law was in force, nothing would stop the girls from leaving and Kamalamba would have to face an uncertain future with specter of poverty in old age a looming possibility. But Muthu had persuaded her that as long as there were rich, bored Mirāzdārs, there would be patrons and he would be there forcing them to pay. Radhai's arguments, his gentle voice, held no authority against the much more forceful and vociferous Muthu. Kamalamba had no idea how to gauge the future and with no vision, took the wrong advice.

Radhai believed the time had come for him to move on. He went to his room and opened the cabin trunk from under his bed. There, wrapped in silk, were Saroja's letters. He had not communicated with her for five years now and the last address was from Madras. What if she had moved? He sat near the window where there was more light and began writing. If she received the letter and he got a response, then he could plan to leave. From his window the gate was in plain view. He glanced up as he finished writing and was surprised to see Mohan running out. Where was he going? Did he not realize he was being watched? Radhai licked the envelope and got up to leave when he saw Bala slipping out through the gate as well. Oh Lord! Were they crazy? If Muthu caught them together again it would end in calamity. He would not think twice about killing them and no one would ever find out. He ran out the door, and as he left the house, he could see Bala ahead of him walking rapidly. He watched her turn right at the end of the narrow lane. Radhai wasn't in the pink of health, and his knees always hurt, especially while walking, but he was terrified in case they planned to run away. Unassisted, they wouldn't get far and God forbid one of Muthu's henchman saw them. *Children, I tell you, were plain crazy!* He glanced over his shoulder as he reached the end of the lane. Good ... no one else had left the house. As he turned onto the main street, he could see Bala's green pāvādai as she quickly navigated the crowd. He saw her cross the street and increased his pace. She seemed to be going in the direction of the Kamakshi temple. As he took the corner, he thought he spotted her entering the temple. That was even better. She was in the temple and none of Muthu's goons would hang around there. These two, Bala and Mohan, they might be young but were certainly smart. They had picked a place they knew would be safe from prying eyes. But this was no time to push their luck. Barely a week had passed since the showdown and the atmosphere in the house was still tense and the mood suspicious. Any slip could have disastrous results.

Radhai entered the temple complex, his eyes searching for Bala's green pāvādai, but he couldn't see her anywhere. He entered the main *sannidhi* and looked around, but there was no sign. Where could they have gone? Perhaps they had not planned a rendezvous and were each going somewhere else. No ... that was not possible. It was too much of a coincidence that they both left within five minutes of each other. They had to be around here. But where? He walked around the outer courtyard twice, his eyes searching for either one of them but he couldn't spot them. Then he saw the rear *gopuram* and headed there. Crossing into the back he saw a copse of trees and could discern the glisten of water through the leaves. Very slowly he made his way there.

In plain view, seated on the mud floor, the two were holding hands and talking. Bala's meandering tears made the swollen contours of her face glisten and dance. Radhai's heart went out to them. Two *krauncha pakshis,* in love, but not permitted to stay together.

In a voice soft and full of compassion he whispered to them, "Dear, dear children, what madness has caught you? *Paythyamaa puduchurku?* Why do you not realize that meddling eyes are everywhere? You absolutely cannot meet like this. If an old man like me can follow you and find you, how long do you think it would be before Muthu's goons get you?"

Both children stood at attention, appalled at being caught the very first time they arranged to meet, so sure they had escaped without anyone seeing them. Mohan heaved a sigh of relief when he realized it was only his father. "Appa we had to talk. In the house it's impossible. We can't get within ten feet of one another. We have to make some plans for the future."

"What plans? Do you really think you can run away without help? It would take the police two days to hound you down and haul you back. Come on now, before anyone sees you, let's go to the temple and at least put some kumkumam on your foreheads as proof. That way I can say I took you both to the temple for *prayashchitham*." Heaven knows why one needs to repent love, but this was the situation. His son was obsessed with a girl he could never marry, and he had to save him from the dire consequences that would follow if he was found out. In spite of his warnings, he feared they would somehow try to meet. It was just a matter of time before Mohan was caught, and Radhai had to make some concrete plans very quickly to get his son away from here. Distance would give Mohan some perspective and he might leave Bala alone.

When Radhai and his young charges returned home, they were surprised to see Kamu, Kunju and Rajam in the living room with Kamalamba. On seeing Bala, Kamu hurled herself into Bala's arms.

"*Yenna aachu* Bala," exclaimed Rajam, shocked at seeing her contorted face. The swelling on Bala's face had closed one of her eyes, and it was pretty clear that someone had hit her, but she couldn't admit to that openly.

"*Onnum illai*, it was nothing, the silly girl ran into the door that's all; she'll be fine in a few days," said Kamalamba forcing a laugh.

"Really?" asked Kunju in disbelief. "That's strange." The imprint of Kamalamba's fingers were still clearly visible on Bala's cheek, and Kunju knew there was much more behind the excuse, but knew better than to probe.

Kamu reached out and touched her face tenderly. In the last year she had grown and almost reached Bala's shoulders. "My, how you've grown Kamu, you're not a baby anymore."

"No!" retorted Kamu, miffed at being called a baby. "I was never a baby. I'm in the sixth standard now. And you know what, Bala, I don't have to return to Bombay anymore. I can stay here as long as I like." Bala and Kamu sat on the floor chattering away, and Radhai grabbed Mohan and took him inside.

Suddenly he had an idea. He would ask the Inspector for help. Both Kunju and Kamu adored Bala, and if he explained the situation to them, perhaps the Inspector could help him locate Saroja.

He put his hand into his front pocket and noticed he had forgotten to mail the letter. Fool that he was! With all this excitement, he was so focused on getting the kids home safe, he had forgotten to post the letter to Saroja. He headed back out and saw that the Swaminathans were leaving. Should he approach them now? He walked swiftly catching up with them. "Namaskaram, Kunju Mami, Rajam Mami. I am Radhai," he introduced himself.

"Namaskaram," they greeted almost in unison. "We have seen you around but were never formally introduced," remarked Kunju.

"I play the *thavil* for the group, and my son Mohan plays the flute. You may have seen us at the Arangetram. What brings you to our home?" he enquired politely.

"Nothing much. Our brother is getting married in a fortnight, and I invited Kamalamba Amma and Bala to attend. We would invite you except really it's going to be a small wedding and we are not calling too many people," Kunju said, the embarrassment audible in her voice.

"No, no, how could you? You only just met me. I wouldn't expect an invitation to your family wedding," replied Radhai, putting the two sisters at ease. "I needed some help from Inspector Saar. Do you suppose it would be all right for me to drop in now?" he enquired.

"Appa is always eager for company. I'm certain he would have no complaints. Radhai Mama, I shouldn't be asking this and I know it's really not my business but my love for Bala is forcing me to inquire. Is she okay? Is there any problem? It's quite clear she was beaten." Radhai yearned to unburden his heart and tell them everything, but he had just met them and he wasn't sure how strong their ties to Kamalamba were. Besides, their story wasn't a topic for casual conversation while walking the streets. He knew Kunju and Kamalamba met regularly and that every other month provisions were sent to the Inspector's home. He didn't want anything to get back, as it would only cause more problems. His life was already too complicated.

"What can I say? Bala was disobedient, and in anger Kamalamba slapped her. I'm really not at liberty to tell you more. Perhaps some day she will tell you herself." He left it at that, allowing curiosity to play out. Perhaps they would question Bala and she could reveal what she wanted to. He certainly did not want to be the source of gossip.

"Amma slapped her?" said Kamu, shocked at hearing this. In her entire life no one had ever hit her. In fact, she had never witnessed anyone hit another person.

"Shh Kamu, don't butt into adult conversation. You must not repeat this to anyone, do you hear me?" admonished Rajam.

But Kamu was not finished. "It's not nice to hit someone. I like Kamalamba Amma, and Bala is the nicest person in the world. Why would anyone hit her?"

"Well, Kamu, you are a child and haven't seen much of life, but you should remember that in life bad things happen to good people. May Narayana bless you so no one says or does anything bad to you ever." Radhai blessed Kamu, touching her lightly on the top of her head.

"If bad things happen only to good people, then perhaps I should be bad," she declared, only to add, "just joking ... just joking," when both Kunju and Rajam glowered at her. They reached the house and found their father fast asleep on his easy chair in the thinnai. Rajam gently shook him, and he was instantly wide awake and alert declaring, "I wasn't sleeping. Just closed my eyes that's all." Looking at Radhai, he beamed. "Good evening ... who is this?"

Radhai introduced himself and sat down. It was time to ask for help, and, after the others left, the words just poured out of his mouth in one streaming monologue.

CHAPTER THIRTY FOUR

RUKKU
CALCUTTA – MAY 1946

LOVE AND LONGING

Rukku sat by the window waiting for her husband to come home. *Husband!* Even as she thought of the word, her body heated up in excitement. She had achieved what she always believed she would. From the time she was a child, she had promised herself she would never marry in the conventional Indian way. A free thinking soul, she could never envision herself as an obedient, Indian wife, and settling for someone her parents recommended was out of the question, especially after Vani's experience of a loveless marriage. Once she found love with Arun, there was no option of looking anywhere else. It didn't matter that he was not what her parents wanted for her. They had no idea who she was and what was good for her. She knew she could look forward to a thrilling life with him. Witty and full of life, she knew that marriage to Arun ensured excitement and fun each day, and that was worth a lot more than simply settling for financial security.

Daddy was not very happy. He used every argument in the book; *We are distantly related, he hasn't studied enough, he looks arrogant, he's far too dark, I think it won't work.* But Rukku stayed firm. She finished her Senior Cambridge exams, and when Arun moved to Calcutta with a job as a salesman in a company called Brookfield, she boldly went to her parents and told them she had found the person she wished to marry.

That wedding had taken place a week ago, and now, here she was in the tiny apartment she shared with Arun. The accommodation was not terribly extravagant, but it was centrally located off Rash Behari Avenue, with easy access to shops and theatres. It had a small bedroom and bath, a living space that doubled as a dining area, and an ample kitchen. Mahadevan offered diamonds, silver, and a lavish wedding, but Arun had other plans. He was starting out and had absolutely no money, so instead he bargained for a motorcycle, apartment rental for a year, and some cash. Rukku was initially a little peeved at being denied a luxurious wedding, but she concurred with Arun's much more sensible decision. After much banter and argument, they decided to have a simple civil ceremony at home. The mood in the house in the days leading up to the wedding was tense. Mahadevan, unaccustomed to continual confrontation, was ruffled when Arun challenged everything he said. Mahadevan wanted to celebrate Rukku's wedding as he had done Vani's, but instead, he found himself negotiating a business deal. It just felt disgusting and common and alienated him even more from his son-in-law to be. For her part, Dharmu didn't care either way. On the brighter side, she was spared the agony of arranging a wedding, and they could use the money for Kandu's marriage whenever that came up. Perhaps they would host a small party in the couple's honor but after the way Arun had spoken to him, Mahadevan wasn't in the mood for a celebration.

The registrar came to their home and Mahadevan invited his close friends from Rangpur—Nabagopal Das and his wife—to act as witnesses. Vani arrived the night before, and the whole ceremony assumed a flavor of solemnity rather than celebration. Rukku looked beautiful as usual, with high color in her cheeks, and one could gauge from the coy looks she darted at Arun that she was very much in love. In the evening, Mahadevan arranged a small, intimate dinner for the immediate family and a few colleagues. Rukku floated in such a tizzy she could scarcely recall whom she met that evening and what they said.

One image, however, kept returning to her. Rukku recalled looking up during the ceremony and noticing Vani, whose gaze moved continually from bride to groom. She couldn't quite tell what Vani was thinking, but she caught the distinct flash of envy and longing in her expression. It hurt momentarily to think that Vani wasn't happy for her, but how could Rukku blame her? Her life was miserable. Her husband was distant and cold, and what every young girl longs for in marriage is to be with the ultimate handsome partner, the perfect mate, the best friend and most innovative lover. Vani didn't get any of that. Almost a decade had passed since her marriage, and she had miscarried thrice. A child would have helped to refocus her energy. With nothing else to occupy her time, all she thought about was her sad and miserable life, her disenchanted relationship with her spouse and her interfering in-laws. Her dark mood seemed to attract even more unpleasant situations making her even more disgruntled. Life certainly had dealt her a rough deal. Rukku sighed, feeling her sister's cycle of discontent.

She glanced down at her watch. They were to meet Kandu and Vani at the club, and after a round of drinks, go to the Mocambo on Park Street for dinner. When Arun and Rukku entered the club, as usual it was bustling with activity, mainly with Britishers and a few Indians. They were privileged to belong to this club, as most clubs in Calcutta weren't open to Indians. Kandu had arrived earlier, and after playing badminton had showered, and now looked dapper in his white, full sleeved shirt and pleated trousers, cigarette in one hand and a fresh lime soda in the other.

Vani looked quite beautiful in a pale green, Mysore crepe sari with a contrasting puff sleeved blouse. She had maintained her slim frame, and when she smiled her face lit up. All three siblings had inherited Mahadevan's heavy lidded eyes, and seated in the same room, it was easy to conclude they were related. Rukku took a moment to admire her brother. She really loved him and they shared a special bond. If only Mummy and Daddy hadn't favored him as a child, even Vani would have had warmer feelings towards him. He had just started college and his recent passion was weight lifting. That, combined with badminton and table tennis, had leached all of his puppy fat. At seventeen, he looked confident and oh so very handsome. All her friends had their eye on him and always wished they were younger. But Kandu was strange. In spite of English girls at the club eyeing him, he never gave them the time of day. He simply was uninterested in them. He was so stylish, Rukku wondered whom he would end up marrying. A traditional match didn't seem to fit in with his lifestyle, yet he shunned society types. Perhaps he was not ready for girls yet.

"Hello everyone, are Daddy and Mummy joining us today?" Rukku enquired, a lilt of joy in her voice.

"No," replied Vani taking a sip of her gimlet. "I think they are quite happy to see us leave the house. Both of them had settled down with their usual scotch when we left."

"That is going to take a little getting used to—a mother-in-law who enjoys her scotch and a father-in-law who encourages it," remarked Arun wryly, one eyebrow cocked.

Kandu winced at the comment. His parents' drinking was irksome, but an outsider making a remark was unacceptable. Arun was still the outsider, and he needed to watch his tongue. Arun somehow rubbed Kandu the wrong way with his random comments. He thought he was being funny but said whatever popped into his head, and this tendency got progressively worse when he had a few drinks inside him. Arun liked his drinks as well and never stopped at one or two, which made his remarks about Mummy's drinking even more hypocritical. Rukku had better watch out and monitor his liquid intake. He knew Arun's parents were extremely traditional and would faint with grief at seeing him drink. On his starting salary at Brookfield, he probably couldn't afford to drink, so maybe he was taking advantage of all the free booze at his in-laws. A retort was on the tip of Kandu's tongue, but he bit it back and let it pass. Rukku had only been married a week and he didn't want to begin something which could quite easily turn nasty.

Driving from the club to Park Street, they stopped at the traffic light. As usual, there were *morchas,* large groups of people protesting something. One group yelled, *something-something cholbe,* and the other, *something-something cholbe naa.* But all that Kandu heard was, *Cholbe ... cholbe na, cholbe, cholbe naa.* Calcutta seemed to have continuous protests. Bengalis loved *hartals* and morchas, and were quick to congregate for any cause. The independence movement was in full swing, and it seemed just a matter of time before its momentum carried India to freedom from the British.

At dinner, Kandu watched everyone cut little pieces of fish and chicken and slide it into their mouths. He and Arun were both in western attire and a jazz band played Glenn Miller's *Moonlight Serenade.* He smiled, marveling at the irony ... *colonial slavery; we might throw the Brits out of India but will we be able to throw them out of our heads?*

CHAPTER THIRTY FIVE

MAHADEVAN
CALCUTTA – JULY 1946

INSULTS AND RESIGNATIONS

As Mahadevan punched holes in the letter to file away, he read it once again.

My dear Sir,

In view of the happenings yesterday morning in the presence of Parliamentary Secretary, Mr. Ethel and others, I feel I cannot consistently with my self-respect continue to work in this Department any longer. I am, therefore constrained to take steps separately to ask Government to release me from my present appointment as soon as Stevens returns or in the last resort to move the Secretary of State for India for permission to retire from the service under the Premature Retirement Rules.

I might add that, although this is the first occasion during my long service of 22 years under the Crown on which I have had to make a complaint of this nature, I am also voicing the feelings of other senior officers of this Department in registering this protest against the treatment received by us.

Yours sincerely

N. M. Ayyar

To: Hon'ble Mr. H. S. Suhrawardy,

Minister Civil Supplies,

Government of Bengal.

He attached the handwritten apology note from Suhrawardy that the minister had written back to him the very same day, in fact almost immediately. He recalled how in the meeting that followed, Suhrawardy apologized profusely and persuaded Mahadevan to stay on. But Mahadevan had made sure that Suhrawardy understood how unnecessarily insensitive his comments were. He recalled that unpleasant time in his life as he read Suhrawardy's letter of apology to him once again.

My dear Ayyar,

I am thunderstruck to receive your letter. I am frankly not conscious even of the least desire of hurting you or having done anything to give you offence or annoyance. I have, as everybody knows, the highest regard and respect for you, and I have quite forcefully expressed that opinion before successive Governors and Acting Governors. As I had no wish to offend you, I really do not know to what you have taken exception. But I must have done something very bad indeed to have upset you, who are generally so equable and unruffled. For whatever I have done, I express my sincerest regrets. And I hope you will accept them and consider the matter closed.

At the same time, as I do not want to fall into that error again, I shall feel much more at ease, if you could tell me what it is all about. I shall be grateful if you could talk this matter over with me. I am always ready to be corrected and to correct myself—otherwise I shall lose all those whom I hoped to make my friends for all time.

Yours Sincerely

H.Suhrawardy

Mahadevan put the file away and made his way to the verandah of their new Elgin Road home to read the morning paper and enjoy his cup of coffee. Hussain was like all others whose prejudice was so deep seated, clouding the ability to realize they said things to offend other communities. He was extremely ambitious and, while a senior member of the Muslim league, was building his own following to become head of state in the new East Pakistan. An erudite man, he could speak very well and already the Muslims of Midnapore and Noakhali were rallying behind him. He reviled Brahmins and resented Hindus in general, although he would vociferously deny it. *Prejudice is a strange disease with its unique conditioning,* Mahadevan thought as he sipped his coffee. It gets embedded in one's subconscious and then comes to the surface involuntarily in comments and barbs. Hussain didn't understand he hurt the sentiments of those around him who couldn't continually pass off his innuendoes as jokes. He continually referred to his staff as "bloody, Brahmin, pen-pushing clerks." Was he blind? The bureaucracy was filled with Brahmins from all states, and it was these *bloody, pen-pushing clerks* that ran government. That day at the meeting, he referred to the carefully assembled report on hoarding and distribution during the famine as a "compilation of rubbish" and insinuated that only Hindus benefitted from Government disbursements, implying that his staff joined others in the system to deliberately siphon off funds. Mahadevan felt directly insulted, as he was the *pen pushing Brahmin* whose name was at the bottom of the report. Hussain was the head of department, and ultimately bore responsibility for its actions, however, he couldn't resist passing on the blame to his staff and shrugging off all responsibility. Numbers were revealing. Yes, someone was profiting from black marketeering, and if Mahadevan listened to gossip, all rumors pointed back at Hussain, which made his voluble and definitive protests sound hollow. When his Muslim League leanings were brought up at the meeting, he told the Governor that at least he had an ideology and was not like the brown sahibs—spineless, Hindus with burgeoning middles, growing fat on British meat. At that point Mahadevan was ready to get up and excuse himself, but his secretary, Bose, stopped him. And to think that Hussain did not have an inkling about his overtly sectarian comments was just amazing. Despite his education and seniority in the pecking order, Suhrawardy had allowed his success to go to his head. Although his letter was beautifully penned with just the right amount of humility, his arrogance in person was overbearing. He never failed to comment on Hindus, the privileged class, on Brahmins whom he thought were spineless and of course all the men who worked for him who only provided "conjured-up" reports. Ironically, more than anyone else in the department, *he* was the proverbial "Brown Sahib" that he made fun of.

Enough of Suhrawardy, thought Mahadevan as he opened the morning paper. Jinnah had called Muslims to revolt against the May 16th resolution in which the Congress was trying to avoid Partition. Jinnah wanted a separate state in Muslim-dominant northwest and parts of East Bengal. In his earnestness to become Prime Minister, Jinnah was willing to move to a country he had scarcely seen. August 16th was to be a day of nonviolent protests throughout the country. Here in Bengal the protests would be led by none other than Suhrawardy. Mahadevan was quite convinced the call to action would urge irate Muslims to go over the edge. Already there were sporadic incidents that police were trying to control, and he hoped that Suhrawardy would call in the army to prevent unnecessary bloodshed.

He knew the Anushilan group had switched gears with morchas and organized meetings exhorting the Hindu faithful to protect themselves against Muslims. Bengal had a greater percentage of Muslims overall, but Calcutta itself was predominantly Hindu. Unfortunately, the poor lived in shanty *bastis* both either Hindu or Muslim, and now with tensions running high, the situation was ripe for the savagery and agony of communal riots. Bengal had suffered a lot with the famine and needed breathing room to recover, but politicians like Suhrawardy with their powerful rhetoric moved mobs and incited hatred. This worked really well for the British, who stood apart and enjoyed the spectacle. *Let the natives kill each other* was their attitude. The Crown had lost interest in India, and it showed with their apathy towards the genocide of millions in Bengal. It was rumored that when the Governor sent a report about the millions of deaths in the Bengal famine with an urgent request for assistance, Churchill wrote on it asking, *Why isn't Gandhi dead yet?* Never having seen the document himself, Mahadevan wondered if there was any truth to it.

He made a mental note to speak with Vaithee and get a heads up on the situation in the streets. Hopefully his former employee wasn't in the business of killing people and wasn't planning anything for August 16th. Mahadevan felt vulnerable with Meera here and hoped the couple would move. Vaithee said he had found a place in Bhowanipur and was planning to take Meera and the kids there once things quieted down. He begged Mahadevan to keep Meera till independence was achieved, possibly sometime in the following year.

In a way, Mahadevan was glad his resignation hadn't been accepted. He wasn't ready to retire from Government service. He had always lived in Government accommodation and had not yet thought of buying a property for retirement. Kandu was still young and needed to finish college and perhaps also go to Cambridge for his studies. At least the girls were settled. Once Kandu was old enough to marry, he would find a really nice girl for him, one who would respect family values and blend nicely with them. Vani's husband Ganesh, was chosen by his father, educated but *personality-less,* if that was even a word and Arun? Arun made his blood pressure rise. He always held an opposing view and didn't wait even a minute before proffering his outlandish ideas. Mahadevan felt as though he were continually mocking him. But Rukku loved him, and though his son-in-law wanted a registered marriage and a motorcycle instead of a diamond necklace for Rukku as dowry, Mahadevan had no choice but to accept grudgingly, but with all the grace he could muster. Like Hussain said in his letter, he was always—what was that? *Equable and unruffled.*

Kandu would marry a beautiful south Indian girl from a good family, one who wore flowers in her hair and sang beautifully. He wondered how far away that day was.

CHAPTER THIRTY SIX

VAITHEE AND NANDU
CALCUTTA – AUGUST 1946

THE CALL TO ACTION

Vaithee locked the door to his tiny room with a padlock and headed down the narrow street. He had a bedroll and few shirts and pants, nothing of real value, but he secured the room anyway. His quarters were right at the back in the last row of rooms in the basti. Behind that building sloped a small embankment, beyond which was a narrow canal. The monsoon rains hadn't arrived in Bengal yet, and an excuse of a rivulet meandered aimlessly under a broken stone bridge which hung precariously between the two banks. At some point this must have been a flowing river, the bridge built by some bygone Rajah. With the basti boasting of one solitary bathroom, the canal was used freely by all for their morning ablutions and the stench was intolerable, which is why he was able to rent the room for a pittance. He picked this place because the Ayyar family had moved residence to Elgin Road, which was a fifteen-minute walk, making it easier for him to meet Meera and the children.

The narrow access road was almost empty. Shopkeepers had shuttered their stores expecting trouble. Even the tea shop had opened only for an hour after which the terrified owner rushed home. The only thriving business seemed that of the knife sharpener. Vaithee could hear the steady hum at varying frequencies, which meant there was more than one working here. Soon enough he passed one such unit, a simple contraption using a wheel and pedal. In addition to knives were all kinds of implements, including rakes, hoes, cleavers, hatchets lying in a heap awaiting the knife sharpener's attention. Apparently people didn't trust the police to take care of them and were preparing for the worst. The atmosphere was really tense in Bhowanipur. All the *Dadas*, gang leaders in each *Para*, were preparing for the imminent battle. Vaithee's basti was too small to have its own Dada, and he believed that the gang leader lived in another basti further down the road.

Vaithee and Nandu were heading towards Rash Behari Avenue, where a meeting had been called by the Anushilan group in the wake of Jinnah's call for "Direct Action". The streets were not crowded; most people were huddling indoors wary of trouble starting. Vaithee knew what to expect at the meeting. Like all the Dadas, the Anushilan group was preparing for a blood bath. Vaithee wanted Independence, and he believed in targeted political assassinations, but he wasn't a killer. He had to keep reminding himself that when he murdered for Revathi's sake, he was a different man, and that had happened a long time ago. Now a father and husband, he didn't want to throw his life away for a lost cause. Nothing would come from killing Muslims. If you slaughtered a hundred, then the next hundred would surface. Massacre was meaningless and solved no problem. It was just a group of frustrated, poverty stricken people venting. As he walked he could hear radios from every home. Everyone was waiting to see what Suhrawardy was planning for Bengal. He was sure to arrange a rally, and heaven knows what would follow. More and more, Vaithee believed that the fight for Independence was becoming too expensive in terms of human lives martyred. He had a sinking feeling that something terrible was going to happen, an overpowering emotion of impending doom.

He glanced up at Nandu standing on the street corner using his knife to pry dirt from under his fingernails. Passersby looked at him suspiciously and hurried away. He was a newcomer to the basti, having arrived just last night, and they weren't sure if he was Hindu or Muslim. Nandu's shoulders had broadened, and he was almost as tall as Vaithee. He spoke very rarely, preferring to listen intently. His speech was a hybrid of Tamil and Bengali—*Tengali*, Vaithee called it. This worked for Vaithee who didn't really want to be bothered by unnecessary conversation. The dialogue in his head was animated enough.

"Nandu, I don't think we should involve ourselves in the Anushilan fight. You are a trained assassin, and I don't want you wasting your talent on killing poor Muslim butchers. *Inniki meetinglai yenna nadaka pordo?*" Vaithee wasn't sure what would be asked of them today. One thing was certain, he was determined not to kill anyone.

"*Kolai kolai thaan, Ki porbah* how many I kill?" murmured Nandu wryly. Vaithee agreed. Murder was murder and the more one killed the less it mattered to the killer. Vaithee glanced at Nandu and felt really sad. So young and so hardened. The only real connection he had in his life was with Vaithee, and suddenly it felt wrong for Nandu to be trained for murder. After all, every action had its own repercussions, and he felt a moment of guilt having led Nandu down this path. In contrast, his own son led such a sheltered life, with adequate clothing and shelter and so much love. He could never imagine asking Prashant to kill anyone, and it felt wrong to ask this of Nandu. Still, he could hardly blame himself entirely for Nandu's predicament. Nandu had enlisted and had been working on behalf of the group for over a year before Vaithee even met him. They needed people to do their dirty work, and a hundred Nandus mushroomed each day, disconnected from consciousness, unable to emote naturally and quite easily conditioned to hate. This was poverty's birth child.

As expected, Subroto Ghosh, Sumit Panda, and other leaders made emotional speeches. The group meeting today was much larger than usual. He could recognize many as gang leaders of their Paras—their neighborhoods. These men had strong followings in their respective localities and were useful assets.

The plan was to prevent the minority Muslim community from attending the speech. They were to use any means necessary to frighten Muslims into staying home and therefore nullifying the effect of the call to action. *Any means necessary,* thought Vaithee. All these Dadas were power-hungry sociopaths. Giving them so much leeway could mean killing hundreds of innocents, not just a few, which could easily spiral out of control. He found the distribution of all kinds of weapons at the end of the meeting even more shocking: choppers, hatchets, battle axes, cleavers—it was terrifying!

Nandu moved forward to grab a cleaver, but Vaithee held him back. This was not what Vaithee signed up for. He was a political activist, not a mass murderer. And if he could help it, Nandu was not going to be party to this. Nandu looked at him puzzled *"Kano nebo na?"* he enquired.

"Aami tomake bolchi, tar jono." Vaithee instructed, and his word was law in Nandu's world. Nandu didn't understand why his mentor was stopping him from grabbing a weapon. If there was going to be a bloodbath, they needed to defend themselves. Who knew what was going to happen? But the younger man didn't question him any further, and they left without another word.

Vaithee couldn't sleep that night. Thoughts about his village, about Revathi, and then Meera and the children kept him awake. These were tumultuous times. And the effects would remain long after the British left. Hatred between the two communities was like a latent bomb waiting to explode, and the British were lighting the fuse. By supporting the Muslim cause, the rulers were riling the normally complacent Hindu community. The Muslims wanted Calcutta to be included in East Pakistan, and the Hindus would die fighting to keep it in Hindustan.

We are born and then we die. How we conduct ourselves in the interim constitutes life, and Vaithee was determined to live the rest of his life well. On his deathbed he hoped he would have no regrets.

CHAPTER THIRTY SEVEN

KAMU AND BALA
THANJAVUR – AUGUST 1946

THE WEDDING AND THE MIDNIGHT CALLER

T he wedding ceremony was short. The *muhurtham* was scheduled very early in the morning, and taking a bath in the cold wasn't her favorite thing to do, so Kamu pretended she bathed, allowing the water to splash vigorously around her, ensuring her face got thoroughly wet. Neither Rajam nor Chithi were very watchful as they were busy dressing the bride Jayam. It was strange to have both the bride and the groom from the same family; destiny had played a bizarre trick on them. On a more positive note, Kunju did not have to worry about providing Jayam with an elaborate dowry.

Jayam was Kunju's youngest daughter, named Jayalakshmi after Swaminathan's grandmother. Names tended to repeat in families as it was considered respectful to name a child after her grandparents, thus honoring them but leaving little room for new and innovative names. Jayam had two older sisters. Sundari was the first to marry. Swaminathan was still working at the time, so the wedding was celebrated really well and Kunju was able to give her oldest a modest dowry. Lalitha was well past marriageable age, but every time the matchmaker brought a good *varan,* it would slip through their fingers when they could not meet the groom's demands. Technically it was not the groom's demands, it was his family's. Most often, the boy would just sit uninterested in the whole proceedings while the parents bargained to fix a price for the girl. Ten grams of gold, ten kgs of silver vessels, a dozen saris and the list often became quite interesting, some asking for land, provisions and even for bicycles and motorbikes. Once they began listing their requirements, Kunju would simply switch off. Her inability to provide an ample dowry filled her with so much melancholy that she heard a high pitched wailing instead of the list of demands. It was her way of coping with her frustration. Having three girls to marry off was a huge burden on Kunju, and she had done well so far, but she worried about finding a match for Lalitha *and* providing an ample dowry. She had saved a few pieces of her mother Mangalam's jewelry and some of her silver vessels, but her own dowry was long gone. With so many mouths to feed and only her father's meager pension supporting the family, she was forced each month to take out one more piece of jewelry or silver to sell. Both girls had gold chains and earrings, which she vowed never to sell. There was no way Kunju could dream of buying new silver vessels and making diamond *thodus*. Each time the grooms' side walked out, Kunju would descend into dejection, but Chithi was permanently optimistic. She always said, "Don't fret, Kunju. This is not the right boy. The man destined to marry your daughter is born already and he will come and marry her even if you have nothing to offer. Your girls are diamond thodus themselves, why would they ask for anything more?" Kunju knew these were just comforting words yet wondered what the future held. At times she cursed her departed husband for burdening her with six children and then just absconding, leaving her to deal with the mess. Thank heavens Venkat was almost done with college. Next year he could certainly look for a job, and when she searched for a girl for him, it would be her turn to ask for diamond earrings which she could use for Lalitha's dowry. It was really a blessing she didn't have to give Jayam anything. Her thali was on a yellow thread, which she could later attach to her gold chain. Kamalamba had lent some dance jewelry, the *thalai sāmān* and *jimiki,* which framed Jayam's petite face and made her look really pretty. The flowers added the necessary embellishment that converted a girl into a bride and, thanks to Rajam's generous contribution, her bright maroon Kānjeevaram sari with gold checks added the final touch.

Kamalamba had really been Kunju's savior. Without her help, Kunju could have never run this household. When she met her, she was deep in debt and their meals had been reduced to watered down thayirshādam and pickle, but for the last couple of years, the children had been eating well and actually ate vegetables with each meal. They all looked so much healthier and rose from each meal satisfied and full. If only she had the ability to earn some money … but that was not an option. Girls, especially from Brahmin households, never went to work. What could she do anyway at this late age? She knew only how to cook, sing and play the harmonium. Unless she walked the streets singing and begging for money she couldn't conceive of any way of earning money to improve their life.

Luckily Rajam did not have to sell the odiyānam. Somehow Partha came up with a thousand rupees. The burden of Rajam's family fell heavily on Partha, but as Rajam would not be traveling and would stay with her father for a while, he borrowed money from friends and gave it to Rajam. Rajam, however, sold two silver plates and in exchange bought Jayam a beautiful *poojai* set. No child should start off life without a silver poojai set. It was really beautiful: two small containers for sandalwood and vermillion powder, a small plate, a rose water sprinkler and a *panchapatram* and *uddrani,* the essential vessels in any Brahmin household to purify everything prior to beginning a poojai. She had not shown it to Kunju yet; she wanted to surprise her at the wedding.

Rajam had been here in Thanjavur for a month now and saw how much Kunju struggled to run the household. Although Kamu was loved by everyone, her schooling was really suffering. Instead of studying, she spent most days learning dance from Bala and singing from Kunju. She was very tuned into the arts and really enjoyed both dancing and singing. Rajam knew this would be short lived, as Partha was not in favor of girls from his family dancing in public. He associated dance with Devadasis, and would never allow his daughter to perform in front of an audience. Rajam indulged her anyway because she knew how much Kamu doted on Bala, and dance practice kept her busy and out of her hair. Rajam had started feeling that she and Kamu needed some stability in their lives, and thought that living in Madras near the steadying influences of Sushila and Nagamma was perhaps a better option. She had written to Sushila informing her that she would like to come to Madras soon, and just yesterday had received a note back saying that a small house was available just down the street, a few houses away from Sushila's. The rent was very affordable, as the house belonged to their lawyer friend who only wanted a nominal amount as long as they took good care of the place. Rajam was actually happy about moving back to Madras. She had tired of her six month sojourns in Bombay especially with her struggle in speaking Hindi. It was disconcerting to have one leg here and the other nowhere. Besides, she and Partha never seemed to see eye to eye on anything. He was always pressed for time and so exhausted from the commute to and from work that evenings were fraught with tension. Rajam found she inevitably said the wrong thing or did the wrong thing and remained in a permanent state of stress from the continual sparring. She had no idea what he wanted from her or if that would even please him, as he seemed permanently discontent with her.

All the love and togetherness that marked the first decade of their marriage had been replaced by the harsh realities of life. Their beautiful life together had become a cesspool of anxiety and suffering. She felt guilty about her desire to be away from him. Perhaps it was a blessing. Maybe he needed time alone to figure out whatever was plaguing him, perhaps find a better job and then they might have a glimmer of hope of reviving the old connection. Till then, she had to make a life for herself and Kamu. Living with her father was a very comfortable and warm experience, but he already had the huge responsibility of raising six grandchildren, and she didn't feel right in imposing on him as well. Yes, on balance, a move to Madras seemed the best option despite the fear of banging heads with Nagamma again.

Jayam's wedding took place in the open thinnai with immediate family and friends as the only invitees. The swing that stood on one side of the thinnai was positioned perfectly for the *Oonjal* ceremony. Kamu loved this ceremony especially when they made it difficult for the bride and groom to exchange garlands. Once the couple came and sat in front of the fire, Kamu sat down near Bala, tired from all the excitement. The clamoring of the *getti melam* startled Kamu from her sleep. She had dozed almost through all the wedding events, having woken up very early that morning. In the beginning, she watched the proceedings, but the drone of the *mantrams* lulled her to sleep. Bala laughed at her puzzled and confused expression. "Good! At least you woke up for the important part." she giggled.

"This is sleep time, not the time to get married. Why couldn't they have chosen a later muhurtham?" Kamu complained.

"Anyway, it's all done and you can go back to your dream world."

But Kamu's stomach was rumbling with hunger. She would have to wait till the ceremonies were over, but the thought of delicious food—*muhurtham shāpādu*—made her mouth water. Preparations had been afoot since yesterday and she had helped with shelling peas and peeling potatoes. They had hired a cook too as they knew there would be no time for the women to enter the kitchen in the morning. The aromas were escaping into the thinnai, and Kamu wandered into the back rooms hoping to grab a morsel.

Bala watched wistfully as Jayam and Mani took the sapthapadi, seven steps and seven vows to remain faithful to one another as long as they lived. That would probably never happen to her. She was married to a stone lingam who could never demonstrate any affection. Life was so unfair. Who decided which girl could marry and which one needed to be a prostitute? Was it the same God she was married to? What people said was all wrong. God was deaf and cruel. He never heard any prayers and he never granted any wishes. He was just a piece of rock and it was useless praying to a rock. In fact, there was no point in praying. She was born a Devadasi and would die a Devadasi, perhaps squished to death under her stupid benefactor's bulging, overweight body. She longed to be with Mohan but was terrified in case they hurt him. For the most part, she remained confined to her room, but Kamalamba had to bring her for this wedding and she was delighted to leave her cramped room which had recently transformed from a sanctuary into a prison. She had to speak with Mohan at least once, perhaps tonight. Kamalamba was sure to be tired ... maybe she could sneak out at night. Comforted by that thought, she turned her attention back to the panorama around her, watching and absorbing silently.

Lunch was a royal treat, seemingly replete with every possible food item, and everyone ate heartily. By the evening everything had been cleared, the thinnai swept and swabbed, and Kamu busied herself preparing the bedroom for the *Shanthi Kalyanam,* the couple's first night together. Her job was to generously decorate the bed with rose petals, which she did with enthusiasm. Two glasses of warm milk were placed by the bedside and a few beedas. Camphor and incense perfumed the room, and once the priest had completed the ceremony they closed the door behind the young couple and settled down for the night in the corridor on the far side of the thinnai. Everyone was so tired they were instantly asleep.

Rajam first thought the banging was in her head but she woke up and realized someone was at the door. It was late. Who could be here at this unearthly hour? She arose to answer the door. Kunju and Chithi were also awake and everyone a little apprehensive.

Yaaru? Chithi enquired opening the door a crack.

Outside, Radhai stood bent forward with the weight, his shirt covered in blood flowing from the still form slung over his shoulder.

CHAPTER THIRTY EIGHT

NAGAMMA AND SUSHILA
MADRAS – JULY 1946

SUSHILA'S REVENGE

Nagamma casually glanced into the open courtyard in front of Siva's home and noticed a foreign car parked on one side. This was the third time she had seen the automobile parked here. She knew Siva was traveling and also recognized the car as belonging to Advocate Panchu, their family friend. What was it doing here? Had he bought a house in the same courtyard? That didn't seem likely. Panchu was a very successful judge in the High Court and lived in a beautiful home on the waterfront in Adyar. There was no way he would move into a tiny home in the Brahmin quarter. Nagamma's mind crawled with all kinds of suspicions as she crossed the road to pray at the Kabaleeswarar temple, part of her morning routine. It was nice to get away from screaming children at home and find a little peace and quiet. But today there was a special function at the temple, and the silence she needed couldn't be found. The deity had been placed on a huge chariot, and hundreds of people were pulling this *ratham* around the outer courtyard. It was beautiful to watch, all the men bare bodied, covered in ashen vibhuti stripes, and the women in colorful saris, but the noise was deafening.

Nagamma was pleased that Rajam and Kamu were returning. She missed them when they left for Poona and Bombay, and in spite of her outward demonstration of fairness, she had to admit she saved a soft spot in her heart for Kamu. Kamu was just different from all the other grandchildren and loved her Nagamma Paati, spending as much time as possible in her company, preferring to eat thayirshādham fed by her instead of the delicious meal her mother customarily prepared. In a way, Nagamma loved it when Kamu stayed over to eat knowing that Rajam would be anxiously awaiting her return. Rajam was a foolish girl, not really good enough for the *laddu* that Partha was. Who could tell at age twelve how a girl would grow up? She hailed from one of the best families in Vizhupuram yet was a dithering fool, who spoke too much and never got anything right. But she was willing to put up with Rajam's foolishness if it meant she could clasp Kamu to her breast to her heart's content.

She had carried a coconut and bananas in her poojai basket and stopped at the flower shop to pick up a garland for the *archanai*. Today she would dedicate the archanai to Partha and Kamu and of course Rajam. God knows he needed all the blessings he could get to secure more remunerative employment. She would pray for him to find a good job here in Madras and then, like old times, they could all live together. Nagamma patiently waited till all the married ladies completed their archanai before handing her basket over to the priest. She had grown accustomed to being an *amangali*. Widowhood, which had crippled her for a while, slowly became more acceptable as she learned to step aside and accept her situation. She just never attended poojais during Navaratri or Varalakshmi nombu festivals. That way the awkwardness of people avoiding her while offering the other ladies manjal-kumkumam was circumvented and so was her pain. At weddings, she seated herself right at the back knowing that the family could simply stop one row in front of her when they walked the aisles with the marriage sari and thali seeking the blessings of relatives and friends. In the beginning, it irked her and brought tears into her eyes. A year ago she was the first person they came to, what with her being the oldest Sumangali, and now that her husband had passed, the same blessings had apparently become evil omens. Nothing within her had changed; she still blessed others wholeheartedly, yet she had to accept that the parents of the bride feared bad luck for the whole family and possibly widowhood for their daughter if they were to accept Nagamma's blessings. Tradition and custom existed for a reason, and though it hurt, over a period of time Nagamma just learned to live with it and limit her interaction with the outside world. Even here in the temple it bothered her for a long time that the priest never took her offerings before that of married ladies. What hurt the most was noticing how people hurriedly returned to their homes on seeing her. Widows were considered *abasagunam*, and if you stepped out of your home and spotted a widow, then whatever you planned for that day would go wrong. In the beginning, tears pricked her eyes but then she recalled the million times before that she had turned back home on seeing a widow and realized it was payback time. Now here she was at the temple, allowing younger sumangalis to go ahead and finish their prayers. This was what widowhood stood for. If she wanted the Lord to accept her prayers, she had to swallow her pride and await her turn patiently.

Nagamma pulled her coarse, mud colored sari over her bald head and fastened it behind her ears. She hated it when the fabric slipped revealing her hairless head. Her hair had been thick and long, almost to her waist when she shaved it off, and she missed the ritual of oiling and washing with *shikakai*.

She missed so many things, but she had no alternative other than accept it all. This was the Brahmin agrahāram. These were the rituals and beliefs that had held this society together for thousands of years, and nothing was going to change. She had treated other widows in the same way, yet when it was her turn, it hurt.

Basket in hand she made her way down Mundakanni Amman Kovil Street. As she passed Siva's house, she glanced once again, and to her utter shock she saw Panchu come out of the house and get into his car. What was he doing in the house when Siva was not there! Sushila had no business entertaining men in the house when her husband was not home. She could feel the anger rising and her nostrils flared with each violent exhale. Nagamma waited outside the gate until the car turned at the end of the street and then marched in to confront Sushila.

"Sushila!" her voice boomed.

"*Yenna* Amma? *Varen*," Sushila rushed in from the bedroom coiling her hair into a bun. She looked a little flushed, but that could have been Nagamma's imagination. Nagamma glanced in and noticed the bed was half made.

"Making the bed so late? Have you been sleeping in?" she enquired sarcastically, one eyebrow cocked. *Had they just been having sex in that bed?* The very thought made her wince.

"Sorry I ... was just tidying up," Sushila dithered, gulping and keeping her eyes peeled to the floor. "Siva isn't here and I woke up early, but I wasn't expecting visitors so I didn't bother to make the bed," she finished.

"That's strange, since I just saw a visitor leaving," said Nagamma, her voice rasping.

"Oh him? Advocate Panchu? Oh he was here because of Rajam. She is going to stay in a house he owns. Number 42. He was here to drop off the keys, so I gave him some coffee."

This was news. She had no idea Sushila was making Rajam live separately. There was plenty of room right here in Siva's house. Balu was in school and there were no other children. You needed a place in your heart to accommodate others. People were so different these days. They all wanted to live in their own private homes. Nagamma didn't know what that was like. All her life she had slept with ten others on a bedroll on the floor. So many years had passed since she had her own bedroom, it felt like that happened a lifetime ago. Perhaps Sushila didn't want Rajam meddling with her rendezvous with this stupid advocate.

"He just came to give the key and nothing else? I don't like strange men coming here when Siva is away. We may be poor but we have impeccable reputations in this neighborhood. Don't do anything to take that away. *Maanam mariyadhai poyidum.*"

"No no," stuttered Sushila, protesting a bit too vehemently. "What are you talking about? How can you say that? I don't like your tone. What are you accusing me of? Come out openly and say it." Sushila had been married long enough to lose her fear of Nagamma. She was not weak like Rajam, and this was her house and her life and no one was about to interfere, least of all Nagamma. At the same time, she did not want an open confrontation. Respect and politeness was ingrained into her and she had to deal with this situation tactfully. She was well aware of prying eyes and knew the neighbors noticed Panchu's car coming so often. She didn't really care about them, but knew she must be a little more prudent. Either he needed to park elsewhere when he visited or they needed to find another love nest. She didn't want to explain her actions to the whole world. Who could understand the years of humiliation of knowing her husband slept with all kinds of women and still be forced to subject herself to his nightly advances. She had sworn to seek revenge and now she had the opportunity. She would sleep with another man under the same roof on the same bed and Siva could do nothing about it, not when he owed Panchu so much money. This was her moment, but Nagamma didn't need to know any of this. This was her personal triumph and she wasn't about to allow anyone take that away from her. Panchu was neither good looking nor young, and neither was she in love with him. She slept with him merely to exact vengeance, the only way she knew.

Nagamma was really irate, sensing disrespect in Sushila's voice. This was still her family and Sushila was still her daughter-in-law. "Do I need to accuse you of that? There is never any smoke without fire. I'm a patient woman, but I have seen that car here more times than I need to. Yes, I am accusing you of carrying on with that hook-nosed fool."

"That's just perfect! Barging in here and accusing me of infidelity. Where were you with your morals when your dear son came home with kumkumam from other women on his veshti? Everyone knew he visited prostitutes and they were all laughing at me. Don't pretend you were unaware of it."

Nagamma sat down on the floor banging her chest. Her deepest fears were realized. What had so far been a suspicion was true. Her daughter-in-law had the gall to sleep with another man. She began flailing her arms and beating her chest dramatically, all the time wailing and lamenting, *Ayyo Ayyo en mātuponnu thevadiyāvā māritā. Mānam pochu mariyādhai pochu. Nān yen uyiroda irruken?*

"Stop it! Stop it I say!" Sushila held Nagamma's arms and shook her. "Stop this drama. I have not said anything about being unfaithful to your son so how did I become a *thevadiya.* Stop calling me that. I am no prostitute and you have no right to call me one. I told you he came to give me the key. Here, let me prove it to you." She ran into the room and returned with the keys, jingling it loudly. "Satisfied? Stop saying all those horrible things. You should have reserved those comments for your precious son. How come you had nothing to say to him? Answer me! Why are you silent … answer me?"

Nagamma had nothing to say. She knew she had no argument. Deep within she did not want Sushila to confirm what she knew to be a certainty. Of course Nagamma knew, but the rules were different for men. They were the breadwinners and could do as they pleased, but women were dependent on them. It would take two minutes for Siva to turn Sushila out, and then she would have nowhere to go with the stain of infidelity. Even her parents would refuse to accept her back. Even if it were true, here was a terrible secret that she could not share with anyone; one more burden to shoulder alone. Again, it remained a question of maintaining respect at all costs. Somehow Sushila had won this round but Nagamma wasn't about to leave without giving her a mouthful.

"Don't be a fool Sushila. Don't throw everything away. You don't have to become a prostitute to prove a point. It's not worth throwing away your reputation. I will never support you and neither will I ever take you in if Siva throws you out."

"Amma, for the last time, don't *ever* call me a prostitute again," she warned, her voice menacing and low. "Neither will Siva throw me out, nor will you ever have to take me in. I am perfectly capable of taking care of myself and don't need an old woman to be my moral shield. Even if I were having an affair, and I'm not, it's no one's business but mine. I will not answer to you or anyone else. I hope that is clear."

Triumphantly Sushila smiled at Nagamma. There was nothing more to be said. She held her back and lowered herself gingerly onto the easy chair. Almost immediately Nagamma realized she was with child.

Are you pregnant? she asked querulously.

"Yes! How insightful of you! Four months now and I hope the baby looks like his father."

CHAPTER THIRTY NINE

MOHAN AND RADHAI
THANJAVUR – AUGUST 1946

THE SAGA UNFOLDS

"Help ... help me please. I'm so sorry to come at this hour, but I had no option. I didn't know where else to turn for help." Radhai could barely speak. He was bent over and wheezing for air. In the moonlight they could only discern his shape, but the dark stain on his otherwise spotless veshti and shirt was clearly perceptible.

"*Ayyuyo,* what happened?" Chithi turned to Kunju, "Wake up Venkat. Radhai needs help."

The women were visibly disturbed. A knock on the door at this hour always meant bad news. They had no idea what to do and how to react. Radhai lumbered into the Swaminathan's home and slowly with Venkat's help lowered Mohan down onto the floor. Mohan was barely conscious, his breath sharp and rasping. Blood streamed from a broken nose and from a deep gash on his temple. His fingers were a bloody mess and from a gaping hole in his thigh, a branding, emanated the acrid odor of burning flesh.

Radhai squatted, holding his head in his hands, sobbing pitifully, his body a cry of pain, heaving and shaking with emotion. Swaminathan searched for his glasses and hobbled up, aghast at the sight confronting him. As a police officer he had seen plenty of blood and gore, but those were strangers and he could be impersonal dealing with them. Now, looking down at Mohan struggling to breathe, he felt his chest rise in anger. What could this young man have done to warrant such a bloody punishment?

Rajam felt the bile rising in her gullet, yet she had to help. While Chithi stayed with Mohan, she ran inside to search for disinfectant and some clean muslin cloth. After Rajam dropped the scissors for the third time and toppled the pot of water, Kunju asked her instead to get water for Radhai, seeing that she was a bag of nerves and no use to anyone. Kunju began the process of washing away the congealed blood from Mohan's face. The gash on his temple was deep, and no amount of pressure could staunch the bleeding. He would definitely need stitches, but how were they to find a doctor at this unearthly hour? Kunju looked at the watch in the hallway. It was 4:30 in the morning. They dare not go into the cantonment clinic till at least six or seven in the morning. She asked Venkat to press down on his wound while she moved to Mohan's leg to see what was happening there.

His thigh had been branded with a spoon, and the fabric of the veshti was stuck tight to the open sore. What were they to do? They cleaned the wound with coconut oil using soft muslin cloth. Kunju knew he was hurt very badly and feared they might not be able to save his life. Who knew how badly he was hurt internally? They needed a real doctor to see him, and every minute they delayed put his survival in jeopardy.

"He needs to go to a hospital, Appa. The wound on his head is deep and God knows why his breathing is so shallow. Maybe his ribs are broken."

"Venkat will go in an hour. Till then, make sure he is comfortable." Swaminathan gave Radhai another glass of water, which he drank thirstily. Carrying Mohan had been no easy task. Exhaustion and fear of not being able to save his son left him trembling with his throat dry and sore.

"Are you better now? Take it easy. It's alright … I'll take care of everything." Swaminathan rubbed his hand over Radhai's shoulders, comforting him the best he could. "Tell me what happened if you can. I need to know."

Radhai kept shaking his head and slapping his forehead, lamenting pitifully, unable to speak for several minutes. Then he told his story.

"I knew this morning when the glass slipped from my hand and crossed the threshold of the house clanging into the courtyard that something bad was about to happen. All day I had this feeling of foreboding, and in the afternoon I spoke to Mohan again, warning him to stay away from Bala. He promised me, but the fool that he is, he didn't follow through on his word, and this is the end result.

"Bala had been confined to her room and Mohan too. I was to make sure he didn't come anywhere near the girl. I don't know what she was thinking. She is desperately unhappy, poor child. She longs to see her mother and is in love with a man she can never marry, while forced to bed another. God knows why she was born into such a miserable destiny. The Leela of Lord Krishna is incomprehensible.

"Anyway, I think she wanted to meet Mohan to find out what was happening. She knew I had asked you for help locating her mother and wanted Mohan to run away and tell her mother to come and rescue her from her incarceration. She had somehow sent word to him through one of the girls to come outside her window so they could speak. Mohan knew I had warned him not to go, but in a moment of weakness he slipped out and met her. I don't know who betrayed them, but the deafening noise of Mohan wailing and pleading for mercy awakened me.

"Muthu and three others beat him and kicked him senseless. As I walked into the hallway, I had the miserable misfortune of watching as they held him down and smashed his fingers, and if that wasn't enough, Kamalamba Amma brought a heated spoon and branded him on his thigh. The sight of him writhing and his screams of pain are still ringing in my ears. When he stopped moving, they locked him in the store room. I was terrified because I knew there are rats in the store room and the smell of blood may attract them to attack. I couldn't leave him there. They don't know it but I have a copy of the keys to the store room. I waited for some time until there was no more noise and then I unlocked the room, picked him up, and ran. I left the house not knowing where I was going. All I knew was that I had to save him at all costs, and then I thought of you and here I am.

"I don't know how things have become so bad. I was Kamalamba's right hand, I have always been peace loving and never hurt a soul in my life. God alone knows why this has happened to my sweet and gentle son. By morning they will discover I have gone and I can't go back; Muthu will kill me. And ... oh lord what am I to do, what am I to do?"

Radhai was overcome with dread, his fears of a dismal future too difficult for him to bear, given his present emotional state. Swaminathan let him weep and release his built up stress. Swami didn't know what to do either. He needed to think clearly and make some plans.

Should he go to the police? No, perhaps that wasn't such a good idea. That would serve no purpose. He would need to file an FIR, and that would mean involving himself legally in the affair. If that happened, Kamalamba would never forgive them and he didn't want to upset her. After all, her generosity had kept the family fed for the last year. No, she could never know of this. It was unfortunate that Radhai had brought Mohan here, but he really had no other option. They could shelter one person, but two? That would be very difficult.

The family went back and forth trying to come up with a viable plan. Finally, after much discussion they decided Radhai would take a bus to Vizhupuram. Swaminathan would send him to Muhammad Salih's house with a letter explaining everything, and Salih could then help Radhai get to Madras. Swaminathan had sent a request to an old colleague still stationed in Madras to locate Saroja but hadn't heard back yet. Mohan needed medical attention urgently and that was paramount. The children had to be warned to hold their tongues, especially

Kamu. Bala would be crazy with worry but it was better she didn't know anything for now.

What a tragic turn of events. Just this morning he celebrated his son's wedding … and now this. Swami sat down in his easy chair. Life was just too full of opposites. In his career as a police officer he had taken lives and saved lives. Today it was his turn to save lives, and that was what he resolved to do.

CHAPTER FORTY

MEERA
CALCUTTA – AUGUST 16TH, 1946

THE CALM BEFORE THE STORM

Meera was uneasy. People said there were going to be riots and Boythee (Vaithee) had not yet shown up. He promised to return by Thursday night at the very latest and now it was Friday morning and that made her uneasy. It was past ten o'clock when she finished most of her chores. Maybe she would have time to walk to his quarters and bring him back. It was risky, but the Muslim meeting wasn't till noon and she was sure to return before then. She was caught between asking for consent and just slipping out. It was foolish to step onto the streets with so much tension in the air, and memsahib was sure to refuse permission. She couldn't risk that. If Boythee's life was in danger, then she had to be by his side. She couldn't let him die alone. She would find and bring him back. He would not perish for such a stupid reason and abandon her and the children. Meera walked swiftly to the servant's quarters located in a row to the left of the main house. Govindhan squatted outside noisily drinking his *chai* from a saucer. The children were playing inside and she hugged them both whispering she would return before long. Then she came out and told Govindhan, "I'm going to bring my husband back. I'll return before noon."

Paagol na ki? he asked, as only a crazy person would risk stepping outside, that too as a woman, she was asking for trouble.

"No, no, the streets are quiet now and I'll return before noon. I can't leave him alone in the basti, not with the fear of rioting in the streets. I just have a nasty feeling and I have to go." As she left she turned and said, "*Shono*, if I don't return, you take care of my children," leaving Govindhan dumbstruck. All he came here for was his cup of tea and now he was saddled with two children? The Gurkha warned her as she stepped out, but she once again assured him nothing would happen and she would be back before long.

Suhrawardy had declared August 16th a public holiday, which meant shops had to be closed and shuttered and no public transportation would ply the roads. Trams and buses stood like silent spectators all along the street, the atmosphere eerily silent, forcing Meera to quicken her pace. She had never seen Calcutta so empty and had no idea what would unfold over the next few days. Meera was focused on reaching Vaithee's quarters and bringing him back to Elgin Road, safe and sound.

❧

Mahadevan sat with Kandu in the verandah. The morning paper had not been delivered, and he knew for the next several days nothing would be available. There would be no milk, no groceries, no paper, nothing. The city would come to a standstill. As a senior ICS officer, he knew that additional armed reinforcements would soon arrive to protect their home, and these policemen were similarly placed in all British homes. Two battalions of soldiers had reached Calcutta, but Suhrawardy, who was now Prime Minister of Bengal, said the police were well equipped to handle any small skirmishes, and he was quite certain that the Call to Action would not have any violent repercussions.

"That Hussain is crazy!" Mahadevan exclaimed loudly.

"Who, Suhrawardy? Why? Because he's talking at the Esplanade?" asked Kandu.

"No, he has to do that as the leader of the Muslim League. It's the police *bandobast* I'm talking about. He has no idea how this can turn out. He should have called out the army yesterday. He really believes that there will be no rioting in the streets and thinks he can control frenzied mobs."

"My friends are saying that both Hindus and Muslims have spent the last month collecting weapons," said Kandu. "They actually saw someone unloading a truck in Lal Bazaar in broad daylight filled with swords and huge knives. They had petrol containers too. I suppose it's for burning shops and stuff. Scary! Do you think our area will be affected?" An involuntary shiver went down Kandu's spine. He abhorred violence of any kind.

"Once they are done with killing, the next step will be looting. The people are poor and with no police around they are sure to start attacking the shops and affluent homes. I don't mean to scare you, Kandu, but anything can happen unless the police bring in the army." He knew the battalions would flood the city on the Police commissioner's command and he hoped Suhrawardy didn't try to prevent them from acting prudently. He was an idealist and could be extremely persuasive, but erring on the side of optimism bordering naiveté, made him a horse with blinkers on. He had no real idea what could come to pass.

"Do you have a gun, Daddy?" Kandu asked, the fear visible on his face.

"No! And I don't need one. Police are coming here and they will be armed with rifles. I don't think we will face any trouble, but still, we should be vigilant."

"The thought of rioting terrifies me. What could persuade a regular person to go on a killing rampage?"

"Two things," said Mahadevan holding up his fingers. "Property and religion are two things people kill for. If they are riled up enough and they fear getting killed, then the survival instinct kicks in and they act without thinking; that's what converts a group into a mob. Kill or be killed, simple as that."

"I could never hate anyone enough to kill."

"Never say never Kandu. Just thank God you have never been in a situation where reason has fled and instinct taken control. I just hope Suhrawardy knows what he's doing and the speech isn't too rousing. Today is Friday as well; the talk will be after prayers."

"That's what I hate about Islam. How could a religion endorse killing? All this jihad stuff makes me so angry. See, they feel they're doing the right thing because they're killing for Allah and God is okay with their terrible acts," said Kandu, dourly echoing a common belief held by Hindus.

"Don't for a minute think Hindus are any less. I have seen the aftermath of killing in Rangpur. People can be vicious regardless of faith. Muslims have a name for it and Hindus do it anyway. The fault lies in the politicians who rile the crowds, and the poor and the unfortunate pay the price."

Vaithee and Nandu had woken up early morning to scout out the exit routes from the Esplanade. The police were just beginning to arrive in a trickle, one car here and one half empty truck there. It seemed by their slothful movements that they were not expecting anything and had all the time in the world to set up barricades to control the crowd. The maidān looked quiet other than the stage which had been set up for the Prime Minister's talk. A few even more lethargic fellows were tying loudspeakers to posts, and at the rate they were going it would probably be ready only next week. It had taken Nandu and Vaithee more than an hour to reach this place, and Vaithee wished he could have borrowed a bicycle. But he was new to the *Para* and knew no one would lend him their precious bicycle, especially if he told them where he was going. He marked out the main routes and possible exits on a sheet of paper, based on the placement of barricades. This done and now the daunting task of locating a phone to call Ghosh Dada.

Most shops were shuttered, and they would probably need to get to the office behind Park Street to give their information in person. They had no idea how many people would finally show up at the rally. At the last meeting, the instruction had been crystal clear. They were to stop as many people as they could, using any means at their disposal. Hopefully the skirmishes would be nonviolent, but Vaithee knew that he was just dreaming. He almost felt a premonition about the next few days and tried not to pay attention to his emotions. He had heard that buses and truckloads of Muslims armed with spears and brickbats were being transported to the city to attend Suhrawardy's speech. Vaithee had no idea if these were just rumors to get the Hindus worked up into a frenzy or if there was any truth to it. There was no means of communicating with local areas, and one could only hope the Dadas had done their job. Vaithee was quite clear. He was going home right after and then would head over to Elgin Road before any of the madness broke. Then he remembered he had to go to the Park street office and groaned in irritation.

The police were working very slowly, and at ten in the morning, the barricades were still not in place. Vaithee glanced at his watch anxiously. He needed to leave before the hordes arrived. They would be here shortly, as prayers would start at noon. By ten thirty, as they made their way back cautiously, groups of people had started arriving. They looked harmless enough—peasants, butchers and leather workers who but for their beard and hat were just Bengali. Vaithee sighed in angst. Such a pity that politics pitted neighbors against neighbors.

As they reached New Market they heard an earth-shattering scream. On the other side of the road a young Hindu boy was running for his life with a mob of forty strong at his heels.

For a moment Vaithee froze in his tracks; the scene in front of him so horrifying it congealed his blood and immobilized his muscles. The look of terror on the boy's face and the expression of hatred on the faces of the assailants shocked him. Never in his life had he witnessed such a petrifying scene. Nandu tugged at his arm, "*Dada ... Dada ...*" he kept repeating while dragging Vaithee behind a stairwell. The furious mob caught up with the man under the clock tower. Forty men hacked one unfortunate soul to pieces.

Vaithee was silent, beads of perspiration breaking on his temples and meandering aimlessly over his face till they dripped to the floor. He looked at Nandu crouched on his haunches, his hands on his thighs. Nandu's eyes were narrow slits, and his face betrayed no expression, which is why he was able to react faster than Vaithee. They hid behind boxes of fruit till the mob passed on their way to the Esplanade. Forty men on their way to pray after chopping someone to pieces. They looked crazed, their eyes popping out of their sockets. In their arms, spears and cleavers already dripped with blood. *Hindustan Murdabad, Pakistan Zindabad. Down with India, Long live Pakistan.* They were literally screaming, their passion and frenzy now expressed through every part of their being.

It was beginning, and this was no place to be. Muslims dominated the area and they needed to get back to the relative safety of Bhowanipur. The main streets were safer perhaps with a police presence, but if they were caught by a mob, they had no way out. They went down Bertrand Street, hoping to cut through Park Street and reach Bhowanipur from Camac Street. Avoiding main thoroughfares, they stuck to side roads. Both of them were walking briskly, stopping at each cross street to peep and look both ways before crossing.

When they reached the next cross street, four Muslim youths stopped them. One minute they were walking and the next, four skull-capped, lungi-sporting youths armed with butcher knives were in their face. There wasn't even time to think about being scared. *Tumi Musalman ki Hindu?* they demanded. Vaithee couldn't think. If he or Nandu spoke one word, their heavily accented Bengali would be a dead giveaway, more dead than giveaway. His whole life passed before him in flashing images. He said goodbye to Meera and the children, and closed his eyes waiting to feel the pain of the blade connecting with his body, when they heard the loud roar of a truck. Momentarily the Muslim boys got distracted, worried it might be a police truck, and Nandu reacted like lightning. He yanked Vaithee's hand, *odungo!* he switched to Tamil as they turned and scampered down back from where they had come. Vaithee had no idea he could run this fast. They had about a thirty second head start, but Nandu kept throwing garbage cans, baskets, and anything he could lay his hand on behind them as they ran for their life. They swerved into the next side street and saw that the building had no gate. Without a moment's hesitation, they turned into the building and then took the stairs three at a time. When they reached the third floor they paused, their breath a spindly wheeze. Vaithee's stomach churned but there was nothing to throw up. They leaned forward and looked down through the latticed window onto the street below. It was just a matter of time before the boys climbed up the stairs—and then? They had no idea what they would do. "*Dada,* I should have picked up another weapon that day. I knew we would need it. My pocket knife can't do much when there are so many people," Nandu hissed.

"Shh don't talk … there they are." Vaithee clamped his hand over Nandu's mouth. The four men were down below on the street, deciding which way to turn. Vaithee and Nandu could hear more people approaching with the familiar cry that told them the real mob had arrived. The two watched through the diamond openings, a group of a hundred or more angry Muslims, each armed with some weapon and screaming in unison, *"Maar-ke-lenge Pakistan, mar-ke-lenge Pakistan, leke rahenge Pakistan. La ila ilalha nara i takbi allahuakbar."*

Nandu and Vaithee stared hopelessly at each other. This was going to be a long day and night and neither knew if they would make it.

CHAPTER FORTY ONE

NANDU AND VAITHEE
BHOWANIPUR

THE HORROR OF HATE

They were shocked to see Meera sitting on their doorstep outside Vaithee's quarters. It was close to sunset and Vaithee had lost track of time. For sure this felt like the longest day ever. After the crowds had diminished he and Nandu waited patiently and only stepped back onto the streets after they had regained their strength. Throughout the ordeal, a relentless, all-consuming fear had kept their hearts pumping and perspiration running. Every time they made an attempt to escape, they heard the dreaded chanting of slogans and would scamper back to their hiding place on the third floor. They stayed there for a long time until the danger died down, after which they warily made their way to the Anushilan office. It was a miracle they were able to reach the office and deliver the road maps. There was water and some *Shenghadas* (samosas), and they were so hungry they wolfed everything down in seconds. Vaithee sat with Ghosh Dada and explained what he saw. It was past five o'clock before they left for Bhowanipur.

Vaithee mopped his face, wiping the sweat off his brow as they entered the basti. It was such a relief to finally arrive home. He would let Nandu into the quarters and then head to Elgin Road. As he turned into his lane, he saw her. What in heaven was she doing here? "Meera, what happened? Is everything okay?" He shook her awake.

Meera had been fast asleep resting her head against the door, and Vaithee's voice seemed to be part of a dream. When she realized she was awake and Vaithee was in front of her, she screamed at him, "Where were you all day? I have been waiting here for you for hours. You promised you would be at the Bangla by sundown yesterday ..."

Vaithee let her vent. The good thing was he was fine and so was Meera. But Meera still couldn't stop yelling. She was repeating herself and Vaithee patiently listened and apologized at appropriate intervals. Finally, they were inside and

Vaithee put a pot of water to boil on his small stove. They would drink some tea and rest a bit before leaving. It was better if they hurried, but they had another hour before darkness descended. Besides, both Nandu and Vaithee were exhausted from the day's events.

Fifteen minutes later, a neighbor walked in. "Did you hear?" he blurted, completely breathless, his eyes wide open in fear. "There are buses burning on Elgin Road. Apparently the meeting had to be called off as Suhrawardy received reports of bloody skirmishes all over the city. You had better lock up and sit indoors. Who knows what could happen?"

Vaithee thought for a moment. Should he take a risk and accompany Meera back or wait until tomorrow morning by which time the police were sure to have taken action. Finally, he made a decision. They would stay here behind locked doors and leave for Elgin Road at the crack of dawn. There was no food at home and Nandu went out to see if he could borrow something from the neighbors. He came back half an hour later with six bananas and a half-rotten apple. That would have to suffice. Nothing was open. Normally Vaithee ate at some tea stall or tiny restaurant. There were always *thelas* with someone selling food for a few *annas*, but today, he had no hope of finding anything. The streets were empty and bananas would have to be their staple.

It was close to midnight and Nandu felt claustrophobic. The room was really small and felt even more cramped with three of them sleeping. The air was heavy and muggy and so very still, partly because they had closed the solitary window. August was a humid month, and with no ventilation he couldn't breathe. He sat up and decided to step outside for a breath of fresh air and perhaps a *bidi*. He unlatched the door gingerly and peeped out. The gully was empty. He slipped out and went behind by the embankment. There was no noise other than the chirping of crickets. He sat down against a tree and lit his bidi. Taking a deep breath, Nandu felt relaxed and stared up at the stars. When his fingers burned, it was time to flick the bidi away. It was nice to have some peace and quiet after their narrow escape this morning. He leaned his head back and looked up once again at the millions of stars. He must have fallen asleep because he was woken up by loud screams. He sat bolt upright and turned around. Spirals of smoke were coming from the front of the basti, which tendrils of fire had lit up. His first thought was that he had left the room unlatched. In a second he was up, switchblade in hand, sprinting up the embankment. He turned the corner and his heart sank when he saw light coming from Vaithee's room. As Nandu reached the entrance to the room his heart was pounding. Meera was on the floor writhing and screaming and a man was on top of her, holding her arms down as he raped her. His rutting, bulbous backside was ludicrously exposed under a loosened lungi. In the far corner was another Musalman holding a knife to Vaithee's throat. Vaithee was sobbing helplessly and pleading with them to kill him. *"Aami dekhte paachi na ... aamake mere dao ..."* Nandu didn't stop to think. With a mighty roar he rushed in towards Meera, held the assailant by his hair, and slashed his throat in one swift motion. Then without even pausing, he picked up a meat cleaver from the floor and with all his strength using both hands chopped the second man's arm off. With a mighty wail the assailant spun around in horror. Nandu slashed again, this time ripping him open.

Meera was screaming as her rapist gurgled to death on top of her. Dropping the bloody cleaver, Nandu pulled him off her, urging Meera to stand up. Meera clung to Vaithee sobbing helplessly. "Come on," he yelled. "There's no time for this. There may be others, we have to go now." Nandu peeped out. He could see activity on the main street with people running back and forth. Their best bet was to get down the embankment and cross the river. "Come ..." he whispered indicating with his head. "It's clear ... hurry." As Vaithee and Meera walked into the narrow gully by their quarters which led to the back, Nandu went back inside the room to pick up the cleaver and was about to follow them when four Muslims armed with spears and knives turned from the main road towards him. He stood there wondering what to do. He could follow Vaithee, but the men would follow too and then both Meera and Vaithee would also be killed or ... he could stand and fight. He had all of three seconds to make a choice. Swinging the cleaver, he ran towards them shouting, *Muhammad, Allah, shuorer bacha!*

Vaithee pulled Meera under the bridge, waiting for Nandu to arrive. After five minutes, when he heard no sound of anyone coming, his heart sank. If Nandu wasn't here by now, there's no way he was alive. The blood curling screams and yells from the basti horrified him. What could they possibly achieve by murdering a bunch of people they never even knew? Scenes from earlier today kept flashing before him. He felt so powerless. His Karma had hit him hard and fast. God knows why the door was unlatched, because those two men were in the room even as they were sleeping. The first man raped Meera while the second forced Vaithee to watch. Vaithee had a knife at his throat and was scared to breathe. Then they switched places, and the man holding Vaithee cornered against the wall was taunting him telling him how much he enjoyed fucking his wife. And then like an angel Nandu appeared. But where was he?

Vaithee couldn't leave Meera alone here. Nandu was a fighter and a survivor. He knew how to kill, so he would probably be alright. Vaithee began chanting the *Vishnu Sahasranamam*, something he had not done in years. Vaithee was born in a Brahmin household, but after Revathi's death had lost faith in religion. Now in the midst of all this madness he returned to his source, to his childhood, and the words rolled off his tongue and once again he was in Vizhupuram with his father and mother. He wondered if they were still alive and if they ever thought of him. So much had taken place in one day. Twice his life was spared, and he couldn't help thanking God for taking care of him. The sound of the mantra calmed Meera, and soon her sobs subsided to an occasional hiccup. By the time he finished fifteen minutes later, she was fast asleep on his shoulder. Vaithee looked down at her, exhausted from the ordeal. The blood from the dying Musalman was still wet on the front of her sari. He felt tears well up in his eyes. She was raped and he could do nothing to save her. They should have killed him first; the memory of watching her screaming as a stranger forced himself on her would be the subject of his nightmares as long as he lived. What must he have done in his past lives to witness such horror? And all the others in this basti? It was sheer madness. He drifted in and out of sleep exhausted by the emotional toll, screams and blood curling yells awakening him from time to time. Calcutta was burning and bleeding. He could smell the acrid fumes of petrol and burning bodies and wanted to go back and check up on Nandu but was terrified to do so.

The sound of gentle rain woke him up. The sky was a lighter blue. Dawn was not far away. Other than the hiss of dousing fires and wail of lamenting men and women, he could hear nothing else. The troublemakers had probably gone by now, or better still, were dead.

He slowly eased himself out from under Meera. His shoulder was numb from inaction. Meera stirred, *Kothai jaccho?* she murmured, still half asleep.

"Shh ... you sleep. I want to check on Nandu. I'll be back I promise."

"Noooo," Meera began wailing and Vaithee clamped her mouth with his hand. "Don't make a noise. I think the Musalman have left. *Aami aschi,* I have to see what happened to Nandu."

Vaithee tentatively climbed up the embankment. The rain washed the blood from his neck in tiny red streams to tinge his shirt and he realized the blade must have nicked his neck. He could hear his heart thumping in anticipation as he stepped into the gully. His room was still open and he peeked in. The two men were still sprawled on the floor, very much dead, one face down and the other belly up. Most of the houses further down were burning and as he reached the main gully he saw him. His face was unnaturally twisted to one side, his lips drawn back in a snarl and his eyes half closed. His neck had almost been severed from his body and the butt of three knives protruded from his body. Countless stab wounds were patterned all over his motionless form. Around him in a heap were around seven or eight dead Muslims. Vaithee kneeled down and cradled him, sobbing helplessly. What a brave boy. Unmindful of his own fate, he wanted to save Vaithee and Meera. Nandu had no one except Vaithee and ultimately his last act was one of sacrifice. "Oh Nandu … Nandu … *ki kando, ki kando,* you should have come with us … you shouldn't have done this … you shouldn't have done this," Vaithee kept repeating, rocking his lifeless body back and forth. Then he turned and looked down the street littered with bodies. Incredulously, he walked down the main street. Two or three old women and men were squatting outside their burning homes lamenting and beating their chests in heart rending cries. *So much carnage? For what? To prove Allah was better than Krishna or Pakistan superior to India?* Silently he walked down the street, but all that he encountered were corpses and more corpses, their blood now forming red rivulets on either side of the narrow street. The drizzle had stopped and Vaithee returned to Nandu's side.

Nandu was not going to rot here. He would cremate him with honor due to a hero. He went into his room and returned with a bed sheet. What was he to do with the knives? He couldn't cremate him like that. With superhuman effort he dislodged the knives one at a time crying and screaming maniacally with each extraction. Then he wrapped Nandu's body in the bedsheet and carried him into the next lane where the houses were still burning. He stopped in front of one and rolled his body in through the flaming aperture that once was a door. He watched the body ignite and whispered, *Go my friend, go in peace, you are a hero, a martyr. No one else knows how brave you were tonight, but I will always remember your sacrifice.*

Then he turned and found his way back, stepping between the bodies of so many unsung heroes whom history would never remember.

CHAPTER FORTY TWO

THE AYYAR FAMILY
AUGUST 17, 1946

REELING FROM THE AFTERMATH

With no traffic and no one in the streets, the deadly silence hung heavily in the air like a faceless monster. No one had slept properly for the last two nights, not with the ominous sounds of sporadic explosions and screams punctuating the intense silence. The mind conjured up grizzly images behind the sounds that converted in slumber into vivid nightmares. Who knew what was happening in the streets and gullies of Calcutta as it rotted and burned. The night was warm and their bodies heated up even more as they tossed and turned in an attempt to find refuge from disturbing images of fear and death.

Meera's disappearance made Dharmu wild with rage. She raved and ranted for hours, knowing that only a complete idiot would leave the sanctuary of the bungalow to play with death. She couldn't believe Meera had the gall to leave without permission and all day they didn't hear the end of it. She yelled at Kandu and Mahadevan, but it was Govindhan who bore the brunt, all with the expected humility and acquiescence. They were used to Dharmu's rages and knew that she would cool off soon enough.

Dharmu and Mahadevan were especially concerned about Rukku, as three days had passed with no word from her. She had no telephone at home and would have to go to a neighbor's house to call. It was probably too dangerous to leave the house, and while they understood her dilemma, they worried nonetheless, anxiously waiting day after excruciating day for the elusive ring. Closeted all day at home, everyone in the household suffered from worries and anxieties fluctuating in intensity, sometimes a panic attack and at other times, a numbing feeling of dread.

It was a relief when the first rays of the sun pierced through the dark, foggy, smoke-filled air. When they stepped out onto the verandah, Kandu was already looking through binoculars, trying to get a glimpse of the street, but there was no movement. The morning brought with it a stillness that was even more ominous. The air was still and foggy from the fumes of the *choolas* and burning homes. Govindhan set the tray down on the table with biscuits and toast, and the clinking of china sounded like cymbals in a marching band.

"Has Meera come back?" Mahadevan enquired.

"No sahib, still no news of her. I told her she mustn't leave, but she wouldn't listen to me. The children are crying and I don't know what to do with them." And he muttered something more in his native *Oriya*, vociferously indicating his disapproval.

Dharmu scowled. "She must be dead!" she declared volubly, making Kandu and Mahadevan wince and look at her with piercing disapproval, all of which escaped her. "Serve her right for not asking permission. I would never have allowed her to leave."

"Mummy, come on … how can you say something like that? You people don't think servants have feelings. She must have been concerned about Vaithee. Wouldn't you be?" Kandu hated Mummy's flippant comments which brought out her selfish, callous nature.

Mahadevan had a feeling this was going to turn into another name-flinging confrontation and quickly interjected. He knew it was a bad idea to keep Meera, what with Vaithee involved in all sorts of nefarious activities. So many times in the last year he had spoken to Vaithee, asking him about his future plans, but Vaithee had pleaded with him to be patient for a while until he decided what he was going to do. Besides, Dharmu liked Meera and was really happy to have her back, and peace in the home was paramount. When Dharmu was in a bad mood the whole household trembled. The young, frail, girl he married, had grown, and along with her burgeoning size came supreme self-confidence and a need to control. She was slow to rise to anger, but when she lost her temper it often lasted for days and was quieted only by continual cajoling and profuse apology. When she screamed, her booming voice shook the foundations of the house on the next street, and Mahadevan did whatever was needed to keep her placated. It was quite amazing how tables had turned and now she was the power-house controlling their relationship. As the years went by, he became more reticent allowing Dharmu to make most decisions, happy to have some peace and quiet when he returned home from work, whenever possible. Allowing her to keep Meera meant a little more peace for him. But it was extremely irresponsible of her to leave the premises without permission, and leaving the children behind? What was she thinking? What was he going to do with them if both Vaithee and Meera were actually dead?

Servants were a great help as long as they knew their place, but he had no time or energy for additional headaches from their personal problems. Kandu never understood the conventional relationship between master and servants. How could he? All his life growing up without playmates his age, the house servants became his friends. That was a lesson he needed to learn. If you allowed them to, servants could take full advantage, but perhaps, now was not a good time for that lesson, not with Meera missing.

"I'm sure she will be fine. It's only been two days, let's wait before we mentally cremate her. You people have no compassion. Mummy is only concerned about herself. Selfish pleasure-seekers both of you! Any way I'm going to the terrace to see if I can get a better view of the streets." Kandu got up to leave.

"I don't need this talk from you. *Yenna?*" Mummy turned to Mahadevan, her anger making the wrinkles on her broad forehead crease into deep ridges. "Are you going to just sit while your son backchats and disrespects me?" Just then the phone rang and Mahadevan was spared the agony of resolving this spat. Recently Kandu was becoming more and more vocal with his opinions. Growing up had made him more aware, and Mahadevan hated being sandwiched between his son and wife, having to resolve their differences.

Dharmu jumped up to take the call. It was Rukku. Dharmu could barely hear her with Kandu and Mahadevan interrupting every few seconds asking if she was fine. She closed the mouthpiece and said, "Yes yes, she's fine, the line is terrible so could you please keep quiet so I can hear?"

Dharmu came back a few minutes later. "She is all right. I could hardly hear what she said she was crying so much."

"Why what happened?" Mahadevan asked, anxious to hear the news.

"Well for two nights they stayed indoors. She stepped out this morning to go next door to make this phone call and see if the provision store was open and right across the street, a Muslim fruit seller had come to try his luck selling fruit, thinking all was well and the streets were safe. Rukku was terribly upset because she buys fruit from him all the time. A group of young boys clubbed him to death with cricket bats right in front of her eyes. She is so upset she can barely breathe. And what mortified her more was when no one came to help him. Every window had people peering out, and they all just stayed silent while he was murdered right in front of them."

"Oh lord, poor girl!" Mahadevan knew she would not be able to forget this for a long time. The memory would haunt her. She was a very sensitive person, and all her life had been shielded from the realities of life. So far, not much news had filtered in from outside. They had been confined indoors with few calls coming in. As time went by, more and more horror stories would come to light. The newspapers would be filled with such stories of apathy, hatred and violence until people simply lost interest in hearing any more gut-wrenching stories and would move on until the next violent outburst. "We haven't heard the worst of it yet," he muttered under his breath.

Dharmu was still seething, but she remained sullenly silent, distracted momentarily by Rukku's call.

The stillness of the morning was broken by loud voices. There was some commotion by the front gate. He could hear the sound of someone wailing. Mahadevan's heart skipped a beat. Had the police left? Were plunderers trying to enter?

Chowkidār kya ho raha hai? he yelled, attempting to get a handle on what was taking place but the chowkidār merely signaled that he should wait with a hand gesture and continued talking. Some more voices and wailing and Mahadevan became more anxious by the minute. A sweat broke on his brow, and he didn't know what to expect.

He saw the gate opening allowing them to enter. Two figures bent over, the man supporting a howling woman who could barely walk. Their clothes were drenched in dark brown blood but when they looked up at him, a smile anointed Mahadevan's face.

Yes! They were alive! Miracles did take place.

CHAPTER FORTY THREE

RAJAM AND KAMU
MADRAS – AUGUST 1947

P. KAMAKSHI

"P. Kamakshi ... P. Kamakshi...."

Kannan looked up shaking his head in disgust. *Idhu yenna anyāyam Kamu. P. Kamakshi nu koopudanama?*

Kamu briskly rubbed talcum powder on her face and shouted back, "Chithappa, we have three Kamakshis in our class. So I'm P. Kamakshi, my friend outside is D. Kamakshi and we also have an S. Kamakshi." Frankly, she was tired of the P. Kamakshi jokes. That was her name, and there was not much she could do about it. All her cousins now called her that and it really made her mad.

"Why P.? Every time I hear it, it makes me wince. Why don't you drop the P and change your surname to Arthasarathy. A. Kamakshi definitely sounds better than P. Kamakshi," retorted Kannan, now vigorously polishing his shoes.

Kamu giggled. "Talk to Appa and ask him to change his name. Stop bothering me." She quickly glanced at herself in the mirror. Her long hair had been braided into a plait that reached her waist. The talcum powder on her face was a bit much, but that would fade away soon enough, eaten up by the Madras heat. It was August and the humidity made the air thick and heavy. But Kamu didn't mind that. The morning walk to her school was long, but Lady Sivaswamy High school was the most prestigious school in this neighborhood and she was so happy to be there.

She picked up her school bag and, giving Rajam a quick hug, ran out to meet her friend. As she walked past the gate onto the main street, Rajam ran out with her lunch. She had packed *vathakozhambu shādham,* Kamu's favorite and spent the morning making the potatoes crisp and spicy, just the way Kamu liked it. Having a few minutes to spare, she decided to fry *vadāms,* which went perfectly with vathakozhambu, and now this girl was leaving without the food. She yelled out for her but Kamu was already half way down the street.

Kannan looked at his sister in law, a caustic expression on his face. "I guess I have to go and give it to her," he grumbled.

"Yes, you do," replied Rajam dumping the lunch box in front of him.

"And drop this important task I'm busy with?" continued Kannan.

"The shoes look fine. Hurry!" said Rajam, grabbing the shoe and throwing it on the floor.

Rajam wiped her hands on her sari and sat down in the easy chair. Her hands had a distinct tremor. The first time she had a full blown attack was on the night Mohan was brought bleeding into their home. The sight of blood and thoughts of what must have happened to him played in her mind like a real-time movie and the confusion in her brain was overwhelming. Kunju found her sitting in the kitchen laughing strangely, her whole body shaking almost as if she were having a seizure. Nothing could calm her down. When the laughing stopped, she began crying uncontrollably. Kunju didn't know what to do. In the hall, Mohan lay bleeding, and here Rajam had lost her mind.

The doctor said she had hysteria and he gave her some pills to calm her down. For so many years she had lived in a continual state of anxiety, unable to deal with her emotions, never capable of pausing to actually voice her fears, and the chatter in her brain had become nonstop. Thoughts of scary situations in the past and unreal fears in the future would alternately plague her, and the resultant emotions served as an accelerant, raising her heart rate and causing her to sweat excessively. Everything, it seemed, would spiral out of control—and that's when the tremors would commence.

At first they were imperceptible, but that one time in her father's home, her whole body went into shock, and later on she had no memory of it. She was mild and very sensitive, and she thought too much about everything that happened around her. Things were much worse after they left Poona because she felt shaken by the uncertainties of living partly in Madras and partly in Bombay. It didn't help that her relationship with Partha had gone downhill. She felt the burden of life like a huge concrete stone pressing down on her chest. Even the smallest incident triggered a fear response, and seeing Mohan bleeding and barely conscious made all kinds of weird scenarios pop into her head; of Mythili dying because of her neglect, of Partha meeting with an accident, of Kamu being struck down by a motorcar. Things that perhaps might never take place became real and plausible in her mind. It became impossible for her to discern what was factual and what was part of her imagination.

Now that she was in Madras, Nagamma was her biggest trigger. In spite of the medication, in spite of living independently, the very sight of Nagamma would raise her blood pressure and increase her heart rate. The last time she had an attack, Kannan was home and could run for help. The doctor clocked her blood pressure at 250 over 110. Now in addition to the medication she took for her hysteria, she was taking another tablet to control her high blood pressure. She was unhappy and really ill. With nothing else to occupy her time, once Kamu left, she began praying. She chanted and prayed and cooked for the gods for two or three hours each day. Yet in the midst of her chanting *Narayana Narayana* she would find herself imagining Nagamma walking in and shouting at her on finding the house in a mess or a sāmiyār coming by and casting a spell on her. And then the symptoms would begin afresh making her chant even louder to drown the conversation in her head.

Kamu was too young to understand, and Rajam's ranting and nonstop chatter drove her away to find refuge either at Sushila's or Nagamma's. She only came home at night to sleep, having eaten whatever meager meal was prepared in their homes, foregoing the sumptuous fare Rajam made each day, and unfortunately leaving Rajam alone for the most part, lost in her world of make-believe.

CHAPTER FORTY FOUR

KAMU AND FAMILY
MADRAS – AUGUST 14TH, 1947

THE DAY BEFORE INDEPENDENCE

K amu was too excited, her mood soaring all week, ever since they informed her she would be dancing a solo item as part of the Independence Day function, that too in front of the actor Ranjan. Besides, last week Kunju Periamma, Thatha, and Jayam had decided to visit. After a long time, the house was filled with noise and commotion and she didn't need to run away to Paati's to have fun.

Both Swami and Kunju missed Kamu and Rajam ever since they left for Madras. Kunju had been particularly worried about Rajam's health, knowing there was no one in the house to really take care of her. They wrote to each other weekly, but letters were never enough. The inland letter was filled up before they penned the list of happenings for that week leaving little room for thoughts and feelings. Those were better expressed in person anyway. Kunju never got a break from household chores, and when Swaminathan expressed a desire to be in Madras to celebrate Independence Day, she decided to join him. He had aged considerably, and it just wasn't safe to allow him to travel all by himself. The children had college to attend and couldn't miss classes, but Chithi was in charge and she knew they would be well cared for. There was another reason they were here. Mani had found a job as a salesman in Porur, a suburb of Madras, and on finding a room for rent, he had asked for his wife Jayam to join him. Kunju felt she needed to accompany Jayam and set her up in her new home as every mother should do.

Swaminathan kept walking up to the front door to see if his visitors had arrived. He was expecting all of his friends from Vizhupuram: Velu, Pandyan and Salih. They had arranged a reunion of sorts and Swami had been dressed and ready from five in the morning for a meeting that wouldn't begin until ten. Obviously, all his friends had aged as well and were tied down with family matters. Meeting each other over the years became less of a priority, and though they intensely longed to meet in person, it was often not practical. Velu and Pandyan had been active revolutionaries, arranging anti-British morchas and demonstrations in the south on behalf of the INC. For the last few years they had taken a less proactive role, counseling newcomers in need of guidance. For all four of them, independence from the British was a deep longing, one that they were prepared to lay down their lives for. They knew they had to celebrate this day together and had been planning this since June. At long last, after going back and forth, they decided to celebrate Independence Day together in the city.

The atmosphere in the city was particularly festive. Thousands of people were in the streets, already holding paper tricolor flags and wishing one another *Happy Independence Day,* although that momentous event wouldn't take place until midnight. Every government building in the city was lit up, the illumination particularly impressive against the darkening skies. There was a prediction of thundershowers and a collective hope that this wouldn't dampen the festivity. In preparation for the grand moment, the entire street had been covered in a shamiana decorated with festoons of orange white and green. Tonight no one would sleep. It would be a night of celebration.

Rajam and Kunju had tears in their eyes as they watched the friends greet each other. They knew this day meant something really special to these folk. This was a group of people who had fought for the freedom of the land with a passion. Perhaps never again would this spirit of patriotism rise in the nation against one common enemy. No one could ever understand the depth of feeling and the deep love for the land shared by this band of revolutionaries. Never again in their lifetimes would the longing for Swaraj (self-rule) inspire poetry that tugged at one's heart strings making tears stream down one's cheeks. These were very special people, this a very special time, and they were indeed privileged to live through it.

Swami did not return till evening, and when he did, his friends were with him. They were determined to be together as much as possible. After dinner Sushila and Siva came by with the new baby and Kamu was fully engaged playing with him. It was a really happy time for the family, and it seemed as though Siva and Sushila were much closer.

Yaaru maadri irrukaannu chollave mudiyaliye? said Salih, trying to figure out if the baby resembled mother or father. Baby Ramji was much darker than his parents and his thin lips and hooked nose were clearly apparent, making everyone wonder which combination of genes he had inherited.

Appa maadri daan, Sushila insisted, stating a fact. He did resemble his father. There was no denying his paternity and Rajam wondered if Siva was ever suspicious. When she arrived here, she did think it odd that several times a week she spotted Sushila going somewhere in a blue Pontiac. Many times she wanted to find out where she was off to but never gathered the nerve to question her. Perhaps she had doctor visits. Advocate Panchu was a close family friend, and she didn't feel right doubting Sushila. Rajam could never suspect another of behavior she would never dream of considering. It was morally reprehensible to even entertain thoughts of adultery, therefore committing such acts didn't enter Rajam's cycle of thoughts. So she just left things, not bothering to question or enquire. Besides, given her state of health, she had no time to think of anyone but herself. It was a full time occupation and others, Kamu included, merely danced on the periphery of her thoughts.

Ariyakudi Ramanujar Iyengar was singing, and the strains of *Kamboji Rāgam Thanam Pallavi* wafted into the open courtyard where the family had congregated in a motley of chairs, the unluckier ones on the floor with no backrest but nevertheless listening intently to Swami and his friends share anecdotes from the past.

Hindu astrologers were very unhappy with the choice of August 15th as Independence Day. Apparently neither the 14th nor the 15th were very auspicious. But somehow, as they usually do, they found a loophole in the charts. A 48-minute window which they called the *Abhihjeet Muhurtham* which commenced at 11:51 p.m. Somehow Nehru, the first prime Minister of Independent India, had to finish his speech and ensure that the actual transfer of power took place exactly at midnight at which time the Holy Conch was to blow, frightening away bad spirits and heralding an auspicious birth of a nation protected by the Gods and cocooned within Universal energies.

The nation was bursting in anticipation and pride, which was reflected in every street and every village, an outpouring from their hearts overflowing with feelings of love for land and liberty, irrespective of religious faith. Two hundred years of subjugation, of determined impoverishment of its natural resources and its treasury, but much more importantly, of its cultural identity and tradition, was about to end. Throughout history, Indians had fought foreign invaders and yet maintained an age-old tradition that could never be deleted from its communal memory. They were Indian. Their way of life had been so for five thousand years and was not about to change. They may have learned to speak English, but the foreigners could never eject the Indian out of them, as much as they tried. Never in the country's history had an entire nation united in their common goal of emancipation.

Mundakanni Amman Kovil Street was a microcosm of the nation, alive and buzzing with activity. Radios were blaring, transmitting live from various locations all over India but at 11:00 p.m. that night, every radio in the country would tune in to one station broadcasting Jawaharlal Nehru's speech live from the Council Chamber at the Parliament House in New Delhi.

This is all India radio … That was all they needed to hear for voices to hush. The broadcast was about to start. Almost immediately no other sound other than radio static was audible. People hunkered down in the streets, in their homes, and in public maidāns, not wanting to miss a single minute. The invocation began. Someone was singing the song *Vande Mātaram* written by the great Bengali poet Bankim Chandra Chatterjee. Kamu knew this one and was tempted to sing along, but the mood was somber and it didn't feel right to burst into song and disturb the trance they were in.

"Who's singing? Indira Gandhi?" she asked Rajam.

"No, her name is Sucheta Kripalani. She is Acharya Kripalani's wife," whispered Salih.

Both names meant nothing to Kamu. Her life consisted of school, home, cousins, and fun, and here, burrowed in the deep south far from the hub of revolutionary activity, she remained relatively clueless, barely exposed or affected by the nation's cry for independence. Her life would remain the same regardless of who ruled the nation. Kamu's thoughts centered on looking pretty and dancing for Ranjan tomorrow, but she shook her head knowingly and then proceeded to draw pictures of the flag with a broken twig on the dusty floor. They could hear the Cabinet members officially taking an oath of dedication, and after a hushed silence the historic speech commenced.

Long years ago we made a tryst with destiny, and now the time comes when we shall redeem our pledge, not wholly or in full measure, but very substantially. At the stroke of the midnight hour, when the world sleeps, India will awake to life and freedom. A moment comes, which comes but rarely in history, when we step out from the old to the new, when an age ends, and when the soul of a Nation, long suppressed, finds utterance. It is fitting that at this solemn moment, we take the pledge of dedication to the service of India and her people and to the still larger cause of humanity.

Cries of *Jai Hind* and *Vande Mataram* rang all around them, and then they stood, one nation, one voice. For the first time as free Bharat, they heard and sang *Janaganamana*, the melodic and evocative song written by Rabindranath Tagore, and adopted as the nation's National Anthem. It was indeed a very special day, one of hope and of dreams as they stood together singing the national anthem. Every citizen, rich or poor, would have tears in their eyes, a combination of painful remembrance and visionary imaginings.

They were all in the streets greeting each other, laughing and cheering. The temple doors were open and people were pouring in to give thanks to the gracious God that had granted them the honor of this momentous day. Sweets were distributed and firecrackers lit the sky. The family was going to see the city lights, but for others, fatigue crept in and slowly the streets emptied and everyone found their way indoors, exhilarated yet exhausted from the emotional festivity.

As Swami lay down he couldn't sleep for a long time. He led a sedentary life, and this was too much excitement for him. He thought about all the great martyrs who had died for this cause from Bhagat Singh in the north to Vanchinathan in the south, and he reminisced about his attempt to aid the struggle despite wearing a British uniform. For many, their minds had been kidnapped and brainwashed, leaving them with diminished self-esteem and questionable loyalty. Added to that was so much pain. The searing pain of communal riots and hatred, the partition of the land and the creation of Pakistan.. The nation had suffered, and it would take tremendous effort to begin the healing process. The scars of colonial slavery would take a long time to mend. But people had faith that the leaders were good and were ready to follow the guidance of stalwarts and erudite intellectuals like Nehru, Gandhi and Patel who would lead them from darkness to light. India would awaken to freedom and enterprise, to belief and tolerance, to hope and dignity.

CHAPTER FORTY FIVE

KAMU
MADRAS – INDEPENDENCE DAY

THE DANCE

K amu couldn't stop crying—the shame and foolishness was overwhelming. She hadn't slept very well that night and was very tired, but the excitement of getting ready to dance woke her up bright and early. Siva and Salih had arranged for two cars, and after listening to Nehru's speech, the family crammed into both cars to drive around the city and join in the celebration. In spite of being cramped and sitting on one another, they all enjoyed driving around Egmore and Fort St. George, admiring the beautifully lit Government buildings over which the tricolor flew proudly in place of the Union Jack. Restaurants all over the city were feeding the poor, and temples were brimming with people offering thanks to various deities. They finally made their way to Marina Beach and joined thousands of others by the ocean front enjoying the breeze and the feel of soft, grainy sand beneath their feet. It was well past two in the morning when they finally returned home.

The program was long and tedious. They had built a stage in the center of the street, and people were seated on beautiful *jamakālams* on the floor. The Chief Guest was the actor Ranjan, who was conspicuously ensconced in a chair in front of the stage. Every family on this street had contributed towards the event, which was to be followed by a sumptuous meal. Kamu wore a beautiful orange and green pāvādai and a white *dhāvani;* and in her hair she had arranged garlands of kadambam, a mix of three colors: orange kanakāmbaram, white malli and green *maru*. Each flower had its own unique fragrance and today the scent of the maru leaves was overwhelming. Rajam had stitched the pāvādai herself, attaching a bright green border torn off from an old Kānjeevaram sari to a piece of orange China silk. Kamu's performance was later in the day. She had practiced all week and now waited anxiously for the music to begin. The dance was set to Bharathiyar's *Aaduvome pallu pāduvomen, Ananda sutantiram adaindu vittom enru.* Preempting the eventuality of independence from the British, Bharathiyar wrote this song envisioning the celebration of this elusive event. *Let us dance, let us sing this song, let us dance now that we have achieved glorious freedom.* He died in 1921 before he could see that glorious day, but his inspiring poetry lived on, and set to lilting music was sung and danced to all over south India.

Everyone was clapping, keeping rhythm, and Kamu smiled and danced her best. Somewhere towards the end of the song, in a step where she danced around the central lamp, Kamu, to her utter horror stepped on her *pāvādai*, lost footing and found herself falling. As she fell she noticed the boys in the front row clap and guffaw at her discomfiture. Utterly mortified, she picked herself up and continued dancing, only bursting into tears once she was off stage. Even worse, was after the performance when the boys mimicked and ridiculed her, "Ey Kamu *aaduvome* ..." and they fell to the floor with their legs kicking up into the air. Kamu couldn't figure out if she was angry with herself for falling or with the boys for teasing her. Either way, she felt thoroughly humiliated. Her Big Day was ruined. With her head buried in Kunju's lap, she relived the moment for the umpteenth time.

Idhai pāru, said Kunju attempting to calm her down, *nānga ellārum romba rasichom.* "Why do you worry if the boys laughed? That's what silly boys do. You danced so beautifully and you looked so lovely. *Dhristhi pattirkum.*" Kunju took a little mai from her eye and smeared it across Kamu's tear stained cheek attempting to remove any evil eye that may have caused Kamu to miss her step in the dance.

Swami came into the room and saw Kamu still disconsolate. "Still crying? Yenna Kamu, don't be silly. No one noticed. I tell you everyone in the hall was talking about how well you did. Stop it. Come here, let's get you a nice *laddu.* Come ... a sweet laddu for a sweet girl." But Kamu wanted to be left alone to cry in peace, and she ran from the room preferring to sit outside in the back courtyard, where she could ruminate to her heart's content, undisturbed.

Swami sat down on his easy chair and fanned himself with his *angavastram* but pretty soon realized this top cloth was better suited to wiping the rivulets of sweat trickling down his bare chest.

"Anyone home? Hello!" It sounded like Salih, and Swami raised himself swiftly out of the chair. "I have some surprise visitors for you." Swami was taken aback but beamed from ear to ear on seeing Radhai and Mohan.

"Rajam, Kunju *va ... paaru yaaru vandurkaa!*" he called out to them, knowing they would be pleased to see Mohan healed and healthy.

"I meant to ask you about them yesterday, but with all this excitement of Independence Day, it slipped my mind."

"I didn't want to say anything because I thought I would bring them here as a surprise." Salih's kindness went beyond anything Swami could envisage. He had asked for him to keep Radhai for a few days till they found Saroja, but Salih had kept both Radhai and Mohan for almost five months. Mohan had to be admitted into the hospital as he had two fractured ribs and his fingers were in a bad shape. Thankfully there were no breaks, as setting the bone would have been an expensive proposition, one that Swami could not handle financially. Before leaving Kamalamba's house, Radhai had the sense to take his letters and all the money he had saved, almost two hundred rupees, which he handed over to Swami for Mohan's treatment. Almost all of it was used up within the first month. Mohan came back to their home after two weeks, still weak but able to breathe a lot better. He still needed a lot of help bathing and eating. Sometime later, Kamalamba and Bala decided to drop in. Kunju was in a panic but Chithi, on seeing them closed the door to Mohan's room. Bala looked ragged and bone thin. Kunju's heart went out to her. They had not informed her that both Mohan and Radhai were alive and well. It was time she knew. While Swami kept Kamalamba occupied, Kunju asked Bala to come inside and help bring out the coffee. Nothing could have prepared Bala, for when she saw Mohan; she was so weak and so overcome with emotion, she fainted. Leaving Chithi to attend to her, Kunju went back to the thinnai. She had Kamalamba to think about.

Their reunion was magical, a gift from the divine. Chithi left them alone for five whole minutes then; not wanting to rouse suspicion, she called out informing her it was time to leave. The change in Bala's demeanor was revealing, and even Kamalamba commented that her face looked flushed.

It was a relief when Swami put Mohan on a bus bound for Vizhupuram. Swami had no luck locating Saroja. This was really disappointing for the both of them, but Salih had managed to get Radhai a job at a dance school in Adyar. Through the INC network, he pulled in a favor, and the two of them had been living in Madras for the last few months.

Kunju held Mohan's hands looking at his fingers. The bones had healed, but his fingers were not straight anymore and he could not bend the middle and forefinger in his right hand. "Are you able to play the flute Mohan?" she asked tentatively, knowing what his response would be.

"No Amma, that belongs to my past. But I am really happy to tell you that I have joined school. I am taking classes privately and right now I am in the tenth standard, but in December if I pass the test I can do my PUC. " (Pre-University Course)

"It must be difficult with all the children younger than you," said Rajam.

"Yes, they make fun of me and obviously I can't play with them at break time. But I am studying really hard and maybe I will get be able to skip another grade and finish college in three years."

"And what do want to do after?" enquired Swami.

"I want to build bridges. I will study engineering."

Swami raised his eyebrows in surprise. None of his children had studied more than high school. "Big plans! That sounds so good. God bless you. It's a new beginning, a new opportunity."

"See, I told you bad things happen for a reason. You would never have left Thanjavur or even thought of going to school if you were still playing the flute," Kunju said with a smile.

"But Kunju Amma, I really suffered these past six months. Without Salih Mama's help, we could never have survived. There is no way I can ever thank him enough for what he and all of you did for me and Appa. Perhaps one day I'll pay you all back in some way."

"There is no need to pay back, you only have to pay forward," said Salih. "Allah is kind that he gave me an opportunity to really help someone. What did I do? My wife cooks enough to feed an army and if you didn't eat the food it would have been wasted. What's two more mouths to feed? There is always lots of food in our home, inshallah we are blessed."

"And what of Saroja?" asked Swami, sad that he had failed them.

"The vocalist in our group recognized her picture. He said she always comes to all the dance recitals held in December. We are very hopeful we will see her in one of them," replied Radhai, still optimistic.

"Keep your hopes up. I'm sure you will find her." Kunju added. While the others began talking about last night's speech, Mohan came up to Kunju and Rajam. "Kunju Amma, how is Bala?" he enquired, his voice low although there was no one here who didn't know about their forbidden relationship.

"I haven't seen her in a while but when I go back I will surely tell her I saw you."

Mohan slipped a folded envelope into her hands. "I have a letter. Could you give that to her? She can read a little, but you may have to read it to her. I hope you don't mind. It's just that I can't send a regular letter in the mail." Kunju assured him that she would, promising to visit soon.

Kamu heard the visitors leaving, but she was still sulking, so she didn't want to come out and meet them. After the dance, Ranjan had given her a hug and presented her with a book and a bouquet of flowers. She was still so upset when she returned home from the dance that she had thrown the flowers in a corner. Normally, Kamu simply loved all flowers. She never spent a waking moment without flowers in her hair. Clearly she couldn't let them rot in the corner and went back to retrieve them.

Carefully she unwrapped the cellophane paper and looked for scissors and a vase. Filling it to the brim she cut each flower with care, arranging them in concentric circles so each bloom was clearly visible and then stepped back to admire her handiwork. One flower, a red rose, was awkwardly sticking out from the top. On impulse she cut it and then using two bobby pins she fastened it behind her ear.

It looked perfect and the fragrance was deliciously strong. Each petal was pristine and faultless almost as if it were made from a porcelain mold. She reapplied mai to her eyes and rubbed fresh talcum powder on her face. Her lips pouting and her eyes half closed, she romanced the mirror, imagining she was a film star, fair and beautiful. Kamu loved what she saw and forgetting that she was supposed to be sulking, smiled mysteriously into the mirror.

I love it. From now on this will be my signature ... a red rose!

SECTION-III
1947-1952

CHAPTER FORTY SIX

MAHADEVAN
CALCUTTA – SEPTEMBER 1947

LAURELS FOR A BROWN SAHIB

Mahadevan rubbed his fingers over the gold CIE medal, which he had received in January of '41. The Viceroy had presented it to him in a grand ceremony in New Delhi. The bright red and green enamel work depicted a flower, which kind he had no idea, but the crown and insignia shone elegantly. He needed to hold onto this, a legacy of his years of service for the British. The suit he had tailored in a military style didn't fit him anymore, at least not around the middle. It still hung in the closet, dark blue with gold embroidery around the collar and sleeves, and nine shiny, brass buttons down the front. Mahadevan walked to his room to search for the sword and cord that went with it. The sword was still at the back of the steel almirah, but the cord was long gone. With so many moves, God knows where it lay now. He returned to the study to look for the parchment from George the Sixth, ordaining him as Additional Companion of "Our most eminent Order of the Indian empire." He needed to keep that safe and ensure it didn't land up in the pile of papers for disposal. Perhaps one day his grandchildren would look at it and remember his day of honor. With care, he rolled up the certificate and tied it with a red ribbon, placing it in the carton half packed with files for moving.

The children had not accompanied him to the service, which he had attended with Dharmu. Right after the Grand Ceremony, they went to a photo studio in Connaught place and took a memorable picture with him proudly displaying the medal, dressed in full military regalia, sword and all. Dharmu had worn a beautiful peach georgette sari with a bright silver border and looked quite regal. Unfortunately, the dull colors in the photo hardly matched the brilliant hues locked in his memory. Perhaps one day someone would develop cheaper technology for colored pictures which would really bring it all to life. He was truly honored to receive the award, a small token of appreciation for all his years of faithful service.

Independence ended up being a solemn affair. Many of his colleagues went to Delhi to witness the actual transfer of power, but Mahadevan was quite happy celebrating the event in Calcutta. The recent riots and Vaithee and Meera's trauma had left a bitter taste in his mouth. He was in no mood to attend all the ceremonies and celebrations and turned down every invitation much to Dharmu's chagrin. The only ceremony he attended was the actual hoisting of the tricolor. That too required tremendous self-effort; he just was not in the mood. Soon after, he was informed he would take on the post of Chairman of the Calcutta Port Trust. The family would be moving to a grand mansion in Portland Park by the Alipore Majherhat Bridge. The house had ten bedrooms, five garages, a dozen servant's quarters and two kitchens. They didn't really need all that space, and it was quite astounding what the British Raj offered their employees overseas. Every home was a mansion, and even the most junior officer lived in regal splendor. Most British officers came from humble beginnings and couldn't boast of a home even a third this size back home but here, for the last two hundred years they lorded over the natives, living lavish, pseudo-millionaire lives. Well ... Mahadevan was about to enjoy that pseudo-millionaire life although he wasn't sure what changes the future held. Would he have five cars in the garages or a dozen servants? The economy was in shambles, what with the recent famine. Besides, Nehru's plans of closing down the economy and planning a financial structure that was semi-socialist had everyone worried. How would it feel to serve the country run by Indians? Would the earlier perks he enjoyed be revoked? Would the bureaucracy be free from petty politics? So many questions were buzzing in his mind, destroying his motivation to work. Perhaps it was time to retire, but Mahadevan didn't want to act hastily. He had to think of his future and ensure that his pension was not affected in any way.

Mahadevan placed the medal back in the blue velvet container and sat down at his desk. He wasn't really sure how he felt, but he realized he was troubled. For more than forty years he had worked as a civil servant loyal to the crown, and his allegiance to the British astonished him. The advent of independence resulted in an upsurge of many conflicting emotions within him, and it was unpleasant and disconcerting because he was customarily clear thinking, and was usually not swayed by his emotions. He wasn't quite sure if he felt any national pride with the British leaving India. As soon as that thought popped into his mind, he felt guilt and shame, for every citizen in this land longed to be free from the British. Why was he feeling this sense of doom on their departure? For so many years, by adapting to British ways, something within him remained comfortable and content. He loved his Johnny Walker Red label and Yardley talcum powder and hated bidding farewell to them in addition to the other host of British goods the family had used and enjoyed for so many years now. How foolish to give so much importance to trivia! After all, whiskey and talcum powder didn't compensate for deliberate depletion of the country's national resources. Even so, he could not shake off the melancholia that had attacked him like a slow and painful virus.

Slowly but deliberately, he had become a colonial slave. Somewhere deep within him was an acceptance of his inferior status and an admiration for the white skinned. This didn't happen overnight. Over time they had chipped away at his confidence and placed themselves at the pinnacle of the caste system. The pride he took at being Brahmin paled in significance to being English. Speaking the language, hobnobbing with British officers, being included in the inner circle, had over time become paramount for his self-esteem. Every time he was insulted or humiliated by his British superiors, he silenced that little voice within him, muffling the protest. He could think of a dozen times he stood on the brink of throwing it all away and joining the fight for freedom, but the cowardice within him triumphed each time, never allowing him to act on his bold impulses. *Yes, I am a second-class citizen in my own country.* He could never allow that thought to manifest and take root within him because pandering to the British, and a deep need for acceptance by them, took precedence. Intellectually he knew he was wrong, but this was an intuitive choice he made without his own volition, and now here he was, wondering if the new India cabinet of ministers was good enough for him. He had turned into an intellectual snob! That was appalling! He cringed inwardly at this consideration.

For the first time in his life he reflected on the values that laid the foundation for his work ethic and wondered how he would adapt to the new way. Change was imminent, and he was the quasi-white-skinned-Britisher looking down on natives.

What were his choices? He could either remain utterly miserable working for those he believed were a cut below his caliber or he could adapt. Somehow the second choice was the prudent one. After all, transforming into a British *bumsucker* was his way of surviving within the system, and it had worked well for him. He just needed to change his mindset. Work was work. What difference did it make whom he reported to? He would silence the superiority dialogue in his head and move on. It was time for a reality check. The British had left. It had been good for him while it lasted, and now, he needed to ensure his mind was steady. No more audience to those ugly voices that longed for the past and were scared for the future. Just like Appanshayal always told him, he would bring it all back to the present. Now, now, now!

That was all he had. And it wasn't so bad. A great job, an accomplished wife, and three healthy children. Life was good. The mental shackles of colonial slavery needed to be released. Mahadevan sat at his desk and wrote three liberating words.

I am free.

CHAPTER FORTY SEVEN

VAITHEE AND MEERA
SEPTEMBER 1947

THE AFTERMATH

Vaithee was tense. The rocking motion of the train had lulled Meera to sleep, but any moment now the nightmare would begin, and his body was on high alert to silence and comfort her. He didn't want to cause any commotion on the train. A year had passed since that horrible night, and still the nightmares wouldn't subside. Meera had been affected far more deeply than he had envisaged. It was a miracle they had escaped with their lives, and he was so thankful to be alive and come home to the children, but for Meera, the nightmare never ended. For the first several weeks she sat in the bathroom rubbing and cleaning herself, yet was unable to rid herself from the stench and stain of the brutal assault. She wailed and moaned continually and for months now couldn't sleep peacefully. Which meant Vaithee didn't sleep much either. At first the people around them had accepted her wailing and crying with a lot of compassion, but as time went by the servants were tired of it and made their displeasure evident. They were really blessed not to be out on the streets even though Meera was in no mental condition to work. The Ayyars were very kind, and had given Vaithee more time till he figured out what to do with his life. Now he was sure he had outlived his welcome in the city, and for sure in the Ayyar household.

For the first week after the riots, he drove around in an ambulance provided by the Anushilan group and picked up the injured from all corners of the city, shuttling them to the Municipal hospital for treatment. Each time he went out, he never knew what they would encounter. The first two days were the worst, as they had to cut down the men lynched and strung up on trees all over the city. It was difficult work that made his resentment of Muslims ferment and boil over. The city stank of death and destruction almost as if it were a war zone. For the most part it was a war, where innocent lives were taken in a flame of insanity.

On the third day they had no driver, so he asked if Kandu baba would be willing to drive the ambulance just for this day. Mahadevan was not happy, and Dharmu refused outright, but Kandu wanted to help. All of his friends were volunteering in camps that had sprouted in every neighborhood, providing the homeless and injured with food and medicines. Dharmu was absolutely firm in her decision not to permit Kandu, but he prevailed on his father's softer side and drove the ambulance, but only for half a day. As they turned into a gully near Kalighat, they saw a man across the street seated unconscious under a lamp post. Vaithee asked Kandu to stop the ambulance so he could take a closer look. He was definitely injured, evidenced by the blood all over his shirt. Before Vaithee could reach him, a passerby, a Muslim, judging by his cap and lungi, looked at him and then lifted the man's head clean off and placed it back. Kandu was at the wheel when the man indicated to him with a quick flick of his hand that the victim's head had been severed.

Kandu couldn't breathe. Never in his life had he witnessed anything so terrifying. He got out of the car and retched violently on the side of the road. His whole body was trembling, and Vaithee didn't know how to console him. Now Dharmu would certainly kick them out once they heard of this horrible incident. There was a man selling coconut water by the street corner and Vaithee ran and bought him one. *Daab* was good for the stomach and would cool him off. Right now he looked a mess. For several days after, Kandu could barely function, and Vaithee felt guilty about having exposed him to such horror.

Na na āmāke chede daao ... aaah ... aah! Meera's screams shocked him back, and he held her, rocking her gently and comforting her.

"*Shob theek aache,* everything is alright ... it's me ... I'm here ... there's nothing to worry about ... shh ... calm down, it's fine ..." but Meera sobbed heartrendingly and Vaithee sat with her rocking her gently. The children awakened as well and stared at her blankly. "When will Ma become okay?" his son Prashant murmured, half asleep.

"Soon ... soon ... we have to be kind to her. Go to sleep." Words he had repeated a million times this year. Meera had not been much of a mother this past year. In fact, she had not been much of anything. She was literally a memory of a human. Who knew what thoughts were flickering through her mind. She sat in the corner of her room staring into space, rocking back and forth. The only time she spoke was in the grip of a nightmare. Vaithee had no idea how to deal with her. He could not leave her alone for a long time, but if he didn't work there would be no way to live. Daytime was better than nights. He had found a job as a pharmacy assistant, but made sure he was home before dark, as that's when the demons came.

Independence Day was an anticlimactic let down. For the last decade Vaithee had dedicated himself to the cause of freedom, working tirelessly, doing the bidding of the leaders in his group, and now, when the day had finally arrived, his personal life was in shambles. The cause of freedom had taken a heavy toll on his psyche, and Meera? She was just a mess. It was not worth it. Nothing was worth losing familial harmony. Right now with Meera so ill, he had to be everything for the children. She simply stared at them blankly and was incapable of even giving them a glass of water. Pushkin, their daughter, was terrified the first few times Meera screamed in her sleep, unable to understand what happened to her mother who was perfectly sane just two days ago. But over time, she just turned to the other side, covered her ears with a pillow, and fell back to sleep. Everyone was losing interest in Meera. But Vaithee couldn't. He had to do something. He couldn't stay here forever. He had to go back home.

When he finally wrote to his parents, it was after exhausting every other option. He had no idea if his parents were still alive or if they even lived in the same house. But he was drained from sleepless nights and worry, knowing he had asked Ayyar Saab for time till Independence. That time had come and he had to move now. When he received a letter back from his father, he wept in relief. They still lived in Vizhupuram and had never given up hope of finding Vaithee. They couldn't wait for him to return home with his family. Vaithee wrote another letter to his father pouring his heart out. He talked about his involvement in the freedom struggle without offering too many details. He didn't speak about Meera's rape, which was better explained in person. He only said she was in a bad way because their basti had been burned and attacked during the riots and that he needed to return home because he couldn't manage. He knew the real reason though. He was tired of running and longed to be home. He longed for the smell of earth with the first rain, the feel of running in paddy and cornfields, the sight of temples and village fairs, and most of all for the sound of his native tongue, Tamil. When he informed Ayyar Saab about his plans, that was his first question: "How will Meera cope with Tamil?" to which Vaithee replied, "I coped with Bengali."

As Vaithee held Meera, he felt deeply grateful to Nandu. If not for the young assassin's bravery, she would not be alive, and neither would he. He swore to himself to keep Nandu's memory alive. Perhaps he would look for his family and give them some money or something in Nandu's memory.

There was so much healing to be done, so much pain to be released, a new life to be forged, and so many new ties to be nurtured. Vaithee ran his hand gently through Meera's hair, "Everything will be alright," he whispered. But he was unsure if he was reassuring her or himself.

CHAPTER FORTY EIGHT

KANDU
CALCUTTA – DECEMBER 1947

HANGING OUT WITH FRIENDS

Kandu slammed shut the door of his Dodge, slung his jacket over one shoulder, and sauntered into the house, pausing to throw the car keys at Govindhan, who deftly caught it.

Aah dekha Kandu baba, *giraaya nahin.* This was a game they played ever since Kandu was licensed to drive. *Kya lena* Kandu baba, *chai ya coffee?*

Ek gilass whiskey ho jai. Kandu was joking of course, again this conversation a daily recurrence.

Whiskey piskey ham to nahin de sakta, chai bolo ya coffee ha.

But Kandu wasn't in the mood for anything. It was too early in the afternoon. He was meeting his friends later that evening. First a drive to Diamond Harbor with the car top down and the wind in everyone's hair followed by a couple of drinks and then back to dinner at Trincas on Park Street. Daddy wasn't home yet, and there was plenty of time to fill up his hip flask. It was Kandu's turn to provide the drinks. They were all underage and would not be served in the restaurant, so it was always wise to get pumped up somewhere else to ensure a bright and raucous evening. Kandu liked to drink but never ever drank more than two pegs. Witnessing his parents' slavery to drink and suffering the humiliation of the bearers and drivers lugging them to bed was warning enough. The last thing he wanted was for the bearers to carry *him* home. He was so large and muscular now that no one would be able to lift him. They would have to leave him to sober up in the car. Saturday evenings had always been booze nights for his parents for as long as he could remember, and he hated waking up on their return. But now, since Independence, he was glad to note the parties had slowed down. No more flowing alcohol at British residences, just quiet evenings with friends, which meant both parents remained sober and in control, home by nine p.m. instead of midnight. No, he never worried about getting drunk. He knew that would never ever happen. He had joined St. Xavier's college this year and was doing his B Sc. in Chemistry. Naturally, he was hanging out with a lot of new fellows. Tucky was still his closest buddy, but recently he had been hanging out with Mickey a lot. Mickey too liked to drink; he was great when sober and even greater when drunk, but Kandu always stopped him after his sixth.

After a quick shower, he changed into white linen pants and a sky blue shirt, both a trifle loose. Somehow tailors here assumed your waist was as big as your shoulders. Kandu's latest fad was weight lifting, and with 46-inch shoulders, his tailor simply couldn't taper the shirt enough to fit snugly over his waist. The style anyhow was pleated linen pants and loose shirts, so Kandu never complained. He knew he looked dashing no matter what he wore. A broad forehead, large, heavy lidded eyes, an aquiline nose and a superbly muscled body. All six feet of him were an exquisite example of manhood. At least he thought so! A dash of Brylcreem and a smooth run with the comb and he was ready for action. Hearing the front door creak, he knew his friends had arrived. It was six o'clock and dark already.

"Mummy," he yelled, hoping she was in. She played bridge on Fridays and sometimes the game delayed her.

"I'm here in the verandah," came the call back. Kandu popped his head in, "I'm off," he said, saluting her. Dharmu put down the magazine she was reading and eyed him over her glasses. "Again? What time will you be back?"

"By eleven latest," he replied over his shoulder hoping to slip away before she lined up something for him to do.

"Are you driving?"

"Yes and I'm not taking the driver with me." Kandu had reached the stairs, but could hear her still. "Okay okay, don't be too late. We are dining with the Venkatachars, but it will be an early evening." Kandu felt relieved. The Venkatachars were vegetarians and teetotalers, so both Mummy and Daddy would return home sober and fresh.

Tucky was stridently singing *Amapola,* a popular song, and was completely off tune. Thank heavens the breeze was strong and carried the sound of his voice away.

"Bugger, you haven't even had one drink and you're already singing off key," remarked Dilip Sarkar, who hailed from a very well-known family, owners of the famous New Theatres in Calcutta. Knowing how much his mother Dharmu loved movies, he handed over to Kandu three tickets for a new release; *Ramer Sumati.*

"Now I'll sing the same song after a drink and watch, I'll be completely *on* key." replied Tucky, going full throated into the chorus. *Amapola ... amapola....*

Mickey joined in, *Amma polaam, Appa polaam, Thatha polaam Paati polaam.* Kandu and Mickey were hysterical, the only ones in the car who understood

Tamil. They shouldn't really have been laughing because what Mickey said could literally be translated as "mother and father can go" but they could also "go" as in dying. It was so corny they laughed anyway.

"Hey! What are you saying? Calling me a *maadarchot*? Don't think I don't know Tamil. I understand Amma you buggers … cursing at me in Tamil?" protested Tucky.

"Relax, all he was saying is mother can go, father can go, etc. etc. Nothing insulting here," said Kandu lighting his third cigarette.

They reached Diamond Harbor and parked by the water, admiring the stars. It was quiet, and no one would disturb them. Kandu stubbed out his cigarette out and opened the trunk to retrieve the glasses and soda. Tucky lumbered out, his jutting lower jaw thrusting forward even more as he stretched and yawned noisily. "Now all we need is a couple of babes."

"No babes," said Kandu. "They add tension to an otherwise peaceful evening."

"What's wrong with you man? Do you like men?"

"Yes," said Kandu lunging for him and pretending to kiss him chased after Tucky, circling twice around the car.

"Seriously man," said Tucky, a little out of breath. "If I had your looks and money I'd have a different babe every day of the week. It's so wasted on you."

"Waste of time. I couldn't be bothered." Actually Kandu was bothered. Ever since the incident with Rani Aunty, he had lost faith in women. Her infidelity had slashed his heart and felt like a personal betrayal. After that, whenever he encountered a modern girl in stylish western dress, she automatically reminded him of Rani, causing him to withdraw into himself. Outwardly he appeared flamboyant, and for the most part he was—he drank and smoked—but when it came to girls, he never let down his guard. It didn't help that girls at the club threw themselves at him. He would talk to them politely, but nothing more. Kandu saw most things as black or white: men were either faithful or unfaithful, and he belonged to the first category. He had adopted his grandfather's and Appanshayal's strict ideals and values, which made him even more admirable to the world at large. His friends, on the other hand, had a weakness for girls, and some even visited prostitutes.

"So what do you want? A good south Indian girl from the village who does pooja to you each morning?" Tucky was unrelenting.

"Okay, why must you go to the other extreme? I just want a good girl. The girl I show interest in is the one I'll marry. Why can't you understand that? I can't play around."

"That Sheela has been eyeing you—at least do a practice run with her."

"That's disgusting! Man … she annoys me. She's at the club whenever I go and corners me every time," said Kandu shaking his head in distaste.

"Have you ever seen him with Sheela? He keeps stepping back, and she moves forward one pace, and he steps back again. It's hilarious!" chuckled Tucky. "You're a crazy bloke, that's all I can say. Just don't see your opportunities. Would she settle for me?"

"Take her … please, I'm tired of her waylaying me. It's even more awkward because our families are friends."

As Kandu drove back after dropping off the others, at a traffic light, a young boy came up to him selling flowers. There were bunches of multicolored dahlias, white chrysanthemums, but Kandu's eye was drawn to the bouquet of roses. He reached into his pocket for change and then threw the bouquet he just bought into the back seat.

It was past eleven when he drove past the gates, the crunch of gravel under his tires sounding incredibly loud in the stillness of the night. He opened the back door and reached for his sweater and noticed that one single rose was wrenched out of the bouquet and stuck to it. He paused to carefully disentangle it. What an incredible bloom! And the fragrance … just heavenly.

He looked at it under the moonlight and a flash of something momentarily crossed his mind. He couldn't fully grasp the thought, but the sensation it created was disconcerting. He didn't understand why he felt this sense of anticipation whenever he saw a red rose. Perhaps it was nothing.

After all, that's all it was … *A red rose.*

CHAPTER FORTY NINE

PARTHA
BOMBAY – MARCH 1948

LONGING FOR CHANGE

Partha sincerely believed that gaining independence from the British had changed his luck. After Rajam left, he'd been very despondent. For some unfathomable reason, his boss seemed fixated on giving him a hard time and each day hauled him up for some trifling error. It was remarkable how he managed to find a new blunder every day and took great pleasure at belittling him in front of his coworkers. It made Partha so annoyed he could not think clearly; all he could think of was how satisfying it would be to smash his boss's head. Savarkar, his supervisor, was a bald, portly, spectacled Maharashtrian who belonged to the right wing RSS—Rashtriya Sevak Sangh—a blossoming political party determined to promote Hinduism at all costs. Savarkar hated those he referred to as *Madrasis*, i.e. anyone hailing from the south of the country. According to him, they were like vermin, flooding the city and taking all the jobs that should have otherwise gone to good, God-fearing Maharashtrians. More than Madrasis, he hated Muslims and ranted each day about Gandhi being a Muslim bumsucker and how Mohammad Ali Road should be bombed. Partha thanked his lucky stars that he wasn't a Tamil Muslim from Madras! Being Hindu redeemed him to some extent in his boss's eyes. In many ways he felt bad for the man. He must be deeply unhappy with a wife that took the broom to him every time he made a false move. Tigers in the office usually were mice at home. They flexed their muscles where they knew they could wield power. Savarkar's poor, demented mind must have been so filled with frustration, he needed to pick on others to affirm his self-worth.

Partha was least interested in politics and even less interested in religion. All he wanted was a secure job so he could bring Rajam and Kamu to live with him again. It was really lonely living with Thambu. Since Rajam decided to leave, Thambu's wife Vaalam had moved permanently in, and on most nights,

Partha found himself on a bedroll in the corridor with a host of others in similar circumstances.

Bombay didn't have the best weather, and Partha felt he slept better outside than indoors. It was just the injustice of paying for a room and sleeping outside that he resented. With work being so stressful and nothing really to come home to, he really longed for a break. In addition, Vaalam's cooking was no patch on Rajam's expertise. Rajam could take water and make it taste like nectar. She certainly had *kaimanam*. Her rasam was quite unlike anything he had ever tasted. Even his mother's rasam paled in comparison to Rajam's. A simple meal with beans *paruppu ushili* and *aloo orappu* curry became a treat for the palate.

Quite by chance, a few months earlier, he met an old friend, Rama Iyer, at VT station. Rama lived in Calcutta now and ran a very profitable hotel in one of Calcutta's popular neighborhoods on Rash Behari Avenue. Partha invited him home, and on the train ride he talked about how unhappy he was with his current job. Rama listened to his woes patiently, not offering any suggestions then, but a week later, he sent Partha a letter saying that some boarders at his hotel worked for a Swedish company called Geigy, that was hiring salesmen. Partha applied immediately, and the following week took a train to Calcutta for the interview. He was hired right away and his train ride back to Bombay was the best ever. He felt light and free. Now he could go back and spit in Savarkar's face and ask him to shove his RSS up an appropriate orifice.

There was not much to pack, just a suitcase of clothes. All the vessels and bedding belonged to Thambu. He wrote to Rajam in utter glee. He could not ask them to join him just yet. He needed to settle down and ensure the employment was permanent before asking them to take the long train ride north. Right now he was on probation for three months. From Howrah he made his way to Rash Behari Avenue, where Rama was delighted to see him and gave him one of his best rooms on the second floor, overlooking the back. Partha was overjoyed because, finally, he had a room to himself with an attached bathroom, which he didn't need to share with a million others. After a hot bath, he went down to the restaurant for a delicious meal served traditionally on a banana leaf. It was incredible! A piece of Tamil Nadu right in the heart of Calcutta.

Most of the people lodging in the hotel were long-staying customers who had traveling jobs and found it convenient to crash here in between trips. His office was near Dalhousie, and it was an easy tram ride. For the next six months he would be traveling extensively and he didn't want Rajam to arrive in Calcutta and feel isolated. After six months he was to be stationed at the head office, needing to travel only for about a week a month. It would have been much more convenient for them to come in January after the completion of the school year, and Rajam was really disappointed that he had moved their arrival date to March. Her letters demonstrated her excitement. Apparently Kamu asked her each day when she was going to see Appa again. Partha felt really gloomy when he thought of Kamu. She must have grown up considerably; she was almost thirteen years old. Partha was unable to go home when Kamu matured. Rajam didn't have the ceremony that was customary, keeping the good news confined to family members with a small service at home.

Partha felt badly that he had spent such little time watching his daughter grow up. But life had been unpredictable with jobs so hard to find. At least for the couple of years they lived in Poona, he'd been able to spend quality time with her. He swore to himself that this would be the last time. He was not going to send her away again. In a few years she would marry, and he wanted to be with her for as long as possible.

For six months Partha travelled along with other salesman all over the eastern states, mainly in Orissa, Bengal and Assam. Through Rama Iyer he met a few of his Tamil brethren, but as he traveled all the time such meetings were sporadic. Finally, last month, he learned his beat would be confined to Bengal and that's when he wrote to Rajam asking her to buy her train tickets.

Rajam was excited to move to a new place. Her life in Madras had been lonely. Kamu was always occupied with school and music classes and spent all her free time playing with friends and cousins, only returning home for dinner. By December Rajam sold all her furniture and packed her silver and jewelry in a large cabin trunk. The other trunk was already half full with their clothes. Even though they planned to leave in March, she wanted to be ready to leave at a moment's notice. They had shifted to Sushila's for the last couple of months, which was perfect for Kamu, who loved playing with the baby.

The train ride seemed interminably long as a result of their eagerness and anxiety to reach Calcutta and be a family again. They had booked a coupé so they could lock the door at night and wouldn't have to worry about someone creeping in and stealing their luggage. Nagamma would have disapproved thoroughly that they didn't carry home-cooked food with them, but both Rajam and Kamu enjoyed the food on the train, and every station on the way was a chance for more refreshment. Tea, coffee, samosas, vadas; the list of available food was endless. For lunch and dinner they shared a veg plate, eating the dal, rice and vegetables with a spoon! They met one interesting couple who lived in Calcutta and were happy for the company for a few hours.

On the other end, Partha was equally anxious for their arrival. He was irritated with everything that delayed him. He had rented a taxicab, but the traffic was slow-moving because of some commotion ahead. Someone had hit a cow and the road was blocked for fifteen minutes. He wished he had stopped to buy flowers, but that would have delayed things further. As the train pulled into the platform Partha looked into every passing window to see if he could spot them.

Then he saw her descend from the carriage. She was not wearing a pāvādai dhāvani as he expected but was in a lovely orange and white cotton sari. His Kamu all grown up and wearing a sari. She was looking all around searching for him, and it struck him hard that Kamu was not a child anymore—she was a young woman. Her hair was braided, and she had an orange rose behind one ear, a trifle wilted but nevertheless making her look divine. In many ways she resembled Rajam, but her bone structure was all his. She was a perfect mix combining the best of each parent.

Partha walked up to her, and her anxious eyes melted into the loveliest smile. "Appa!" she exclaimed. Partha held her at arm's length admiring her. His daughter … his creation! He took in everything from her flawless, pearly complexion to her shapely, dark eyebrows, her narrow forehead and almond shaped eyes, from the small gold drops in her ears to the simple gold chain around her swanlike neck. She was dressed like an adult, but there was a childlike innocence that sprung from her bright, animated eyes. Partha's heart burst with pride, admiration and love.

Then he did what he had never done before. He planted a kiss on her forehead, and held her tight. Kamu held him close as well. "I love you too Appa," she whispered.

CHAPTER FIFTY

KUNJU
THANJAVUR – MAY 1948

THE FUTURE LOOKS HOPEFUL

By the time she finished reading the letter, her hands were shivering in excitement. She ran out into the thinnai where Swami lay half sleep in his easy chair. *Kaduchurthu Appa, Venkat ku velai kaduchurthu!*

Swami half opened one eye unable to make sense of her outburst. *Yaaru … yenna?* he muttered sleepily, completely disoriented.

"Venkat … he got the job with the shipping company. If I tell you his starting salary you will die," exclaimed Kunju.

"Then don't," said Swami, "I'm not ready to go yet."

"Of course I didn't mean it like that. But do you see what this means? It means we can close this household and live with him."

"All of us? Poor boy. I hardly think he will be able to keep us all. This is a huge house and we are lucky to fit so many people. We can't all land up with Venkat. It would be too much of a burden."

Kunju knew he was right. Many changes had taken place in her life, mostly involving her children. Lalitha, her oldest daughter, had met a boy in college and wanted to marry him. He was Tamil, but not from their caste, and the idea of protest died as soon as the groom's family offered to pay for the wedding. The marriage took place in a large hall rented for the occasion, and all of their relatives and friends attended. All Kunju's daughters were married now, and a huge burden had lifted off her shoulders. Venkat, Kunju's oldest son had found a job at the Cochin shipyard after graduating from college, but for the past few months wanted to better his employment prospects. Shipping companies paid very well, and some friends there recommended him for a desk position. Only Visu and Natarajan remained here, and life was easier with fewer mouths to feed. For so many years she struggled to make ends meet. What started in her head as a random idea became a way for her to earn a little money. She had started teaching young children to play the harmonium. At first, she only had three students, but word spread, and pretty soon there were more than a dozen students. It didn't transform her life, but at least it helped to buy an extra kilo of sugar. The supply of provisions from Kamalamba had dwindled over the past year, and Kunju hadn't received a gift from her in six months. The last time they spoke, Kamalamba said that her nephew Muthu had been arrested for roughing up a client. The Mirāzdār wasted no time in filing a complaint and Muthu was in prison, leaving Kamalamba alone to deal with her household without any male help. There was no one now to force the Mirāzdārs to pay, and she was in a bad situation herself. One time when Kunju met her, she talked to her about starting a school of dance, but as the original suggestion had come from Radhai, who was persona non grata, Kamalamba refused to act on it, although she knew the time had come to disband the old household and let her girls go free. The bill banning prostitution had been passed in Parliament, though the girls had no idea what it meant for them. One time, the police had the gall to raid their home and take the girls into custody. What a shame! They knew very well that this was no brothel, yet they enjoyed treating the girls badly and shaming Kamalamba, as if she were a cheap Madam. The grand style in which Kamalamba had been living all these years was slowly slipping away.

Kunju received and delivered Mohan's letters, and for the most part, Bala was able to read them. Last December, Radhai spotted his sister Saroja in a dance recital and it was an emotional reunion. He told her about Bala and her condition and asked for her help, but Saroja was in a bind. She had children by Raja Varman and didn't know what he would say if she brought up the topic of rescuing Bala. Radhai had been so sure she would instantly come to their aid, he couldn't believe his ears when she said she needed to think. After all, Bala was also Raja's child, and he had married a prostitute himself, so what was the terrible dilemma? He didn't want Bala to know this, as she would be terribly hurt, and told Kunju only in confidence. Six months had passed and they hadn't heard from Saroja. Mohan still needed to finish school, and they didn't have the money for college unless some miracle took place. He couldn't marry Bala just yet, but they needed to do something soon. Bala was getting increasingly despondent, and he feared she may be tempted to end her life. Kunju had just received another letter from Mohan and needed to deliver it. Perhaps she would stop by later that afternoon.

Kunju opened the sugar jar and poured out a half cup of sugar. She roasted the rava and then on impulse poured out the rest of the sugar. Today she would make *rava kesari* the way it was supposed to be prepared, with lots of sugar, ghee, cashews, and raisins. Good news like this was an elusive event in their family, but this year, the gods had been kind. Lalitha got married, Venkat had a job, and Visu would graduate by December and hopefully find a job. Mani had held onto his job, and her daughter Jayam was pregnant. Both Chithi and Swami had aged, and though Swami looked feeble, Chithi was still as strong as a horse. She was reed thin but still quick on her feet. Kunju had no idea how old she was, probably younger than Swami, but hard work had made her body resilient to any disease. She ate a good meal only once a day, preferring to drink only a glass of watered-down buttermilk at night, and could remember details about people and events that surprised Kunju. She would send Chithi to stay with Mani and Jayam to help with the delivery. Chithi had already delivered over twenty babies and was the perfect person to care for Jayam. Kunju had to make some plans soon. Once Visu graduated, she could move with her father and her youngest, Natarajan, to Venkat's. Swami was becoming frailer, and things were getting too expensive in Thanjavur. It was time for change.

Kunju took a small portion of the kesari and decided to visit Kamalamba. When she reached the house, she was surprised to find it in darkness. Normally, they had lights blazing from every window, making the bright, blue living room shine like the evening sky. She knocked tentatively on the door and Vyjayanthi came out to receive her. Kunju was happy that Kamalamba was out. She could deliver the letter to Bala without any major subterfuge. Bala embraced her and on receiving the letter proceeded to tear it open, hungrily reading each word. As Kunju watched, it broke her heart. She was as old as her daughters, but her fate was so rough. She prayed the letter had some good news for her. "What does Mohan say? Did he hear back from Saroja?"

"Yes Kunju Mami, there's good news and bad. Saroja Ma and her husband met with a motor car accident, and for the last few months she has been recuperating from broken ribs and legs. Her husband was in a coma for several weeks because of a head injury but is recovering now. See? I knew she wasn't a bad person. I was confident she would want me to join them as soon as she heard about me."

"So what's the good news?" urged Kunju.

"She wants me to go and live with her!" Kunju and Bala hugged each other in sheer delight. Kunju was overjoyed, but knew things were going to be difficult. With Bala gone Kamalamba would be in dire straits, as the other two girls who remained with her didn't have regular patrons. Yet, this was Bala's chance to escape. "So have they said when and how you can go?"

"No, only that I should wait for the next letter for detailed instructions on what to do."

"You have never traveled alone. How will you go?"

Bala was silent. Despite everything she loved Kamalamba Amma. She was the only mother Bala had ever known, and for the most part was kind and loving. The only time Bala could recall Kamalamba being harsh was when she discovered her and Mohan together. This year had been especially hard for Amma. She never entertained any talk about Radhai, but Bala knew she really missed his calm presence. It was what anchored her life in this house. Most of her musicians had left for Salem and Madras, knowing there was no future here in Thanjavur. Only the mridangam player remained, and he was turning deaf. Kamalamba had no one here to really help secure and maintain rich patrons. The girls had heard about the new bill and would have run away if they could, but being illiterate with no ties to any place else, they were doomed to remain here with Kamalamba. But it wasn't the same for Bala. She needed to pluck up the courage to just break the ties and leave without bidding farewell to Kamalamba. If she knew where Bala was going, she would most certainly hunt her down just so Saroja didn't get to keep her. This was going to be hard, and Bala and Kunju needed to keep this completely under wraps, not sharing a word with the other girls.

"Today is the day for good things to happen. Venkat got a job in a big company and now your mother is ready to keep you. I will sleep very well tonight, Bala. By December, we will move from Thanjavur. Hopefully you will be gone by then. My heart goes out to Kamalamba. She will be lost without you."

"I know Kunju Mami, but this is my only chance. If I don't go I might as well commit suicide."

"Shh … Don't talk like that. If the Lord wills, you will see Saroja soon and will marry Mohan. Till then, don't breathe a word."

Bala tore the letter into little shreds and put it along with strips from all his previous letters. One day, she would piece them together again. One day, when her dreams came true. One day, she would hold her mother tight. One day, she would be free. One day, she would marry and have children. One day….

CHAPTER FIFTY ONE

PARTHA
CALCUTTA – AUGUST 1948

MEET 59 SOUTH END PARK

Pinniduven yenna nanaiche, yen ponnai kannu adikariya? Bhadua rascal! Partha was ready to tear off his scrawny neck. He was livid that the young boy had the gall to wink at Kamu. There was pin-drop silence in the dining hall as Partha held the skinny youngster by the collar, his fist pulled back, ready to throw a punch. Kamu and Rajam were screaming, *Porum porum ... avan onnu pannalai ... vittudungo!* "Appa stop! He didn't do anything ... Enough, stop embarrassing me ..." This was the third time Partha had drawn his fists on a would-be suitor. He was a big man with a powerful 50-inch chest, and none of the puny Bengali *para boys* hanging around wanted to take him on, but Rajam worried that one day he may get into a real fight and get injured. He looked huge, but had never slapped anything other an unfortunate insect in his life. Yet he was so protective towards Kamu that he had his fists up at the slightest provocation.

This was all very new for Kamu. In Madras she never ventured out of their neighborhood, and her male cousins were so well known, no one ever bothered her. But here in Calcutta, ever since she landed, someone was either whistling at her or winking or passing some random comment in Bengali, which she didn't completely understand, but knew was something suggestive. In a way she was flattered and really didn't quite feel insulted. After all, everyone was free to admire beauty! But she did not dare to let her father know how she felt about it.

At their hotel was a young boy who had been interested in her ever since they landed and constantly attempted to get her attention. Kamu wondered how he timed his breakfast and dinner with theirs each day. Avoiding eye contact with him was becoming increasingly awkward. Wherever she sat, she could feel his eyes boring in through her back. She casually mentioned it one day, and Partha had been on high alert waiting for any sign. The boy was persistent and did all kinds of silly things from changing seats so he could look at her to dropping his hanky near their table and excusing himself while he picked it up. Today at

dinner he once again switched seats so he was facing Kamu diagonally. He was
making all kinds of strange faces, stretching and yawning noisily, trying to catch
her eye, and when she turned her head towards him, he winked at the exact
moment Partha chose to join them for dinner. That was it! Partha completely
lost control. Thank heavens he didn't hit him, but he certainly called him some
choice abuses—ones Kamu was hearing for the first time. On being released from
Partha's iron grip, the terrified boy ran from the room never to be seen again.
Kamu was so embarrassed. Everyone was looking at her and whispering. She
sulked for the rest of the meal, and once they went into the room, she gave her
father a piece of her mind.

Partha was shocked. Nobody other than Nagamma had ever spoken to him
in those raised tones, but he quietly listened to his young daughter tick him off
about his behavior. Fatherhood was strange. He loved Kamu so much and was so
protective of her that he was suspicious of any interest directed at her, continually
ready to save her honor. This hotel was completely filled with young men and
perhaps was not the right place for Rajam and Kamu. It was time to look for
other lodgings, a flat with two bedrooms, but that was not easy to find. For the
last two weekends they had responded to several ads in the paper, but either the
area was too dangerous or it had no proper bathroom, or something else was
not right. Rajam contacted the couple they traveled with on the train to Calcutta,
who invited Rajam to stay with them for a few days till they found a place. They
had a beautiful flat near Park Street, right in the center of the city, and Kamu was
quite overwhelmed by the lights and social activity in the area. Rajam and Partha
came from a family that didn't think twice about hosting long-staying guests.
Their homes constantly boasted a floating population of cousins and friends and
even strangers distantly connected to some cousin, some staying for a few days
and others for months. They loved the company and were honored to serve
their guests. However, they made a mistake in incorrectly assuming the whole
world had their pure and generous disposition. The Ramans were civil enough
for the first few days, but fifteen days into their stay, the innuendoes began, and
all three of them began to feel uncomfortable. Clearly they had outstayed their
welcome, but with no place to go, they swallowed the insults and began praying
for a solution.

When they drove in through the gates of 59 South End Park, they knew they
had arrived home. Something about the red circular steps at the entrance signaled
a warm welcome. The owner, Dr. Ghosh, came out to greet them, looking elegant
as ever in his *dhuti pānjabi,* a crisp long kurta over yards of a flowing, white
muslin dhoti. His salt and pepper hair was slicked back, and his spectacles gave
his empathetic face an affable, intellectual demeanor. His wife was wearing a

cream *tangail* sari, the typical cotton weave from Calcutta, with a blue and red border, draped in the traditional Bengali way with her keys thrown over her right shoulder. Her hair parting was smeared with *shidoor*, bright, red vermillion, and her forehead sported an oversized *bindi* from the same vermillion. Their gentle, radiant faces proclaimed that this was going to be a very happy home, made for beautiful memories.

Dr. Ghosh had faced trouble in the past with renters from Delhi, but as soon as he saw the Parthasarathy family and learned they were south Indian, he knew there would be no problem with timely payments or raucous behavior. He reduced the rent on the spot by twenty rupees and said they could move in the following week once the rent agreement was registered. They walked into the house with animated anticipation. An ample living room was flanked by two decent sized bedrooms, each with its own bathroom. Kamu giggled on noticing one bathroom had a western style toilet, knowing for sure they would never use this. Who could sit on a chair and actually defecate? It was ridiculous! The hall opened into a large dining room so big that one could easily fit a table for thirty people. The kitchen in contrast was really small with very little storage. In the old days most people cooked outside, so this room must have been added as an afterthought. But Rajam said she would manage. They would use the dining space to store groceries and vessels. In any case, they didn't own very much, and the space far exceeded their expectations. What stole their hearts was saved for last. A long corridor which ended with collapsible gates led onto a patio tiled with the same red oxide flooring, with steps leading down into the back garden. The expanse of green bordered by beds of colorful flowers took their breath away. "Look Amma, this is so beautiful!" Kamu exclaimed, running down the steps and twirling around in sheer glee. "I can even play badminton here with my friends."

"You certainly can," said Ghosh Babu indulgently smiling. "I have two nieces who live down the street and they actually come here to play badminton. You will meet them soon."

Kamu and Rajam hugged each other in utter happiness. They didn't want to wait another day to move in. The very thought of returning to the tense atmosphere with the Ramans filled them with gloom. When they explained their situation to Ghosh Babu, he permitted them to move immediately even before any papers were signed. The trust and friendship between them was instant and mutual, almost like a reunion of soul mates. That settled, they returned to pack their belongings, and the very next day arrived with their luggage. Three trunkfuls. They had no bedding, no furniture, no vessels, not even fresh water, but they felt like royalty in their new palace.

It was evening when they arrived and too late to go shopping, but the Ghoshes' hospitality extended beyond borders and custom. Ghosh Babu invited them for dinner, and for the very first time in their lives the family tasted authentic Bengali cuisine. Knowing they were strict vegetarians, Mrs. Ghosh had prepared an elaborate vegetarian fare, *alur dom, alu potoler dalna* and *cholar dal* with soft Basmati rice and Kamu's favorite, soft, fluffy rasagollas for dessert. But it didn't end there. As they left, she asked the servant boy to carry down two bedrolls and pillows with bedspreads to cover themselves. The boy kept returning, first with towels, then a jug of freshly boiled and cooled water and then a handful of vessels, some fruit and vegetables to get started. Rajam's faith in humanity was restored.

That night Kamu slept between her parents as usual, and as she stared out the window at the gibbous moon, life seemed perfect. For the first time in their entire lives, they were in their own home, just the three of them. She touched Rajam's soft cheeks and then reached over to rub her hands over her father's broad shoulders. Both were fast asleep and pretty soon with a smile anointing her face Kamu succumbed to her fatigue and drifted into deep, dreamless sleep.

CHAPTER FIFTY TWO

DHARMU
CALCUTTA – JUNE 1948

THE FAMILY GROWS

Dharmu completed her morning ritual, which included cleaning and polishing her diamond jewelry, her nose rings, and earrings. Then, as usual, she retrieved her comb from its muslin bindings and combed her hair into a bun. She looked at herself closely in the mirror and could discern three visible white hairs in front. Next year she would be forty, and today she was celebrating her granddaughter's first birthday. It was a fleeting yet frightening thought that perhaps half her life was over, but Dharmu never gave audience to negative thoughts. She didn't like to contemplate issues involving death and seamlessly turned her thoughts to something current which required her immediate attention. Focusing on enjoying her life gave her little free time to ponder serious issues, which didn't interest her and floated only on the fringe of her mind. She just lived to enjoy the good things in life: good food, wine, vacations, parties, and the list went on. She knew there were several issues that needed her attention—she was overweight and given to tantrums. But Mahadevan loved her regardless, and when she was angry he did anything in his power to make her feel better, from buying her jewelry to arranging a European vacation; so really, there was no problem at all.

She was content and her life was full. She played bridge on Tuesdays and Fridays and tennis on Mondays and Thursdays. Every Friday and Saturday they went out for a party or to a restaurant. *Yes! Parties!* That's what she really missed. It was so nice when the Europeans were around. They would dance and drink till the early hours of the morning. Now that the British had left, the drinking was much less, though when Mahadevan came home each day, they always had a couple of *chotas* before dinner, which usually eased her headaches. In the beginning, the migraines had been terrible. It was hard drinking less alcohol, but Dr. Walters had prescribed a new medicine that was working well. For the last three months she could only recall one severe attack when she was vomiting all day—that was a good sign. The doctor said the migraines would lessen once her periods stopped, but that would not be for another ten years or so. Till then, she would have to darken her room and ride out the pain.

Last June, Rukku gave birth to a daughter whom they named Shyamala. Rukku had beaten Vani to it. So many years had passed since Vani's wedding, yet there was no sign of a baby. She couldn't have inherited Dharmu's genes. Dharmu was so fertile she had her first baby at fifteen. Delivering the baby was so much easier these days with hospitals and English doctors. They gave Rukku something called twilight sleep. It gave her that little rest in between contractions. Dharmu was not allowed inside the room, the nurse came out from time to time and informed them that both mother and daughter were safe and well.

That was so different from Dharmu's deliveries. Every house in the village had one room reserved for the *prasavam*—or childbirth. In Dharmu's home in Porambur this was the darkest, dingiest room. They would keep hot coals under the bed, and when she asked, her mother told her the heat made the baby come out faster. The heat didn't bother her as much as the fumes when they added the incense. To begin with, she had trouble breathing with her belly pushing up on her diaphragm, and the vapors made her choke, but her mother insisted that sulphur was healing. No one argued with elders. They had experience delivering babies, and the midwife even knew how to move the baby in the belly in case it threatened to be a breach. Even though they used boiling water, they cut the cord with a kitchen knife. None of this was hygienic—and it was no shocker that so many women died at childbirth. It was fine as long as everything else was normal, but if there were complications, then everything was left to God. Dharmu had easy deliveries for both Vani and Rukku, but Kandu took his time coming and was such a large baby that she ruptured and bled for days. It was a miracle she survived and recovered. At the time she was young and healthy and she remembered how her father was at her bedside night and day praying and urging her recovery.

Calcutta was steaming hot, and Dharmu decided to wear a Mysore crepe with a simple border, but when she attempted to put her hands into the sleeves they barely went up her forearms. She had put on a lot of weight, and now that she was almost forty pounds heavier, her arms were loose and flabby and refused to enter the sleeves. She yelled for Meera, then remembered there was no Meera. She had no time to send the blouse for alteration, so instead she searched her stack of neatly organized blouses for one that would contrast well with her sky blue sari. She found a nice navy blue one, and her arms slid through easily; the front buttons were a problem, but nothing a couple of safety pins couldn't fix.

Dharmu wanted to have the full ceremony with a *homam* fire and the rest of the rituals, which were part of the *Punyavajanam*, a child's first birthday, but she had to bang heads with her son-in-law, who believed it wasn't really necessary. This was her first grandchild, and the celebration of the first birthday was traditionally very important, so Dharmu stood her ground. A new priest had come to the area who agreed to bring all the necessary vessels and other items for the rituals. She only needed to prepare the *havis* at home and buy fresh flowers and fruit. Their Brahmin cook was on leave and so Dharmu boiled the rice herself because these priests were particular that the havis be prepared by a Brahmin. The khansama from Nepal was there, but he cooked meat and she didn't want him hovering around. The kitchen in their home was so large she had divided it into two. One side was for south Indian Brahmin food prepared by the Brahmin cook and the other reserved for fancy British and meat items. Kandu needed his fish or chicken every day, and it was challenging when the khansama went on leave.

The servants had cleared and wiped down out one area in the enclosed verandah. It was easier to have the ceremony here so the fumes from the sacred fire could escape. As she walked into the verandah the priest arrived. *Vāngo Sundar Sāstrigale*, she welcomed him.

Namaskaram Mami, vandāchā kuzhandhai, ponnu, māplai?

Dharmu made some excuse, annoyed that Rukku and Arun hadn't arrived yet. She had sent the car for them hours ago, and they should have been here by now. Just then Mahadevan walked in dressed appropriately in a veshti and white kurta, his forehead smeared with three even rows of vibhuti, adorned in the center with a perfectly round kumkumam pottu.

Following him was Kandu, who looked like he had just stepped out of a Hollywood movie, sun goggles and all. Kandu absolutely refused to wear a veshti and was in his customary linen pants and shirt. Dharmu could hear the car arriving and was certain they were here. She hoped and prayed that Arun wouldn't create a scene. He was unpredictable and quite capable of being rude to the priest ... somehow she had a feeling something untoward would be said by the end of the morning.

It was inevitable.

CHAPTER FIFTY THREE

VANI
MYSORE – JANUARY 1949

ABASAGUNAM—INFERTILE AND BAD LUCK

T he mirror smashed into a million pieces, some of it falling on Vani, but she couldn't care less. She was so angry with the world, with stupid, religious, Hindu bigots, but most of all she was angry with life that had treated her so unfairly. Why was the whole world doing so well while she was stuck in a dark, dirty place filled with envy, resentment, and anger as her sole companions? They could have married her off to anyone, but no—they chose Ganesh, and here she was barren and unable to have a child, having to sit mute and dumb while being insulted and made to feel so redundant.

Vani was thrilled when Shaila, a school friend from Kurseong, had married and moved to Mysore. For a few years now life was slightly more tolerable. She still couldn't stand Ganesh or her in-laws, but at least she went to play tennis with Shaila and sampled the delicious Mysore rasam cooked by her mother, Vanaja. Vani hated cooking and wasn't very good at it. How could she be? She was so consumed with resentment that she hardly knew what she put into her food. The salt was missing or there was way too much chili powder, and she didn't really care. She had lost almost ten pounds since her marriage partly because she was depressed and partly because the food in her home was so bad. Her mother-in-law ranted about the tasteless fare, but Vani didn't seem to be bothered.

Meeting Shaila three days a week was the only time she forgot to be miserable. They went shopping and to the movies, ate crisp vadai at the corner tea house and candy floss and colored ice cream by the zoo, almost as if they were reliving their childhood.

On those days Vani finished cooking and cleaning early and dressed up in her best velvet blouse, actually putting a little *mai* in her eyes. Inevitably they landed up in Shaila's home, and if her mother was there, they would enjoy a sumptuous meal if it were lunchtime and fried pakodas or vadais at teatime. Shaila had been married recently, and her husband worked in a factory outside Mysore. They had taken a small house on the same street as her mother's, which was convenient, because her husband kept long hours, leaving her with a lot of free time. Shaila's father was in the army and because they moved location every couple of years she had joined the same boarding school for girls as Vani. Having grown up in the north, Shaila was more liberated and westernized than most local girls and actually wore slacks and shirts, which Vani could never summon the courage for. One time Vani tried on Shaila's slacks and was shocked at how good she looked. She even wore lipstick and curled her hair that day. Their meetings were such fun, always full of laughter and gaiety.

But Shaila wasn't just her fair-weather friend. She was there embracing her in her darkest hours when the muck seeped into her life from the leaking sewer of her mind. Like the time she heard her sister Rukku was pregnant. Shaila held her and comforted her, assuring her that her time would come. She would be a mother when she was ready, but first, she needed to release all these negative emotions she had for her sister. Shaila was right. It wasn't Rukku's fault that she married a man she loved and like clockwork a couple of years later was pregnant with her first child. It's just that Vani couldn't help wondering how things fell so perfectly into place with others, yet for her each day was drudgery with absolutely nothing to look forward to. Many times she contemplated having an affair thinking that perhaps Ganesh was the one who was sterile, and if she had sex with another man at least she would conceive a baby. All these thoughts were exciting enough, but she never had the courage to go through with on any of them. She hadn't a clue how to approach a man, and, so far had not seen anyone she would like to jump into bed with—so that was that.

When Rukku gave birth to a daughter, Vani tried her best to feel happy, but the tears came on their own. She cried so much she had a headache for two days. That day Ganesh couldn't stand seeing her that way. He loved her and just didn't know how to evoke the same response from her. No matter what he did he could sense her revulsion. He couldn't change his face; perhaps he could build his body, but where was the time for all that with his heavy schedule? In addition to working at the palace, Ganesh had opened a clinic in town and worked there in the afternoons, only returning at night for dinner. His work day was always twelve or fourteen hours long, and on returning he would find Vani as usual with a sour face complaining of a headache or dying to sleep. How was it even possible to conceive a baby when she avoided contact with him? Added to which was the dreadful memory of miscarriages.

Ganesh promised to take her on vacation to Kashmir in the summer. It was so beautiful there. They could rent a houseboat on the Dal Lake and even try skiing at Gulmarg. The next day he returned with a beautiful, red crepe sari with a matching velvet blouse. He was trying so hard, that much was apparent to Vani.

Then, six months ago, Shaila got pregnant. Vani knew she should be feeling happy for her, but the old feeling of envy and resentment resurfaced. Immediately, she told herself that she mustn't feel any antipathy for her, but she couldn't deny the vacuum within her. She hid everything really well and never let her friend know that she felt anything but pure joy for her. Each time on returning from their home she would think of Shaila's swelling belly and pummel her concave one, crying helplessly.

Vanaja Mami, had been planning Shaila's bangle ceremony for weeks now. She wanted everything to be perfect. She had bought glass bangles and was decorating them herself with glitter and stones. The week before, Vani went sari shopping with them. They bought the loveliest Kānjeevaram sari in black with small *jarigai* checks, and then knowing how finicky Vanaja Mami was, they bought a matching bag, slippers and bangles to match. Shaila was very insistent that Vani come early to help her dress, even though the ceremony would start at 8 a.m. sharp. Vani ironed her sari and kept a matching ruby necklace out on the dresser. She would wear the new sari Ganesh had given her, which would look just fine with the jewelry. She was surprised when the doorbell rang. It was Vanaja Mami. "What a surprise!" exclaimed Vani. "Please come in. I'm so happy to see you here, what with the Valaikāpu tomorrow."

"That's exactly what I wanted to talk to you about," replied Vanaja Mami, her face looking somber.

Vani's heart skipped a beat. Had something happened to the baby? Were her negative feelings responsible? Was it even possible to kill a baby in someone else's uterus just by crying and lamenting? She had a bad feeling but knew she wasn't the root cause of it.

"Vani," began Vanaja Mami, "I don't know how to tell you this. I know you are Shaila's closest friend and I know you both love each other very much. But this has nothing to do with the fact that you both are so close. That is undeniable and I'm very fond of you. But Shaila is my only child and this is her first baby. I just don't want you to come there tomorrow."

"Wh ... what? Why?" stammered Vani, too shocked at the request.

"It's *abasagunam* with you being childless. Please try and understand. Your very presence may result in some harm, especially since we are doing the religious ceremonies."

The whole room began to spin. Vani couldn't believe what she was hearing. The acid rose up her gullet and the poisonous words teetered on the tip of her tongue. *You evil witch! How dare you come and tell me where I can or cannot go? What kind of demented, contorted mind do you have that makes you believe that my very presence will make her instantly abort? How could you … you an educated, modern, woman who has socialized and been exposed with western thought, actually believe in such superstitious garbage?* So far she had only thought of herself as unfortunate, but the truth was she *was* childless. She wanted to slap Vanaja Mami hard in the face and make her face reality. She loved Shaila so much she would never wish for her to lose the baby. She knew after three miscarriages how it felt to lose a baby. Though in the beginning she felt the pangs of envy, it was not for Shaila's good fortune but for her own unfortunate state.

No one spoke until Vani asked, "How will I explain it to Shaila?"

"Tell her you got your period. She will understand. Please, she must never know I came to you. You are like my daughter, which is why I felt free to tell you, knowing you would understand. Please don't mistake me."

And while you protected your own, you didn't think twice about stabbing me in the heart. But again Vani said nothing. And Vanaja Mami departed.

Like a zombie, she entered her room, put on the red sari and ruby necklace, and on impulse covered her lips in ruby red lipstick. Then she placed a pillow under her sari and looked at the false image of herself in the mirror. But the reflection that confronted her only confirmed what she already knew. She was *barren* and *childless!* Hurling the pillow on the floor, she snatched a perfume bottle and threw it with all her might against the mirror, shattering it instantly, the golden liquid oozing menacingly down the jagged contours of the broken glass.

She cried for hours. Then from her drawer she took out a picture of Jesus that the nuns had given her in school. She would never enter a temple again or willingly participate in any Hindu mumbo jumbo. Jesus would be her savior and he would place a child in her belly.

And Shaila and Vanaja? She didn't need such people in her life.

CHAPTER FIFTY FOUR

RANI
CALCUTTA – JANUARY 1949

THE SURPRISE VISITOR

Dharmu simply loved knitting. Her friend Dorothy from the bridge group had taught her the basics, and ever since then, Dharmu's knitting needles were clacking all day. Her problem was gauging size, so both Kandu and Mahadevan had identical, oversized sweaters. Kandu's sweater was big at the shoulders and Mahadevan's had adjustments for his belly; either way nothing fit anybody, but no one was about to complain. She had diligently knitted for the last six months and was proud of her handiwork. She was making a sweater and cap for baby Shyamala, and was busy knitting away when the bearer came in to say there was a visitor.

Kaun hai? Dharmu asked, slightly irked to have an unexpected caller.

Koi memsahib ... bola Chatterjee memsahib. Dharmu put her knitting down. She was puzzled. She knew many women with that last name—Reema, Deboshree and Sanjukta, but they would always call before coming over. She walked into the hall and stopped in her tracks. Dharmu never expected to see Rani, not in a million years. She could barely recognize her. The Rani she knew and remembered—beautiful, svelte, debonair—was gone. That charming, vivacious woman was replaced completely and only because she knew to expect a Mrs. Chatterjee that she realized it was Rani from Shimla. Her hair was wiry and almost white, her skin sallow and wrinkled, a shade between gray and blue. Her arms stuck out of her blouse sleeves like little sticks, and as for the rest of her, everything had shrunk until she looked like an eighty-year-old, wizened geriatric.

"Rani!" she screamed unable to believe her eyes. "I can barely recognize you. What happened to you? Why are you so thin? I tried contacting you for so many months, but Sudipto would not allow me to talk with you. Then after we came here, I asked Mahadevan to call but he kept forgetting."

"Oh, Dharmu, it's so nice to see you after such a long time. What can I say? It has been a very difficult time, Dharmu, and I know I should have contacted you earlier, but I didn't have the strength to do anything. I leave for Mother's Ashram in Pondicherry next week, and I was thinking of you and Kandu and Rukku and wondering how you were doing, so here I am."

Dharmu asked the bearer to bring some tea, and they sat in the hall just looking at one another. "I can't believe it. We haven't met for five years and I've swollen like a pumpkin and you have shrunk. Tell me what happened."

"Well, Dharmu, where shall I start?" Rani cracked her knuckles noisily before continuing.

"It was a horrible time. Sudipto refused to let me go to my mother's home, and I had to live there imprisoned for almost two years. The door to my bedroom was padlocked because he was afraid I would run away. As you can imagine, this had a terrible effect on Deb. He would sit outside my door and we would talk sometimes from either side of the door without seeing each other. I met no one and was only allowed down for dinner. If I was depressed, Deb was doubly depressed. Being locked up for such a long time played on my self-esteem and made my mind play tricks. I couldn't exercise or even go for a walk, but I ate three meals a day. When I looked in the mirror I saw myself putting on weight and that made me feel even worse. Then the vomiting started. I don't think I ever forced it, but food just couldn't sit in my stomach for more than a few minutes. I would eat and throw up, eat and throw up."

"Could you not use the phone? Why didn't you call me? I can't believe Sudipto would be that cruel. This is terrible!"

"Well ... he was scared I would run away and embarrass him and I think it was my open rejection of him that made him resolute. He wanted to punish me without hurting me bodily. I was cared for. I had a beautiful room and bathroom and could eat what I wanted as long as I didn't leave the room."

"Did Sudipto know about your vomiting?"

"Well he could hear me in the bathroom at night. Everyone knew about it. Sudipto thought I had some stomach problem. I must have ingested dozens of bottles of sulphaguanidine, but nothing worked. I was admitted to the hospital for two months and fed with a tube because I couldn't consume anything and keep it down. Finally, the doctor said that this was a nervous disease and that I needed a vacation. After I'd been a prisoner in my own house for two years, my husband sent me to Calcutta to stay with my mother."

"And did you improve?"

"My stomach was used to heaving, so it took a while to begin eating. For almost two years more I could only drink soups and juices. No solid food would go in. Lack of nutrition does horrible things to your body. My skin became dry and scaly and my hair was falling out in lumps. I even lost two teeth; thank heavens they're molars. I couldn't meet anyone, not looking the way I did. Then one day, I was with Deb and I pushed his shirt sleeves back and noticed cuts on his arm. Horrified, I made him show me his legs and there were cuts on the inside of his thighs too. My poor Deb, my poor Deb," Rani began sobbing and Dharmu put her arms around her. "What a horrible thing to happen! He felt so bad about me that he wanted to hurt himself."

"You see, Deb was terrified of his father and was totally attached to me. Not being able to talk to me and hold me, plus the psychological trauma of me wanting to leave him created terrible pain inside him which he couldn't express to anybody. So he would cut himself, as that physical pain was worse than the pain in his mind. Only it wasn't. He was going crazy, and Sudipto never even noticed." Rani needed a few minutes to calm herself. The bearer brought tea and Dharmu poured her a cup. After a few sips, Rani continued.

"Then on one visit last year to Calcutta I went to a friend's home where she was leading a group meditation. Both Deb and I had a beautiful experience and we kept going back. For the last year we have a yoga teacher who comes home thrice a week, and we learn pranayama and yoga with him. I can't tell you how much it has helped us both to release the pain and built up stress. Deb is done with school, and we are moving to the ashram. I don't know what he wants to study, perhaps medicine. There's a fine medical college right there in Pondicherry. I'm sure I will live there for the rest of my days."

"What a turnaround. What will you do there? Won't you miss the social life?"

"What social life? I only had myself for so long now, and other than my mother and father I have not met anyone. This world filled with lust, greed, and ambition has taken the juice out of me. Now I need to recuperate and really find some meaning."

"But meditating? I don't know how that will help. I think you should go to Switzerland to one of those spas. Everyone is going there these days."

"No, Dharmu, I won't try to sell meditation to you. It only comes to certain people and most often when all other options fail. In my case, the circumstances were so miserable, the earth beneath me had opened up. I was falling, and then like a miracle this branch appeared for me to hold onto."

Just then, Kandu walked in with his buddies Tucky and Dilip. He was always with at least a couple of his five friends. Ram and Mickey were not there, but they would soon arrive. Almost every night they were here playing billiards or table tennis. The house was big enough, and Dharmu liked the ruckus having the kids around. "Come Kandu, you remember Rani Aunty from Shimla?"

"Rani Aunty? Oh my gosh, I would never have recognized you? How are you? And Deb?" Kandu was really shocked to see Rani. All through his youth he had admired her beauty and looked up to her as a role model, and seeing her like this shattered the remnants of admiration he had held onto.

Rani hugged him, and he felt he was holding a skeleton in his arms. "My ... !" she said stepping back to admire him, "what a strapping young man you have grown into. I always knew you would. I will certainly tell Deb I saw you."

"Do give him my best," said Kandu excusing himself.

All the while Tucky's eyes were popping out of his head and his jaw protruding disjointedly. "Oh man ... Oh man!" he kept repeating unable to actually voice his thoughts.

"I know, I can't believe it's her. You remember looking at her through binoculars?" Kandu remarked when they were safely outside.

"Kilimanjaro has become poached eggs," lamented Tucky recalling the time he was obsessed with Rani. Kandu walked into the game room and turned on the lights. Then he lit a cigarette and let it dangle from the corner of his mouth as he bent to pick up a 60-pound barbell. Dilip looked at him disapprovingly. "Don't do that." he said.

"Do what?" muttered Kandu.

"Lift weights while smoking? It's bad for your heart. You need to stop."

"Stop what? Lifting weights or smoking?"

"Smoking ... it's going to kill you one day, and combining the two is like signing your own death warrant."

"Aah its fine—nothing is going to happen to me. Stop nagging me." Kandu was young and full of life. His entire future was waiting to unfold. He felt like nothing could stop him. Kandu was convinced he was invincible.

CHAPTER FIFTY FIVE

PARTHA AND KAMU
CALCUTTA – OCTOBER 1948

OH! CALCUTTA!

Kamu had a blinding headache. The noise level in the movie theater was ear-splitting, but she was celebrating her thirteenth birthday with her friends who insisted on seeing this particular movie as the songs were catchy. She had seen *Chandralekha* once before with her parents and was singing along with the now familiar songs in spite of her throbbing headache. Partha wouldn't hear of her going alone with a bunch of girls for a movie. She kept reminding him that she was now a teenager, perfectly capable of caring for herself, but Partha wanted to be present to give any young man who glanced at her a black eye. Chandralekha was a blockbuster and this year's favorite movie. The story was about two brothers falling in love with the village dancer, and Partha wondered what might have chanced if one of his brothers liked Rajam. *Ugh! What a distasteful thought!* He glanced at Rajam eating a *samosa*, or as the Bengalis called it a *shengada*. Her hands were steady and all signs of tremors had vanished. It was hardly a wonder, considering how happy she was. Mrs. Ghosh had taken Rajam under her wing and introduced her to all the neighbors. Though Rajam knew just a smattering of Bengali, she combined it with the Hindi she had learned in Bombay and the resultant mishmash was still acceptable and welcomed by this warm and vibrant group of ladies.

Their *Para*, the neighborhood they lived in, was very close knit. Most families had lived here for generations, and all the children knew one another. Doors to their homes were typically left open, especially in the evenings, as the children wandered from one home to another, playing badminton here, listening to music at another's, or settling down for some warm *chai* in the others'. The young men in the para were highly protective of the girls and zealously watched out for them, allowing Partha to relax a little, secure in the knowledge that Kamu could roam the streets without any fear of being kidnapped or assaulted. Yet when she wanted to go to the movies with her friends, Partha insisted on taking them.

It was a short tram ride to Priya Cinema on Rash Behari Avenue, and Partha bought two seats for himself and Rajam four rows behind the girls. That way he could discreetly keep an eye on them while watching out for any potential trouble makers.

He looked at a family seated on the first row. He had seen them at the movies and at Carnatic music *katcheris* several times before, always seated in the first row. The father was portly and balding, but sported an air of authority. The wife was big, too, and surprisingly tall for a woman, with a colored string of flowers in her hair. The flowers were different each time, matching her sari. She must have an amazing garden to change flowers each time according to the sari she wore. It was her double nose rings that always got his attention. The incredibly large diamonds caught the light, emanating streaks of lightning every time she turned. Neither were very handsome in the traditional sense, but they had an air of authority, or was it superiority? Partha couldn't tell. Sometimes their son was with them and at other times their daughter and husband. Three or four times he saw the son slink off, perhaps to smoke a cigarette. He had seen him outside standing against the pillar his legs crossed Krishna style, blowing smoke above people's heads. He was tall and surprisingly handsome, but what a wretched habit. Partha made a mental note to find out about them. Judging by her choice of saris and her nose rings, they were certainly from the south. He didn't know too many locals yet, but Rajam had just become a member of the south Indian Ladies Club and was excited about attending their first meeting. As they pushed their way out of the overcrowded theatre, he watched the family climb into a huge car, a Dodge or Chevrolet perhaps. Posh! Just then Kamu nudged him. "Appa can we go to the lakes for *puchka* and *muri*?" she pleaded. Puchkas were a very creative snack. Small wheat flour *puris,* fried and puffed were piled on the side in a pyramidical marvel. The vendor broke the top and stuffed it with spiced, mashed potatoes and dipped that into the spiced water, the *pani,* and then served into small *bel* leaf cups each customer held.

Partha wanted to say *no, it's unhygienic. God alone knows what water went into making them,* but Kamu's request with beseeching eyes forced the words down his gullet and, instead, he found himself saying cheerily, "Yes, why not?" When Kamu looked up at him with those doe eyes, he was putty in her hands.

There was a nip in the air as they walked towards the food vendors, and Partha could tell the weather was changing. The winter would be here soon, and it was certainly welcome after a scorching summer. The vendors by the lakes were very well known, and for generations recipes had been handed down from father to son. Each family had their favorite muri person and puchka person who knew whether they wanted their puchkas sweet or a little spicy. They had the correct specifications recorded for posterity in their heads: extra onions for *boudi,* no oil for *dadu,* cucumbers only for *didi.* It was quite interesting to watch them furiously doling out puchkas and muri. They were here by four in the afternoon and went home with empty vessels and happy faces by sundown.

The lakes were a popular destination: most people living in the area congregated here in the evenings. You could clearly discern the regulars, walking briskly in their saris and dhotis, wearing mud-stained, worn-out tennis shoes and flashing walking sticks to scare stray dogs. Visitors tended to amble along, staring cluelessly, deciding what to do next. Groups of young men and women had the spicy water pouring down their faces and staining their clothing, but most were unmindful, fully absorbed in the delightful sensations evoked in their taste buds. Aromas of all kinds made the air thick with odors, from pungent mustard oil used for the muri to onions and coriander, including a host of other mysterious fragrances. You could tell the army men by their waxed and twirled handlebar moustaches and erect bearing, many walking their prized Alsatians along the boardwalk. The older *babus* were seated under the lamps on benches spaced sporadically throughout the area, attempting to read the newspaper through thick, horn rimmed spectacles, in the failing light.

The girls ran around choosing their hawker with care, and then it was time for a puchka-eating competition. After eighteen rounds Kamu's friend Champa had stuffed herself with the most puchkas. Rajam and Partha opted for *loochi-alurdom* offered by one vendor. It was typical Bengali fare served hot and certainly much more wholesome, which and would fill them up till they could top off their burgeoning stomachs with cooling thayirshādham and *oorgai* when they got home. No matter what they ate or where they dined they always had a little bit of rice and yogurt with lime pickle at the end to settle the stomach. No meal felt complete without this. The girls ate two and three helpings of muri, puffed rice with condiments, and then finished their meal with cool and very sweet daab, coconut water.

On returning home, Kamu sat outside on the steps as each of her friends was picked up by their parents, and soon most of the para girls had joined her. Kamu loved Calcutta. She was not bored for a minute. In the beginning she was a little diffident when talking to the local girls, who seemed to chat only in Bengali. But the Ghoshes introduced her to their nieces Pinaki and Ketoki, and they became Kamu's badminton pals. She went with them for walks down one street and up the other and by the end of the week curiosity got the better of the para girls. They all came up in turn and introduced themselves, and within a few weeks, Kamu had a hectic social life. In Madras, other than her school friends, she tended to play with her male cousins and their friends. It was really nice to have girl friends with whom she could exchange gossip and beauty tips and just hang around chatting and singing, whiling away the time. For the last few months, she had attended National High School, which was far from home, but Rajam had sent her there on hearing that all the south Indian girls went there. Kamu didn't like the bus ride to school, and somehow she found a cultural difference between girls in Madras and those brought up in the north. Besides, each one lived in a different neighborhood, so meeting after school was very difficult. She complained to her parents, and in the beginning, Rajam and Partha ignored her, assuring her that things would improve over time. But each day Kamu would delay getting ready and dawdle over breakfast, missing the bus, leaving Partha no choice other than to drop her off in his Jeep. This went on for three or four months and eventually Partha realized she wasn't very happy in school.

All the girls in the para had private tutors and would sit for their Junior or Senior Cambridge exams by registering in a convent. Many came from traditional families, and the school had allowed them this privilege, giving them access to a list of private tutors. Partha signed Kamu up at a prestigious school, La Martinière, and hired an Anglo-Indian lady to tutor Kamu in English, Math, and Science. The big advantage was that Kamu didn't need to learn Bengali, and though she couldn't write it, she was speaking Bengali fluently in six months.

Partha was barely connected with the south Indian community, and his only regular friend was Sundar Sastrigal, the priest from the temple who would drop by every other day just to chat. Sometimes it seemed he really dropped by just to taste Rajam's rasam. He never came alone and inevitably brought a couple of other priests so that Rajam had to make the meal stretch, but she didn't mind. She liked having company, and as long as they were not robed in saffron garments, she had no problems welcoming them into her kitchen. So far, she had not seen any sāmiyārs whom she dreaded encountering. Mrs. Ghosh said the sāmiyārs or sādhus as they were called up north, came down to the plains from the mountains in winter when their caves in the Himalayas froze, and then stayed till the ice melted. The thoughts of being around one of these frightening characters made Rajam nervous. She felt her old fears returning when she visited Kalighat, the Kali temple at Dakshineswar, which was filled with weird looking, half naked Kali worshippers, some even wearing necklaces made of skulls. The place scared her, and she resolved never to return there. It was nothing like her Mundakanni Amman Kovil, her temple back home. Some said they sacrificed goats at Kalighat too. But Sundar and his gang were great company, and their presence seemed to bless the house even more. Next month she would have the honor of hosting a great saint, Anatharam Deekshithar, and was excited to have him visit.

Partha watched the girls from the open doorway, a smile lighting up his face. The sound of laughter and casual banter was so heartening. Life was really good. But Kamu was growing up. Pretty soon he would need to find a suitable groom for her. He would have to speak to Sundar Sastrigal tomorrow and find out what was the best way to secure a good alliance.

Life presented itself in cycles. There was a time he was supremely happy as a teenager and when he first married, and then the down cycle hit him making him dread each dawning day. But pretty soon the up cycle began again and the days seamlessly flowed into one another. Partha wondered how long this would last, and hoped, no ... he believed, really believed, that this would last forever.

CHAPTER FIFTY SIX

KAMU
CALCUTTA – OCTOBER 1948

DURGA PUJO

Dhin thadhina Tak dhina dhin Dhin thadhina Tak dhina din. The rhythmic beat of the *dhak* was mesmerizing and all the spectators at the pandal in South End Park's *Durga Bari* clapped in time. The air was thick with incense and fumes from smoldering coconut husks scented with *Dhuno*, or benzoin resin, cocooned in earthenware pots, filled the air. The sound of cymbals rang loud and clear, keeping beat with the dhak drummers. Their pandal boasted of six expert dhak drummers who had come from remote villages and would tour the pandals in the area. Their forefathers had been *dhakis,* and their children would carry on the tradition. Almost in a trance, they beat their dhaks, drums decorated with silk and velvet with golden tassel trimmings, their bodies swaying to the tempo. All of them were dressed in traditional yellow dhotis, their foreheads smeared with turmeric and vermillion. The beat was getting even more frenetic as they prepared to watch the *dhunochi* dancers perform.

Kamu and Rajam had never attended a Durga *pujo* and were scared to blink lest they missed something. For the last four days they had faithfully come for each pujo(poojai) in the morning and for the celebratory *ārthi* at night. It was customary to visit other pandals as well, and a large group of them went pandal hopping, eating fruits at one Durga Bari and *bhog* of warm *khichuri* and *labra* at another. The fragrance of the *labra* filled the nostrils even as one entered the pandal. Large vats of khichuri—rice and lentils cooked together and flavored with pungent *garam masala* stood on one side as volunteers doled out the bhog in bel leaf plates along with a generous helping of labra, a mixed vegetable curry. This was the season for sweets, and Bengali sweets were famous all over India. They lost track of the number of *shandesh, notun guder payesh, rasagollas and panthuas* they ate after the tenth Durga Bari. It was a feast of sugary delights, a diabetic's nightmare with each para offering a different variety, which of course had to be sampled. For four days Rajam had not entered the kitchen to cook, which was a miracle, because their home boasted a constant stream of visitors who always stayed for lunch or dinner. This was a week of rest and festivity for all the women in the area.

Preparations had been afoot a month before with the para boys collecting *chanda*, donations for their neighborhood Durga Bari. In Hindu mythology, Durga, the consort of Shiva, would return to her mother's home during the holy festival of Navaratri and for five days from holy *Shashti* through *Shaptami, Ashtomi, Nobomi* until *Bijoya Doshomi,* her presence would vibrantly embellish and honor each home in every corner of the state. Each neighborhood took great pride in preparing for the festival and eagerly awaited the arrival of their idol, which would have been ordered a year in advance. Anantharama Deekshithar had taught Kamu the Mahishasura Mardhini stotram, and the family recited it every evening during the course of Navaratri, but the Bengalis chanted it differently, because their intonation differed. Kamu knew the story well, but the Deekshithar's explanation had imprinted the myth[5] behind the festival forever in her mind.

Weeks before the idol arrived the pandal decorations began in earnest. Each year the splendor of the Durga Bari seemed to improve, and neighborhoods vied to outshine each other in intricacy and size of the idol. Calcutta was splendidly dressed for the festival with streamers, flowers and fairy lights lighting up the city. Loudspeakers blared from each pandal, broadcasting chants from the holy chandi sutras, songs and chants sung by several different Bengali singers. Every para had its own Durga Bari, a community pujo which would bustle with activity, and be

---

5   Mahisha, an evil asura, was causing havoc on earth and in the heavens. Unable to fight the demon, the celestial devas and ordinary humans prayed to Parvathi, the consort of Shiva, who took the form of Durga, a warrior with ten arms, each wielding a different weapon. While the Goddess and Mahishasura were engaged in a fierce battle, Mahisha's two generals, Chando and Mundo, attacked Durga from the rear. Durga's shakti or feminine power had first revealed her as glowing and beautiful, but her anger changed her color to inky blue, and from her third eye manifested the fierce goddess Kali. For ten days the fight between the combatants rocked the universe, but finally Durga vanquished the evil demon with the help of Kali, whom she had generated from her own spirit. Mahisha's general, the terrible asura Raktabija, seemed invincible because he had the ability to create a new demon from every drop of blood that was shed. Ultimately, Kali drank his blood, allowing Durga to vanquish all the accompanying demons and establish peace on earth. The gods were relieved and cosmic balance was restored. The festivities began on Mahalaya, the last day of the previous fortnight and would carry on through Lakshmi Pujo, Kali Pujo, ending in Bhai Dhuj almost a couple of months later.

home to the neighborhood for the next five days. All offices and schools were closed, and the atmosphere in the city was electric.

Kamu's friend Shathi lived a few doors down, and their home had their own special idol and pujo, which was their family legacy. The entrance to Shathi's home from the main street was tiny, but after the first few rooms, it opened up into a huge courtyard. The giant eight-foot idol had been brought in from the back entrance, and their home was an open house for the community. All the children from the para were there, blowing on conch shells, ululating, and dancing to the dhak. Shathi proudly showed her friends the five saris she had bought, one for each of the holy days. Kamu mentioned this to Rajam, and two of them went sari shopping and bought two beautiful white and red tangail saris for Kamu, so she wouldn't feel left out.

The ārthi would begin shortly after the dance and she could see the ladies preparing. They were dressed in exquisite matching tangail saris, and in each hand held earthenware pots in which nestled smoldering husks. Their movements were slow and undulating to begin with, but what fascinated Rajam was the way they held the pots upright in spite of complicated arm movements. The husks appeared to be glued to the pots because nothing fell from them in spite of the increasingly complicated dance moves. The dhaks began to beat faster and faster and the dance seemed to explode. People stood up, swaying to the rhythm, and shouting *Joi Durga ma ki jai*. The collective devotion was astounding; it was what held the community together irrespective of social background. People from all castes prayed together and celebrated together. At first Kamu merely watched, but the clanging of the cymbals and sonorous drum beat was mesmerizing, and she ultimately stood up, clapping and swaying to the music. Finally, after the ārthi, the sound of Vedic chanting filled the air. Kamu didn't recognize the chants, but everyone seemed to know the words.

Rajam turned to Mrs. Ghosh, "Last night around midnight we heard loud noises like firecrackers and cannons booming. Was something happening?"

"It was not last night, it was the night before. That was to announce the Sandhikan."

"What is that?" Rajam had never heard of it, Navaratri being celebrated very differently in the south.

"Sandhi Pujo is performed at Sandhikan, which is after midnight between the eighth and ninth day. That is supposed to be the exact moment the demon Mahisha was killed by Durga. It has to be done for exactly 48 minutes. The first 24 minutes is spent on evoking the Goddess and the next with the pujo. The exact timing is important, and some zamindārs still fire the cannons which they received from Robert Clive after the battle of Plassey, but the firecrackers are more commonly used to tell everyone it's time to begin Sandhikan."

"So what do you do? Were you here for the Sandhi pujo?"

"We were at the Banerjee house, you know Shathi's parents? It's an elaborate pujo with 108 earthen lamps, 108 lotus flowers, a single fruit, rice, clothes, and jewelry. In fact, we were up all night making the hibiscus garlands and the bel leaf tridents. Then after that a goat is sacrificed."

Rajam covered her ears and her mouth. Animal sacrifice! That was terrible? The horror she felt was clearly evident, and Mrs. Ghosh realized it. "Okay, okay, don't be so shocked. Kali is always associated with bali—animal sacrifice. I know you are all vegetarians. We are too, until Sandhikan. Then once the goat is killed we eat meat." Loud clamoring of cymbals distracted Rajam, and they looked up at the central stage where the priest was doing something with a fan close to the idol.

"What is happening now?" Rajam whispered.

"Today is Dashami, the tenth day. The priest is removing the soul from Durga, which has now gone back to her husband in Kailash. After this, we will all take *shidoor* and feed Durga Ma with sweets and then soon it will be time for Bishorjon."

"Are you going with the truck to immerse Durga?"

"No it gets too crowded. I have been as a child but some of the men will go. We bid farewell right here." The line was forming to offer flowers, and Rajam pulled Kamu close to her as they patiently waited for their turn to worship this beautiful goddess, asking that she return the following year. After that, suddenly all the ladies went crazy smearing shidoor, red vermillion on one another hugging and greeting each other with "Shubho Bijoya," and forcing shandesh and sweetmeats into each other's mouths.

Kamu ran up to Rajam. "Eighteen!" she mumbled unable to speak with a stuffed mouth.

"Eighteen what?" asked Rajam utterly perplexed.

"Rasagollas."

"Seriously? *Nejamava?* Stop now, you will be sick. Keep some space in your stomach for the bhog. And look for your father. Make sure he is not eating too many rasagollas."

After the tearful farewell ceremony for Durga Ma, Rajam finally found Partha, and they walked home. Once the Ghoshes left, Rajam sat down and declared, "It's horrible to think of how sacred Durga Ma is and a poor goat has to be killed to please her. It just doesn't make any sense."

"I know," piped up Kamu. "Bengalis have strange customs, and if you realize how they made Durga you probably won't ever go back to the Durga Bari."

"What do you mean?" asked Rajam.

"Shathi was saying that their family orders the idol from a village called Kumortuli. Every year they take clay from the Ganga, add cow dung and cow urine to it, then they go to the red light area in Shonagachi and take mud from the front of the prostitute's home. She called it "Nishidho Palli." Mud from a red light area is an essential ingredient while making the clay idol. Can you believe that?"

"Why?" asked Rajam, puzzled beyond reason.

"Apparently that mud is supposed to be the purest because men leave their virtue and goodness at the doorstep before entering a prostitute's home."

"I think it's because they realize that men release all their base and violent tendencies with prostitutes, which leaves women from good homes safe," said Partha, drinking the remnants of his *moru*, buttermilk spiced with salt, sugar and asafetida. He needed something to settle his stomach after all those sweets.

"So if there weren't prostitutes, we would all be raped daily?" remarked Kamu, her eyes flashing and her chin jutting out defiantly.

"Something like that," replied Partha wryly, leaving the room.

"Men are weak and these women have a dreadful life, said Rajam, "and it's good they are being honored like this. I love that Bengalis respect women so much. It's a refreshing change from our Iyer traditions."

"Bala is a prostitute too," remarked Kamu.

"Yes, but she has only one benefactor. It's different. It's almost like being married to one man."

"All this talk is making me very depressed," remarked Kamu wryly. "I'm going to bed."

"I know. It's been so nice all week. Why should we spoil our dreams by thinking of horrible things like killing and prostitution?" But, as much as she tried, Rajam could not escape her thoughts. Why did such bad things happen to people? Why were some girls so privileged and others forced to be sex slaves? Poor Bala, would she ever escape her predicament? Her thoughts looped in chains, and finally she nudged Partha, who moaned, annoyed at being disturbed. "*Yenna* ... have you ever visited a prostitute?"

Partha's eyes opened and his heart involuntarily skipped a beat. No, he wasn't going there. There was no need to open a can of worms or in this case, a can of scorpions, which would only sting him and poison his perfect life. "Go to sleep," he groaned, covering his head with a pillow. "Think about planning for Deepavali. The Deekshithar will be with us for ten days."

That's right. Deepavali was just round the corner, and Rajam had so much to do. Tangail saris wouldn't do. She reminded herself to write to Sushila to send

Kānjeevaram saris for her and Kamu and a silk veshti for Partha. She might as well send three or four veshtis. They would need to honor the Deekshithar at the end of the Bhagavatam discourse.

Rajam drifted off to sleep, and all thoughts of prostitutes and blood sacrifice were immersed and purified along with Durga Ma in the cleansing waters of the Ganga.

CHAPTER FIFTY SEVEN

SWAMINATHAN
COCHIN – JANUARY 1949

VANDE MĀTARAM

Today marks the first death anniversary of our beloved Father of the nation. Bapuji was a towering figure and key player in the nation's bid for freedom and his absence is felt by one and all.

"Thatha! Are you listening?"

"Hmm ..." said Swami, who had actually dozed off but his grandson's gentle nudge awakened him. "Yes, I'm awake ... keep reading. Is there anything else?"

Natarajan continued. *The last act Gandhiji did was to lift both his hands as a sign of prayer in the direction of the large gathering which had assembled for the prayer. Thereafter, he was speechless and the loss of blood, at his age and so soon after his fast, made death inevitable. He was beyond medical aid even from the start, when shock had its effect. Lord Mountbatten and Cabinet Ministers, including Pandit Jawaharlal Nehru, Sardar Vallabhai Patel, and Maulana Abul Kalam Azad and others soon arrived.*

"Even in death he thought of the Lord. That is why we should recite the name of God continually. Who knows when our time runs out?" Two solitary tears oozed out of Swami's eyes and rolled down his wrinkled cheeks.

"Thatha, stop this. Stop talking about death!"

"How can I? You are reading to me about the death of the greatest man that ever walked the earth. Do you know where most people die, Natraju?"

"In hospital?"

"No ... in bed. That is why you must chant the names of Vishnu before going to sleep. That way if you die in the middle of the night you get salvation at the lotus feet of Vishnu."

"Okay, Thatha, stop being so morbid. I'm not going to read to you if you keep talking like this."

Swami felt around for his spectacles. They were lying on his lap hidden in the folds of his veshti, but his eyesight was weak because of high blood sugar and he couldn't find them. Natarajan picked up the glasses, which had remnants of every meal he had eaten in the last week clinging to them. "Thatha, even if you could, you would not be able to see a thing through these glasses. Let me wash them." He was back a few minutes later, and, even after donning his glasses, Swami could barely discern a furry shape, which he knew to be his grandson.

Swami's move from Thanjavur had aged him considerably. After so many decades of being in charge of his household, he had to let go of the reins to his grandson. He knew that his time was over, and it was now his grandson's responsibility to take care of the family; and now a sense of uselessness had overcome him once he reached Cochin. His heart was failing, and every time he walked he found himself gasping for breath. Then a few months ago, the doctor said his blood sugar was up, and he needed to take additional pills and control his diet. Kunju knew how much he enjoyed his morning coffee and added a teaspoon of sugar to it in spite of the doctor's instructions. But his sugar levels must have been high for a long time. He had very little sensation in his fingers and toes, and things would slip out of his hands all the time. But he kept his spirits up, sitting on his easy chair by the entrance and watching people walk by while he read the newspaper from end to end. But a few weeks ago he found he was unable to read. Venkat took him for an eye checkup, and the results showed that cataracts were blocking his vision, but the doctor did not want to remove them until his sugar levels were under control.

Swami knew his body was failing one organ at a time, and now that he couldn't even read, he had no wish to live. Everyday Natarajan, his youngest grandchild, read to him excerpts from the English newspaper, and in the afternoons, Kunju would read to him from the Tamil one. She also took care of his other needs. He needed help walking and eating and even using the toilet. Swami hated depending on others for even his basic needs. For so many years he had been the backbone of the family, and now the life he knew and loved seemed to be slipping away.

"Thatha?" he heard Natarajan and wished he could see his soft, beautiful face. "Shall I read something else?" Swami nodded, and Natarajan turned to another section of *The Hindu*.

Gandhi's towering moral reputation tends to blind us today to the role he played in the minds of his contemporaries in the British Empire—that of a political activist. This raised issues that Orwell grappled with in this penetrating examination of Gandhi's career, published in the Partisan Review in January, 1949, a year after Gandhi's assassination. Orwell struggled to balance his natural skepticism of those held up as saints: ("Saints should always be judged guilty until they are proven innocent")

"What is this?" asked Swami, not able to figure it out with no visual reference.
"Some book review of some author called Orwell."

"Never heard of him. They must have taken something from a foreign paper. Ask Kunju to come and read the Vishnu Sahasranamam to me."

Natarajan ran in to find his mother but she had stepped out to buy vegetables. "Thatha, she's out. I need to do my homework now. Do you need anything … water? Moru?"

"I need nothing, I want nothing I have nothing," he said to his perplexed grandson.

Swami closed his eyes and leaned back in his easy chair. It was time to relax. *No point trying to cram my head with all kinds of trivia which I won't even remember tomorrow,* but as he closed his eyes he thought back on his life. So much had happened. He remembered meeting Mangalam, so many years ago. She was just a child then, but what a burden she shouldered and what a support she had been through his life. He really missed her. As he closed his eyes he could see her in a yellow and red *madisar,* her big round kumkumam pottu anointing her face. She looked so real. Swami reached out and tried to touch her soft face, but the image vanished. "Mangalammmm!" he cried out. *Yennai thaniya vittutu poyitiye….* If he could hold her just once, touch her silky smooth skin, hear her soft voice. Oh, how he longed for her presence and just now, her form seemed so authentic.

Natarajan shook his head as he heard his grandfather rambling away. *Vanchinathan … Pandurangan … Hey Sivakumar!* He put his math book away and reached for his composition notebook. Thatha was talking to himself again. *Blabber, blabber, blabber.* He had really become senile. *Achamillai achamillai acham inbadilliye….* He heard his voice, a hoarse croak attempting to sing one of Bharatiyar's famous songs. Natarajan smiled to himself. Bracing for his grandfather's next words he began writing. There it was … *Vandeeee Mātaram.*

That's it! I'll write about something from the freedom struggle. He took out his pencil from behind his ear and scribbled … *Swaraj is my birthright and I shall have it.* He wrote down the famous quote but for the life of him he couldn't recall who said that. Thatha was sure to know. He raised himself and walked towards the outer thinnai. "Hey Thatha, which freedom fighter said Swaraj is my birthright?"

But Thatha was travelling through a tunnel of light meeting with martyrs and forefathers. His grandson shook him several times and when he didn't respond, he knew he had passed on.

Then, suddenly, he had the answer. It felt as though it were whispered in his ear in an inaudible voice.

Bal Gangadhar Tilak.

CHAPTER FIFTY EIGHT

DHARMU
CALCUTTA – APRIL 1949

THE PHOTOGRAPH

D harmu's knitting needles were flying at top speed. In front of her, Rukku's daughter Shyamala sat openmouthed on a lopsided pouffe, completely mesmerized. The clickety clack of the needles fascinated her, and she looked up soulfully at her grandma. Timid by nature, she barely spoke, added to which was her fear of her Paati. Dharmu's booming voice frightened her, and her large form intimidated her into silence. To begin with, Shyamala's vocabulary was limited. Dharmu had aired this concern with Rukku several times. Girls always reached landmarks faster. They crawled and stood faster and definitely spoke much earlier, but Rukku was not terribly concerned. Shyamala was a quiet one who was happy to sit and play with her dolls for hours, with little or no supervision. She ate and drank what was put in front of her, never really asking for anything. Even more gratifying, she slept right through the night. Even when she cried, which was rare, she sounded like a cat mewing, not really disturbing anyone yet maintaining her inner protest somewhere in the deep recesses of her body.

Yenna? Yenna pākarai? Shyamala jerked as Dharmu posed the question gently enough, yet she could not gather the nerve to tell her grandma that she was merely watching her knit. She stared for a moment, her little heart fluttering in fear, then crawled behind the sofa, happy to listen to the sound of the needles safely ensconced, away from her grandma's looming presence.

Kandu and Rukku walked in together and flopped on the sofa. They had been playing table tennis for a while and Dharmu curled her nose up at the smell of sweat. In utter glee, Shyamala ran and squeezed between the two of them, pushing her hand into her mother's. She beamed at Dharmu from her safe haven. Kandu pulled her ponytail, and she whirled around, but not before he pretended he didn't know what happened. As soon as she turned her head away, he did it again, and Shyamala mewed in protest.

"What? Why are you squealing?" shouted Kandu. "Did Govindhan pull your ponytail? Let me catch him and beat him up."

"No Govindhan you ..." she said with a shy smile.

"You mean like this," he said pulling it again, and the two rolled on the sofa with Kandu tickling and cuddling her.

Rukku leaned forward and picked up the album on the coffee table. "You should keep a magnifying glass with the albums. Everyone looks so small I can hardly tell who is who." Rukku peered through her glasses, which were a latest addition to her wardrobe. "This is a good one of Gayatri Paati and Thatha," she remarked, admiring one of the few pictures Dharmu had of her parents. "You should frame this. Tell your son to get off his lazy bum and do some work. I heard the new Kodakcolor picture shop on Park Street can enlarge the picture for you."

"I don't need that. I can always look at the album," remarked Dharmu wryly.

In truth it had been a while since Dharmu caught herself thinking about her parents. Almost a decade had gone by since her father passed away, but the circumstances surrounding his death were so nasty that she couldn't bring herself to think about him. She felt really sad when her mother passed away a few years later. In the interim, she had been so consumed with fury about her father, she just did not visit home. And when she did, it was too late. Her mother died without Dharmu getting a chance to clear the air.

Gayatriammal wrote to her every month, and in each letter would beg her to forgive her father and to come and visit, but Dharmu just didn't want to return home. The whole incident had been so shameful with all the neighbors snickering and gossiping openly. She was so angry with her father for his weakness, especially since the hypocrisy of noble status and social standing was his proffered veneer. She hated that he flaunted his station as manager of the estate, vibhuti smeared across his forehead in a pretense of being Brahmin, yet he was nothing but a cheat and masquerader causing everyone ignominy, demeaning his wife openly, even in death.

The incident had scarred her for life, and for a long time, she could think of little else. Which is why she chose not to see her mother. Seeing her would only dig up buried memories, and she didn't want to relive that miserable time in her life. She knew that her mother really needed her, but she just couldn't bring herself to face her.

"I miss going to Dindigul." Rukku remarked. "How many years is it since Thatha passed away?"

Too many thought Dharmu lost in thought.

The children were small at the time. Kandu couldn't have been older than eight or nine years, maybe older. Her brother Venkat and his new wife were also visiting, and the reunion had been a happy one. But that was soon to change.

That night was etched in her memory. It was warm and she couldn't sleep very well. Waking up from a disturbing dream, she heard some noise in the living room. When she entered, the room was in semi-darkness, but light from a bright moon bathed the floor near the open windows. She could discern the silhouette of her mother leaning against the window, but couldn't see the tears glistening on her face. The clock announced the midnight hour as Dharmu walked up to her mother and threw her arms around her neck.

"He isn't back yet," she stated with evident disgust.

"No, I thought I heard something, so came to see if he had come home."

"Why, Amma? Why do you wait up for him? Have you eaten?" Dharmu could tell by the look on her mother's face that she was waiting for him to return before eating. She was superstitious and only ate when her husband was safely home, and Dharmu was sure *he* had eaten. "I can't understand this. You know he has gone to meet her, yet you starve and await his return. Why?"

"That's how we were brought up. Women in our homes don't eat until the men have eaten. You know this. I cannot eat unless he comes home. I know he must have eaten there, but still, unless I am sure, I cannot eat. Don't question me. I know you and Mahadevan eat together, but those are all British customs. No Brahmin woman worth her salt would dream of eating before her husband does."

"At least have a glass of moru. You can't sleep on an empty stomach." Dharmu went into the kitchen and brought a glass of buttermilk spiced with salt and asafetida. Against her will, Gayatriammal drank the moru. She knew she needed some sustenance. Still the uneasiness that made her rise from her bed and sit by the window wouldn't abate.

"Come on, Amma, let me take you to the room. I refuse to allow you to sit and wait for that debauch to return."

"Don't speak of your father like that. It's not respectful."

"And his actions are? For heaven's sake, Amma, he doesn't deserve my respect. Be thankful I haven't told the children."

"No!" exclaimed Gayatriammal. "They must never know. Don't make that mistake."

"I won't, but only if you come and sleep." Gayatriammal relented, but as they left the room they were startled by the urgent banging on the door. Dharmu peeked out of the window and saw it was a young man. She had never seen him before, but her mother seemed to know who he was. He must be one of the children of that hateful woman. She opened the door a crack and looked at him. He must have been in his teens, dark and pimple faced, but his expression seemed harrowed. "Gayatriammal?" he spoke, panic palpable in his voice. "You need to come immediately. Something has happened to your husband." Dharmu broke into a sweat. Now what had happened? Her mother pushed her aside. *Yenna aachu?* she asked, trepidation apparent in her tremulous voice.

The young man broke down, wiping his face against his already damp sleeve. "*Ayya* has passed on. *Avar poyitar,* I'm so sorry, *Ayya* is no more."

Gayatriammal couldn't move. There was no expression on her face. Of all the places in the world, this despicable man had chosen to die in a prostitute's bed. But her face was placid. "Wake up Venkat," she instructed Dharmu. "He has to go and bring back Appa's body."

Venkat was thoroughly disoriented, but he washed his face and left with the young man. The next few hours stretched on endlessly. Gayatriammal wouldn't speak, and no matter what Dharmu said she couldn't evince a response from her. She simply stared into the distance, lost in the highway of her own tormented thoughts.

Dharmu didn't want to wake up the children yet, but Venkat's wife Seetha woke up and sat with them. The conversation was awkward. Dharmu couldn't vent because Seetha had no idea about her father-in-law's philandering. She wasn't quite sure what to say. She felt like crying, but the overriding emotion was anger. How dare he put Amma through this torment. *Bastard bastard!* She was so happy he was gone, but even in death he rubbed his sins into his wife's face. Amma would have to live with this knowledge, unable to face her friends and neighbors. Such a pure and gentle woman, she certainly didn't deserve this. In the early hours of the morning, they heard the sound of the bells from the bullocks. Venkat entered thoroughly agitated. "Amma, do you have any money or jewelry at home?"

"Why?" asked Gayatriammal, nonplussed by this strange request. "Where is Appa? Why don't you have his body? What do you need money for? We cannot perform the kriya till the priest comes and have to wait for morning."

"I can't explain too much, but that damn *thevadiya* won't release his body till she's paid." Seetha, completely unused to such language, covered her mouth in horror. Dharmu couldn't think clearly, but she noticed her mother's chest heaving with emotion. Then Gayatriammal pulled her thali off her neck and threw it on the floor. "Take this!" she screamed, and proceeded to throw her gold bangles as well. *Maanathai eduthaachu ippo baaki yellam eduthukatum!*

She was sobbing for the first time, and both Seetha and Dharmu ran to her. Compared to the loss of face, a few pieces of jewelry meant little. The noise and commotion woke up the children, and they all wandered out completely confused. Dharmu went to her brother, who was sitting red eyed and completely dazed. "I think you have to take the Jameendār with you to bargain. How much are they asking for?"

"Too much!" He exclaimed. "200 grams of gold and 50,000 rupees, plus they want the house they live in."

"Do we have the money? And in whose name is the house?"

"Who knows? Appa never told me anything. I'll have to speak to his lawyer and look through all his papers. Right now we have to get his body back somehow."

All these years he had been the "Manager Ayya" and now they were referring to him as a body. What a mess! Dharmu was so angry and so ashamed of him, but she had to make sure the woman was placated and out of their lives forever. "Just give them what they are asking for. We have to bring him home for the last rites. Speak to Jameen Amma. They will know how to handle it."

At regular intervals, both Vani and Rukku kept asking what happened, but in what words could Dharmu explain it to them? They could tell there was a problem but didn't care to probe further. And Kandu had forgotten about his earlier spat with Sendhil, her father's son with the Devadasi woman. It was best she say nothing to them and allow them to have a good living memory of their grandfather.

Dharmu opened the steel almirah and took out all of her mother's jewelry. There were several gold chains and rings, and she picked out the solid gold ones and gave them to Venkat. At noon the contingent returned with her father's body, and the ceremonies went by in a blur. Venkat returned a few pieces of jewelry to Dharmu. Taking the Jameendār and his wife turned out to be a blessing, as they were able to bargain and pay only 20,000 and some gold. When they looked at the deed for the house they were shocked to see it had been bought in Gayatriammal's name. The shame of it all! Buying a house in your wife's name to keep your prostitute. It was unforgivable, and no matter how much they tried to keep it a secret, everyone heard soon enough. Dharmu could tell by the look in their eyes, either filled with pity or scorn. Whichever, it made her so resentful she wanted him out of her life forever. But her mother deserved much more … much, much more.

"Kandu," she said picking up the album with the photograph. "Will they be able to enlarge the picture of Paati only?"

"I can ask," replied Kandu, shrugging his shoulders.

"Then do that. Get me a big picture of Paati only."

"And Thatha? What about him?" enquired Kandu, a little confused.

"What about him?" replied Dharmu derisively.

Chapter Fifty Nine

Vaithee
Vizhupuram – June 1949

The Pharmacy Connection

"Come, come Sahib, your prescription is ready." Vaithee went over to the shelf and pulled out two bottles, scribbled instructions and handed them over, carefully counting the money before he placed it in the safety of the partitioned drawer.

He was really lucky to get this job and he thanked God for it each day. It was only three streets away from home, and he could run back whenever needed. In the first six months after he came to Vizhupuram, Meera was really in bad shape. She wouldn't speak to his parents and didn't eat unless Vaithee fed her. Then, quite by chance, the family goat gave birth to a kid, and that bleating animal was able to touch Meera's soul as no other human could even contemplate. She held the kid goat rocking back and forth, crying and wailing. She watched over it and even slept with it lying by her bed. This was not very well received by his parents, who were Brahmins and considered all animals unclean. Having a goat inside the house was a travesty, and Meera finally understood their body language, and, without saying a word started sleeping outdoors in the thinnai with the kid goat.

Vaithee said a special prayer to the goat each day. If there had been a Hindu god with a goat face, he would have broken a 101 coconuts for it each week, but as there wasn't one, he treated Babu the goat with sacred deference. The first few normal words Meera spoke were to her goat. It's lame bleating was comforting in some way to Meera and she felt safe in its company. The villagers called her the "goat lady," which once again bothered no one, least of all Vaithee.

That was a turning point for Meera, after which each day she spoke more and participated more. It was wonderful to watch her chatting away in broken Tamil with his mother. They understood each other, and Amma was happy for the help in the house. For so many years she had managed alone and was grateful for the extra pair of hands and the company. She had picked up a smattering of Bengali, but Vaithee was really surprised how well Meera could communicate in Tamil.

The children of course had become fluent in Tamil within the first six months.

Prashant was growing fast, and his shoulders were filling out. He was much darker than his sister Pushkin, and finely muscled, a legacy from his father. The local children had welcomed him into their fold after they realized he had a foolproof square cut. Always the top scorer in all their cricket matches, his peers sought him out especially before an important upcoming cricket match.

Pushkin on the other hand took a while fitting in. She followed her mother everywhere, and the local children teased her calling her *aattukutti,* referring to her being with the goat lady. She hated the move, pined for her friends in Calcutta, and missed the comfort of living in the Ayyar's quarters. The school in this area mainly had Brahmin children whose mothers had told them Pushkin was a "half breed." The children never attempted to mix with her and were deliberately cruel. She came home each day in tears, and with Meera so disoriented, Vaithee needed to find a way to console her. Between comforting Meera and Pushkin, Vaithee felt thoroughly overwhelmed.

After six months Vaithee changed her school to one on the other side of town, where children from different backgrounds attended. That was when she made her first friend, Razia. Vaithee was terrified his mother would object if Razia came over to play, but thankfully, Brahmin rules of purity didn't extend to children. Either that or his mother saw how lonely Pushkin was and welcomed this friendship in spite of it being with a Muslim girl. Razia hailed from a wealthy family, who lived in a large house on the other side of town. It was too far to walk, so, on the days she wanted to visit her friend, Vaithee took her by bus, a quick journey that took only five minutes. Razia's family was very welcoming, and Vaithee would while away the time walking in the fields surrounding the main house. His favorite spot was by a small stream. He would sit on a rock by the banks and watch the water gurgle by. It was the only peace and quiet he got, and he relished the meditative reprieve.

On one such day Razia's great-grandfather interrupted his lone pondering. The old man leaned on a cane and peered at him over his rimless spectacles. His embroidered skullcap hid his bald pate, but he exuded dignity and demeanor. As he hunkered over an oak walking stick, his black *shervani* clung to his bent form. The long, white, perfectly trimmed beard and round, rimless glasses further heightened his venerable bearing.

"I see you have found my favorite retreat," he proclaimed, surveying the landscape.

"I'm sorry if I disturbed you. I am Vaithee, Pushkin's father. I wandered here and it was so peaceful. I hope it is alright; I will be off in a bit as soon as the children are tired."

"And I am Muhammad Salih, Razia's great-grandfather." Thus began a most unlikely relationship, but to his surprise he was never at a loss for conversation with this octogenarian. Salih Sahib knew everything about everything. He read voraciously in spite of failing eyes, and his mind was razor sharp. The conversation became much juicier when Vaithee realized he had been a revolutionary although he belonged to the Gandhian tradition of non-violence. Vaithee was careful about sharing too much, but the discussions on politics kept him thoroughly engaged. After their initial encounter, Vaithee eagerly anticipated each week to bring Pushkin to play, and once she scampered in, he waited for his friend on the banks of the stream.

Razia's father owned a pharmacy and it was Salih's kindness that secured him a job. Even so, every time the old man came to the store to pick up his medication, he insisted on paying. This was his grandson's business and every rupee counted. The medication was for his arthritic knees. Salih was chairman of a Constitution Recommendations Committee, and every month he went to Salem for a meeting. The collective recommendations were then sent to Dr. Ambedkar, who was in charge of drafting a complete Constitution for the new nation. Once the new document was adopted, India would then be declared a Republic. Vaithee started accompanying him to his meetings and was grateful for the opportunity to hobnob with the elite of the south. One afternoon, Vaithee accompanied the old man to Salem in the comfort of his large Chrysler sedan. The committee's work was done, but it's members continued to meet to maintain friendships. After the meeting, as they sat down to eat a sumptuous lunch, a young boy came up to them to beg for alms. He couldn't have been more than eight or nine years, and his clothes were unsoiled, which was uncommon for a beggar. Immediately, Vaithee thought of Nandu. He must have been around this age when he had run away. His destiny changed forever, replacing a child with a hardened assassin. Reaching into his pocket, he took out a few coins. "What's your name?" he asked the young boy.

"Raju, saar," said the boy saluting in gratitude.

"Raju, why are you begging? Where are your parents?"

"They are in the village saar. It's very difficult. This year the crop failed and the landlord still wanted rent. I was too hungry for too long so I ran away. I thought I could find some work in the city and feed myself."

"Do you have brothers and sisters?"

"Two of my younger brothers died and my sister is sick. I don't want to die."

Vaithee's eyes teared up. Heaven knows how many families have children they can't support. This boy was new to the city. You could tell by looking at his eyes, the gaze was still soft. But Vaithee knew the hardships of survival would teach him tough lessons, and soon stony eyes would replace this soft gaze. "Do you want to go to school?"

The boy nodded.

"Will you come and stay with me? I can feed you and send you to school."

"And what do I have to do in return?'

"You can certainly help on the farm. We have cows to be milked and there are always vegetables for delivery. You can earn your keep."

The young boy agreed immediately.

What innocence! Vaithee thought. He trusted the whole world and could easily have become prey for some sexual deviant. It was his good fortune that it was Vaithee and not some predator who offered him sanctuary. Salih Sahib had no objection, and after lunch, they drove home to Vizhupuram with one extra, overjoyed passenger.

"What are you going to do with this boy?"

"Nothing ... bring him up and educate him I suppose."

"And your wife and parents? What if they object?"

"They will protest but he can sleep in the shed with the cows for now."

"So remind me again, why you are doing this?"

"There was a boy I once knew, whom I couldn't save. This is for him. This is for Nandu."

CHAPTER SIXTY

KANDU
CALCUTTA – JANUARY 1950

THE ACCIDENT

K andu couldn't breathe. The events of last night were so traumatic and so overwhelming, he felt completely overrun with emotions. *Why? Why? Why?* That too on New Year's Day. How was Dilip going to live with the guilt? It should never have happened, and although Kandu wasn't directly responsible for the accident, he felt morally accountable. It was a horrible end to an otherwise pleasant evening, and now he had the disagreeable task of telling his father what took place. Kandu looked at his watch, beads of perspiration dripping off his face—and it wasn't even hot. It was almost eight o'clock. He had checked several times, but Daddy wasn't awake yet. They had been out to some party but were home before Kandu returned. He had to speak to him before the police arrived. The Police Commissioner Mr. S. N. Chatterjee was Daddy's friend, and he was sure to be lenient, but taking a life was a terrible crime and they were collectively responsible. Kandu kept repeating the words *why why why* and banging his head on the desk.

Yesterday was a great day if you left out Sheela Ghosh and her antics. The party was in Sheela's friend Usha's home. Usha's father also worked in government, and they were to bring in the New Year at their palatial home on Burdwan Road. Kandu was sure she too had a crush on him. It was really quite awkward, all evening trying to avoid Sheela and Usha at the same time. His friends were guffawing watching him sidestep and duck. Each time he moved away from Sheela, Usha would appear seemingly from nowhere. Kandu found himself running from room to room providing entertainment for all his friends. They called it the 'Shusha dance'. Tucky had even set it to rhythm, and Mickey would add percussion. Kandu was not amused. He was just not interested in either girl. At least Usha kept her distance while speaking to him. Sheela on the other hand came up too close, and the duo literally danced around the room with Kandu back-stepping continually. It was really shameful the way she threw herself at him, Kandu mused. Any other man could have taken full advantage, and there would have been no objection coming from Sheela, but he just wasn't interested. She was pretty with classic Bengali features, but she annoyed him.

Food and drinks were flowing, and even Kandu had downed plenty of beer, unusual for him. The food was fabulous and helped to reduce the buzz in his head. He was quite sober by one in the morning after drinking six glasses of water. Kandu never liked the feeling of sleeping with an alcoholic high. He drank water and peed till he felt normal. Beer was alright, like drinking water. The bathrooms were constantly busy, and the boys had no compunctions relieving themselves in the bushes. Ammonia was good for plants anyway, Tucky argued.

After the party was over they hung around in the car park horsing around. No evening was complete without a drive to Diamond Harbor and about twelve of them piled into three cars and made their way past the Majherhat Bridge onto Diamond Harbour road. Kandu loved car racing but today he knew his Dodge was no patch on Dilip's Chevy. It would take them over an hour to reach, and Kandu wasn't sure if he wanted to go all the way to the harbor. Maybe they could turn back in half an hour. The Diamond Harbour road was narrow but desolate. Nobody lived near or used this road, especially at night, and it was perfect for drag racing. There were only one or two spots where one could safely overtake a rival driver, and this had to be done skillfully to avoid going off into the sludge which banked the road.

Kandu was leading the convoy for the first fifteen minutes. They had the windows down and, other than the sound of the breeze and the revving of engines, nothing else could be heard. Mickey was slumped at the back. He had imbibed way too much and was snoring rhythmically. Ramu and a couple of other fellows from the party were in Kandu's car. Kandu adjusted his rear-view mirror swerving to preempt Dilip's every move to pass him. As they approached the part of the road which was a little wider, Dilip accelerated, and there was little Kandu could do. Kandu knew his Dodge couldn't match the Chevy's 120 kms/hour. The boys were hanging out the window booing and yelling, thrilled at passing Kandu's car.

It happened suddenly. A body slammed into Kandu's front bonnet and careened off. He slammed on the brakes and swerved crazily trying to avoid Dilip's car, coming to a screeching halt on the side of the road. It required all of his driving skill to prevent the car from going off the road. The third car was a quarter mile away and came to a slow stop behind them.

No one understood what happened. In a few seconds every boy was cold sober. Dilip got a flashlight out of his trunk and they walked back down the dark road searching for the body.

"What happened?" the boys asked. They had not seen the accident in the pitch darkness. Kandu asked Dilip, "Was it me that hit him?"

"No, I hit him and he went up in the air and landed on your bonnet," Dilip replied somberly.

"Jesus, this is terrible!"

It was an old man, dressed only in a dhoti which was now covered in his blood. From his contorted resting pose it was clear he was dead. The boys didn't know what to do. They were so nervous they took turns peeing by the side of the road, returning after they were done to confer.

"What do we do? Do we leave him?"

"How can we do that? What if he is still alive?"

"Shit, shit, shit, this is horrible!"

"Listen guys, the police *lafda* will be terrible. It will go on our permanent record. Its best we just leave and pretend it never happened."

"What kind of man are you? This guy is bleeding, we can't just leave him."

"Look guys, it was an accident okay? It was dark and this man had no business crossing the road."

"You could hear the sound of our engines miles away. He should have stayed on the side."

"But he didn't ..."

"Yes, and now he's dead."

There was a moment of silence

"We have to take him to the hospital. It's the right thing to do," decided Kandu.

They placed their jackets in Dilip's Chevy to prevent the blood from staining the leather seats. It took four of them, all terribly unsteady on their feet, to carry him and put him in the car.

"Wait!" said Dilip. "We can't say we hit him. The story has to be that we found him like this and brought him to the hospital. They will see the tire marks on this road and the blood, so we have to say we found him on Taratala road."

"What about the blood on the car?" asked Ramu.

"We have to wipe the damn thing down. Thank God we didn't crash into one another and there's no damage to the car. When the police come to examine the car, it has to be shining and clean. We were driving and saw something on the middle of the road and stopped to pick him up. No one can say anything else. Got it?" Dilip instructed.

Kandu searched for a rag and wiped as hard as he could, but the echo of the body slamming into his bonnet churned his stomach, and he turned to the side and retched violently.

They drove in silence to PG Hospital. Kandu stayed in the car chain smoking, shattered by the turn of events. They could have left the man bleeding on the side of the road but they didn't. They brought him here and perhaps the police would be able to locate his family. That was comforting, but in no way did it relieve the overwhelming feeling of guilt at having taken a life. Dilip filled out the police report, and they returned to their cars and parted ways.

Mickey was too drunk to go home and would have to crash with Kandu. Govindhan and Kandu hauled him up the stairs. It was no big deal; Govindhan was used to doing this.

But Kandu's moral dilemma didn't let him sleep. Should he tell his father the truth or go with the story Dilip asked them to share? Never had he lied to his Dad except perhaps about his smoking when he first started. But on the other hand, it was better his father knew nothing. That way if questioned by the police, he wouldn't have to lie. Dilip would be fine. His family was very well connected. The man who died looked poor and homeless, so there was no question of his family reporting the accident. There were no witnesses except twelve drunk boys who were now partners in crime.

Kandu was drinking his third cup of Darjeeling tea when his father came in.

"Happy New Year, son!" he said hugging him.

Kandu had almost forgotten it was the New Year. He certainly wasn't happy. "Hey Dad! Happy New Year to you too. When did you guys get home?" he asked cheerily.

"Around 12:30. How about you?"

"Oh a little after that. I lost track of time."

"Anything interesting happened that you want to share with me?" Mahadevan queried casually.

He knows ... he absolutely knows! The police must have already advised him.

"What do you mean?" Kandu asked nervously.

"Nothing in particular. Why do you look nervous?"

"It's just ... it's just that ... we f ... found a dead man. He had been hit by some car." (That was true.)

"So we took him to the hospital and that's all. I mean if the police come, you can tell them we found him."

"That was decent of you. Where were you?"

"Taratala road."

"Why all the way there? Isn't the Kapur house on Burdwan road?"

"Oh, I was dropping a friend off." One lie leads to another, and Kandu knew he needed to change the subject soon or he could get wound up in knots.

All day his heart skipped a beat every time he heard the gates open. But the police never came. Neither to his house nor Dilip's. For a few months both Dilip and Kandu suffered terribly in the turmoil of guilt. Then slowly ... the nightmares stopped. Within a year the poor dead man was completely forgotten, relegated to a hateful nightmare.

CHAPTER SIXTY ONE

KAMU
MARCH 1949

SAPTĀHAM WITH THE DEEKSHITHAR

"**N**o, no, no, you can't do it!" Kunju yelled from the verandah on seeing Kamu pick *tulasi* leaves from the sacred tulasi madham.

"What? Why can't I do it?" Kamu stopped in her tracks, her chin jutting out rebelliously, wondering what was wrong with picking a few basil leaves.

"Only men are allowed to cut the leaves from the tulasi plant. They are supposed to be an embodiment of Goddess Lakshmi," was Kunju's unacceptable response.

"Kunju Periamma, how is there space in your head to remember all these million rules?"

"What is there to remember? Everyone knows it."

"I don't understand it. If Amma and I are the only people who care for this plant, then how come we can't pluck the leaves to make a garland? It doesn't make sense," grumbled Kamu. They had bought several bunches of sacred tulasi leaves from Lake Market, and Kamu wanted to add a few leaves from their plant at home while making a garland for the Rama Navami celebrations.

"Please listen to me. Ask Venkat; he will happily pluck the leaves, then you can make the garland. Venkat…." Kunju called out to her son.

This is all rubbish, Kamu thought to herself, but she didn't want to make a scene. Tomorrow morning was a big poojai in the house celebrating the beginning of Rama Navami, a celebration commemorating the birth of Rama, the seventh incarnation of Vishnu on earth.

The Deekshithar was in Calcutta at this auspicious time for a *saptāham* at National High School. The week-long festivity was in honor of Lord Rama, and the Deekshithar would be giving a discourse each day celebrating the stories of Rama.

This was the seventh time Sengalipuram Anantharama Deekshithar was visiting their home. Sundar, their local priest, was his cousin, and, as he was so close to the family, each time the Deekshithar visited Calcutta, he was invited by the family to preside over some poojai at the Parthasarathy home. Rajam never complained, as she believed it was an honor to have such a learned man bless their home. The Deekshithar had received this title after years of arduous study of ancient Sanskrit texts. He had travelled the length and breadth of the country conducting week-long *saptāhams* singing the praises of the Lord. An ardent disciple of Krishna, he glorified the essence of ancient Indian texts, such as the Ramayana and the Bhagavatam. The last time he visited, he had spoken from the Bhagavata- Purana, which celebrates the incarnations of Lord Vishnu. His description of Vishnu as *Narasimha,* half-man and half-lion, was almost as if he were painting a picture. Chanting from sacred texts and singing in his deep melodic voice, he dramatized the scene, breathing life into the ancient myth of the devotee Prahalad's love for and singular faith in the Lord. The Deekshithar's name and fame had spread, and tomorrow about fifty people were expected to get a private *darshanam* and a special *Pravachan*—a discourse by a spiritual giant.

Kunju Periamma had been visiting them for the last month. She was still broken with grief from missing her father. Swaminathan's passing created a huge vacuum in her life, and she was left completely bereft and emotionally drained. He had been for so many years her source of strength. Life had not been easy, especially since she was widowed so young. The burden of raising six children was shared in equal part by her father, and now she felt exposed and lost. Rajam thought a change of scene would do her good, and after the first month ceremony had been performed, she asked Kunju to come to Calcutta. The two sisters cried and lamented together, and Kunju it seemed had an endless repertoire of anecdotes to share. Kamu especially enjoyed the stories. It was hard for her to believe she would not see her Thatha again, but hearing and speaking about him was a celebration of his stellar life, and the crying brought closure to all of them.

It was good they had this big poojai to plan for. It distracted them all, and especially gave Kunju a break from her grief. The previous day they bought all the vegetables and flowers needed for the event. Kunju really enjoyed shopping at Ganesh Bhandar, the local provision store. She ordered as much as she needed, perhaps for the first time ever. It brought back memories of her visits to Perumal's store in Thanjavur, and she could feel the familiar clenching of her gut as she recalled her previous anxieties of figuring out ways to pay for groceries. Never in her life had she ordered such lavish quantities of food, and she enjoyed the sense of abundance for a change. A fleeting thought about Kamalamba flashed through her mind, but she didn't heed it.

As Kamu sat down to weave the tulasi garland, Kutti Ramu, Sundar's cousin and apprentice, walked in. Ramu had finished his Vedic studies in Sengalipuram and was staying for a while with Sundar, helping him with his busy schedule. He was just a few years older than Kamu and the two were very good friends. He was bone thin, his white veshti standing in sharp contrast to his dark body. In the beginning, he always turned up bare bodied, so Partha bought him his first two white shirts, one of which he was wearing today.

Yenna Kamu, tulasi malai kattariya? he asked, squatting down on the floor.

"*Aama* Ramu. How come you are here? Making sure we are preparing correctly according to *Manushastra*[6]?" asked Kamu, tongue in cheek, always ready to poke fun of the million rules of conduct enunciated in this ancient text, laws which had survived millenia.

"No, no ... tonight Deekshithar Mama comes and things will be very busy. I had some free time so I thought I would drop by." In the past few months, Ramu had become a permanent feature in their home. He hung around helping Rajam with chores and going marketing with Partha, but what he loved most of all was playing badminton with Kamu. His *kudumi* shook vigorously as he ran around the yard hitting the shuttle and inevitably the top knot would come untied making him pause his game to tie it up again. Like any other teenager, he loved to discuss movies and film stars, making Kamu forget at times that he was a priest. Rajam suspected he was sweet on Kamu, but she was blissfully unaware. Kamu had always played with all her male cousins and didn't treat Ramu any differently. As usual, Sundar arrived just before lunch. Accustomed to his regular visits, Rajam always had enough rice prepared. Food in this home was plentiful, mirroring the love and generosity in their hearts.

Kamu had finished making the garland and placed it in a silver tray along with the other fruits and offerings in preparation for tomorrow's event. Then she filled the bucket outside for Sundar and Ramu to wash up before eating. A loud burp at the end of the sumptuous meal indicated Sundar's appreciation of Rajam's cooking. There was no doubting her culinary skills. She loved cooking and feeding others, but there would be too many guests tomorrow, so they hired a Brahmin cook who would begin preparations hours before daybreak.

Frenetic excitement marked the next morning's activity. Rajam and Kunju would fast until the poojai was over, but Kamu enjoyed the steaming hot idlis and chutney made by Ramadurai, the cook. The ladies were dressed in traditional madisars and the men tied their veshtis in the *panjakatcham* style. When they

---

6   Manu-smriti (Laws of Manu) traditionally the most authoritative of the books on the Hindu code based on Dharma or right action, supposedly authored by Manu, the progenitor of mankind.

heard the gate creak, they knew the Deekshithar must have arrived. The huge, black Oldsmobile entered the driveway. Their mutual friend G. V. Raman owned Underwood typewriters, a very successful business headquartered in Calcutta. He had a massive mansion with several bedrooms and always hosted the Deekshithar whenever he visited Calcutta, loaning his Oldsmobile to take him around. Their mutual interest in religious activities had brought them together, and Partha felt honored to count Raman as one of his closest friends. It made no difference that Partha was only a salesman and Raman a successful tycoon, the two frequented each other's homes and held one another in high regard.

They came in three cars—the Raman family and several of their friends along with a retinue of nine priests. Rama Vādhyār was the last to get out of the car. He was the Deekshithar's younger brother who would be ordained as a Deekshithar very soon. Partha washed the holy Deekshithar's feet on a silver plate and led him into the living room where the poojai was to take place. The room was almost full, and once the poojai was completed, the Deekshithar began his discourse with the birth of Rama. This was a story each child in every corner of the country knew well, yet his rendering added a special flavor, and the whole crowd silently absorbed each word. Kamu glanced at Ramu Vādhyār standing by the doorway. He was as fair as the Deekshithar but much slimmer and more finely muscled. His veshti bordered in bright red was tied impeccably and he stood tall with a royal bearing. Everything about him was perfect, from the width of his broad shoulders to the narrow waist, his upper body in perfect proportion to his lower. His lofty brow was lined with three rows of ashen vibhuti almost as if they were painted on. A perfectly round kumkumam pottu adorned the center of his forehead. Even the lines of vibhuti on his arms and chest were perfectly lined with no stray marks. Rows of gold chains and *Rudrāksha mālais* hung from his neck and in his ears were large diamond earrings. His face was sculpted perfectly from his long straight nose to his heavy-lidded eyes and perfect bow-shaped mouth. Everything about him seemed perfect. Kamu looked at him for the longest time and couldn't help thinking this is what Lord Rama must have looked like. After the discourse, everyone lined up to offer their namskarams and get the Deekshithar's blessings.

Nanna iru Kamu, he blessed her, placing his hand on the crown of her head.

Kutti Ramu piped up. "*Mama,* this year Kamu made the tulasi malai for the poojai."

"Oho!" remarked the Deekshithar. "That's why it looks so perfect. I was wondering whose tiny fingers wove it so well. I should have known. Your devotion is heartwarming and making this garland? *Rombo punyam rombo punyam.* For this act alone you will get a husband who is just like Rama. But perhaps you won't be matched with Rama. The perfect consort for Kamakshi is Shiva. Kamakshi will get a *Nilakantan.*" He smiled at her benevolently.

Kamu blushed. *"Illai Mama, ippo vendaam.* Let some more time pass. I'm not ready for marriage. I'm too young."

"Yes that is true, but very soon your Nilakantan will appear," said the Deekshithar handing her a red rose as a blessing.

Kamu was so happy. How did the Deekshithar know she loved roses more than any other flower? She scampered off to her room and pinched off the bloom, leaving a short stem attached. The rose was pristine, dewdrops still glistening on its concentric petals. "Aaha!" She exclaimed in delight, admiring nature's perfection. Kamu placed the striking bloom in her hair behind her left ear. She looked at the mirror appreciating the vision more than was wont.

Nilakantan wherever you are, you don't stand a chance. One look at me and you will be my dasana dasa; my slave. I'm just too beautiful!

CHAPTER SIXTY TWO

KAMU AND SHATHI
SOUTH END PARK – JULY 1949

THE BALD GIRL AT THE WINDOW

I t was really hard to focus when Viju and Vatsal kept peeping in to see if she was done. Their making funny faces at her didn't help. Kamu had two tutors who came to teach her every other day. Mrs. D'Costa taught her Science and Math, classes which she absolutely abhorred. She had no head for numbers or logic, but she had to pass her exams. There were still two years more to prepare for her Junior Cambridge exams, and if she went by her recent test scores, she wasn't going to do well in either of these subjects. She loved classes with her other tutor Mrs. Davis, an Englishwoman who had lost her husband and decided to stay on in Calcutta. She received a pension from the Government and supplemented her income by tutoring young girls and boys for the Board exams. It was Saturday afternoon, and the history lesson had been boring enough, but Shakespeare was just too much when all Kamu could think of was hanging out with her friends.

"The quality of mercy...." Mrs. Davis began.

Show some mercy on me, thought Kamu, unable to stop fidgeting. The next half hour dragged by agonizingly slowly. As soon as Mrs. Davis left, the girls ran in.

"Finally," said Viju, collapsing on the sofa. "She stayed much longer than usual."

"Honestly, I have no idea what she said. Saturdays are bad days for tutoring, but there's no other time. You girls didn't make it any easier by continually peeking."

"Anyway she's gone now, so what's the plan?" asked Vatsal, helping Kamu stack her books on one side of the dining table.

"Well ... Shathi has invited us over to play badminton, and after that we will go to Panchamda's house. He has some musical evening planned, so it should be fun."

"Ooh, I'm so excited," exclaimed Viju. "Maybe some famous film stars will be there. I would love to meet Kishore Kumar. *Marne ki duayen kyon mangu....*" she crooned, a song sung by Kishore Kumar in his debut film Ziddi.

"Don't pray too hard. Kishore is the singer. Did you mean his brother, Ashok Kumar? Anyway, both brothers live in Bombay ... not here. I've been to Panchamda's house many times and mostly his father Sachinda invites Bengali singers. I met Hemant Kumar once. He sings so beautifully," reminisced Kamu.

"What did he sing?" asked Viju, her voice filled with excitement.

O Nodire ... ekti kotha something *tomare,* sang Kamu remembering the tune far more easily than the lyrics. "I think Sachinda composed that, or I may be mistaken." Gathering their racquets, they stopped at the corner shop to buy new shuttles and proceeded to Shathi's house.

Shathi's home was the largest Kamu had ever seen and perhaps one of the oldest in South End Park. The huge courtyard was flanked by rooms and, with so many people coming and going, it seemed as though hundreds of people lived here. The Banerjees had an extended family. Four brothers, their wives and all their children lived in separate wings of the house. The servants' quarters were massive, with at least ten rooms, and a small courtyard in front, where they dried their laundry. Food was cooked on an industrial scale, and the smell of fish and other seafood bothered Kamu a bit, but as Shathi was her close friend, she overlooked this.

A maidservant brought out a jug of ice-cold lemonade and placed it next to the clay pot filled with cool water. They would need all of that, what with the humidity so high. Saris were a bit cumbersome while playing, and Kamu folded the sari at her waist hiking it up several inches.

As she played, out of the corner of her eye, she could sense being watched, but every time she looked up, the young girl peeping from one of the windows would hide behind the curtain. Kamu and Shathi won the first game 21-7. They were tired and out of breath, happy to take a break and sip the ice-cold lemonade. Kamu wiped her face with the end of her sari and surreptitiously glanced up again without so much as moving her head. The young girl had no idea she was spotted and she stood there looking down longingly. She appeared very young, perhaps not much older than Kamu and was wearing a white sari with a small blue border. But she didn't have on a blouse, and when the sari slipped from her head Kamu was shocked to note she was bald. She jerked her head up and waved, but the terror in the young girl's eyes was evident as she hurriedly closed the window and disappeared.

"Who is that?" Kamu asked Shathi.

"Oh her. That is Sharmila, my cousin's widow. Don't look at her; it's bad luck."

"Surely you don't think looking at her will bring you bad luck. Come on, Shathi," remarked Vatsal scornfully.

"Well it hardly matters what I believe. I have to follow the rules, and the rule about not looking or talking to her is very important here. She married my cousin last year, and within six months he got some fever and died."

"Yes I remember you told me," recalled Kamu. "Sometime around March wasn't it?"

"It was really tragic. She is only sixteen, but she has to shave her head and can't come out of her room."

"Are you friends with her? Can we call her to play badminton with us?" asked Viju innocently, not having listened too closely to the prior conversation.

"Are you mad? My mother would kill me. No, no, no…. She is here only till the end of the month then my uncle will take her to Kashi. There is a family house and she has to live there with the servant."

"Alone?" asked Kamu in shock, one eyebrow cocked.

"Naturally. There are a few other widows who live in the house. Distant cousins."

"What will she do there?" enquired Vatsal.

"She has to do penance for being a bad *shagun* and stay there till she dies."

"That's terrible. Why can't she stay here? There's so much room. She could easily hide in one corner and not be noticed."

"I don't know, Vatsal. I really feel bad for her, but her father-in-law, my uncle, is very traditional and blames her for the death of my cousin, so he is anxious to get rid of her."

"Can't she go back to live with her parents?" said Viju, assuming that was only natural.

"Chii … no! She is bad luck. Her parents don't want to even look at her."

"That's just terrible. My aunt, we call her Chithi, was widowed very young, but she stays with us and takes part in almost everything. In fact, she is the midwife in our family and has helped with almost thirty births. We never do anything important without consulting her. I suppose it's a little different in the south."

"Can she come to weddings and poojais also? I also have a widowed grandma, but she must remain indoors whenever we have some function at home. My mom says it's better that way. People can be very cruel, and if she's not there she doesn't need to hear any harsh words." The rules were different in Vatsal's home.

"My Thatha was very progressive. My aunt Kunju Periamma, who is visiting us now, was widowed early, and he wouldn't even hear of her cutting her hair. She even wears normal silk saris. Both Periamma and Chithi attend all functions, but Chithi never sits down with us. She stands beyond the doorway, and that itself bothers me because I love her so much, but this is so much worse," lamented Kamu.

"Don't break your head about Sharmila. She was very shy to begin with. We spoke but not much. I think she'll be happier in Kashi. My aunts and uncles are quite mean to her."

"How could she be happy there in the company of widows? She is so young she has her whole life ahead of her," said Kamu, really sad to hear how widows were treated even in this modern age.

They played two more games, and after freshening up left for Panchamda's home. All the para girls and boys were there mainly for the free food. The Bengali fare was largely seafood, but Kamu and her friends enjoyed the dal and two vegetables and polished off the *Aamer tok* made from *Langda* mangoes. Viju was sad Kishore Kumar was not there that evening, but she recognized a young, upcoming actor named Arun Chatterjee. Kamu had not seen his lone film *Dhrishtidaan*, probably because it flopped in the box office, but she knew his younger brother Tarun, who was Panchamda's friend.

Partha accompanied the girls home after dinner, and Kamu was tired from the day's excitement. Kunju Periamma was sharing her room, and the two chatted each night before drifting off. Kamu sat on the bed as Periamma brushed her hair. She never liked oil remaining in it and had read in a magazine that a hundred strokes with a brush kept the hair shining. "Periamma are you sad being a widow?" she asked quietly.

"Not anymore. For a while it was hard, but Appa was so kind."

"Today I saw Shathi's cousin, and they are sending her to Kashi to live forever. She is only sixteen! It's so sad!"

"I know. There are hundreds of widows in Kashi. Thank God we don't have those horrid customs in the south. But what can we do? We can only pray for them."

And that's what Kamu did. She prayed that one day Sharmila would meet a kind man who would marry her and give her a new lease on life. She knew she was asking for the impossible, but if one didn't ask, how were the gods to know what you wanted? If only that could happen....

CHAPTER SIXTY THREE

KAMU
CALCUTTA – DECEMBER 1949

THE DINNER PARTY

Kamu was super excited. Partha had a Swiss delegation visiting, who wanted to sample Indian food in an Indian home, so he had invited them on Saturday evening for dinner. All week long Kamu had been decorating and then redecorating the house. It was the first time foreigners were coming to their home, and she wanted everything to appear just right. She rearranged the sofas at angles, placing a lamp behind the longest sofa in one corner. Then she put everything back the way it was, lined up against the wall. This morning she changed her mind again and put everything back in angles.

Partha was getting exasperated. "Every time I come home I'm not completely sure this is my house. What are you up to Kamu?"

"I'm doing it. I'm not troubling you. Don't worry, everything is going to be just perfect." And then flippantly humming a tune, she skipped off. She walked into the dining room and surveyed the scene. Hmm…. The room was large, but the view of the kitchen spoiled it. Maybe this was not the perfect spot for the dinner. That evening she rounded up all the para boys and shifted her bed into the verandah and made them move the dining table into her bedroom. They complained nonstop when she said they also had to move the bedside table and her huge dressing table. But she sweet-talked them into this by promising homemade *mysorepak*, one of Rajam's most famous delicacies. That evening Partha returned to find a bedroom in the verandah, making him go crazy. "Kamuuuuu," he screamed. "You really don't have to turn the house upside down just for a dinner party!"

"Did I ask you to do anything? Did I? Come and see my room. It looks perfect. I borrowed a tablecloth from the Ghoshes and their crystal glasses and forks. Those will go really well with our *peengang* set." She was chattering nonstop and Partha was not a happy camper.

"Please don't call it peengang in front of the visiting *vellaikārā;* it's called china."

Kamu made a mental note and then busied herself with the paintings, moving everything around till it looked just right. Partha walked back in after discovering Kamu's clothes strewn all over his bed. "So are you planning to sleep outside, dear?" he asked, a beatific smile on his face.

"Er.... No that's the only thing I'm going to trouble you with. Could you? Pretty please? it's only for one, no, two nights. Sunday morning, I promise I'll have everything back where it was."

Kamu took five rupees from Rajam and ran down to the stationer's store. No dinner would ever be complete without a menu. That's what they had at all restaurants. She bought card paper and colored pencils and got to work. She had to make four identical ones, one for each guest. She struggled with a few descriptions especially with idlis and vadais, but in the end it really looked fantastic. The guests were sure to be impressed, and she was quite sure this would result in a good promotion for her father. It felt really good to do her bit.

Menu at the Parthasarathy residence—

Appetizers
Vadai with chutney
Fried lentil delights with coconut chutney (Non-spicy)

Main Course
Onion Sāmbār
Lentil and vegetable soup (Little spicy)
Dal
Bengali lentil soup
Rasam
Mulligatawny soup (Little spicy)
Alu Curry
Sautéed potatoes spiced with turmeric (Tasty)
Kos Poriyal
Lightly tossed cabbage garnished with coconut flakes (Not at all spicy)
Kosmari
Lentil cucumber and carrot salad (Garnished with coconut and hing)
Idli
Steamed lentil cakes (Bland, best eaten with sāmbār and chutney)

Desert
Semiya Payasam
Semolina in milk garnished with raisins and cashews (Sweet)

ENJOY

Kamu was hyper-excited and ready by six o'clock, though the guests would not be in till much later. She had chosen a mauve voile sari, but her orange rose did not match at all. Impulsively she decided to wear her new French chiffon sari. The *sariwallah* had offered a great price and she persuaded Rajam to buy it. All her friends wore chiffon saris and she didn't possess one. It was beautiful really, white with sprays of orange roses all over. It would go perfectly with the orange rose in her hair.

Partha came by at exactly seven p.m. and reluctantly Rajam shook hands with the men. Kamu had already trained her to say, *How do you do* like she saw in the movies. Partha looked at her strangely during the dinner but was otherwise absorbed in conversation with his guests. Kamu barely spoke English, and the men's strange accents forced her to ask them to repeat themselves. The food was delicious, making the evening a complete success. Partha dropped them off at their hotel and was back by ten o'clock. Kamu and Rajam were lolling around getting ready to sleep.

"Kamu!" said Partha his voice a little sharp. "How could you dress like that, and that too in front of guests? Have you no shame? Haven't we taught you anything about decorum?"

"What are you talking about? What is wrong with what I wore?" replied Kamu feeling the heat suffuse her face. This was serious and Appa looked really angry.

"That sari showed your skin completely. How could you come before my guests half naked?"

"HALF NAKED? Appa I was fully covered. I was wearing a sari not a dress." Tears of anger already sprang into her eyes. Appa was completely spoiling the evening.

"I don't want to hear of it. You can NEVER wear such a thin sari ever again— do you hear me? Not as long as you live in the house."

Kamu didn't hear the rest of what he said, but the anger and pride within her were dangerously colliding, and she picked up the neatly folded sari and ripped it in two, staring at her father defiantly. "There.... Happy?" Then she threw herself on the bed crying uncontrollably and swore to herself not to speak to her father ever again.

CHAPTER SIXTY FOUR

KANDU
MARCH 1951

THE UNREAD OBITUARY

*J*ohnny was a chemist, but Johnny is no more; for what he thought was H_2O was H_2SO_4. Kandu smiled. Someone had shared this morbid joke with him in school, and now this was inscribed on top of every page of his Chemistry notebook accompanied by doodles of Johnny the Chemist in various stages of distress. He had one more exam to write, and then he was done with college. He would officially be M. N. Ayyar B.Sc. Hons. His whole future lay ahead of him, yet he had no idea what he wanted to do. Mickey had already found a job with Bird and Co., and Ram and Dilip had their father's businesses to fall back on. Daddy wanted him to go to Cambridge if he could, but Kandu had his heart set on going to America and had already applied to Harvard University. No one he knew had ventured to America. The legacy of colonialism in India made it every young man's virtually unattainable aspiration to secure degrees from Oxford or Cambridge, but for some reason Kandu was much more fascinated with America. People said it was *God's own Country,* and he longed to see for himself. Hollywood movies had painted an exotic picture of America, the land of dreams, but his personal fascination with American cars was much more significant. He drove a Dodge and longed to drive a Buick on those famous American highways. He hadn't mentioned any of his plans to his parents and wasn't even sure if Daddy could afford sending him there. It wasn't the right time; he would wait to see if he was admitted before speaking to his father.

Kandu sighed and leaned back in his chair. He reached for his silver cigarette case and lit a cigarette, inhaling deeply and blowing smoke rings. It was a dull day. He had been studying all day, and his mind was filled with numbers and equations. Though mentally exhausted, he knew he would do well in this exam. Chemistry was his passion, and he never needed to work hard. Perhaps he should consider doing research. After a while, he slapped the book shut and went out into the verandah to smoke the rest of his cigarette, opening the doors to his room so the encapsulated smoke could escape. Right now, it looked as if his room was on fire.

"Govindhan," he yelled. "*Ek* cup coffee *lana.*"

Aaya saab, he heard Govindhan reply. Kandu stared mindlessly at the Majherhaat Bridge, watching cars and trucks roar by, the engine resonances surprisingly comforting. His trance was broken by the deafening sound of a thud followed by the clanging of the steel tumblers on the floor. He spun around, shocked to find Govindhan lying unconscious on the floor.

Springing to action, he ran to Govindhan, calling out to the servants for help. Kandu was sweating. What should he do? He tried sprinkling water on his face and slapped him gently, but there was no response. His pulse was weak, but other than that, Kandu couldn't make any further guesses. Govindhan didn't look good; his breathing was shallow and his stillness scared Kandu. With the help of the *bawarchi* and driver, they put the comatose servant into the back of the car and rushed him to the Government Hospital. Dharmu had gone out to play Bridge, and Kandu left a message asking her to come to the hospital, although he knew there wasn't much chance she would cut short her game for a servant. Once he brought Govindhan into the hospital, the doctor shooed him out, and he waited anxiously in the verandah chain-smoking. His throat felt raw and he hoped he wasn't falling sick. The corridors were littered with supine, sick patients waiting to be seen, which didn't help. These unfiltered cigarettes were no good for the throat. He had one last exam tomorrow and hoped to stay healthy till then. He popped a mint into his mouth enjoying the soothing menthol vapors sending cooling waves down his throat.

Kandu knew he had to go home soon, but the doctor had not made an appearance and he hoped Govindhan was all right. He couldn't be very old, perhaps in his mid-forties. Govindhan was such a loyal servant. In all those years he worked for them in Delhi and Shimla, he only went home a couple of times, the journey to his village too long and arduous. But in that time, his wife gave birth to four children. Kandu tried to explain to him he was being cuckolded, but he would hear none of it. *Shob Bhogowan ka den,* he insisted, accepting God's blessings of plentiful progeny and refusing to believe otherwise. Poor Govindhan, such a simpleton. So full of energy and positivity. God alone knows what malady was afflicting him. The servants never complained about their health and preferred natural remedies. They were terrified doctors would give them *Injishuns*(injections), and preferred to suffer in silence rather than be taken to hospital or a clinic. In any case, Mummy dealt with the servants and their problems, and Kandu felt sad that he never ever asked him about his life or even how he was feeling, not ever. Govindhan was just always there, jumping to attend to everyone's needs. The Ayyar household could never have managed without his energetic presence, always flying to everyone's aid, finding lost spectacles and newspapers, arranging almirahs and polishing shoes. And all of this he did with a beatific smile. Happy. That was Govindhan. Always happy.

Kandu looked anxiously at his watch. It was almost five o'clock and he really should be heading home. He decided to call his father from the hospital and tell him what happened. Perhaps he could send someone to relieve him. Kandu was nervous about tomorrow's exam, and it didn't help that his throat hurt. He wanted to go home, yet he was anxious and needed to find out what was wrong with Govindhan

He didn't have long to wait. The doctor came out of the surgery, and the look on his face spelled bad news. Kandu listened and tears just streamed off his face. Govindhan had died of a ruptured abscess in his stomach. The doctor said he would have suffered intense pain for a few weeks before his collapse, but Govindhan had borne his suffering in silence.

Kandu was stunned. Govindhan's family lived in some village in Orissa, and Kandu had no idea if his parents even knew how to contact his wife and children. They would probably have to cremate him without even informing his family.

Mahadevan arrived with a couple of peons from the office who would make all the arrangements for his cremation. On the ride home Kandu cried copious tears, his body heaving with overwhelming emotion. Govindhan had been his playmate and friend when he was young and some part of him believed he would always be there. He was surprised at himself. Normally he was composed and never given to emotional eruption. Perhaps he was tired from the stress of exams or maybe he was just sad—really sad that Govindhan suffered so much and he had no inkling what the poor man was going through. If only he had said something, perhaps they could have saved him, but what was the point in thinking of dead possibilities when Govindhan himself was dead.

When Kandu reached home, he was exhausted. Poor Govindhan, no one to celebrate his life or even remember him. He opened his diary and wrote an obituary reserved for his own eyes. This would not make newspaper headlines. Govindhan was ordinary but so special, at least in Kandu's grieving eyes.

Today on the 14th of March, 1951 our loyal and hardworking servant Govindhan died after intense pain. He cared for me from childhood and will always be remembered fondly.

CHAPTER SIXTY FIVE

PITTUDA
CALCUTTA – MARCH 1951

THE LITTLE SAUSAGE

A fit of coughing woke him and he sat up, groggily reaching for the glass of water. *"Koi hai?* Anyone?" he croaked. *Pani chahiye.* His head felt heavy and his throat raw and terribly parched. It hurt to swallow. He must have slept with his mouth open and really felt awful.

Saab abhi laatha. A scrawny young man whom Kandu didn't recognize brought a jug of water and changed the glass.

Kaun ho tum? asked Kandu, half dazed.

Durjodhan, Saab, said the young man saluting him.

Kandu was amazed. Mummy had already replaced Govindhan. Only three days had passed and his stand-in was already here. That was so sad! Well, no one was indispensable he guessed, certainly not Govindhan. They must have been lining up outside the gate on hearing there was a vacancy. He looked for his cigarette case on his bedside table. It had fallen onto the floor. Darn! It was empty. He was quite certain he had filled it only yesterday. He had a couple of tins in the dresser and he asked Durjodhan to get it. *Udhar se mera cigarette ka teena le ke aao.* Durjodhan searched but couldn't find the tin of cigarettes. Kandu was sure he had four tins. "*Dekho theek se,* look, goddammit!"

Durjodhan slapped his head as he remembered. *Oh Boudi hamko bola kitchen men rakh do. Jabtak bukhaar thik nahin hota, cigarette nahin peena, aise bola.*

Kandu was annoyed. It wouldn't have occurred to Mummy to hide his cigarettes. Rukku must be behind this. *Kon Boudi?* he asked, his voice crackling with phlegm.

Voh chotawala, confirmed Durjodhan. Damn Rukku! Why did she have to hide his cigarettes? He knew it wasn't good for him, but one wouldn't hurt. After Govindhan died, Kandu came home and by evening the fever began. When he took his exam, he was running a high temperature. God alone knows how he did! Right now, he didn't really care. He had slipped in and out of sleep for two days now, and by the sweat on his kurta it looked as if the fever had finally broken.

Kandu shuffled into the bathroom and took out another tin he had stashed away that Rukku didn't know about. He lit a cigarette, but was thrown into another coughing fit. Taking a few quick drags, he stubbed it out, splashed some cold water on his face and stumbled out, walking to the windows and opening the curtains for some fresh air. He could hear sharp barking but was sure it must be from the neighbors. After a few minutes, he heard it again. His door was open a crack and he thought he was dreaming when he saw the smallest dog or, rather, the nose of the smallest dog peeping into the room. Kandu stared transfixed. What was this ... a dog or a rat? Then it took a few unsteady steps into the room and stared at him with soulful eyes. It *was* a dog, the cutest ever; a tiny, black Daschund with the sweetest, most adoring floppy ears and the saddest eyes.

"Hey doggy, did you get lost? Come here," coaxed Kandu, flopping down on the floor. For a minute the little dog just stared and then barked a soft, friendly bark almost as if he were introducing himself. Kandu crawled over and picked him up, his soft, velvety fur jet-black with a few brown spots. The little pup whined happily, enjoying the fondling. Daddy peeped in, "I see you have been introduced to our new friend."

"He's so cute; where did you get him from?"

"Major Kar's dog littered and he gave us this one. I thought it would cheer you up after this past week's events. What are you going to call him?" Just then the little sausage escaped from Kandu's weak grip and ran across the room, his long nails tapping rhythmically on the wooden floor. In Kandu's feverish state it sounded like *Pittu pattu pittu pattu.*

"I think I'll call him Pittu. Pittuda because he's a little Bangla doggie."

Pittu turned towards him and yapped his approval. For the next few days, Kandu had to continually watch where he walked. Pittu was really tiny but he just followed Kandu everywhere, even into the bathroom, sitting patiently until his master had finished his business. It was a little weird being watched, and Kandu had to constantly remind himself Pittu wasn't human. It was easy to forget because the emotions he displayed were more than human, so apt—barking at all the right times and growling at the right ones. Kandu felt a little silly talking to his dog all day and actually felt guilty leaving him home. In his absence, Daddy said he whined and sat near the front door, then, on hearing Kandu's car arrive, he would bark and run around in circles, rushing into the kitchen, barking at Durjodhan, telling him Kandu Baba was here and it was time to make his chai. And when Kandu entered the house he would go crazy, jumping up and down over and behind the sofas and up and down the stairs, barking until Kandu stooped to pick him up and cuddled him. So much unconditional love was refreshing, and Kandu was basking in it, enjoying the warmth and not minding the cuddles and licks one bit. Pittuda had touched a side of him he never knew existed. He brought out a gentler, more emotional aspect of his nature that had remained hidden so far.

Kandu picked up Pittu and went upstairs. He climbed into bed and the enthusiastic little puppy promptly jumped up and snuggled under the covers. Kandu giggled. *Whoever married him would have to share the bed with a dog!*

CHAPTER SIXTY SIX

KANDU
CALCUTTA – JUNE 1951

ONLY PITTUDA UNDERSTANDS

Kandu was really excited because this week he received acceptance letters from both Cambridge and Harvard. The only downside remained that his scholarship application was turned down because of his father's income. Daddy earned well, but they also lived lavishly, and Kandu's suspected he hadn't put away much in savings. In fact, he had not thought about retirement. Most of his colleagues had already purchased their retirement homes, but Daddy kept procrastinating. He wasn't sure if he wanted to settle in Delhi or Calcutta. Many people were talking about a quaint little hill station in the south where the British had their cantonment base. Bangalore was a sleepy town with excellent weather. Daddy was planning a family vacation in Bangalore later in the year, which would be convenient as they could also visit Vani at the same time.

Now that he had graduated, there was a lot of pressure on him to get a wife, but Kandu felt he was not ready. Dharmu was against him going abroad either to the UK or to the US. He was her precious son and she wanted him right here where she could be with him and enjoy his company. Once he went abroad, she was terrified he would marry a white girl. One thing was certain: if he left the shores of India, he would leave as a married man. The arguments over the last week had been long and arduous, but no one was capitulating. It was like an unstoppable force against an immovable wall. Daddy felt he was much better off just finding a job, and Kandu couldn't understand why his father was so much against him going to Harvard given that he too had a foreign degree. It just made no sense.

In the meantime, Rukku was annoying him about Sheela, pushing her case as she was her friend, which made those arguments even more agonizing. The whole world was waiting for him, and here they wanted him to settle down and marry the one girl he hated. In the beginning Sheela's advances merely annoyed him, but with Rukku bringing her over and arranging "casual encounters" in the club and at restaurants, it was becoming unbearable. He didn't know how to explain it to Rukku. He wasn't against marriage; he was just not interested in Sheela. Why was that so hard to digest? Then Vani descended and decided to present a new girl, some bumpkin from Mysore who had a crooked nose and teeth like a staircase. Apparently, she was studying to be a doctor, so Kandu was supposed to be highly impressed. He took one look at her and guffawed, making Vani extremely irate. Honestly, did she expect him to close his eyes when he slept with her? There was no way he would agree to her even if she were the last woman on earth and people were lining up for her. Vani was so unhappily married she couldn't bear to see Kandu with a pretty girl and told him as much. "You have very high expectations, Kandu. I don't know who you think you are…. This girl will do you fine. You are never going to get anyone better."

"Then marry her yourself," Kandu's replied, leading to another verbal battle with no one willing to back down. Everyone had their own agenda and seemed to know what was best for him. Only Pittuda understood him. Kandu wanted to make something of his life, and when he married, it would only be to the most beautiful, gentle, wonderful girl who would be his soul mate. On hearing this, Pittu always barked in agreement. Now if only the rest of the family could see things from his point of view for a change instead of from their own selfish perspectives, but that was a tall order.

It was 10:30 when Mahadevan and Dharmu came home that night. Kandu was in his room with Mickey and Ram listening to music. Mahadevan peeped in. "Hello boys," he said cheerily, vigorously fanning the air attempting to dispel the thick smoke. "All of you are going to die if you sit in this stale smoke. Smoke outside in the verandah for god's sake—not in your bedroom where you sleep." He exchanged pleasantries with the boys and then asked Kandu to come outside for a bit.

"Kandu, I met the Chairman of a British chemical company called ICI," Mahadevan began.

"I know Imperial Chemical Industries; I have heard of it. They have a plant in Rishra."

"Well I told him you graduated with Chemistry Honors and he is willing to take you on as a Covenanted officer if you do well in the interview."

"And when is that?"

"It can be next week if you want."

For a while, Kandu remained silent. He was tired of fighting them. But he couldn't accept that America was not in his destiny. "And what of Harvard?" he asked knowing full well what Daddy's response was going to be. He had heard his argument a million times.

"Honestly, Kandu, it's too much to expect me to pay so much money. Forget Harvard, it's a fool's dream. ICI is a growing company and you could be earning an honest salary as early as next week."

It was the end of the day and Kandu was tired and mentally defeated. "Let me think about it, Dad. I'll tell you in the morning."

Both Mickey and Ram were all for him taking a job locally. "Think about it, Kandu, if you go abroad you have to get married immediately, and the only available bride is Sheela."

That decided it for Kandu. The following week he attended the interview and joined ICI as a Covenanted Officer.

CHAPTER SIXTY SEVEN

NAGAMMA
MARCH 1950

CROSSING THE "SNAKE LADY"

The Parthasarathy household always overflowed with guests. Partha worried a little because his savings at the end of the month was minimal. Kamu was growing up and in the event of her marriage being suddenly fixed, he had no idea where he would get the money. Yet the family behaved as though the coffers were overflowing, cooking for a banquet each day. This was a very happy time in their lives, and they were eager to share their good times with whoever wished to partake of their company. Kunju stayed for almost six months, and her departure was followed by a steady stream of visitors from both Cochin and Madras. Siva's son Balu came for both the winter and summer vacations. Virtually brought up by Rajam, he felt much more emotionally connected to Partha than his own father. Balu was the older brother Kamu never had, and the two enjoyed his time in Calcutta going to movies and music *katcheris* or just hanging around playing badminton and chatting.

Kamu was especially excited, as her uncle Kannan and his young wife Sachi were visiting along with Nagamma Paati. It was quite a trip for Nagamma, forcing her to leave behind all her million rules of *Madi* when she boarded the train to Calcutta. Kannan, like Rajam's brother Mani, never had much luck holding jobs. He didn't complete his school finals, saying studies were not for him, and made do by taking odd jobs here and there. Siva got him a job in his company as a peon, which was when Nagamma seized the opportunity to find a good girl for him. Sachi was recommended by Sushila, who was related to her in a distant way, and the marriage took place almost five years ago. Sachi was very pretty, and the two made a handsome couple, but so far, their marriage had not produced any children. Nagamma felt cursed in a way because all her sons had trouble having children. There was absolutely no problem for her daughter Pattu, who had produced six children, whom she could barely afford to feed. Life was unfair! She often wondered why God just couldn't give two babies to each of her children?

Tired of peeping out the window, Kamu finally decided to sit outside on the steps leading up to the entrance. They had not visited Madras recently, and in these two years Kamu had transformed into a young woman. She had replaced her adolescent pāvādai-dhāvanis with saris and had filled out considerably. Paati was sure to be surprised.

Nagamma beamed from ear to ear as she descended from the car, and Kamu threw herself into her strong embrace. The two connected in a very special bond that had been cemented in the years Kamu spent in Madras. They shared similar characteristics in their personality. Both were headstrong and domineering and both had their self-pride bordering at times on arrogance. Both were extremely capable and lived life to the fullest. Nagamma had no patience for the weak, and to some extent Kamu was like that too. Besides, she was Nagamma's first granddaughter, born to her favorite son Partha, and that placed her on a pedestal reserved solely for her.

This was the first time Sachi was visiting them and Rajam had the *ārati* plate ready to welcome them to her home. *Va Saachi, eppadi irundhudu train?*

"*Parava illai.* It was long, but I was very comfortable. Besides we are all so excited to see Calcutta, we hardly noticed the journey," she replied with a fatigued smile. Sachi was much fairer than Kannan, who had taken after his father Muniswamy, his skin burnt to a dark ebony in the Madras sun. She had long, curly hair neatly braided and a beautiful smile that lit up her eyes. Most of all, Kamu admired her little button nose. Kannan had lost his job again and would stay in Calcutta for a couple of weeks before returning to Madras to search for a new one. He didn't seem too upset about it. Over the years he had changed so many jobs that it felt normal. Partha was happy to find him something in Calcutta, but Kannan wasn't ready to move from Madras either.

Nagamma would be staying for a couple of months, at least, and Rajam could feel the now unfamiliar tremors returning. Almost a week had gone by and while Nagamma hadn't said anything offensive, yet, the sound of her voice made the nervousness return. Her mere presence triggered old memories. She knew it was just a matter of time before she started doing things wrong, prompting the familiar censuring.

It was an exhausting day. They had spent almost the entire day out visiting the zoo and Victoria Memorial, and Nagamma's feet hurt with the activity. Kamu brought hot water with Epsom salts to soak her feet. Then she wiped them dry and brought out the homemade pain oil—coconut oil with camphor dissolved in it. Sachi grabbed the bottle out of her hands and vigorously began massaging Nagamma's feet. Her strong fingers made Nagamma wince as she pressed and kneaded tender spots. Sachi was fast securing a stronghold in Nagamma's heart.

Of all her daughters-in-law, she was the most capable, running an efficient home on a tight budget and that, Nagamma really appreciated. Sachi attended to her mother-in-law assiduously, giving her head and foot massages when needed, serving endless cups of coffee and moru, rolling out her bedroll after dinner, none of which went unnoticed. Utterly content, Nagamma sighed and slipped into a delightful slumber. She awakened sometime later on hearing voices outside. They were sitting on the steps in the verandah chatting. Nagamma rose and made her way there, but on reaching the dining room she heard her name mentioned and stopped instinctively, pausing to hear some more.

"How is Nagamma treating you?" asked Rajam casually.

"Oh I know exactly how to deal with her and I think I have managed to make her adore me," replied Sachi cockily.

"You were upset with her at your wedding I recall," said Rajam.

"Who wouldn't be? My parents meant nothing at all when they asked Sushila and Siva to eat first. After all, she is the eldest sumangali and Nagamma is a widow. Who serves amangalis first I would like to know? We hardly expected Nagamma to scream like that. What vicious words, so hurtful! I tell you, she is full of venom that serpent Nagamma. I can never ever forgive that outburst. One day, I will get my revenge, but first I have to make sure she is in the palm of my hands."

"Shh ..." whispered Rajam, her nervousness peaking. "Don't say all that, she might hear." It was actually quite shocking to hear Sachi speak such mean words even if they were about Nagamma.

Kadakara kazhavi, interjected Kannan coming to his wife's defense. "She's an old crone now and has lost her sting. I don't care about her and am certainly not frightened of her like you all are. If she says one mean thing to my wife, she'll have to deal with me."

Two solitary tears rolled down Nagamma's big nose and fell noiselessly to the floor. She recalled the incident Sachi was referring to at her marriage. It wasn't proper to call the daughters-in-law before the *sambandhiamma*, and she did let them have it. That was what was done at weddings. It was the only time the boy's side could get a little extra attention and she didn't remember saying anything that wasn't true. She hadn't given it a second thought, but that snake Sachi, she kept it in her heart. All her currying favor was nothing other than flattery. No one held Nagamma in the palm of their hand. She was going to be very surprised. So far she had seen a gentler side, but it would not cost her anything to switch demeanors. She was sad to learn Sachi was two-faced, but to hear Kannan call her a kazhavi—that was really heartbreaking. She had always fiercely defended him, no matter what trouble he got into, and he was always in trouble. Now this chit of a girl had stolen her place and he was willing to cross paths with his mother on her behalf! She would speak her mind. Let's see if he had the gall to be a man. Nagamma was furious and very hurt. She took a deep breath and walked forward standing in the doorway. She didn't speak. Not one word. She would reserve her words for a later spat. She stood and stared at Kannan and Sachi. The expression on her face said it all. She didn't look hurt ... far from it. She stood proud and tall. She was Nagamma, and no chit of a girl could speak of her like that and get away with it.

Kannan stared openmouthed. He knew she had heard his words. His lower lip trembled, and with a wail he ran and fell at her feet begging forgiveness, groveling incoherently.

Nagamma looked down sardonically at her pitiful son.

"Yes son, that is where you belong ... at my feet. Don't you ever forget it!"

CHAPTER SIXTY EIGHT

BALA AND MOHAN
MADRAS – JUNE 1950

THE MIRACLE UNFOLDS

Bala held onto the round green bars of the window in their South Mada Street home in Thiruvalikeni and watched the world go by. Starving cows and potbellied Brahmins, young giggling girls, bawdy, *rowdy pasanga* and more cows. The street outside was buzzing with activity. People going somewhere, talking and laughing. Hundreds of people, each with their own ongoing story. Time went by so fast just watching the activity in front of her.

They lived in the Brahmin quarter, renting two rooms in a small house on the corner of Periyaalwar Kovil Street. It was a stone's throw away from the main Parthasarathy Temple, the only temple where Krishna was sculpted with a moustache. The owner, a retired priest, lived in the main house with his aged wife, the additional income useful as he could no longer officiate at functions. It was quite surprising they rented the place out to Radhai, who certainly hailed from a much lower caste, but economic need preceded caste rules. She felt something move, like the flutter of a butterfly and touched her soft round belly. Bala was in her fourth month of pregnancy and elated to be with Mohan.

Many things had happened in the last year.

After Kunju Mami and Inspector Saar left Thanjavur, Bala was thrown into a deep depression. Kunju would deliver letters from Mohan and now with her gone, Bala had no way of contacting Mohan and Radhai Mama. Times were really bad. Karadi had been released from jail and was sponging off Kamalamba Amma. He was still very much the bully. In fact, his incarceration had made him rougher and meaner. Bala's benefactor Mudaliar Saar kept his monthly appointments with her but her friends Vyjayanthi and Vasanti were not that lucky. They were forced to have sex with random people that Karadi dragged off the streets, and Vyjayanthi already had the beginnings of some dreadful disease. Mohan needed to hurry. If Mudaliar Saar stopped his payments, Karadi would have no compunction forcing her to become a common prostitute. The very thought made her tremble.

The house had crumbled into complete disarray, covered in moss with paint flaking off everywhere. They had not paid their electricity bills, and now they had to rely on petromax lamps. Kamalamba was always angry, always screaming at the girls. It was hard for her to accept her life of poverty and her resultant frustration, which she took out on the girls. It seemed as though she had aged ten years when only a couple had gone by. Her hair had turned grey and her skin wrinkled. She couldn't see very well and squinted all the time but would not spend money for spectacles. She must have lost at least twenty pounds and looked like a ghost of her previous self. What a fall from grace. It was difficult for Bala to look at her without compassion in her eyes, but Kamalamba was too proud, and on detecting an ounce of pity would fly into a rage. Every month Karadi sold something from the house. The jewelry and silver were first to go followed by furniture and vessels. The house echoed emptiness and desolation. The girls mended rips and tears in their saris, as there was no money for anything new. The prosperous era of Devadasis was long gone.

Bala knew it was just a matter of time before Mudaliar Saar stopped paying. He realized they were in deep financial trouble and had been steadily reducing the grains he sent and the money he paid each month. Bala knew if she left, the only source of steady income for Kamalamba Amma would disappear, yet she had to escape. Each day, she went to the Kamakshiamman temple, praying for a miracle.

A few months later her prayers were finally heard. Radhai and Mohan came to town. She had just finished praying and was on her way out when she saw them both. They were by the entrance scanning the crowd. Mohan knew she was here every evening, and this would be the ideal place to meet her alone. It was as if the whole world were moving in slow motion. She couldn't believe her eyes. Dropping the plate containing the offerings, she ran until she stood in front of them.

"Finally ..." she whispered. "Finally you came. I have been waiting and waiting...."

All three of them began hugging and crying, trying to speak but unable to say anything coherent. The plan was for her to meet them at the end of the road at five o'clock in the evening the following day, so they could make the seven p.m. train to Madras.

Bala couldn't contain her happiness and spent the whole night wide awake and planning. She envisioned the rest of her life filled with happy moments. She would marry Mohan and have his children. She would finally meet her mother and her sisters and brothers if she had any. Life would be perfect, just perfect.

Kamalamba sensed something was up because instead of her usual glum face, Bala was singing and skipping around the house. She could not wait for five o'clock when she would forever leave this hellhole. She had already bundled her two remaining decent saris and placed them outside the house in the bushes. She collected her poojai plate and was about to leave when she heard Kamalamba coughing. She knew she couldn't leave without saying goodbye. Kamalamba was the only mother she had ever known and by walking out, she was sealing Amma's fate. God knows how she would survive. And Vyjayanthi and Vasanti? What would become of them? They were probably destined to die of some dreaded disease, and if they did survive, what would they do and where would they go? For a minute, she contemplated taking them with her but she could not leave Kamalamba Amma completely alone. Karadi would abscond at a moment's notice and then what would happen to her? Perhaps she could take just Amma with her. But no ... she knew Amma was too proud and would never agree to living with her arch enemy Saroja. Besides, if she found out she was losing her only meal ticket, she would rather have Karadi kill her. Yet Bala couldn't leave without saying good bye.

"Amma ..." she whispered. The petromax light shone on Kamalamba's face at a strange angle making her appear ghoulish.

"I'm leaving," she said without adding the word permanently.

"Mm ..." moaned Kamalamba. "Bring me some *vethalai* on your way back,"

No, Amma, I'm leaving forever, she wanted to say, but couldn't. She just touched Amma's feet and bowed down, placing her forehead on her wrinkled and cracked toes, praying fervently to Kamakshiamman to watch over her.

Then she left.

The journey to Madras was too emotional for Bala. On the one hand, she could not believe her dreams of escaping, and reuniting with Mohan had come to pass. Yet she was forever leaving behind the only memories she had. She was going to miss Kamalamba, yet longed to see her real mother. It was as if she were walking on a cloud in a dream. Would she wake up and be back in the red room with Mudaliar Saar on top of her? Conflicting emotions made her smile and cry alternately till the rocking of the train lulled her to sleep.

On reaching Egmore station, they took a taxi all the way to Thambaram where she would meet her mother Saroja for the first time. Bala kept smoothing her hair down and pressing her sari into place but knew she looked soiled and exhausted. When she saw her mother, she couldn't move. She was more beautiful than Bala could have ever imagined. Fair and diminutive with thick black hair in a braid. Dressed impeccably in an orange and green Kānjeevaram sari, Saroja smiled. Bala felt her knees wobble and then she slipped onto the floor in a dead faint.

The events of the last few days had taken an emotional toll on her, and she had little or no nourishing food in the last year. When she came to her senses, she felt her mother's soft hands smoothing her brow. The rest of the week went by almost as if she were in a fairy tale. Her father was tall and handsome. He was from a royal family and very wealthy, and when she looked into his eyes, she recognized how much she resembled him. She met her two sisters and brother, but they could never know she was their real sister as Saroja had never spoken of her earlier life with them. But that did not matter. She was introduced as a cousin and was ecstatic to finally have a family.

Saroja offered Radhai and Mohan room to stay, but Radhai had most of his work in the Adyar area and preferred to live independently. Mohan still had a couple of years to finish his college education and was still firmly intent on studying to be an engineer. Bala recovered slowly. For the longest time, she couldn't believe she was safe. She thought about Kamalamba Amma often, yet was so absorbed with her fascination for her mother. Everything here was new and exciting, and soon the traumatic memories of her past life became less important. Saroja ran a school of Dance, and Bala threw herself into the classes, teaching beginners the basics and helping her mother to choreograph dances. Saroja had hurt her neck in the accident and didn't have full range as yet. She and her husband were quite lucky to recover, and other than pain in her neck she had no complaints. Her husband had hurt his lower spine and walked with a stick, but he too had recovered better than anyone could have imagined.

Saroja and Bala spent many nights sharing their stories, crying and consoling one another. Saroja understood the love between her nephew and Bala, and in December before the month of *Margazhi*, arranged for them to be married. Mohan was far from settled, but if they waited for him to complete his education, the rest of their youth would be depleted. She saw how they looked at one another, the sorrow in their eyes evident on parting and felt it was best Bala married Mohan straight away. The ceremony took place in the house with very few invitees, though Bala secretly wished Kamalamba could have been there.

Intimacy with Mohan was every bit as she imagined it would be. He was a gentle and considerate lover, and every night they lay in one another's arms in disbelief, unable to reconcile themselves to the turn of events. Radhai slept outdoors to give them space. Bala felt guilty about that, but he wouldn't listen to any of her arguments and was very happy to sleep in the fresh air. Two months ago, Bala realized she was with child. Saroja wanted her to move back to Thambaram, so that Bala would not have to cook and clean in her delicate condition, but Bala couldn't think of parting with Mohan right now. It was only two rooms to keep clean, and both Radhai and Mohan were excellent cooks, helping her with shopping and cutting vegetables as well as cleaning. After her *Valaikāpu* ceremony, she would move back to her mother's home for her confinement.

Yes, many good things had taken place, and her life was complete and filled with happiness. Yet, she thought of her friends Vyjayanthi and Vasanti often. Last month on impulse she wrote a letter telling them she was safe and enquiring about Amma. Perhaps it didn't reach them because she had no response so far. One morning she walked to the gate to check the mail, and there it was. She hurriedly tore open the cover. It was from Vasanti. The writing was a childish scrawl filled with spelling errors.

Dear Bala

You are so lucky to have escaped from here. I wish you had taken us with you. Many things have taken place recently. Amma got herself so worked up after you left she suffered a stroke and now has lost the use of her left side. Each day I oil her limbs and make her move them and right through she laments about you being a traitor leaving her when she most needed you. She cannot bring herself to forgive you or for that matter your mother. Even in her sleep she talks and mutters uttering your names.

I have some very sad news to give you. Vyjayanthi passed away last week. She suffered intensely before dying and I pray she now has the peace she always longed for. I know I will die too if I stay here. For the last few weeks with Amma out of action I have had to put up with Karadi's sexual advances. I suppose I mustn't think too much. After all I am a prostitute and whenever I am with a man I switch my mind off and think about some movie I saw, not caring about my body being ravaged. I beg you, I plead with you, please find a way for me. I will come and cook and clean for you. Anything to escape. You are my only hope. I am praying this letter reaches you.

Your sister

Vasanti

Bala sat on the thinnai and wept tears of rage and bitterness for the twisted destinies of Devadasis. She was overwhelmed at her own fortune and her unbelievable escape. God had provided her one more opportunity, and she would do whatever she could to give Vasanti that chance as well. How, she had no clue, but something would occur to her. It had to.

CHAPTER SIXTY NINE

VATSU'S WEDDING
CALCUTTA – JANUARY 1951

NO THANK YOU!

T he muhurtham was scheduled for very early in the morning, and they hadn't slept a wink all night. It was Vatsu's last night as a single girl, and she insisted all her friends sleep over. They laughed and talked till past midnight. It amazed Kamu that Vatsu agreed to marry Vasu after meeting him just once. It was such a risk she took. What if he was a really awful man who was bad tempered and beat her? But Vatsu said her parents had checked out the family well. They had common friends who knew him, so she was confident he wasn't the beating kind. On the contrary, his shyness worried her a lot more. At least she had a chance to meet him once and speak to him, which was not an opportunity most girls got. They just married whomever their parents selected and hoped for the best.

It was kind of scary. Now that Vatsu was marrying there would be pressure for Viju to get married and then it would be her turn. Kamu shivered in a mix of fear and anticipation. Ever since she turned fourteen, her parents had been getting several enquiries. Every time Sundar mama visited, Kamu would quiz her parents after he left. *Yenna Amma, inniki yenna pudu varan vandhudhu?* It was almost a joke for her because Sundar inevitably had a new varan each week for her. He seemed single-mindedly focused on marrying her off, but Partha felt she was too young and they should wait until she passed her Junior Cambridge at least before vigorously looking for varans. The south Indian community in Calcutta was fairly large and very connected, which made weddings ideal times to fix matches. They could check out boys and girls before the awkwardness of *Ponnpaakal* took place. Although Kamu wasn't interested in marriage, she had picked the best of Rajam's saris to wear, just in case some prospective groom, her elusive *Nilakantan,* was there, and she made sure she had a rose to match each sari. For the muhurtham, she had selected an onion colored sari with a bright turquoise border. The peach rose matched almost exactly; the combination of *malli* and the rose was her signature.

Vatsu's wedding took place on the terrace of the Ramamurthy's Ballygunge home. A huge pandal covered the terrace and a swing had been placed on the far corner. After the ceremony, lunch would be served downstairs in the garden, which too had been covered with an ornate pandal. Kamu had been here for the last three days, caught up in the excitement of the marriage—and even though she hadn't slept much, she wasn't tired.

She spotted her father, who was much taller than the average south Indian, looking dashing as usual in his *mayilkannu* veshti and white bush-shirt. Rajam was nowhere to be seen; she was so tiny and hard to spot. Partha waved at her and sat down with Raman and his other friends. The noise level was incredibly high. Sundar and his retinue were conducting the wedding, but no one paid much attention to the ceremony and ritual proceedings. They had all witnessed dozens of weddings and used the time instead to socialize and chat. Partha noticed the family entering, one couldn't miss them; the portly man and his beautifully dressed wife followed by their handsome son, daughter, and another darker man holding a young child. Perhaps that was their son-in-law. He nudged Raman. "Who are those people? They are always in the front row of all the katcheris," he enquired.

"You haven't met them yet? That is N. M. Ayyar, Chairman of the Port Trust, and his wife Dharmambal. Let them come this way, and I will introduce you."

"Their son," Partha continued. "Is he of marriageable age or is he already married?"

"No, no, I think he is still studying, but a great catch, great catch! Very handsome boy, very fond of Carnatic music."

"Really? He smokes a lot though," Partha remarked wryly.

Raman threw his head back and laughed. "So do I, Partha; that cannot be a disqualification."

"No, it's just an observation. I have seen them at Tamil movies, and the son slips out several times during the show. What is his name?"

"They call him Kandu, I am not sure what it's short for."

"I see," said Partha. He knew they would never consider his family. There was just too much class difference. Where was an ICS officer and where was a salesman! The difference was like that of heaven and earth. But he certainly was a very handsome boy.

Sometime later, the wedding ceremony over, they went downstairs for lunch, pushing and making their way through the crowds. Raman did introduce him to Mahadevan and told him that Partha was from a great family and very dear to the Deekshithar, but apparently, that didn't impress him too much. Either that or he was particularly hungry because he smiled politely then excused himself, hurriedly joining his wife to sit down for lunch. Partha was a little miffed, but there was so much confusion with everyone wanting to sit in the first *pandhi*. Kamu and her friends helped serve lunch. Meals at weddings were traditionally served on banana leaves, and there was an order to how the food was doled out on the leaf. Sweet was always served first followed by salt and pickle then the curries, both wet and dry. On the lower half of the leaf, rice, *paruppu*, sāmbār, and rasam would be served. There were at least fifteen items, but Kamu found herself serving lime pickle, and she followed the line of servers placing the pickle on the top left of each banana leaf. She approached Kandu and was about to spoon the pickle when he placed his hand over the leaf and said, "No thank you," without so much as glancing at her.

Kamu was surprised at hearing him speak in English. All the other young men were dressed traditionally, and here was this one, all fancy in his shirt and pants, his hair parted and gelled back with some swanky English cream. He was certainly not the coconut oil type, and he waved his hand over his leaf without bothering to even look and see who was serving him. That was so arrogant of him! *No Thank you! Can't speak Tamil, British bada sahib in your fancy shirt and pants? Hmmf! Too much of a bada sahib to even look at me. Talking to your lady friend while we poor servers don't deserve the slightest attention.* She tossed her head back in a grimace of annoyance and the rose pinned in her hair came loose and slipped onto Kandu's banana leaf.

Kandu was busy talking to Rukku and then casually looked down onto his banana leaf. There, instead of pickle was the most perfect, peach colored rose. A familiar sensation passed through him, and he searched through nebulous memories, but it passed before he could pinpoint what he felt. He picked up the rose wondering whom it belonged to, but there was a line of girls serving the food and he didn't want to go searching for the owner. He put the rose into his pants pocket, rolled up his shirt sleeves and started eating.

CHAPTER SEVENTY

KAMU
CALCUTTA – MARCH 1951

THE KATCHERI

K amu adored music classes. As a child, she learned music with Kunju
Periamma and realized quite early that, although she had no talent
for playing the harmonium, she was blessed with a melodious voice.
She had learned with several *Bhāgavadars,* honored music teachers including
Venkateswara Bhāgavadar, who had fine-tuned her skills here in Calcutta. He
taught her twice a week, an hour-long class sometimes running over to two
with neither of them realizing it. Often her teacher asked her to participate in
local competitions, but Partha would never hear of it. There was no question of
her getting on stage. Music was for the soul and she could sing as much as she
wanted at home or when she visited friends during festivals. The only time she
could showcase her talent was during Navaratri, when she was invited to other
homes for manjal kumkumam, an excuse traditionally used by women of the
south to socialize, sing, eat, and drink as they celebrated the nine-day festival.
The very first year they moved to Calcutta, the holiday season remained very
low key, as they had few friends. But slowly, they met a few families and became
members of the South India Club, which held events every month that were well
attended by all members of the community. Now with so much hectic social
activity, the south Indian community seemed to be growing exponentially and
their circle of friends was increasing.

Kamu was learning the intricacies of *Kāmbodi* rāgam. Indian Classical music
was very complicated. Songs were set to *rāgams* which used combinations of
five to seven notes. The arrangement of notes created unique patterns typical to
each rāgam, and Kamu had learned songs in virtually every rāgam, her favorite
being Mohanam and Kambodi. Today she was learning *Ma Janaki,* written by
the famous saint and music maestro Thyagaraja in Kāmbodi rāgam. She could
instantly replicate every complicated line, every *sangadhi,* making her master's
head roll in appreciation. Hours after Bhāgavadar left, she was still humming the

tune. It was a very popular song, and her favorite rendition was by the currently popular singer Madurai Mani Iyer. Mani Iyer suffered from leprosy, which for a long time affected his voice, but he altered his style of singing, making innovations which music loving audiences really appreciated. His rendition of Kāmbodi was unique, bringing tears to the eyes of spectators and making their hearts swell with *bhakti* (devotion). They loved him not only for his miraculous voice, given his medical condition, but also the rhythm and complicated level of melodic combinations he used. He would be here for a music concert this Saturday, and Kamu was not about to miss it for the world.

Partha was really annoyed when she made him stop the car at the market to buy a rose for her hair on the way to the katcheri. He was anxious to reach their destination and make sure the arrangements were perfect. She saw him outside, even as she got down from the car, the *English gentleman,* standing outside smoking away. He was leaning against the lamp post, his legs crossed Krishna style, and he didn't bother to turn and look at her. Kamu was exasperated at his inattention. She was used to heads turning in admiration and couldn't believe this posh fellow hadn't even glanced at her. Not that she was interested. She certainly wasn't, but she wanted him to notice her nonetheless.

He came in and sat down in the first row along with his parents. His mother had a pink sari with a matching garland of pink sweet peas in her hair. Kamu saw Viju and Vatsal and moved seats to be with them. Both had studied music and the discussions would be lively. The concert began with Abhogi varnam and almost immediately the air in the auditorium became electric. Mani Iyer had an inimitable style, and the pace he set stayed through the concert. Kamu glanced at the Englishman. His head was shaking intermittently in enjoyment. Good! The cigarette smoker liked music. Almost as if he felt he was being watched, he turned his head and for a minute their eyes locked until Kamu lowered hers, embarrassed to be caught staring. She haughtily raised her head appearing to be involved in the music, but her heart was beating rapidly. She told herself she wasn't going to look at him, but in a few minutes, she found herself staring at the back of his head. His arm was draped behind his mother, resting casually on the chair. *Stubby fingers,* she thought and smiled, and once again he turned. This time there was a quizzical expression on his face. *Darn!* Kamu was horrified but pretended she was scanning the audience and turned her eyes away nonchalantly. She was determined she would not look at him. Instead she would make *him* look at her.

A little later she felt his eyes on her and tightened her lips suppressing a smile. The fifth time it happened, she couldn't help but laugh.

"What happened?" whispered Viju.

"The boy in the front row, the "no thank you chappy" from Vatsal's wedding, remember I told you about him? Well he's here sitting in the first row and he keeps looking at me."

Just then he turned once more and Viju burst out laughing. Unfortunately, her timing was bad and her loud guffaw during a pause in the music made several heads turn in annoyance. Kamu looked down and covered her mouth. This was so awkward, to be caught laughing in the middle of such a great concert. It felt empowering, though, the ability to attract anyone she wanted even if he was a cigarette-smoking-Englishman.

During the break, they went out to buy vadais and drinks and saw the boy outside leaning against the lamp post again. There was another young man with him, a cigarette-smoking compatriot.

"He's talking about you," Viju nudged Kamu.

"How do you know?" quizzed Kamu, keeping her voice casual although the urgency within her bubbled at bursting point.

"He said something and now his friend is looking at you."

"Is the friend good looking?"

"Not as handsome as Mr. no-thank-you. I think he likes you," Viju crooned, making Kamu even more flustered. She was determined not to make a big deal out of it. She would not bother about him. He looked so arrogant and self-assured. Let him not think she was in any way interested in him. She hurried back into the concert hall determined to focus on the music, but the harder she tried, the more difficult it became to concentrate. She hadn't heard a single song fully. She found herself counting the number of times he turned around. She was up to twenty now. He was certainly interested in her.

She saw him standing near the exit. He was so tall his head stood out conspicuously above the sea of bobbing heads. As she passed him, she turned and glanced at him, her expression haughty, with one eyebrow raised. To her utter consternation, he cocked his eyebrow mimicking her. What audacity! He was making fun of her. Angrily she tossed her head back and walked purposefully out of the auditorium towards the car. Her face was flushed and she was really mad. How dare he? Was he making fun of her? She would show him. The next time she would not give him the time of day. Not one glance, not one look. Let him stew in his attraction to her. That would serve him right. Arrogant so and so....

CHAPTER SEVENTY ONE

KANDU
CALCUTTA – AUGUST 1951

AN UNSETTLING FEELING OF LOVE

Kandu was sitting in the waiting room playing with Shyamala.

"It's a boy!" the nurse peeped out and declared.

"And my daughter, how is she? Can I see her?" asked Dharmu anxiously.

"In a few minutes. She is still recovering. Long labor no, she needs rest."

"Hey Shyamala, you have a little brother. What are you going to call him?" asked Kandu, pinching her cheeks.

"Umm … Pittuda I think," she replied.

"No, that name is already taken."

"Okay then I'll call him Kittuda," said Shyamala giggling.

Rukku looked tired. She had been in labor for two days; the baby took his own time to enter the world. When they entered the ward, Arun was holding him, and he opened his huge eyes and stared around. He had the Ayyar heavy lidded eyes and an incredible head of hair. Naturally. He was almost two weeks overdue.

Dharmu had been nagging her for some time, and for the last couple of months Rukku moved into their home so she could get a little rest and some help caring for Shyamala. That meant Arun came every day for dinner, but his concern for Rukku kept him in control, and there were no major spats. The child was fair; it had Rukku's color. Kandu was handed the baby after his parents took turns, and Shyamala came and hung onto him staring soulfully at her new brother. "Isn't he cute?" Kandu asked her and she nodded. "Don't worry, you'll still be my favorite but don't you tell him. It's our secret, shhh…." Shyamala giggled.

They reached home by seven in the evening and Kandu walked into the living room and over to the decanter, pouring three drinks. He was sure his parents needed a drink too. The last two days had been stress-filled for them. Looking back, he realized how fast the last six months had gone by. Govindhan dying during his exams, the arrival of Pittuda, topped by the excitement of a new job. He was thoroughly enjoying his job at ICI. They had a beautiful office on Chowringhee overlooking the *maidān*, and from his room he could see the dome of Victoria Memorial. That year they had taken twelve new covenanted officers, a mixed group. Kandu hit it off with one: Mani Narayanswamy was a short, charming guy with a smile that extended beyond his face. Soon he became another addition to their badminton and table tennis evenings. He wasn't terribly good at those games but always beat them soundly at billiards. Life had been truly hectic but good, and with Rukku's confinement, they thankfully called a moratorium on his wedding plans. Kandu walked out into the balcony, enjoying the breeze, even though it was laden with moisture. August was a bad month in Calcutta as was the rest of the summer. The only time one could feel reasonably comfortable was after sunset. Nothing compared to the feeling of sitting in the balcony with a cool breeze, enjoying a *chota peg* of Johnny Walker. Dharmu and Mahadevan joined him and for a few minutes they simply sat in silence.

"Vani is not going to be happy," remarked Dharmu.

"She will also have children," replied Mahadevan, not wanting to encourage this conversation.

"She has been married for so long, unless there's a miracle, I don't believe it will happen."

"Then pray for a miracle," he concluded.

Just then Durjodhan walked in and placed a bouquet of beautiful multicolored roses on the table.

"Roses? In August?" observed Kandu.

"I didn't know you were well versed in flowering seasons? In fact, you have not shown interest in plants for a long time, not since your childhood when you insisted we leave the plant that Appanshayal gave you in your room at night. Do you remember that plant?" Mahadevan laughed, the pleasant memory brightening his demeanor.

"Hmm, very vague memories. I remember watching it bloom with Banu Mami. What ever happened to that plant?" Kandu enquired.

"No idea, but I don't think we brought it with us. You lost interest in it pretty soon."

"Yes, now I seem to be obsessed with roses."

Dharmu set the empty glass down and got up for dinner followed by Mahadevan. Kandu didn't feel like joining them just yet. He reached forward and pulled out a long stemmed red rose. It reminded him of the girl at the katcheri, the one with a rose pinned in her hair. She was certainly pretty but looked much younger than him. That was an interesting evening, and he couldn't understand why he felt compelled to look at her repeatedly. Something about her unsettled him. He had seen her several times afterwards—at the movies and at some cultural function his parents dragged him to.

If he married, that was the sort of girl who appealed to him: clean and innocent. Mickey thoroughly approved and said if Kandu wasn't interested, he would give it a shot. It was a difficult situation. Lately no one was talking about his marriage, and he couldn't just bring it up out of the blue. He would simply have to wait for the right opportunity and tell his parents he would like to marry her.

It felt strange. A few months ago, he was averse to the word marriage, yet ever since this *belle with a bloom* glided into his life he was considering settling down with her ... and he hadn't even exchanged a single word with her. What if she couldn't speak English? Yet, somehow, it just felt right. That rose in her hair, the double nose rings, her pearl complexion, she was just perfect, a dream come true. At times, he sensed she had manifested from some hazy dream, and he couldn't understand that feeling. It felt as if her soul was reaching down to his soul and that didn't even make any practical sense. It would happen ... when the time was right.

CHAPTER SEVENTY TWO

PARTHA

CALCUTTA – OCTOBER 1951

LUNCH WITH FRIENDS

Rash Behari Avenue was slowly becoming a madhouse. Cars and lorries were parked at awkward angles and Partha could not find a spot for his Landmaster. He was already late—he should have been here a half hour ago—but his meeting with the distributor went on longer than planned. He got every single red light from Dalhousie to Rash Behari Avenue and now there wasn't a single spot to park. He had circled the block three times and finally parked on the parallel street. Hopefully the car would remain intact and he wouldn't return to find a bare shell. Instances of car theft were becoming more commonplace in Calcutta, and when they couldn't break into the car, they stole tires, leaving the car sitting on bricks.

Om namah shivaya, he chanted under his breath as he locked and checked the doors one last time. He was meeting his friends for dinner at Komala Vilas after a long time, and by the ruckus inside, he guessed they were already there. His friend Rama, the owner, joined them, asking an assistant to man the desk. Partha knew almost everyone else. Raman, Vaidhee, Sethu, and Ramachandran, but there were a couple of new faces.

"*Va va,* Partha, we were just about to ask for the food. Good thing you are here." Partha was about to begin with excuses for his tardiness, but his brain was exhausted from its own chatter and it felt futile to prolong the argument. "Raman, you made it. I know this is way below your league but I'm glad you're here." Raman was the only one among them who could afford to eat in fancy restaurants, but he was as happy eating off a banana leaf as he was handling silverware.

"Hello, Vaidhee, how is Vatsal doing? Any good news?" Partha enquired.

"No, none yet. Give her some time. Let her enjoy being married. Of course we are looking for someone for Viju. Please do let me know if you have any good varans. She will be eighteen this year and already Manju is nagging me nonstop. It's not as if I can catch any fellow off the streets to tie a thali around her neck."

"What about the Ayyar boy," said Rama. "Have you considered him?"

That one is for my daughter, Partha thought to himself, but he knew he shouldn't even allow such thoughts to take root. It would only make him feel terrible when they refused.

"Oh that family? They are too hoity toity for us. That mother … I have heard she drinks a lot and dances with men. *Namaku adhu yellam seripattu varaadhu,*" he concluded.

This was worrisome. Partha could certainly not send Kamu into a family who were so ultra-modern. She would be like a fish out of water. That would not work, but it was good to hear this because that gave him additional ammunition to drop the Ayyar boy as a prospective groom for Kamu. Vaidhee introduced him to Ganesh Iyer, who had moved to Calcutta from Madras. After dinner, he joined Partha and Raman, who, reluctant to leave, stood at the entrance chatting away.

"By the way, Partha, did you ever consider the Ayyar boy as a groom for Kamu? He is very handsome and the two will make a striking couple," Raman commented.

"*Yenna shollare Raman? Avaa yengai naan yengai.* There is a difference of heaven and earth between our two families," demurred Partha.

"Who are you talking? Which Iyer?" asked Ganesh.

"N.M. Ayyar ICS. He has a son, a very sought-after bachelor."

"Oh Mahadevan, *nanna theriyume,* I know him very well. Actually, he is from my ancestral village, Nagarcoil. In fact, I need to meet him. I have some papers he needs to sign regarding some property over which our families have joint custody. If you are thinking about that family one thing I can guarantee—he hails from a very aristocratic family. His father was a Rao Bahadur working as Chief Superintendent Engineer for the Travancore Maharajah and his father Appanshayal, I don't have words to praise him enough. Excellent family."

This intimidated Partha even more. "I don't know Raman. Vaidhee was just saying they are ultra-modern, and I'm not sure I want Kamu to get into such a family."

Raman laughed. "That is a case of sour grapes. Vaidhee's wife Manju is angry because Mrs. Ayyar rejected Viju saying she's too short and dark, so they are going around spreading rumors. It's true she drinks, but dancing with men and stuff like that is all exaggeration."

"But seriously, Raman, how can I give her to a family who drinks?"

"Are you just searching for excuses? First you said he smokes, now you say she drinks. Come on, Partha, you drink too. Both of us have shared a peg often enough. Don't spoil a good alliance with stupid reasons."

"I tell you what," piped up Ganesh. "I will be visiting them soon. Why don't I make enquiries and we can see what happens?"

"They are so wealthy. I cannot give dowry," piped up Partha.

"Now reason # 3. Do you want someone for Kamu or not?" yelled Raman shutting Partha up.

Partha walked to his car happy to see all four wheels intact. But when he tried the ignition, it wouldn't start. Every drop of petrol had been siphoned off.

CHAPTER SEVENTY THREE

KANDU
CALCUTTA – OCTOBER 1951

CRUISING THE HOOGHLY

It was a picture perfect day. The sun was rising and the waters over the Hooghly River glimmered as if illuminated by a million chandeliers. The hum of the boat broke the stillness of the morning. It felt as though nature were taking a break and just resting. Everything was so peaceful. The fishermen had set out hours ago and only small boats with lone sailors were poling along. One of them, happy and hope-filled singing a song and, though he was far away the lyrics could be heard clearly. *Mother India with all your bounty fill my palms with gold and silver.*

Dharmu had plenty to celebrate this year. Her first grandson and her dear son Kandu's graduation, his first job and his twenty-second birthday. She had been planning this excursion for weeks. The servants had been up all night making the chicken-and-egg salad sandwiches, cucumber-with-tomato-and-chutney sandwiches for the vegetarians. They had bought virtually every loaf of bread baked in the city, and baskets were laden in neat piles. She had ordered pastries and vegetable puffs from Flury's, and there was the usual *poori sabji* and tamarind rice catering to the Indian palate.

The boat was large enough for fifty to fit comfortably, a retired vessel from the navy which Mahadevan's brother Kannan had arranged for the day. He was there with Laali and his children even before guests arrived, cracking everyone up with his bawdy jokes. Kandu stood on deck admiring the view. It all felt so peaceful, and he wanted to take a moment to simply enjoy the solitary calm before the rest of the company arrived. He knew the morning would be filled with laughter and loud talk. His father had organized a well-stocked bar with three gloved waiters and a music duo to play their favorite tunes for the dancing, which would commence later.

He heard Dharmu calling out to him and joined them by the gangplank to receive their guests. His friends were late as usual and the last to arrive.

"What kept you fellows?" Kandu asked when they finally clambered aboard.

"Mickey was fast asleep when we went to pick him up, hence the delay. You can hammer him if you wish," said Mani apologetically.

"I know he's going to be hammered anyway," said Dilip and they hooted, knowing Mickey would be the first at the bar and the last to leave. Kandu's heart sank as he saw Sheela arrive with her parents. "Who invited her?" he hissed.

"I did," Rukku piped up. "Any problems with that? She's my friend you know."

"Yes I do have a problem, Rukku, since you keep shoving her down my throat," he retorted angrily. "Since you invited her, make sure she doesn't leave your side and doesn't come within six feet of me."

"Kandu, I don't know who you think you are. You think you're so dashing that all the girls are falling at your feet. If that were the case, how come you've never had a girlfriend?"

"That's because he's a homo," chuckled Ram, breaking the apparent tension between them.

Kandu strode angrily to the other end of the boat, followed by his pals, and prayed he wouldn't have to play hide and seek all day. He had been so excited about this party and now this. He was not interested in Sheela, and his sister needed to understand.

Rukku had touched on a raw nerve. Bengali boys from college boasted of girlfriends, but no one from his group ever dared go out solo with a girl on a date. It just wasn't done. Their family ties were really strong, and they knew they would be married soon. Even Dilip, who was the lone Bengali in his group, didn't dare take a girl out alone. Somehow the thought of doing something like that hadn't entered his mind. He didn't think it was right to mix so freely with a girl before marrying her. It wasn't that he didn't have the opportunity to. With girls like Sheela and Usha, he could have done what he wanted, but he had a dream. He dreamt of this perfect girl, and he was willing to wait until she entered his life. Skinny and fashionable women like Sheela were a dime a dozen, but he would wait for that girl of his imagination, perhaps the girl with the rose. He was dying to know her name. It would probably be something long and complicated like Vijayalakshmi or Suryakiranapriya. He had to find out who she was at least. How else was he going to tell his parents about her? Several times he attempted to tell them, to broach the topic, but felt sheepish and just chickened out. Besides what was he going to say? *I saw this girl with a rose in her hair. I don't know where she lives nor do I know her name or her father's name but pretty please, I'd like to marry her.*

Today if Sheela tried anything he would just push her overboard, and perhaps he could push Rukku along with her. Last week at the movies he showed the *rose girl* to Rukku, and she scoffed saying she was no patch on Sheela. *No patch on Sheela!* He had hoped to persuade Rukku to speak on his behalf, but she remained fixated on Sheela. Kandu scowled and Mani put his arm around him. "Forget it Kandu, women are stupid anyway. Today is your day. Come on, let me get you a drink."

The music started and many of his father's colleagues were dancing, but Kandu stood on the port side, far away from the action. Nothing could persuade him to dance. Besides, Sheela was there, and his sister might push him into asking her for a dance. Mickey came up to him and noticed he was still annoyed. "What's the problem?" he asked placing his hand on Kandu's shoulders.

"I don't know her name or anything about her."

"That can be remedied. I'll ask Mr. Raman." A few minutes later he was back. "I have full details. Name Kamakshi, affectionately called Kamu, father Parthasarathy, salesman in Geigy, live in South End Park. Need any more info? I can get vital statistics if you wish," he chuckled.

Kandu was silent. *Kamu* ... he finally he had a name. It had a nice ring to it and rolled easily off one's tongue and rhymed well with Kandu. *Kamu and Kandu.* Now he could do something about it. Several times he had considered tailing them after a katcheri, but there was always some family member with him. He needed to broach the subject with Mummy. The next time she shoved a photograph of some unfortunate girl from Kumbakonam under his nose, he would tell her not to waste her time with these stupid alliances. He would let her know he had someone in mind. She was sure to listen.

They returned home by sunset thoroughly exhausted. Talking was a drain on one's energy, and he needed to recuperate before work tomorrow. Pittuda as usual ran around crazily and just wouldn't calm down. He picked him up, allowing him to lick his face, and then carried him up into his bedroom. "Pittu, I know her name ... Kamu.... Do you like it?"

Pittu cocked his head to one side as if he were hearing intently and then he barked twice.

"Good, that's settled then," said Kandu happy to get his decision approved. Kandu slept deeply but as he slept, he dreamed that same familiar dream.

He saw her once again running down the hillside towards him, but she was grown, tall and lissome. She stopped a few feet away from him and smiled. "I'm here, come and get me," she whispered, her voice soft and sweet. He tried to look at her face, but clouds from the heavens had descended and he couldn't tell who she was. "Come closer," he called.

She smiled and said nothing, merely turned around, ready to return from where she had come.

"Wait," he called out, eager to stop her. "Come back. Don't go so fast. You can't leave this time. You have to stay."

"Come and get me," she said and moved further away, her long tresses swinging about her shoulders, gently cascading down to her hips. She turned around again. He still could not tell who she was but he saw it. He saw the red rose nestled behind her ears. A single ray of sunlight shone directly on it and there was no mistaking the pristine rose.

"It's you, isn't it?"

"Perhaps," she whispered and laughed tantalizingly.

Kandu murmured in his sleep. *Red rose … Rojapoo … why do I keep seeing it….?*

Pittuda raised his head, one ear cocked, and then, as he saw Kandu still and silent once more, he then lay down again.

Both dog and master seemed to know where their destiny lay.

CHAPTER SEVENTY FOUR

BALA
MADRAS – NOVEMBER 1951

FALL FROM GRACE

*V**asanti, I can't believe you're here!* exclaimed Bala, still reeling in disbelief. Vasanti smiled weakly. She was a phantom of her previous self, her sunken eyes holding a haunting look. Her skin, which should have been healthy and vibrant, was now shriveled and yellow. She had aged so much, even her sparse hair had grayed. It was a miracle they managed to rescue her. Now she was actually free, and a month of rest and good food would make a world of a difference.

Ever since Bala received the letter from her she had been pestering Mohan and Radhai to bring Vasanti back to live with them. Six months ago Radhai went to Thanjavur, but the house they all grew up in lay abandoned, occupied by squatters and vermin. Radhai cried bitterly when he saw the dwelling in such an advanced state of ruin. For so many years it had been vibrant and alive with music and dance echoing off its walls. Abundance was overflowing everywhere, from the fruit-laden trees to the flowering malli and champa, from to the plush, velvet sofas and silk carpets to the dancing chandeliers. Food was always cooked for a banquet in Kamalamba's home, such was the glory of a lost era. To see the house broken down, the garden overrun with weeds, left Radhai overwhelmed with guilt. He should never have abandoned Kamalamba. She had been a mother figure and protector for so many decades. It just felt wrong. But Mohan had been beaten beyond recognition and Radhai had feared for both their lives. So many times he had told Kamalamba to change her profession, to give up the old way of the temple Devadasi and establish a School of Dance, but evil counsel got the better of her. She believed that Karadi would be her savior. When times are bad, you can never be detached enough to discern wisely between friends and enemies, and Kamalamba let slip her only chance for survival. Although Bala had sent him to save Vasanti, in his heart he knew he was here because of an inner compulsion to save Kamalamba and give her a chance to see the end of her days with some semblance of dignity. But where was she?

He asked neighbors and was led on a wild goose chase knocking on strange doors in the poorest quarters of Thanjavur, but no one had seen her. Many had heard of her, she was notorious enough, but they didn't mix with the likes of her and were completely unhelpful. After a week-long search Radhai had to accept defeat, and he returned to Madras completely distressed and disappointed. A month later, they received another letter from Vasanti. Her plight was terrible. They had moved to Salem and were living together in a makeshift hut on the outskirts of town. There was no return address, but Vasanti had begged her to please help them out. Karadi had become a full blown alcoholic, and his assaults were getting more and more violent. She believed Kamalamba had broken a collar bone after a beating from him. Vasanti was now entertaining truck drivers and twice had been afflicted with some dreadful disease. It was a miracle she had even survived this far. Both Kamalamba and Vasanti were sick and malnourished and this was their last hope.

This time both Radhai and Mohan went to Salem. They had no idea where to begin. From morning to night they visited every shanty town, every hut, working their way around the perimeter of the city. Utterly exhausted and ready to accept defeat, the duo sat by the railway station contemplating the next train, when they saw Karadi. His bloated face had completely distorted his features. His unkempt beard and uncut hair made him look even more frightening.

Knowing Karadi's vicious temperament, they decided it was best not to talk with him, so they waited until he left the station and discreetly followed him. Karadi made several stops along the way, the longest at an *arack* stand in the north of the city, where he downed pints of cheap alcohol, then staggered down into a *cheri*, a filthy slum. The stench from the overused, open gutters nearly overpowered the two men, who covered their noses and continued to follow him from a safe distance. After about ten minutes or so, Karadi turned into an apology for a house and let himself in. It boasted of a corrugated roof and door but the walls appeared to be made of cardboard. Radhai and Mohan had no idea what to do next. They didn't want to go in and confront him, so they waited patiently until daybreak.

Mohan was shocked when he saw her. Vasanti, who had been so beautiful with radiant skin and long, curly tresses, looked like an old, wizened hag. She had a pot with her and was probably going to fill it with water from the communal tap. When they approached her, she was in a daze and for several minutes showed no recognition. Then she smiled imperceptibly, and Mohan was sad to see she had lost some of her teeth. She didn't want to leave Kamalamba in the clutches of Karadi, but Mohan persuaded her, promising they would return the following day to get her.

As promised, they returned the next day. On seeing them Kamalamba was so angry she wailed in a long, perplexing yowl. She had lost her speech, and the only sound that came out sounded like a child babbling. Almost on cue, Karadi entered, and on seeing them, growled like the bear he was and went straight for the *aruvaal* lying at the far end of the room. Both Radhai and Mohan were out of there like a gunshot, racing down the gully with Karadi ambling after them hurling abuses and brandishing his aruvaal.

But, still, they were not ready to accept defeat. They knew Karadi spent evenings at the arack shop, and they snuck into the hut the following evening, only to find it empty. There was no sign of Kamalamba. This time they had to accept they would not save her. She would have to live her days out the best she could. Radhai cried all the way back, unable to control the memories that kept flooding in. So many good times, so many happy moments. He had tried sincerely, but God wanted something else. He resolved to return again some time, but right now he was too exhausted to think of anything.

It was reward enough when they saw Bala's eyes light up. Bala shared the same guilt of betraying the one person who had cared for them for so many years. But saving Vasanti partly served as atonement, and in the next few weeks Bala focused all her energy bringing life back to her dear friend's atrophied frame. At least she had the opportunity to save Vasanti—Vyjayanthi had passed before she had the chance. Life was very strange, the circumstances you faced, the problems that cropped up, and the choices you made. All of this made her sharply aware of divine *Leela* at play. Who understood the mysteries of existence? Who could fight against the will of Providence? In the end, everyone was just running aimlessly like mice in a maze—and some found an exit and others did not. Tears of gratitude streamed down her cheeks. She was the lucky one, she had the fortune of escaping and redefining her future, and she couldn't get over the miracle of her destiny. It was too incomprehensible.

CHAPTER SEVENTY FIVE

MAHADEVAN
CALCUTTA – DECEMBER 1951

THE ALLIANCE

V*ango vango, Ganesh Ammanji. Yenna? Rhombo naaluku apram parkarom?*
"Good evening, Mahadevan. Yes, it has certainly been a long time, but now I have been transferred to Calcutta, so hopefully we will meet more often."

Mahadevan called out to Dharmu, who was also happy to see Ganesh Iyer. He was a constant visitor whenever they stayed in Nagarcoil, and Dharmu had watched him grow up over the years. It was really good to meet people from one's hometown as they brought all the local news with them. In the early years, she missed home and visited at least twice annually, but as the children grew older, it became harder to get away. Now with all the children's grandparents gone, there seemed no need to go back home, so they used their vacation time for actual holidays.

Dharmu went into the kitchen to ensure there was vegetarian food, while Mahadevan and Ganesh talked about property and business. Thankfully there was no meat on the menu today. Ganesh Iyer was a strict vegetarian, and though she was not ashamed anymore of eating meat she certainly didn't want to flaunt it. People talked about their westernized lifestyle a lot anyway, and she didn't want to give them additional ammunition.

When she returned, Kandu was with them. He had just returned from work and was undergoing the third degree from Ganesh Ammanji. In a matter of a few minutes he had asked Kandu everything about his life including his take-home salary! Kandu excused himself to go wash up, and Ganesh jumped right to it.

"Tell me, Mahadevan, your son is very eligible; have you thought about his marriage?"

"Yes, my wife has a huge file of varans. Someone or another keeps sending us good alliances, but so far Kandu hasn't shown any interest in anyone."

"If you don't mind my suggesting, I met a very good family. They live close by, in South End Park. The girl is sixteen, and next year she will sit for her Junior Cambridge exams. Very pretty girl, and I think she will be a good match for our Kandu."

"What does her father do?" asked Mahadevan.

"His name is Parthasarathy, and they have lived in Madras for a long time although I don't know what their ancestral village is. They are not a rich family like yours, that is the only problem. He is a salesman in Geigy." He paused to gauge Mahadevan's reaction, but there was no change in his expression, so he continued. "The girl sings beautifully and is very well raised. Only child, so they want a good boy for her."

"I don't have any objection at all if the family is poor. For me, the girl and boy need to meet and approve of one another that's all."

"And dowry?" Ganesh asked tentatively, wondering how Mahadevan would respond.

Mahadevan threw his head back and guffawed. "No, no, Ammanji, I would never expect a dowry for my son. I'm against it. In fact, they can send the girl here with just the clothes she owns. We want nothing. The only thing we ask is that the wedding be celebrated traditionally. The reception I will host and pay for, at least that is what I have in my mind. It's all hypothetical at this point because Kandu doesn't seem to like anyone we suggest. Do you have a photograph?"

"No I don't, I thought I would ask if you were interested then I can arrange for you to go and meet the girl. Perhaps you wouldn't mind giving me one of Kandu's so I can show them and I will get you Kamakshi's."

"Sure, we have plenty. I will talk to Kandu and let you know," Mahadevan assured him.

By the time Kandu came down again, Ganesh Iyer had left. He couldn't eat with them because he was expected for dinner at home and promised to be in touch.

"So ... ?" queried Kandu. "What did Ganesh Ammanji talk about?"

"Oh nothing much ... some details about property."

"Now that you are here," said Dharmu opening her file of varans. "We have received a very good alliance for you. The girl is from Madras and the daughter of a High Court Judge. The girl looks quite nice ... here ... take a look at the photo and tell me what you think."

Kandu sighed and leaned back in chair, least interested. This was his opportunity. He had to speak now or else he would never get around to it. Taking a deep breath he began, "Amma I don't think you should be looking all over the country for a girl for me. I have seen a girl. You may have seen her too. She comes for all the tamil movies and katcheris. Maybe you can find out more about her family." There! That sounded casual enough.

"Do you like her?" asked Dharmu.

Kandu was embarrassed, his face now a little flushed. "I think so. You can't tell much by just looking, but yes, she looks really nice and I think she may work."

"Do you know anything about her?"

"Well, her name is Kamakshi, and her father works in Geigy; he's a salesman I think. They live in South End Park, that's all I know."

Mahadevan's face broke into a smile. "I don't believe in coincidences, but this is really an amazing coincidence."

"What is?" asked Dharmu, a little confused.

"Ganesh Ammanji just asked if we would be interested in the very same family."

"Interesting … divine intention I suppose," remarked Dharmu.

"Well then, tell him I'm happy to meet her," added Kandu quickly.

"Happy to meet who?" asked Vani walking in on them. She had arrived last week and would be here for a month. Dharmu explained it all to her, and she clearly wasn't happy. Nothing made her happy. "Honestly," she declared, "I think he should marry my friend from Mysore. She's going to be a doctor." But no one heard her, and she realized that her words were falling on deaf ears.

"If Kandu likes someone then he marries her," declared Dharmu with a finality that pleased Kandu but made Vani visibly angry. "How come you didn't give me that choice?"

"Oh lord! Back to that again," said Dharmu holding her head in her hands. "You have been married ten years now. Stop complaining! You didn't have anyone you wanted to marry, so we suggested someone. If you had, we would have considered it like we did for Rukku. Stop blaming me all the time. I didn't have a choice either when I married your father."

"But that was your generation. You didn't let me choose, but darling Kandu gets to marry whoever he wants," argued Vani, refusing to relent.

Both Mahadevan and Kandu got up simultaneously. They were tired of this constant banter. Every visit she brought it up, and the same conversation repeated itself. "Enough!" screamed Mahadevan. "This is not about you, Vani, this is about Kandu. If you are fed up with your husband, leave him. But if you don't plan to leave him, just keep quiet. I'm sick of this!"

Vani was taken aback. It took a lot to rile up Mahadevan, and she sulked for the rest of the evening, not that anyone really cared. Kandu had escaped from the room a while ago. He ran into his room followed by a yapping Pittuda and lay on his bed staring at the ceiling.

He was happy. He didn't know why he was so happy. Just the idea of being with the rose girl, Kamu, brought a smile to his lips, and when he checked with Pittu, the little sausage looked happy too. He had a smile on his face and his little tail wagged nonstop. Kandu pursed his lips and whistled an entire song. Then, out of breath, he stopped and smiled some more.

CHAPTER SEVENTY SIX

KAMU
MADRAS – DECEMBER 1951

ANOTHER VARAN

Kamu returned home all sweaty. In spite of the cool weather, table tennis was an exhausting sport. In the tournament that day their team had narrowly lost in the semi-finals. Kamu played well, but knew that many others had played better. She should have entered the mixed doubles, where less people had enrolled. She would have stood a better chance of winning, but there was no point regretting her choice now. She was looking forward to a cold bath and some real food. Sandwiches were not enough, given how hungry the exertions of the day had made her. As she approached the front door, she was a little annoyed to hear voices. Sometimes having a constant stream of visitors was exasperating. It was hardly ever just the three of them. Normally she enjoyed company, but today she was in no mood for small talk. She peeped in. Sundar Mama was there, so Kutti Ramu must be lurking somewhere indoors, but the other gentleman she had never met.

"*Vaa vaa* Kamu," said Partha noticing her. "You have come at a very good time. Ganesh Iyer, my friend here, has just brought an excellent varan for you."

Kamu smiled imperceptibly. Was she supposed to be excited? Well, she wasn't. This was not what she wanted to attend to right now given her physical and mental fatigue. She was sixteen, and this was a crucial year; she had been studying single-mindedly for the big exam next year and marriage was the last thing on her mind. She was just too tired, but she couldn't be rude. *Namaskaram Mama, namaskaram Sundar mama,* she greeted them politely. "Appa," she began, a wan expression on her face. "Not now, you can't get me married now, it's not fair. I told you, you can start looking for me next year, after my exams. I'm just not in the right frame of mind to focus on anything you say right now."

Partha turned to Sundar, "I told you she wouldn't be interested."

"What interested?" he responded. "You just have to decide when to fix the Ponnpaakal and tell her to be there, that's all. Why are you asking her? She's only a child, *pacchakuzhandhai*. What does she know about these matters? The horoscopes are a perfect match. It's extremely rare to find such a perfect match. You cannot wait, Partha, you have to snap up the boy."

"That doesn't work in our house. You know Kamu. Nothing happens in this house without her permission. I can't even pick my own clothes to wear. You think she will agree to be left out of choosing her life partner?"

"Let her see the photo at least," said Ganesh waving the photograph in the air, but Kamu was least interested. All she wanted was to fling herself onto her comfy bed and go to sleep.

Mama, na kulluchutu pārkaren, she assured him. That was a good answer. Everything was best done after a purifying bath. This was Kamu's strongest advantage. She knew how to phrase things so she made her point without offending anyone—she spoke to adults with the right amount of deference.

Partha nodded. "Go bathe, you must be tired. Amma is in the kitchen preparing dinner." Kamu ran into the bathroom happy to get out of her sticky clothes. Bathed and powdered, she emerged fifteen minutes later, sharply aware of her hunger pangs. As usual, there would be extra people eating dinner but she couldn't wait for them; she filled her plate and sat down with Ramu.

"So Kamu?" he began, licking the rasam off the back of his hand. "Looks like you will be married off soon."

"I wish you wouldn't say that. *Na yenna ādā kudharaiya?* Seriously … am I a goat or a horse?"

"Don't get offended. Whether you like it or not, you belong to your parents. You don't have be a goat or horse to be sold off. Girls are given away the same way. What do you think *Kanyādānam* is about? Your father is giving you away to your husband."

"That is so offensive. Well, Appa knows he can't just marry me off. If I don't like the boy, then no marriage is going to take place. I think you are mistaken. Kanyādānam is not just a girl being given away. It is a huge sacrifice; at least I like to think I am a prized possession for my parents and allowing another man to take care of me is a privilege for him."

"We will never let go of you Kamu," added Rajam, having just emerged from the kitchen. "In the olden days it was different. Girls were sent off to another village, and it was hard for them to travel home, but nowadays things are different. We will see you regularly, so instead of losing a daughter we will gain a son."

Adhaane! exclaimed Kamu banging her palm on the table. "*Vazhiki vango.* See Ramu, my in-laws will be giving their son as *Kumara dānam,*" she said laughing.

Rajam cleared the table and set four more plates down for Partha's friends. Kamu watched this, shaking her head in despair. "Amma, can we go somewhere for a holiday. I'm so tired of having visitors at home all the time."

"Not for a while. Your Siva Periappa and Sushila Periamma are coming in a few days."

Kamu flopped down on the chair. "Again? For how long?"

"Don't say that, Kamu. This is not how I brought you up. We always welcome any visitors; that is our *sampradāyam,* our tradition."

"Okay, okay. I guess I'm just tired. Do you need help with dinner or can I go and sleep?"

"Go, *ma,* I can manage," said Rajam kissing her on her temple.

Kamu slipped into her bedroom and changed into her nightdress of ultra-fine cotton. Faded from so many washings, it looked overused, yet it remained her favorite. She picked up the Women's World magazine and began reading a new romantic story. English people were so lucky; they could marry anyone they met and fell in love with. There was no question of *jādi* and *sub-jādi.* Indian marriages were so complicated. And your choice was so limited. She had to marry an Iyer, and he had to belong to the *Vadama* subcaste at that. But Kamu knew one thing: she was never going to settle. She would only marry someone tall, dark, and handsome like in her romantic novels. No, not dark; just tall and handsome. She fell asleep with the lights still on and the book lying on her chest. Sometime in the early hours of the morning she woke up and remembered that Appa had asked her to see a photo, and now she was curious. She tiptoed into the hall and turned on the light. There it was on the table. In his hurry to go to bed after the exhilarating time with friends, Appa hadn't bothered to put it away. She looked at the picture and was stunned.

Oh lord! It was Mr. No thank you, her English gentleman!

CHAPTER SEVENTY SEVEN

MAHADEVAN
CALCUTTA – DECEMBER 1951

FAMILY DRAMA

M ahadevan threw the letter down in disgust. It seemed as if nothing he said or did was ever taken in the right spirit. It all began after his father died. Not permitted to leave Calcutta, he couldn't attend his father's funeral and committed the worst crime any Brahmin could conceive of—to be the eldest son and not perform his father's kriya. The guilt and sadness haunted him for days, but he was in such a tight situation then. The country had been in the grips of a severe famine, and his presence in the city was crucial at the time. There was no way he could justify getting permission for leave. Taking off without authorization was his only other choice, but that would have entailed losing his job, which would have created more problems than it solved. His father would never have approved. It was his father's dream that made him study and sit for the ICS exams. Despite financial problems, somehow, Nilakantan Ayyar found a way to finance him, and relinquishing the fruits of so many years of hard work just didn't sit right with Mahadevan. After all, his father's soul departed from his body long ago, so what did it matter if he did the kriya or his younger brother did it. His brothers had made peace with him for the most part, but his sisters were unforgiving, harping on the lapse in letters to one another and boycotting them at family events. It seemed so childish. Each year he called Sundar Sastrigal and performed the *tarpanam,* the annual ceremony on his father's death anniversary, with due solemnity, not leaving out a single ritual, but no matter what he did, it wasn't good enough for them.

A few months before, he learned that his sister Lalitha had taken ill. He was shocked to discover that she had contracted syphilis from that wastrel husband of hers. He somehow was fine, but with Lalitha's delicate constitution, she unfortunately got progressively worse. Her condition was further exacerbated by advanced diabetes, and for the last two months she was bed ridden and showing early signs of bed sores. On hearing this, Mahadevan wrote to his brothers and asked if they could jointly purchase a hospital bed, making it easier to mobilize and turn her. The bed could also be raised and lowered, which would help at mealtimes. His brothers agreed, and his younger brother Dandapani, who was a doctor, arranged for the purchase and transport to Lalitha's village. Lalitha's son made trouble from the start. He wrote an acidic letter thanking "the great Mahadevan Ayyar" for his concern, but he didn't need or want their charity, and they could abandon this idea of a "bed-fund."

Mahadevan sighed. *Bed fund.* Well in one way it was sort of a bed fund, but more than that, all the brothers wanted Lalitha's last days to be as comfortable as possible. As long as Nilakantan Ayyar had been alive, he held a tight rein on the family and no one dared say a word out of place. But now with him gone, the fragmenting family was developing new cracks on a monthly basis. It was exhausting!

Kandu came in to sort the mail and saw his father looking visibly anxious.

"What's up Dad? Office or financial troubles?"

"Neither … family problems, but nothing you need worry your head about," said Mahadevan with a sigh.

Kandu was anxious to find out if any progress had been made on the Kamu front but was thinking of a casual manner to broach the subject. "Something to do with Ganesh Iyer?" He knew Ganesh Ammanji was there to sort out some family property and thought this was the perfect opener.

"No, no. That was a completely different matter."

"So did he come visit again?"

"As a matter of fact he did," replied Mahadevan knowing exactly what Kandu wanted to talk about, but just for a lark made his son sweat a bit. There was an awkward silence…. Mahadevan knew Kandu was bursting, and it was hard for him to keep a calm face when he was itching to smile.

"And?" asked Kandu annoyed his father wasn't filling him in on the news.

"And what?" asked Mahadevan innocently.

"Did he say anything else?" said Kandu, slightly irritated.

"About what?" asked Mahadevan unable to contain himself, his face breaking into a broad smile.

"Oh Dad, you're playing with me now. You know very well what I am talking about."

Laughing, Mahadevan finally told him what he wanted to hear. "Yes he did. Apparently as it is *Margazhi māsam*, they will not arrange for us to meet the girl till January 15th."

"Margazhi māsam huh? What's so special about that?"

"Well we don't do anything auspicious in that month."

Kandu was really annoyed. Damn! He would have to wait a whole month now. He stood up abruptly and stalked off.

Mahadevan smiled. Kandu really liked the girl, but waiting would increase the longing. What was that saying? Absence makes the heart grow fonder. Good, good. Kandu was always so quick tempered. Let him learn the value of patience. Everything would take place in good time.

CHAPTER SEVENTY EIGHT

KAMU
CALCUTTA – JANUARY 1952

THE PRIZED KOH-I-NOOR

The excitement was palpable in the Parthasarathy household. The astrologer was consulted repeatedly to get the perfect date for the Ponnpaakal, and Sundar Mama was an even more regular visitor. Preparations were in high gear to welcome the Ayyar family. The date was fixed and the menu revised repeatedly. Everything had to be just right. The walls were brushed for cobwebs, the curtains taken down and washed. Kamu had arranged and rearranged the living room a million times.

She had seen the English gentleman at least thrice this past month, but both of them kept stealing glances and then looking away nonchalantly, as though they had no idea what was being planned for the two of them. Two weeks previously at the katcheri, she could tell plans were afoot, but tried to compose herself and pretend she didn't know what was happening. Raman uncle introduced Siva and Partha to the boy's father and Kamu could feel their eyes on her several times. All the while, the silly boy was at his favorite lamppost smoking away as usual. Kamu was unsure how she felt. It was an exciting time, but every now and again fear would raise its ugly head masking all else.

Sushila Periamma insisted he looked fabulous. *Raja madri irukaandi,* she exclaimed, on seeing him for the first time. *Nee kuduthu vechirke.* But Kamu was certain she was the one who looked like a queen and *he* should feel privileged to marry her. She couldn't understand why he didn't have the courage to talk to her. Perhaps he was scared of his parents. She knew it was not acceptable that a boy and girl speak to one another before an official engagement, but her romance novels suggested otherwise. For sure, he was not reading those novels.

Kamu alternated between excitement and fear, buffeted continually by rising emotions she didn't know what to make of. She was excited because everyone else in the household was, but she didn't really know why. She should really be sad because she would be leaving her parents and going into an alien home. It felt strange to suddenly drop everything that was familiar and go into an unknown home where she would have to think of two perfect strangers as her parents, but much worse was the prospect of sleeping in the same bed with a man! All her life Appa had done whatever he could to prevent men from even looking at her, and now he was gung ho about marrying her off to a mysterious outsider.

She didn't quite understand much about the love they spoke about in romance novels. She had never experienced anything like that. Her parents did not act giddy and never even came within two feet of each other in front of her. Perhaps she was too young. In her family, married couples never demonstrated any affection, they just lived with each other. Marriage seemed to be simply a convenient arrangement for the division of chores. The man earned the money and paid the bills while the woman cooked and cleaned. Love did not really enter into the equation. No one had ever spoken of it, so Kamu had no clue how it was supposed to feel. She was certainly excited and happy but didn't know what to make of her feelings. Kamu knew all girls needed to get married and this was a perfectly acceptable man. To her, looks meant far more than anything else. All she wanted was someone she could be proud walking next to. That felt a little shallow, but it was the truth.

Sushila called her into the room where she had laid out a dozen saris to select for the Ponnpaakal. They were all Kānjeevaram silk saris, and Kamu didn't want to wear any of them. She wanted to present herself as a modern girl, so instead, she ran into her room, ransacked her closet and came back with a dozen georgette saris. They went back and forth a million times and finally she picked an orange georgette with a contrasted green blouse. Kamu had embroidered the blouse painstakingly in a multicolored running stitch. Amma's coral necklace and her simple pearl tops would be perfect. She wanted to look classy and simple. Of course she had to make sure she got an orange rose for her hair.

Kamu laid out her sari along with all the accessories on her bed. This was fun. Awkward but fun. If everything went well, she would be married soon. This year, definitely. The thought terrified her and she threw herself on her bed sobbing loudly. On hearing her, Rajam and Sushila ran into the room in a panic. The Ponnpaakal was five days away and they had to take good care of Kamu until then. Rajam was terrified Kamu had changed her mind. She was quite capable, and if she had, nothing would persuade her otherwise. "What happened, Kamu, you scared us. Are you okay?" she asked, her concern apparent.

"No I'm n ... not!" Kamu stuttered. "I can't get m mm ... ma ... married Amma, I'm too small." And she began crying afresh.

Both Sushila and Rajam looked at teach other knowingly. Both of them had experienced their moments of fear and panic, only they had been so much younger. Every girl went through this, battling with the fear of the unknown. But they let her cry, attempting to calm her down with soothing words. It was good and liberating to release your feelings. Nothing like a good cry once in a while. Siva and Partha joined them, both wearing woeful expressions. Partha could not bear to see his dear daughter unhappy. When the others left, he sat down and for the first time talked to her about marriage.

"Kamu, you know I would never send you away with anyone who could hurt you—you know that don't you? You are like a prized Kohinoor diamond and if I hadn't got a perfect match, I would never have thought of him as your companion." Kamu nodded, sniffing occasionally, but listening intently. Partha's heart was all mush, seeing tears in his treasured baby's eyes.

"You mustn't cry. There is nothing to be frightened about. You are educated and you are a strong girl. Things in your new home may be strange, but that is all it is; strange. You will get used to it. Kamu, it is my duty to find someone for you to be with, a good companion who will love you, provide for you, and make you happy. I promise, if you don't like him, the matter will end there. No one will force you to be married. I think you are crying because of a fear of the unknown. Don't think too much. Just go with the flow, and in your heart if it feels right you tell me. You will know."

Partha's talk calmed Kamu immediately. She realized she was just overwhelmed with all the recent fuss over the "great Match" and a little nonplussed being at the center of all attention.

She would go with the flow and instead of focusing on the rest of her life, she would think about looking good. That was a lot less stressful. She washed her face and sat in front of her mirror. She looked awful. She picked up the now wilted pink rose and pinned it behind her right ear, applied some lipstick, and put a little on her cheeks. Then she raised one eyebrow and flirted with her mirror. She appeared so silly with rouge on her cheeks added to her swollen, shiny nose. She looked like a buffoon! Wiping off her makeup, she lay down and stared at the fan. Pretty soon she was asleep.

Partha peeped in and turned off the lights. He pulled the covers over her and tucked her in. Kamu moaned and turned on her side, a smile on her face. Partha could tell she was in the midst of a very sweet dream.

Chapter Seventy Nine

Kamu

South End Park – January 1952

The Ponnpaakal

Sleep was impossible with the frantic household activity and intense noise level. On an impulse, Partha had gone shopping the previous week and bought a beautiful, rosewood sofa set in upholstered, red velvet. It was a really attractive addition to the drawing room and contrasted perfectly with the jute rug tucked beneath the coffee table. Everything looked pristine and well-organized in anticipation of the afternoon tiffin.

Rajam added the finishing touches to the most divine *rava kesari* oozing with ghee, raisins, cashews and a tantalizing aroma. The sliced vegetables for the *bajjis* were soaking in water. They would fry these vegetable fritters later to be served piping hot. Rajam ground fresh coconut chutney and then began preparations for lunch. With Sushila's help, the morning went by swiftly.

After a sumptuous three-course lunch, they all retired for a well-deserved siesta, but Kamu's anxiety kept her from sleeping. Her whole life was about to embark on a new trajectory, and it felt strange to relinquish control. The last few years here in Calcutta were her best. Besides remaining financially secure, they were finally completely together as a family, making it even harder to contemplate all the changes that lay ahead. She went into the back verandah and was soon joined by Ramu. While the adults slept, the two of them played several rounds of rummy. After a while, Sushila and Ramji joined them and, judging by the lighthearted banter, no one could gauge what a life-altering day this spelt for Kamu.

Sometime later they heard Rajam calling, letting them know that coffee was ready. No one could prepare coffee as well as Rajam with the right amount of decoction complemented with the correct proportion of milk and sugar. Kamu downed hers and scampered off to get dressed. Today she would use powder on her face as well. She took her time applying her makeup and fussing with her hair. As she pinned the rose behind her right ear, Partha walked in. "Are you okay?" he asked, running his hand affectionately over her head.

"Appa!" she exclaimed. "Don't spoil my hair, I have just spent ten minutes getting everything in place."

"Oops, sorry," he apologized. "I'm off, Kamu. Just relax, and remember, your choice is final."

In her heart Kamu had already agreed to marry this English gentleman, except she could not think of him as Nilakantan. The name sounded too traditional and didn't quite suit the image that she had created in her mind. He seemed more like a Dev or Raj. When she emerged from her room, Sushila had just laid out the colorful Thanjavur jamakalam in the inner room where the ladies would sit. From this vantage point, one could get a clear view of the entrance and part of the living room, so the men could look in, but more importantly Kamu could strategically sit so she could see the boy.

Sundar Mama arrived with his retinue, and after washing up in the back of the house, assembled in the living room to receive their guests. Having fried the last of the bajjis, Rajam wiped her hands and quickly changed her sari. As the clock struck five, they heard the sound of a car pulling up. They were here! These people were certainly punctual. The ladies ran to the window to see who had come. Kamu's heart was beating extra fast. She saw him get out of the front seat wearing the same nondescript, beigish-cream shirt and khaki pants and made a mental note to change his wardrobe. Each time she saw him, he wore the same colorless shirts and baggy pants. His father was wearing a veshti, and his mother had a purple sari with a matching purple sweet pea garland in her hair encircling her bun. The other young girl must be another sister or a friend, but Kamu did not recognize her. As they reached the steps, Sundar Mama and his retinue began a very loud chanting, welcoming them and blessing the event. Kamu giggled when she saw the boy's terrified face. This was perhaps the last thing he expected. He must have imagined a casual cup of coffee and spontaneous conversation, and here was this retinue of Vādhyārs stridently chanting to them as soon as they arrived. Suddenly the pace of the mantrams slowed down but the volume trebled, making him jump in alarm. This was hilarious! Sundar Mama really took his job seriously. He was ensuring the gods heard their mantrams, but in doing so awakened the entire neighborhood.

Kamu rushed back and sat down on the jamakālam just as they entered. She smoothed down her sari and made sure the rose in her hair was visible. After exchanging pleasantries, Dharmu and Vani came into the inner room to meet Kamu. Dharmu looked at her intently for a while, making Kamu feel thoroughly uncomfortable. Thankfully, the ladies began talking, leaving her free to peek into the living room. The stupid boy had taken a seat on the far end so she couldn't see him, but soon enough he moved places, and as he looked at her she quickly averted her eyes, feeling the heat suffuse her face. He was trying to appear nonchalant, but every few seconds his eyes wandered back searching for hers. Every time their gaze locked, she was forced to smile. He was attempting to speak to her with his eyes, raising his brows as if he were asking if she was okay with this arrangement. Kamu shook her head, saying yes, and couldn't stop smiling when she noticed his mortification at being caught by his father making eyes at her. Someone passed a comment about how he was already attracted to the girl inside, and there was a teeter of laughter, making Kandu frown in embarrassment. Just then Kamu was jerked out of her glance exchange by Sushila repeating her name several times. Her mother-in-law-to-be had asked her a question and she hadn't heard a word. This was embarrassing!

"Sorry," she murmured. *Enna shonnel?*

"Can you sing?" Dharmu repeated. Kamu had no time to react because Rajam interjected quickly. "Yes of course, let me fetch the *Shruti box*. Kamu will sing."

It was expected for the girl to sing at her Ponnpaakal, though how that qualified her to be a good daughter-in-law was unfathomable. Singing was something Kamu was confident of and she set the shruti to the correct pitch and began. She chose *Chalamelara* in *Margahindolam* rāgam and sang effortlessly in her sweet yet strong voice. After she finished, she looked up to see if the English boy liked it but was disappointed she couldn't see him. He had moved seats. She wanted to know his reaction. But Dharmu was all praise and asked her to sing another. This time she chose another song *Pranamāmyaham* in *Gowla* rāgam, which would show her expertise. This time Dharmu was even more effusive in her praise. She liked this girl: accomplished, pretty, yet apparently of strong character. *Yennamā pādare Kamu! Yenna bhruga yenna bhruga?*

And then they left. Kamu watched through the window as they got into the car. She could see him searching for her, but he didn't know she was at the window.

It was such an anticlimax. Kamu had no idea what she was expecting, but she felt a sudden plunge of mood. Now what?

In an hour the phone rang, and she could tell they were speaking to her father, who came into the room a few minutes later beaming from ear-to-ear. "Congratulations!" he exclaimed slapping an unsuspecting Siva on the shoulder. "They love you and want to fix the engagement next week."

Kamu felt the room spinning. It was happening … It was happening ….

She wasn't quite sure what she felt and if indeed she felt anything. Everything was mixed up in a huge muddle somewhere in the backwaters of her mind.

CHAPTER EIGHTY

KANDU AND KAMU
CALCUTTA – JANUARY 15, 1952

THE ENGAGEMENT

"So?" asked Kandu, anxiously seeking approval. "What's the verdict?"
"Could you at least wait until we're out of the gate. They might hear us," replied Mahadevan, beaming away, amused at Kandu's urgency. They drove down the road in silence, but Kandu's restlessness was evident by his continual drumming with his fingers on the car seat.

"We're out of earshot now, come on … tell me what you think," he barked.

"I like her very much. Her teeth are so straight and white," declared Dharmu, making Mahadevan look at her in surprise. "So you examined her as one would a horse," he remarked wryly.

"No, no, good teeth are a great asset, and she sang Kandu's favorite song. What did you think of her singing Kandu?"

Kandu grunted and shook his head, which could have meant anything.

"She's a very good singer, there's no doubting that," added Mahadevan. "My only concern is if she will fit in with our family. There is a considerable difference in lifestyle."

"If I could learn your British ways after being raised in a village, then Kamu can certainly do the same, and she has lived all her life in big cities," remarked Dharmu.

"Frankly, Kandu, she's way too young for you and hasn't even finished school. I seriously think you should marry my friend," said Vani, taking advantage of perhaps her last opportunity.

"Give it up, Vani, that is not going to happen. I can't understand how it even crosses your mind to bring that up considering we went to their house with the specific purpose of confirming if I could marry her. Seriously, you need your head examined," interrupted Kandu, irate that Vani didn't appear to like Kamu, not that he particularly sought her approval.

"Vani, leave it," said Mahadevan, his voice sharp. "It's decided then. I'll call

Parthasarathy and fix the engagement as soon as possible, maybe this weekend. Dharmu, you speak to Sundar and fix a good date. It's best to get them engaged soon."

Kandu was thrilled. He smiled all the way home, his cheeks hurt from the effort. Wow! It was unbelievable that he was going to be engaged to Kamu. It was all finally coming together. All day he whistled Pranamāmyaham, the song Kamu had sung, though he was scarcely aware of it. Dharmu spoke to Sundar the following day, and after consulting the Panchāngam, the lunar calendar, he called back to fix the date for Friday, the first of February.

There was plenty to be done before then. Rukku was still staying with them and completely occupied with her new baby, so Vani accompanied Dharmu to make all the purchases. They knew their prospective daughter-in-law liked crepe saris, so Dharmu picked up a sky blue one for her with a deep blue border and then bought two more in the same design for herself. Somehow she couldn't control herself from buying in threes. Since veshtis in the south Indian style were difficult to find, she bought a dozen shirt pieces for the men. She would probably make a shopping trip to Madras before the wedding, but for now this would do.

Kandu went with Mickey to Satram Das, a jeweler on Middleton Row, to pick up a ring for Kamu. Dharmu said there was no ceremony in the engagement function for exchange of rings. Their family was very traditional, and she doubted Kamu knew anything about ring exchange. Even if he bought her a ring, there was no chance the in-laws would even think of a ring for Kandu. But Kandu didn't care and wanted to buy a ring for Kamu with his own earnings. It was hard to do so when he had no idea of her size but the jeweler assured them Kamu could return to the store to size the ring. Kandu's buddy Mickey was hardly the best for advice on jewelry for women, so, eventually, Kandu picked a plain gold ring, not realizing that girls liked diamonds. Kandu would have to live with this decision for a long time! The ceremony was to be in the evening at the boy's parents home as per tradition and would be followed by dinner. Dharmu invited only a few people—there was really no time to plan a big affair. Just a private ceremony where the two families would exchange a written contract agreeing to the marriage.

✻❧⟨❂⟩❧✻

Kamu refused to get engaged in an old sari. She threw a tantrum and didn't come out of her room till Partha agreed to buy her a brand new sari. Then, happily, she traipsed off to Lake Market and picked up a beautiful Mysore crepe in a peach with an orange border. Sushila helped to prepare the *thāmboolams*, gifts to be given to the groom's family during the *Nischyathārtham*. They ordered the *paruppu thenga*, which was molded into a cone shape and arrived on the morning of the engagement along with the rest of the order: 25 *murukkus*, 25 *thatais* 25 *laddus* 25 *jāngris* and 25 *mysore pāk*.

Every day Rajam added another item to the list and Partha had to borrow two thousand rupees from his friend Rama Iyer, the first installment of the very large loan he would take to celebrate this wedding. They argued over buying saris for Dharmu and Kandu's sisters, but finally decided on just a shirt and pant piece for Kandu. They would have to buy saris at the wedding anyway.

The day of the engagement finally arrived. With all the gifts and passengers, the Landmaster was filled to capacity and slowly made its way through Calcutta's busy streets, finally arriving at 16, Portland Park on Majherhat Bridge.

Kamu was astounded when she saw how massive this mansion was. She had no idea her in-laws were so well off. Four cars stood outside, and there were servants everywhere. Kamu entered the main hall feeling like Cinderella entering the ballroom. Arrangements had been made in the living room where they had pushed the furniture against the wall and spread jamakālams on the floor. The ceremony began with Sundar Mama in his loud, raucous voice reading out the *lagnapatrika*, a contract between the two families agreeing to the marriage, with full details including name, *gotram* (family name), their ancestral village, and declaration that Kamakshi and Nilakantan would wed on an auspicious muhurtham on October 31, 1952.

The families exchanged thāmboolams, and Kamu looked sharply at Sushila Periamma when she noticed that there were gifts for Partha and Rajam as well. Oh no! It was too late to do anything about that. The Ayyars were far wealthier, and from the look on their faces, they were not expecting anything and didn't look disappointed.

After the ceremony, they asked Kamu to go upstairs and talk to Kandu, and she followed him sheepishly. They couldn't be left alone so of course Rukku and Vani were seated at the far side, and Ramu and Siva followed a few minutes later pretending to admire the view.

Kandu reached for his pocket and took out the ring and then asked for permission to put it on her finger. Kamu could have sworn an electric current passed through her hand when he touched her, but that might have been because she was all wired up.

To every question Kandu asked in English, Kamu replied in Tamil. She was too scared to speak to him in English. What if she made mistakes? Her brain was fuzzy, and even though she intended to speak in English, only Tamil came out of her mouth. After a few minutes she noticed Kandu spoke only in English and she answered only in Tamil. How were they ever going to communicate? Just then Pittuda came pattering in and sniffed noisily at Kamu's feet. Kamu shrank back instinctively.

"Don't worry, he won't bite. He's a good dog, see? Just pet him," Kandu urged, picking up Pittu. Kamu reached out, but Pittu raised his nose up sniffing wildly making her snap her hand back.

"Just rub his back, he loves that," said Kandu trying to make it easier for her.

"It's like velvet," Kamu said, plucking up the courage to place her hand on Pittuda's soft fur.

"Pittu, this is Kamu. Say hi ... come on ... show your paw." Pittu lifted one paw obediently and Kamu shook it, giggling away and, thus, the ice was broken.

Kandu was happy. If Pittu didn't like her he would have barked, but not a peep came out of him and he happily allowed her a paw shake. As long as Pittu approved, Kandu was okay. This was going to work. He would speak to her in Tamil next time. God knows why he was talking only in English. Nervousness I guess.

Fifteen minutes was apparently enough time for them to speak alone, because both Rukku and Vani came over, followed by Ramu, and then other family members came in turn to congratulate them. As they left the house, Kamu turned around and took one last look at the mansion which would be her new home. What a terrifying prospect!

CHAPTER EIGHTY ONE

KAMU AND KANDU
CALCUTTA – MAY 1952

BLACKJACK IN THE MIDDLE

Kamu came out of the examination hall with a sense of relief and trepidation. It was her last exam, thank God! With all the excitement of being engaged, Kamu had been in no mood to study, one of the reasons she had warned Partha to wait until she finished her exams before looking for a boy. But her destiny took an unexpected turn, and now here she was trying her best to focus on Shakespeare and Shelley, when all she could think of was her next meeting with Kandu. Her teacher had pulled her up a couple of times when she caught her daydreaming instead of focusing on what was happening in class, but she too realized it was impossible for Kamu to give her total attention to her lessons at this time.

Kandu dropped in to see her at least twice a week, but they were never permitted to be alone. Ramu became almost a permanent fixture in their home, always hanging around, privy to all their conversations. A week before her exams, Kamu banned Kandu from visiting; it was simply too distracting. He sort of hinted that she didn't really need to do her exams, but Partha would hear none of that. She had been preparing for these exams for two years now and she might as well finish and do the best she could.

Kandu called her after every exam to find out how she did. Their conversations were stilted, with Kamu continually switching between Tamil and English followed by several long, awkward silences. Regardless, she waited for his calls, which became the high point of each day. Her last exam was on Saturday and Kandu said he would pick her up and take her home to his house for dinner, as he wanted her to meet all his friends. Of course Partha could not allow Kamu to be alone in the car with Kandu, so Ramu was sent off to meet Kamu at the examination hall and accompany her to the Ayyar residence. Kandu had been looking forward to being alone with Kamu, but as he parked his car opposite the college there was a tap on his window, and he saw Ramu beaming and waving. Kandu slumped forward in the car, his head resting on the steering wheel. It was pointless. Ramu would be there no matter where he turned. He would probably pop up in between them on their first night together—there was just no escaping him. *Darn you Ramu – Blackjack,* thought Kandu, referring to him with a name that stuck for a long time. *Vandutiya?* asked Kandu, amazed Ramu had turned up here. *Yennapa aalaiye vidamātengariye,* he complained about not being left alone.

"Sorry, Kandu Saar, Partha Mama sent me. I'm so sorry, but you mustn't be alone before marriage," he apologized beaming away, his white teeth a sharp contrast to his dark skin.

Kamu looked exhausted but flashed a smile when she saw him, waving and crossing to where he stood. "Hi," she said awkwardly as he opened the passenger door for her to get in. Kandu glanced at her profile before turning the ignition on. She was wearing a simple voile sari and had her hair in a braid. Without any makeup she still looked so beautiful. He would never tire of looking at her.

The boys were already there when they reached and gave them a boisterous welcome. Kamu was a little overwhelmed, only speaking when spoken to. She couldn't help noticing that Kandu's eyes never left her, and after dinner when she spoke to Mickey for a little over five minutes, he moved quickly to her side. Of course his friends ribbed him mercilessly for his jealous behavior, but he couldn't help being possessive around Kamu. She was really innocent, and he wanted to make sure he was there to help her, especially because she struggled for words when forced to speak in English. He also wanted to ensure that none of his friends were flirting with her. Once they reached Portland Park, Ramu just melted into the background, only showing up as they were ready to leave.

"Nalla majaa unga friends," said Ramu, complimenting Kandu on his choice of friends.

"Yes, it was a really nice evening," added Kamu. "I like Mickey, he seems to be just like us. Very friendly and funny."

Us thought Kandu. That was a first.

"He's a fine guy. All my friends are nice. Mickey is going to see a girl in Madras this weekend. So he may be the next one to leave the bachelor gang."

Ramu's presence made the conversation easier because Kandu was more inclined to speak in Tamil, which suited Kamu perfectly. As he dropped them off, Kandu said to her, "I want to buy you a gift. Do you like perfume?"

Kamu couldn't remember what that word meant. "P ... p ... perfume?" She stuttered. "What is that?"

"You know ... perfume, scent, eau de cologne," he said pretending to spray himself.

She didn't recognize the last word but supposed he meant "odicolon," which is how they pronounced it at home, but scent ... that word she knew well enough. "I like scent," she said shaking her head from side to side.

"Which one?" asked Kandu.

Lord, what did he mean which one? Scent was scent. She searched for a name. Cuticura ... Ponds ... no they were all powder names then she remembered an ad she once saw in a movie advertising English Yardley perfume, and she told him confidently, "Yardley, I like Yardley."

By the time Kamu got married, in the next five months, Kandu had bought her every Yardley perfume ever manufactured.

But Kamu still called it scent.

CHAPTER EIGHTY TWO

DHARMU AND VANI
TRAIN TO MYSORE – JULY 1952

VANI'S SURPRISE

The train was slowing down as it neared Bangalore cantonment and through the long train ride, Dharmu felt the annoyance rise up in her whenever she thought of her daughter. She wanted to help Vani, but, at the same time, she was really upset with her. Six weeks ago she had received a letter from Vani. When she slit open the envelope, out slipped a photograph of Vani conspicuously pregnant.

Vani was pregnant? She had visited Calcutta only in February, and not a hint from her! What kind of daughter hides such a secret from their mother, especially knowing how anxious everyone was to see Vani start a family! That Vani was a strange one. She had blamed Dharmu for all those years of unhappy marriage and for her misery in general to such an extent, that Dharmu had begun to feel responsible. She had never developed a close bond with her daughters. She was excessively proud of Kandu and never realized she had been pushing her daughters away from her right through their childhood. When they really needed her in their growing years, she was steeped in her own unhappiness. Her own marriage had fallen far short of her expectations, and Meera had always been around to care for the girls.

In a sense, it wasn't really her fault. When she gave birth to Vani, she had just turned fifteen, still a child herself, with no idea how to care for anyone else. Those years were so fraught with the anxiety of being accepted in an alien society, of learning to fit in with westernized ways, of familiarizing herself with English and learning to be an obedient wife; it left little time to nurture her children. To some extent she felt the girls, both Vani and Rukku, had stolen her childhood. As she held the babies to her breast, she longed to be outdoors playing marbles and flying kites. She didn't understand the seriousness of motherhood and treated the babies as if they were mere dolls, feeding and clothing them and then putting them away so she could focus on her other preoccupations. Besides, servants were always there for them, making sure they were comfortable.

She was much older and definitely wiser when Kandu was born. He was so charming it was hard to remain emotionally detached from him, but more importantly, she had badly wanted a son after two daughters. So she threw herself head first into motherhood, cooing and cuddling her little boy, not realizing how it alienated her daughters. And soon, when they were old enough, she sent them away to a convent in Kurseong for some semblance of a stable education, but they read it as an overt sign of rejection. Both girls had accepted Christianity, never having been exposed to Hindu tradition, which Dharmu had herself thrown away in adapting to the colonial way of life.

Vani had never forgiven her for marrying her off to Ganesh. He was a good man, but she did not want to recognize that. She had no idea whom she wanted but it was not Ganesh. Her anger and resentment became even more bitter after Rukku's love marriage and natural expansion into family life with two children born in succession. She never sought advice from Dharmu and only blamed her continually for her own miserable marriage and existence. It was impossible for Dharmu to have a conversation with her because no matter what Dharmu said, she offered a contrary stance, arguing endlessly and creating even more of a divide between them. Dharmu's sanity lay in blocking thoughts of Vani from her mind.

In contrast, there was never any trouble with Rukku because she had sanctuary in a good marriage, although plenty of irritation came their way via her controversial husband. One could never find perfection in any relationship. No, that wasn't true. Dharmu's relationship with Kandu was perfect. She loved him wholeheartedly, perhaps more than she had loved anyone, Mahadevan included. It was a special bond that gave her so much happiness that she preferred to rest in its shadow than confront the glaring reality of a fiery relationship with her girls. And now there was Kamu. Dharmu had completely taken Kamu under her wing and was surprised at her own outpouring of love for this young girl. Already she had placed the order for a diamond necklace for her and had bought almost a dozen saris to give her at the wedding. Kamu was so polite and respectful, always saying the right things and never speaking out of turn; it was really easy to like and even love her. From the expression on her face when she spied Kamu entering the room, it was evident to all that Dharmu simply adored her, although neither Vani nor Rukku approved of this new-found love.

Vani must have been pregnant when she visited, but chose to keep it a secret. Perhaps she didn't want to be too hopeful after several miscarriages. It was really a shame because Dharmu couldn't perform the bangle ceremony for her as the fifth month had already passed. She called up Vani and asked her to return immediately to Calcutta, where plenty of good English doctors could take care of her confinement and delivery, but Vani didn't want any of that. She said Ganesh had arranged for the baby to be born in Bangalore and he was taking good care of her. With six weeks left for the delivery, Dharmu boarded the south-bound train. Maybe her in-laws would be willing to perform the *seemantham,* and she could have an abbreviated bangle ceremony at the same time.

Dharmu spotted Vani at the station with Ganesh, surprised to find her positively radiant. She was sure to have a girl. The ride back to Mysore in Ganesh's Austin was a little cramped, but Dharmu noticed a complete change in Vani's demeanor. She was upbeat and positive and didn't complain once. Dharmu was not very comfortable living with Vani's in-laws, and, thankfully, in a week the three of them would temporarily move to Bangalore where Mahadevan had arranged accommodation in a Government rest house.

The very next day, Dharmu busied herself with arrangements for the seemantham and bangle ceremony with just the family present. Dharmu was quite worried—Vani's belly was low and the pressure might urge the baby to come early. Three weeks were still left before her due date, and their ride back to Bangalore was filled with angst. This time she spent with Vani was the best ever. They didn't fight even once and were able to talk about so many different topics without ever getting on the defensive. It was amazing what pregnancy did to women.

Vani was in labor for two days. Nothing ever came easy for her. At the end of two exhausting, pain filled days, she finally gave birth to a baby daughter. The baby was incredibly fair and so very pretty, and both parents looked so happy holding this perfect pink bundle, that it was hard to imagine there had ever been a problem between them in the first place.

Vani was finally at peace.

CHAPTER EIGHTY THREE

PARTHA

CALCUTTA – AUGUST 1952

THE COST OF A MARRIAGE

Ippo yenna yezhavu pannanom shollu? screamed Partha, at his wit's end. "*Yezhavu yellam shollaadhengo.* We are spending for a wedding not a funeral. How can you speak like that?" Rajam was really upset. Lately, Partha seemed to fly off the handle at the slightest provocation. As the wedding date drew closer more expenses seemed to appear out of the blue and any mention of a payment drove him crazy. The burden of an alliance with such a well-known family was weighing him down. He didn't want to appear a pauper, though he felt he was no better than one. After Kamu's engagement, he realized he possessed only one thousand rupees in his savings and had no idea where and how to raise more money. Loans from banks came with a killer interest rate, and with his meager salary he would never be able to pay it off. He asked Siva, who was able to give five thousand, but that wasn't nearly enough. With a very heavy heart, he held out his begging bowl out and asked each one of his friends for a loan. A thousand here and ten thousand there, he finally had borrowed almost thirty thousand rupees, but even that didn't seem enough for Rajam. Each day she came up with another expense, and he was pulling his hair out in anxiety. Today's plan involved getting the best shamiana vendor in Calcutta to cover the lawn. They would arrive a month prior to the wedding and begin the arduous process of twisting yards and yards of fabric to cover the main canopy over the back lawn where the actual wedding would take place.

Partha checked and rechecked his accounts. So far they had spent over twenty-five thousand, and the actual wedding expenses were not met as yet. He had no idea what to do. He still had to pay the contractors, cook and flower vendors and who knew what additional expenses would crop up. He called Raman and told him he needed at least twenty thousand more. Raman was very understanding and said he would arrange for it but reminded Partha to go easy. He still had to pay back all this money. Of course Partha knew that, but he didn't want to think about it right now. He would deal with repayment when the time came. Right now he needed to ensure that the wedding was celebrated in a fitting manner. After all the Ayyars had not asked for a rupee in dowry. Other fathers would have spent thousands on gold and diamonds, and he felt really lucky to get such a reasonable sambandhi. The least he could do was celebrate the wedding well. Just as the money and loans appeared, God would provide a way for him to repay the debt.

Kamu was his only daughter, and he would celebrate the wedding so well that all of Calcutta would talk about it. The bulk of expenses went in the purchase of diamond earrings, which Rajam had insisted on. Sushila had ordered a pair from their family jeweler in Chennai and would bring it when she came to attend. Then they bought two sets of gold from Satram Das. Kamu didn't want to go to Madras to buy saris, so Arni Silks send a man with a selection of a hundred saris. Kamu was overwhelmed and knew how much her father was spending and as she looked at him the concern in her eyes was very clear. "Buy as many as you need," Partha assured her. Rajam thought he was speaking to her and took it as a cue to spend like a queen, picking up saris for everyone in their family and Kandu's. For Kamu, in addition to the actual wedding sari, her *koorai,* in brick red with thin gold stripes, she picked up almost a dozen others. After the wedding there would be plenty of occasions to wear new saris and, really, this was the only time Rajam could ever be this extravagant.

Partha was seated at the dining table when the duo Kamu and Ramu walked in. Kamu's face was all flushed and she and Ramu were cracking up over some joke. Just looking at her, Partha felt his heart swell. Right then, he didn't care how much money he was spending; it was all well worth it. Kamu looked so happy and so relaxed, it made everything fall into perspective. Kamu ran up to him and kissed him on his forehead. "Yenna, Appa, accounts again? Don't look so worried. It's all going to be fine."

Partha smiled. A good attitude certainly helped, but it didn't take away from the reality of the monstrous loan he would be paying back for a long time. But Kamu shouldn't have to worry about such things. This was a magical time in her life. She was young and in love. This came to a girl only once in her life, and he didn't want to temper her exuberance with his worries. She was special and would get whatever she wanted.

After all, it wasn't every day that Kamakshi(Parvati) married Nilakantan (Shiva).

Partha stood outside watching them meticulously unload the truck—emaciated, bare bodied men carrying ten chairs at a time into the back garden and then returning to fetch another batch. The shamiana crew had arrived almost a fortnight ago and the canopy was almost ready. It was painstaking work twisting yards of green, red, and white fabric and attaching and rotating them strategically so not an inch of sky was visible to the naked eye. The design was geometric, hundreds of triangles intersecting to replicate the Srichakra; the tantric representation of Shakti or female energy. This made it even more symbolic, as Nilakantan was another name for Shiva and Kamakshi an alias for his consort. They would wait another week before laying down the thick carpets, fourteen of them, over which the chairs would be arranged. Partha had been ticking things off his list. Chairs done. Carpets done. Pooja supplies done. Everything was ready. Next week the commotion would begin with the cook arriving, followed by several contingents of family members. It was happening!

*⁂

Rajam was busy with her own list of chores. Supplies from Ganesh Bhandar had arrived; large jute sacks filled with grains and lentils needed for the lavish menu planned for the entire week. The menu for each meal had been carefully crafted so not a single item would foolishly appear twice. She would visit the wholesale market next week to get the vegetables. There was so much to do and so little time. It felt as if the burden of the whole world was placed on her small shoulders. Just then she heard the dreaded call, something she had not heard in a while, which frightened her to the core, bringing ancient, dormant fears to the surface again.

Bhavati Bhikshān dehi.

She called out to Partha, but he had just left the house. Kamu was not home either and panic began to rise within her. Never in all these years had she been completely successful in ridding herself of this age-old phobia, her fear of sāmiyārs—ash-smeared mendicants.

Bhavati Bhikshān dehi. The call for alms echoed within her head, making her cranium feel as though it was about to burst. She sank into a chair, wondering what to do. Her hands were trembling and she couldn't keep them still for a second. They seemed to have a mind of their own. Sweat was trickling down her back in rivulets, but she scarcely noticed that. She could ignore him, but then she might incur his wrath, and a curse right now just before the wedding would be a very bad omen. Or she could face him and give him a cup of rice. What was so terrible about that? She called once more for Partha and Kamu but again … only silence. After three unsuccessful tries, she finally managed to fill a cup with rice, spilling some in patterns all over the kitchen floor. With trembling hands and quaking steps, she walked to the door. She never looked above his feet, gray with dryness, but she could see the orange color in her periphery. With quivering hands, she somehow poured the rice into his bowl, an amazing feat because she was incapable of raising her eyes. *Kalyan ho,* she heard his surprisingly gentle voice blessing her. Then something about *mangalyam and ayushman;* it was all a blur, but she knew she was receiving blessings. For an instant, curiosity overcame fear and she raised her eyes and looked into the kindest, softest, brown eyes she had ever seen. She smiled nervously at first and as the young *bhikshu* turned and walked away, she entered her home, shutting and bolting the door behind her.

It wasn't as bad as she had feared. Then in disbelief and sheer liberation, she began laughing hysterically.

✺ᕵᏻᑫ᠍ᓑ᠍ᕫ✺

The brilliant light from the chandeliers suspended from the ceiling brought out the rich hues of the Kashmir carpets. The sofas were ornate, imported from the occident no less, upholstered in rich tapestry and in each sat a king dressed in the finest brocade, dripping with diamonds and pearls, each with an even more ostentatious turban ensconced on his noble head. Tables were set with crystal vases overflowing with rare and fragrant blooms; jasmine and rose, orchids and camellias, parrot's beak and chocolate cosmos, rhododendron and sweet pimpernel. And then there lay silver plates laden with exotic and rare fruits; grapes and nectarine, rambutan and dragon fruits selected to cater to royal and distinctive cravings. Silver spittoons were positioned strategically and hookahs bubbled furiously. Silver and gold bejeweled goblets of wine were raised to honorable lips and the anticipation of the *pièce de résistance* was vibrant. The scent of the roses adorning her hair wafted in even before the curtains parted to expose her beautiful form. Sounds of *Ooh!* and *aha!* flashed across the room disturbing the harmonious *jugalbandi* of the flute and violin as they competed to outplay one another. But what flight of imagination could prepare them for the vision that appeared? A veritable goddess descended on earth!

Dressed in a resplendent rose pink Kānjeevaram, cinched at the waist by a serpentine, ruby encrusted gold odiyānam, the folds of silk sheathing her nubile, voluptuous frame left the spectators speechless, riveted by her stunning frame. She lifted her netted veil, revealing her face, luminous with a luster that dazzled and blinded them momentarily. From the parting of her jet-black hair, lined with a traditional ruby thalaisāmān to the blinding sparkle of diamonds from her ears and her nose, to the swan like curve of her neck, she was perfection in grace and form. And when she raised her eyes to glance at them flirtatiously, they swooned in ecstasy. As she walked, the sounds of her shalangai, the bells that adorned her ankles, silenced the raptured audience. *Shalaku shalaku shalaku....*

There could be no one quite like Koviladi Kamalamba.

⁂

Nagamma watched Pattu packing colorful Kānjeevaram saris as they prepared to leave for Kamu's wedding. They had booked four bogeys on the train because everyone from the family in Madras was attending the wedding. It was the first marriage in the family, and no one wanted to stay behind. Pattu's son Balu sat on her lap sucking his thumb staring at his mother as she stuffed even more clothes into the already bursting suitcase.

Nagamma couldn't help feeling a little sad. Her saris were all dull and colorless—all four of them—which she wore in turn and she would need to take them all to Calcutta. There would be no new and colorful saris for her. Just four mud-colored saris and a pair of slippers. She opened her almirah and then remembered she had one more prized possession that she had fiercely guarded, refusing to sell against all odds. Her seven-stone diamond nose ring. She had no use for it anymore; as a widow there was no way she could wear a diamond nose ring, yet she held onto it because it reminded her of a bygone era of abundance. At one time, it was a symbol of fortitude, its hardness cementing her inner strength, its brilliance allowing her internal resilience to shine through. But the passing of time had mellowed her: the pride and arrogance that had once been her hallmark were leached out of her and replaced with a deep acceptance of her widowhood. She reached for the velvet box hidden at the back of the cupboard covered in several layers of muslin. The diamonds glimmered with a dull sheen in the dimming light of the bedroom. She took the ring out, spat on it and polished it vigorously with end of her sari. She then replaced it in the box and wrapped it in its muslin bindings, placing it at the bottom of her cloth bag beneath the rest of her possessions: her four saris. She smiled, her large nose crinkling up at the thought. In spite of her abject poverty, she would give Kamu

the most expensive gift compared to all her relatives. That felt good. Nagamma
still reigned supreme.

"I got it, I got it!" Mohan came flying into the room, picked up Bala and swung
her around until both of them spun dizzily onto the bed.

"Got what?" asked Bala completely confused.

"Admission. I'm going to Guindy Engineering College. I will finally be a civil
engineer."

Bala fell silent. She felt like such a burden. Engineering College meant he
would be away for four years at least, which then meant Radhai would have to
take care of her and the baby. Prasanna, almost two, clambered onto the bed
and wiggled in between his parents, making Mohan turn his attention to him,
snuggling and cuddling him while Bala just lay staring at the ceiling. She rubbed
her stomach, now flat, but poised to swell in a few months as the fetus within
her grew. She had not told Mohan yet, and this wasn't the time. She would wait
for a while. Today was his day, let him enjoy the euphoria of good news. She
had other concerns.

"How about money? How are we going to pay for it?" Her eyes were sunken
with worry.

"It's a scholarship. They will pay for my board and tuition fees, but I will have
to take care of food. Scholarships are rare and I'm really lucky to get one. All
the boys entering college are far younger than me, and I should break a hundred
coconuts that they even considered me. Of course they considered Appa's caste,
his status, and annual salary as well."

"What will I do till then? Vasanti is here as well. Appa has to care for us both."

"You should think of teaching dance. We will speak to the owners and see if we
can rent the back thinnai once a week. You can tell people in the area, and I'm sure
that will keep you occupied and give you a little extra money. Balamani School of
Dance. Doesn't that sound good? We can put up a board outside."

Bala was silent. This was the time to tell him about the baby but the words
stayed glued to her throat. How would she dance if she were pregnant and then
… after the baby came? On the other hand, teaching was little effort and Vasanti
could certainly demonstrate steps for her. She was a fine dancer too. And there
was the prospect of extra money, which sounded so tempting. Yes … she would
do it. She would start her own school of dance. If only Kamalamba Amma were
here to see all of this….

Kamu held her arms stiff as a staff and glowered at Rajam. It wasn't fair she wasn't allowing her to see Kandu today. She had taken so much care buying the silver hairbrush from New Market, and she wanted to give it to him before the commotion of the wedding commenced.

Nagamma came into the room and squeezed Kamu's face in affection making her cry out.

Pannādhengo … valikardu! she exclaimed, yelping out in pain.

"Oh! She can talk," said Nagamma tongue in cheek, but Kamu wasn't amused. "What is it, Kamu, what do you want?" asked Nagamma, gently wiping the tears off her face.

Kamu burst into a fresh bout of tears and buried her face in her grandmother's lap. "See …" she sobbed, "I bought him a brush, a really beautiful brush in silver and they won't let me give it to him, it's so unfair! Only five minutes, that's all I need."

"*Kanna,* it's four days before the wedding, why don't you give it to him after?"

"Noooo … I want to give it to him now; otherwise …" threatened Kamu, her voice rising to an alarming crescendo.

"Otherwise what?" asked Nagamma wondering what she would say.

"Otherwise … I won't marry, *na kalyānam pannikamāten!*" she declared.

"*Adeappa! Yenna pudivādham!* Stubborn as a mule aren't you?"

Partha walked in just then. "I wonder where she got that from," he remarked wryly.

"Okay, she's like me, but that doesn't solve the problem. *Paavam kuzhandai,* all she wants is to see him and give him a present. What harm is there if we just drop by for ten minutes? Let's humor her," suggested Nagamma softening up, willing to do anything to calm Kamu down. A girl needed to be happy right before her wedding.

"I have so many things to do, I can't spare any time. One of Kunju's boys can drive the car, but you must go with her and bring her back unharmed," said Partha relenting.

Kamu was all smiles. In one second, the look of petulance on her face suddenly expanded into the loveliest smile. In an instant she was up changing and readying herself to meet Kandu. Partha called ahead to make sure he was home, and then Venkat, Nagamma, and Kamu left to deliver the gift.

"Do I look okay?" Kamu asked, wondering if anyone could tell she had been crying.

"Your eyes are a little swollen, but that love-struck Romeo of yours won't notice," said Nagamma with an indulgent smile. It was so heartwarming to observe young lovebirds.

Dharmu met them at the entrance and welcomed them. Nagamma and Kandu had hit it off really well from the start. Naturally; the two were so alike in so many ways. They waited in the living room while Kamu stepped outside to give him his present. She insisted he open it, and when he did he made all the appropriate noises to let her know he loved it.

"Wait … I have something for you too, but you open it later," he said giving her a package. From the shape Kamu suspected it was more of the same, and she was right.

Yardley English Rose perfume. *Oh no! Another scent.*

Kamu sighed in disappointment. She had said she loved scents and now she had a dozen. If only he could be a little more imaginative with his gifts.

Yenna? Yenna kuduthaan māplai? Nagamma asked, eager to know.

"*Innooru* scent," said Kamu, the disappointment evident in her voice.

It wasn't just another scent, but how could Kamu reach into the recesses of Kandu's subconscious to understand the significance of the rose. He barely understood it himself.

✹⛥✹

Kamu looked resplendent in her green and gold tissue sari and matching gold jewelry. The groom's family was expected, but Kamu needed to remain indoors. Partha and Rajam were at the entrance awaiting the sambandhis, but Sushila wanted to walk with the procession and enjoy the action. At the last minute, she took off her diamond rings and put them on Kamu's bare fingers. The bride's ordinary gold engagement ring was simply not enough. Kamu knew that but didn't really mind. She would get diamonds from Kandu later—there would be plenty of time.

Sushila grabbed hold of her son Ramji's hand and marched down the road to the next street where the groom's party had congregated for the *Māplai azhaippu*. The open Chevrolet was adorned with strings of fragrant *rajnigandha* interspersed with roses. The aroma of these tuberoses combined perfectly with that of the roses. The tuneful sounds of *melam and thavil* rent the air, symbolic of a marriage ceremony. The artist had arrived only yesterday and was blowing away on his instrument, competing with the band Partha had also arranged at Rajam's insistence. The deafening noise had locked Kandu's face into a grimace. It was customary for young children to sit in the car with the groom, and baby Balu, Pattu's youngest was already there on Kandu's right, sucking his thumb and staring wide-eyed all around, fascinated by all the lights and sounds. Sushila hurriedly picked up Ramji and placed him next to Kandu on the other side. Both children were thrilled to ride in such a fancy car. As the band broke into *Jiya bekarār hai,* a popular Hindi melody, the car departed followed on foot by the entire groom's party and some from the bride's party. Sushila glanced at her husband Siva, striding confidently and handsomely dressed in his silk kurta and veshti. Then she looked at her son Ramji. With his hooked nose and crossed eyes, he looked nothing like Siva, and Sushila loved him doubly for that. Ramji was her ultimate revenge. Every day, Siva looked at Ramji and knew the truth, yet he could never say anything to her, and in that she gained her power. Sweet, sweet revenge.

☙❧

Mahadevan tied Kandu's veshti securely, but he still insisted on wearing a belt. It just felt too loose and he certainly didn't want to sport his underwear in front of a crowd, especially at his own wedding.

"Okay, that looks fine," remarked Mahadevan admiring his handiwork. "Now take off your *baniyan* so that I can arrange the angavastram," he added, pleating the top cloth.

"No!" Kandu yelled. He would wear his undershirt, come what may. His chest was so pale it embarrassed him to be bare bodied.

"What? You're going to wear that right through the wedding. That looks so stupid. What is the point of all that body building if you're too shy to expose your body?"

"Leave me alone," said Kandu, "I can't come half naked. I have to wear the baniyan."

So in a baniyan and a veshti, tied with a thick black belt, Kandu married Kamu.

☙❧

Vaithee handed him the scissors, and as he snipped the blue ribbon a teetering of claps and cheers rippled through an appreciative gathering. Muhammad Salih had donated the land to him six months before, and along with other friends and volunteers he had built a small compound wall around the building. Clouds of red, muddy earth rose with all the children running around making the central building nebulous in the haze. The big board covering the front end of the house read:

NANDUKAMALA CHILDREN'S HOME

Salih and Vaithee stood admiring the banner. It was the result of plenty of hard work and the payoff for Vaithee's relentless pursuit of his dream. After he picked up that child at the train station in Salem, he came home every other week with another child, and pretty soon his barn was bursting with children. Vaithee knew he had to find a bigger place. When he spoke to Salih, his proposal was met with almost instant approval. By the time Salih obtained the land, which had been under litigation, Vaithee and Meera were caring for another ten children. The property came to them dirt cheap, and with financing from a local bank, construction of the main building began. The Home was nothing special: four large empty rooms. One to sleep, another to eat, the third to study, and the last one for storage. An open area at the back would serve as a kitchen.

Salih leaned on his stick, his hand thoughtfully stroking his beard. "The name is strange. It's not yours or Meera's," he remarked, stating the obvious.

"No, Nandu was a very special boy who was a runaway. He died saving us during the Calcutta riots and this is in his memory. The story is too long and too painful. Perhaps another day."

"And Kamala?"

"Oh, Kamala, she was Meera's daughter."

"Passed on as well?" asked Salih compassionately; this young couple had witnessed so much pain.

"Yes. She lost her in a tiger attack years ago; a long story. Perhaps someday I will tell you."

❦

The Headline read *Koviladi Kamalamba found dead on the streets of Salem.* Tears of guilt streamed down Kunju's cheeks as she read the article. Kamalamba had saved Kunju's family from starvation, yet Kunju had never gone back to check what happened to her. She had no idea that poor Kamalamba was reduced to such a state as to die penniless on the streets. It was horrible, horrible!

The last of the well-known Devadasis, Koviladi Kamalamba was found dead outside a children's home in Salem, her shalangai clasped in her hands. The proprietor of the Home, Mr. Vaithyanathan, paid for her cremation and asks for any relatives to come forward to claim her ashes and shalangai.

The article went on to describe the plight of Devadasis, but Kunju had stopped reading. She cut the article out and slipped it into an envelope. She would deliver it tomorrow to Bala in Triplicane. Perhaps Radhai would go and pick up her ashes and honor her. Overwhelmed, she wept copious tears, begging Kamalamba Amma for forgiveness. She beseeched her to pardon her selfishness, lamenting for an hour or so, after which the tears subsided. She could not come to terms with her guilt and her prayers would forever include a plea for forgiveness for her neglect of Kamalamba.

Radhai left for Salem immediately, and after picking up Amma's remains, he proceeded to Thanjavur, where he found his way to their old home, now in almost complete ruin. There, crying bitter tears of remorse, he scattered her ashes. She had lived like a queen in this house, and her remains rightfully belonged here.

On the train ride back he cried continually, unable to get over his sense of helplessness. He had tried many times to save her, but in front of Kamalamba's iron resolve his persuasive skills withered. Ultimately, her karma was overpowering.

He took out the shalangai whose rightful place was in the pooja room in their home, a hallowed resting place in her memory. On the inside of the soft cloth, now worn out with continued usage, her name was embroidered in bright red. *Koviladi Kamalamba.* Such a legend and now nothing; just an old, worn out pair of shalangais.

The wedding went by in a blur. It seemed too quick for any lasting memory. And it didn't help that Partha had forgotten to hire a photographer. Kamu sat in front of her triple mirror watching Sushila and Pattu braid her hair, fix her thalaisāmān and encircle her long braid with strings of fragrant jasmine interspersed with kadambam. She would wear her electric blue Kānjeevaram with thin gold lines running through the fabric and change into her red koorai, the traditional nine-yard madisar for the actual wedding.

The oonjal stood by the entrance, and by the time Kamu went out onto the marriage dais, the whole area was packed with guests. It was still dark when Kamu and Kandu sat on the oonjal, swinging back and forth while receiving blessings from the sumangalis for a long and blissful wedded life. Rajam couldn't help feeling they resembled a celestial couple. *Sākshāth Kamakshi Nilakantan.*

Compliments were effusive. Seldom before had Calcutta seen such a grand show. *This wedding will be remembered for a long time. Such a perfectly matched couple! What incredible food! Who picked the menu? What an amazing shamiana! Such intricate work! Partha you have really outdone yourself. What a wedding!*

There were to be two receptions. One in their South End Park home and tomorrow, the glitzy one at Portland Park. For both, Kamu had chosen to wear banārsi tissue saris with contrasting velvet blouses. It was exhausting to greet and smile at everyone when all she wanted was to sleep. Soon enough the reception ended. Kamu and some family members then left for Kandu's home for the *Grahapravesham*, Kamu's entry into her new home and brand new life.

This would be followed by the *Shanthi Kalyānam,* nuptials before their first night together. Dharmu welcomed Kamu into her new home, presenting her with a beautiful diamond necklace. Kamu was overwhelmed—so many saris and so much jewelry—her mother-in-law had showered her with gifts. It was not customary but Dharmu wanted to welcome Kamu into their home in a grand way. Kamu and Kandu then walked out into the enclosed balcony and Ganesh took a beautiful photograph—the only one taken at the wedding.

✸❀❀❀✸

Meera washed the last of the vessels and sat for a while under the shade of the tree out in the front yard. She ran her hands over the goat's back, its soft, velvety skin soothing her nerves as much as its bleating calmed her turbulent thoughts. It had been a long and tortuous journey from the Sunderbans in the east all the way south to Vizhupuram, but she had finally arrived. She was safe and freed from her mental shackles. It was strange what twists and turns her karma had churned out. Kamala, her daughter, mauled to death by a tiger, an unwanted pregnancy, followed by a failed suicide attempt. And then Boythee! Oh Boythee! He was the angel sent to her from Banobibi. Where would she be without him? She choked up in utter gratitude and salty tears rolled down her contoured cheeks. Without Boythee she would never have made it this far. Not after that terrible assault in Calcutta. And Nandu? How could she ever thank him? Each day she cooked and cared for these twenty runaway boys at the Home, and when they ate she felt in her heart as though she were feeding Nandu. He watched over her, she was certain of that.

What a miracle! She was alive! She had survived ... and she would keep going....

✸❀❀❀✸

Rajam and Partha sat opposite one another eating silently, the noise of their loud swallowing and slurping not fazing either of them. The house felt so empty without Kamu's colorful presence, but it had to happen I guess. She had found her *rajakumaran,* her prince, and was blissfully happy. What more could one ask for? After dinner Partha opened his book of accounts. His debt totaled 56,489 rupees. Considering he earned five hundred each month he had no idea how he was going to pay that money back. Rajam came in and saw his worried look. "Don't worry," she said hugging him. "We will somehow pay it back At least it's not money borrowed from a Kabuliwallah."

"No," said Partha. *"It's borrowed from ten kabuliwallahs."*

A whole month had gone by without either of them realizing how easily one day slipped seamlessly into another. He was completely besotted, and spent every wakeful moment with her, attending office only because he absolutely needed to. Her shy smile, the curve of her neck, her supple skin, her lustrous, straight, black hair; everything about Kamu beguiled him. Kamu made the whole world a brighter place—even the sun shone brighter when she was around and the moon expanded its luminous surface even on sensing she was near. Flowers tripled their fragrance and water tasted like wine if she served it. Life was just wonderful, and each morning he rose from his bed with a smile on his face, excited to see her, to touch her. Just being with her was intoxicating, like a draught of elixir.

Kandu stretched across the bed to touch her, but she had already arisen. Half asleep and this being a Sunday, he closed his eyes again and drifted off to sleep once more.

He was running in a green valley, the wind in his face, his soft feet treading on grass that was softer than the softest silk. It was early morning and a cloud had descended into the valley, the swirling mists making shapes appear and disappear in nebulous, floating clouds. Tantalizing dancing peacocks, varied birds of paradise and colorful parakeets emerged magically out of the mist. He walked farther and farther up the familiar path, dragged involuntarily by a magnetic presence. He had been here time and time again in the valley of promise, and he moved amidst the rocks and grass with uncanny familiarity. Sudden brightness and the strong fragrance of roses caught his attention making him glance upwards. The clouds had parted and she stood illuminated in a ray of sunshine in the midst of a rose garden. She closed her eyes submitting to the intoxication of the moment. Raising her hands to the sky in ecstasy, she twirled around slowly, her body responding to a silent rhythm, reacting to the joy brimming within her. She then reached down and plucked from a thorny bush the most perfect, pristine red rose and placed it strategically in her hair just behind her left ear. He stared at her in amazement, walking enticingly closer, as his heart seemed to burst with love for her. Who was this mystery woman who made his heart beat with such passion? He had to see her face. But all he could behold were her ebony tresses in which was nestled this perfect rose. "Who are you?" he groaned, reaching out yearning to solve the mystery of the lady with a rose. "Who are you?" he exclaimed again.

Sahib, kuch chaiye? asked Durjodhan unable to understand what Kandu said.

Kandu sat upright in his bed, annoyed that his eyes had opened before he saw the dream girl's face. The dream had repeated itself many times, but not once could he remember it on being awake or make any earthly connection.

"Memsahib *kahaan hai?*" he asked Durjodhan wondering where Kamu had run off so early in the morning.

"Garden *mein* Sahib, *chai pee rahi hai.*"

Kandu stumbled out of bed and shuffled down the stairs, picking up Pittu as he made his way to the garden. It was daybreak, and a mist had descended on their front lawn. He walked towards the chairs and he could tell she was seated in one of them with her back to him. Pittu jumped out of his arms and made his way to her, his sharp yelps startling her out of her trance.

"Kamu?" he called out to her.

Hearing him she turned around, a smile on her face, her eyes lighting up in anticipation.

He took in the beautiful vision: her narrow forehead over thick arched eyebrows, her eyes bright and twinkling, her soft cheeks rosy with the December chill, and her full lips parted to reveal her perfect pearl-like teeth. Then he beheld the red rose nestled in her hair behind her left ear, and stared in a moment of stunned silence as in a flash the face in his dream was finally revealed.

"*That's it ... that's it,*" he realized in excitement. "*You are her. A rose from a dream ... or rather, the rose from my dream.*"

The End

GLOSSARY OF INDIAN WORDS

Word	Meaning
Abhinaya:	In Indian classical dance where facial expression/hand gestures convey meaning (Sanskrit)
Agrahāram:	A village square around a temple, lined with houses—traditionally occupied by Brahmins (Tamil)
Ambattan:	Barber (Tamil)
Angrezi:	English language/race/person (Hindi)
Aruvāmanai:	A kitchen instrument used to cut vegetables (Tamil)
Basti:	A slum inhabited by the poor (Hindi)
Beeda:	Areca nuts wrapped in betel leaves—Pān (Tamil)
Chawl:	Residential apartment blocks for communal living in Mumbai (Hindi)
Darshanam:	Sacred viewing (Sanskrit)
Darwān:	Doorman— Also called Chowkidār (Hindi)
Devadāsis:	A caste where women are temple dancers or courtesans
Dhāvani:	Half-sari commonly worn by teenage girls (Tamil)
Jamādār:	Cleaner or Janitor (Hindi)
Jameendār:	Plantation owner (Hindi)
Kabuliwāllah:	A man from Kabul, a city in Afghanistan (Hindi)
Kājal (Mai):	Black herbal eyeliner (Hindi/Tamil)
Kāli:	Hindu Goddess to whom blood sacrifices are sometimes offered
Kanakāmbaram:	Crossandra— a plant with orange flowers(Tamil)
Kānjeevaram:	A silk weave from a city in Southern India (Tamil)
Khādi:	Hand woven cloth (Hindi)
Kriya:	Death ceremony (Sanskrit)

Word	Meaning
Kumkumam:	Vermillion powder worn on the forehead (Sanskrit)
Lāthi Charge:	Dispersing a mob using batons (Hindi)
Madi:	Rules governing personal purity and pollution for brahmins (Tamil)
Malli:	Jasmine flowers (Tamil)
Memsahib:	Madam (Hindi)
Mirāzdār:	A rich land owner (Hindi/Tamil)
Mridangam:	Percussion instrument used in Classical Indian music (Tamil)
Nattuvāngam:	Art of conducting a classical dance performance (Bharatanātyam)
Parayan:	An untouchable (Tamil)
Pathān:	A member of the mountainous tribe from eastern Afghanistan
Pāvādai:	Long skirt commonly worn by young girls (Tamil)
Poojai:	Prayers offered as per traditional injunctions (Pooja/Puja/Pujo)
Pottu:	A mark on the forehead worn as a symbol of protection (Tamil)
Pottukattu:	A ceremony in which a young girl is dedicated to God as a devadāsi (Tamil)
Pradakshanam:	Circumbulation of the sanctum sanctorum in a temple (Tamil)
Rasam:	A spicy soup traditionally accompanying rice in a South Indian meal (Tamil)
Sāhib(Saab):	Sir
Sambandhi:	Father/Mother-in-law (Sanskrit)
Sāmbār:	A spicy lentil-based dish served with rice in South Indian cuisine
Sāmiyār:	Mendicant (Tamil)

Word	Meaning
Sapthapadi:	7-steps taken around a pit of fire in a traditional Hindu marriage ceremony (Sanskrit)
Sepoys:	Soldiers in an Indian army
Shamiana/Pandhal:	A colorful tent put up during ceremonies (Hindi)
Sumangali:	A married Hindu woman—not yet widowed and hence considered auspicious (Sanskrit)
Thavil:	A barrel shaped drum used in temple, folk, and carnatic music (Tamil)
Thayirshādham:	Rice with yoghurt (Tamil)
Theetu:	An unclean period after a death (Tamil)
Thinnai:	A raised platform, bordering the front of the house (Tamil)
Tonga:	A horse-drawn carriage (Hindi)
Vaidhyar:	Doctor (Tamil)
Varan:	A prospective groom/bride (Tamil)